CONFESSIONS

OF A

Farmers Market Romeo

JAMES R. DUBBS

Pat, Enjoy the book!

MILFORD HOUSE

an imprint of Sunbury Press, Inc.
Mechanicsburg, PA USA

MILFORD HOUSE

an imprint of Sunbury Press, Inc.
Mechanicsburg, PA USA

FIRST MILFORD HOUSE PRESS EDITION: August 2022

Set in Adobe Garamond Pro | Interior design by Crystal Devine | Cover by Rachel Watson and Victoria Mitchell | Edited by Taylor Berger-Knorr.

Publisher's Cataloging-in-Publication Data
Names: Dubbs, James R., author.
Title: Confessions of a farmers market romeo / James R. Dubbs.
Description: First trade paperback edition. | Mechanicsburg, PA : Milford House Press, 2022.
Summary: The search for love is never out of season in *Confessions of a Farmers Market Romeo*. Follow the misadventures of Jim, an unlikely Romeo, as he pursues "complete unfetteredness." In eight binge-worthy episodes spanning two decades, *Confessions* will leave you laughing as Jim ponders life's eternal question: *Where does love go when it's gone?*
Identifiers: ISBN : 978-1-62006-947-9 (softcover).
Subjects: FICTION / Coming of Age | FICTION / Humorous / General | FICTION / Romance / New Adult.

Product of the United States of America
0 1 1 2 3 5 8 13 21 34 55

Continue the Enlightenment!

For my brethren, the humble farmers market vendor

EPISODE ONE

Title: *Pilot Episode*
Time: *43 minutes*
Synopsis: *A farmers market urchin falls in love with the new girl in town.*

My story begins and ends at the farmers market.

I was conceived in the back of my parents' 1960 Econoline van just minutes after the conclusion of a particularly successful Saturday morning market on the square in Gettysburg. The impetus for my conception? My parents, William and Martha Dubbs, sole proprietors of the fledgling Little Martha's Bakery, sold the last remaining item on their table—a sour crème and chives scone—to a smallish British man wearing a pith helmet. The story's minor details vary with the telling, but in every version, the British man buys the last scone just seconds before the final bell. According to my father, the man wasn't a regular. What's more, he seemed to materialize out of thin air, like foot traffic from heaven. By the end of the transaction, my parents were giddy. Beyond giddy—they were euphoric. Little Martha's sales on that cloud-hidden May morning totaled $142.75. Not only was this a tidy little fortune in 1961, but irrefutable proof that they had latched onto a viable livelihood, and with it, a modicum of freedom.

As the British man padded away, my parents shared an amorous look. They were two years removed from high school, where everyone—even the teachers—had referred to them simply as "Bill-n-Mattie." They were attractive, energetic, and as evidenced by my existence, at least momentarily uninhibited by the realization of their modest dream. A light rain began to speckle the sidewalk. The breeze picked up a smidge, carrying the perfumed scent of Jessica the Flower Vendor's unsold bouquets across the market to my parents' tent, where they stood hand-in-hand, marveling at their empty table. The Econoline van was just sitting there. My father very likely puffed his chest and winked at my mother. My mother very likely blushed. All I can say is thank God for the fifteen-minute grace period on the town's parking meter. Without it, I would be someone else.

The last time I heard my father tell "The Last Scone Story" was eight months ago, on March 26th, 1983, at 11:02 P.M. I'm certain of the date and time because I have two markers. First, it was four weeks before I decided to experience extreme "unfetteredness" and move from my parents' home to the Michaux State Forest, where for a short time I would live in the woods like Henry David Thoreau in *Walden*. And second, March the 26th, 1983, was the worldwide premiere of *Star Wars* on free television. It aired on the CBS network from 8:00 P.M. until 11:00 P.M.

For six years, my father's desire to see *Star Wars* had bordered on an obsession. He'd had countless chances to see the movie in the theater, but in addition to being inflicted with a deep-rooted stinginess, my dad was prone to weird flights of logic that only he could fully comprehend. As a result, when *Star Wars* opened in 1977, my father couldn't bring himself to pay $2.50 to watch it in the theater—not in good conscience. When it was re-released in 1979, he couldn't see his way clear to part with $2.75. When it was re-released again in 1981, he refused on basic principle to fork over $3.25 to watch a four-year-old movie: "A movie is no different than a loaf of stale olive bread," he argued one night at dinner. "You can't sell old and charge new." And, when the movie was re-released yet again in 1982 to promote the upcoming *The Empire Strikes Back*, he argued that if he had balked at paying $3.25 to see a four-year-old movie, he was even more justified in refusing to pay a quarter more—$3.50—to watch the exact same movie a year later.

So that March night, when he was finally able to watch *Star Wars* in his own living room, my father settled back in his chair as though he'd fought the good fight and won. The movie was free—worth no more in trade than a rock-hard, three-day-old baguette—and he had watched it. Watched the hell out of it, in fact, refusing both food and drink as he sat motionless and stared at the television screen for three straight hours. As the final credits flashed across the screen, my dad tried to look unaffected.

"I guess *Star Wars* is okay—with the force and all," he said, leaning back, "and I guess it's a good thing that Luke fella blew up the Death Star. Although I probably would have done it a bit differently."

A moment passed. He tapped his fingers on the arm of his recliner, a strange, post-vindication letdown already dampening his victory. He glanced at my mother. Then he twisted his entire body toward me.

"Yeah, I guess *Star Wars* is okay, but give me a well-attended farmers market any day. Like that market in '61 where *you* were born."

I nodded and resisted the impulse to point out I wasn't born at the market—I was conceived at it—and as disheartening as it was to credit my existence to the last-second sale of a fifty-cent scone to an oddly-dressed passerby, I had bigger problems. I was jobless, penniless, beleaguered in mind, body, and spirit. Plus, I was fatter than I'd ever been. Most soul-crushing of all, I was reduced to crawling back to my parents' house because I'd plunged headfirst into a string of disastrous events—the most recent being that I'd set fire to a chicken coop to make amends with a girl who now hated my guts.

My father tapped the recliner again, then leaned forward and formed his fingers into a small pyramid—his go-to posture for reciting the opening line of "The Last Scone Story." "It was the third market of the season," he said, "and I was playing a hunch."

He waited for us to give him our full attention before continuing.

"It was a tad overcast, but otherwise it was the kind of morning that had impulse buy written all over it. The first strawberries were in. Salad greens were in. Onions were in. And we had the good sense to pawn your brother Trez off on your grandmother so he wouldn't pitch some screaming fit at the exact wrong moment and squelch a sale.

"But here's the heck of it—I hadn't talked it over with your mother, but in my mind, that Saturday's farmers market was do or die for Little Martha's Bakery."

He looked at my mother. At this point in the story, my mother was expected to buttress the narrative by conveying an incredibly nuanced series of emotions, ranging from shock to measured self-reflection to a slow-dawning realization of what-might-have-been-if-not-for—all with a flicker of her eyes. As I grew older, my mother's response to her prompt was my favorite part of the story. She made the required face most of the time, but if she sensed Trez and me growing bored with the story, she would add a comedic touch. She'd replace the nuanced face with a "village idiot face." She'd droop an eyelid and scrunch up her mouth in such a way as to indicate that the entire dramatic thrust of The Last Scone Story was hopelessly beyond her ability to comprehend. This evening, though, she played it straight; she made the nuanced face.

"I'm not going to lie—the first hour or so, I was scared," my dad continued, "the local tomjammery thinned out earlier than usual, but around 10:30, a cluster of tourists made a run on the sweet rolls and muffins. An hour later, a second, smaller clump wiped out the last of the bread. Then your mother said—"

"All we have left is this one scone," my mother filled in.

"And now it's seconds to close, and I'm thinking, please, just one more goddamn customer—some pathetic loser to buy this last stinking sour crème and chives scone. Suddenly, standing there as if he'd materialized out of thin air, was a—"

My dad looked at me. When my brother and I were little, this was our shared line in the narrative. We used to scramble to our tiny feet and scream it at the top of our lungs, trying to outdo each other. Trez was long gone. He was in the Air Force, stationed in Fairbanks. So, it was up to me to carry on the family tradition. "A Limey," I said with as much gusto as I could summon.

"That's right—a Limey. And it was the damnedest thing. He was wearing—"

"A pith helmet," I said dutifully.

"Like he was on safari," my father said. My mother had her nuanced face, and at this point in the story, my father had his. A wistful smile spread across his lips and his eyes focused inward, as if, on cue, it suddenly occurred to him that life was a well-designed mystery—a tapestry viewed from behind—and that every single moment of every one of our lives was not only a knot in that tapestry, but the beginning and the end of everything we were and everything we would ever be.

That was my father: cheap, overly dramatic, and family-centric to a fault. Looks-wise, perfect strangers would comment that he resembled a young William Shatner. As for me, no one would compare me to a television star, much less Captain Kirk. On two separate occasions, girls have likened me to tofu. For those with no knowledge of tofu, it's a near tasteless, white, coagulated bean curd, usually molded into the least inventive of all shapes—a rectangle. Its chief culinary attribute is its ability to act as a conduit for other, far more exciting tastes. The first girl to make this comparison was Doris Messinger. She blurted out "Tofu?" to describe my puckered lips. In my defense, she was blindfolded at the time and had no idea *what* her lips were touching. The second girl—let's call her Alisha—intended her somewhat contemptuous "tofu" jab to describe my personality. If she'd been describing my physique, it would have stung less because, body-wise, I *am* like tofu. I can't deny it. I'm fat. Not morbidly fat—that would make for poor storytelling—but certainly I'm overweight. As proof, I offer this: I chafe easily; the two center fingers on each of my hands rub together below the first knuckle; and if I'm not careful, when I lift my chubby ham-hands skyward, my pear-shaped stomach slips from its T-shirt and dances to a tune only it can hear. And while I prefer hard rock, I imagine my stomach shaking its groove-thing to mid-70's R&B. Something like "What's Going On." And not the original Marvin Gaye version either—I'm thinking of the far-superior Al Green cover version.

Despite my physical limitations, I'm somewhat of a Romeo. I manage this—one could almost say in spite of myself—with only a few modest gifts. I have thick, curly brown hair that girls can't help but touch. I have impeccable taste in music (Graham Parker as opposed to, say, Iggy Pop). And on numerous occasions, I've been told by the opposite sex— young and old alike—that I'm naturally funny. Above all else, though, I've cultivated "The Art of Intuition." I invented "The Art of Intuition" at fat camp when I was eleven years old, and while, in the moment, the concept seemed to come to me fully realized, looking back now, I can trace its inception to a series of events that began with the most common, unextraordinary act imaginable: I straightened my legs.

In the summer of 1974, Little Martha's Bakery was thriving on the square in Gettysburg; my older brother Trez was scorching the local football fields; and I was praying twice a day. I'd never attended a church service, but common sense dictated that God expected my prayers to be not only humble and reverent but also as poetic as Bob Dylan song lyrics. I further reasoned that I needed to pique God's interest with a touch of mystery—a religious double entendre of sorts. So twice a day, I knelt over the foot of my bed, clasped my pudgy paws together, and softly mouthed, "Oh Lord, into this humble life, please deliver a little fat."

Unfortunately, God answered my prayer.

I'd fallen in love with a girl named Doris. It happened at the Farmers Market. For my part, it was love at first sight. I'd like to think that Doris was similarly love-struck, but the truth is, if she noticed me at all that May morning, it would have been the same way one notices a fire hydrant. Her family strolled up to our tent while I was crouched down, digging shoo-fly muffins from the stack of bread flats under the table (it was my job to keep the table stocked). I heard a woman's voice ask my father about the sourdough baguette—*was it crusty?* She planned on fixing pasta for dinner: maybe spaghetti or ziti, but hopefully perciatelli. That was if the grocery stores in Gettysburg carried it. And of course, she added with a trace of a laugh, she would be making her own marinara sauce—or gravy—as everyone called it back home in New Jersey.

I hadn't noticed Doris yet, so my eyes instinctively turned to Troy the Vegetable Guy's tent at the mention of homemade marinara sauce. It was too early in the season for any serious produce, but he had a half-decent display of spring onions, garlic scapes, and overwintered bell peppers—any of which would sauté up nicely and add depth to the woman's sauce. The farmers market code dictated that my parents point out Troy's vegetables and vouch for them—a cross-sell. In theory, he would do the same for us. It had been a slow morning, though, and Little Martha's was sitting on six loaves of spinach garlic bread. So my dad had a choice: he could cross-sell his neighbor's vegetables or up-sell his own product.

He didn't even hesitate. "You may want to consider the spinach garlic bread, too," he said. Then he mouthed his go-to line: "I've always found that if you get the bread right, the rest of the meal falls into place."

I heard the husband murmur his approval and the woman's purse snap open. "Tell me," she asked my father, "this is all so quaint—is the market here every Saturday?"

I began to straighten my legs. At that instant, my eyes fell upon Doris. She was to the left of her mother and father, bent down on one knee, tying her shoelace.

I've since learned that love at first sight is a misnomer. In reality, the whole process takes two-tenths of a second. That's how long the brain requires to transition from visual stimulation to flooding one's bloodstream with "happy" chemicals such as dopamine, oxytocin, and adrenaline, all of which harmonize to create the sensation that everything will work out perfectly. I've also since learned that, co-joined with this chemical overdose, is a phenomenon called "the halo effect." Put simply, the euphoria-inducing chemicals cause a sexual response which in turn causes the pupils to dilate. (Again, this takes two-tenths of a second—about the same amount of time it takes a camera shutter to open and close.) Everything brightens, and whomever you are focused on at the time—the first mover of these somatic responses—appears to be lit from behind, creating the illusion of a halo. This is why we, as humans, assign positive personality traits to individuals we find physically attractive.

So I never had a chance. By the time I'd straightened my legs completely, I was in love. And by the time the mother handed "Doris" the spinach garlic bread to carry, I'd assigned a litany of larger-than-life personality traits to Doris that would have dwarfed a fictional composite of Mother Theresa, Georgia O'Keefe, and Marilyn Monroe.

"Tell me," Doris' father asked, "The public schools. Are the children . . . the right kind of kids?"

My father looked genuinely puzzled. He was a salesman though, at least on Saturdays, so he understood the benefits of playing along. "Yes, yes, of course," my dad said. "My son here, Jim, is in sixth grade."

Doris' parents glanced at each other as if my father's words had given them comfort. "We just moved into—" the mother said, stopping mid-thought.

"Twin Oaks," the father said, finishing her sentence. He was wearing a bulky, silver ring on the pinky of his right hand, and he banged it on my parents' table three times before pulling his shoulders back and imparting the most important detail: "The *wooded* section."

Doris' father may have been new to Gettysburg, but judging by his ring-banging, he'd already deduced the local social hierarchy. Twin Oaks was the most desirable subdivision in town. The cream of Adams County's professional class lived in Twin Oaks. And *their* cream lived in the wooded section: lawyers, college professors, real estate brokers, et cetera—not common farmers market vendors who had the poor taste to earn their meager living by selling bread in a glorified parking lot.

As I watched Doris and her parents walk away, I knew my dad already hated the entire family's guts. They'd stood at his family's place of business and put on airs—an unforgivable sin. It didn't matter to me, though. I felt changed. And not just because my pulse was hammering and my head felt as light as a balloon. It went deeper. It was as if I'd spent my entire life walking past a door without noticing it and now, out of nowhere, I'd noticed it and it was all I *could* notice. And to make my epiphany even more story-like, "Doris" was on the other side of the door, waiting for me. We belonged together. It was meant to be. Why else would I feel it? And if her Twin Oaks parents were better than mine and it read as a Romeo and Juliet thing, then that's what fate demanded.

What I needed was an in. I had one, but it wasn't ideal.

My classmate, Wayne Clark, lived in the wooded section of Twin Oaks. His father was an inventor. He had invented a stainless-steel meat hook that swivels 360 degrees. Over the past decade, the meat hook had revolutionized the slaughterhouse industry. We knew this because every fall, Wayne would bring his father's invention to school for show-and-tell. Over the years, Wayne's presentation grew more and more elaborate. In kindergarten, he'd simply held the hook up and then ran back to his seat and cried. But by fourth grade, he would describe the meat hook's function and purpose in minute detail—from the beginning of the slaughtering process to the end—all the while holding the eight-inch-long contraption aloft and spinning the swivel mechanism with his free hand to demonstrate the hook's fully patented 360-degree "travel" capacity.

At the beginning of fifth grade, Wayne was diagnosed with a lazy eye. The first day he wore his eye patch to school coincided with his turn to present show-and-tell. To the class's shock, Wayne strode to the front of the room without his father's meat hook. I personally was devastated. I'd grown to love Wayne's presentation, especially the way he kept the swivel swiveling with a quick brush of his hand. In place of the meat hook, Wayne was clutching an Elvis Presley record album to his chest.

"This is my lazy-eye patch, and this is an album recorded by Elvis Presley," he said without hesitation. He held the album jacket over his right shoulder so that Elvis's head and his head were on the same visual plane.

"When Elvis was in fifth grade, he too had amblyopia, and he too had to wear a lazy-eye patch. My father told me this."

Wayne paused for us to process that what he was telling us was on good authority—imparted to him by none other than the inventor of the single most essential apparatus ever to grace the slaughterhouse floor. When Wayne was satisfied that we'd grasped what he was saying, he proceeded to recount Elvis's humble Tupelo upbringing and how Colonel Tom Parker—who, in Wayne's opinion, was a music visionary—had discovered "E" driving a delivery truck. From there, Wayne outlined the highlights of Elvis's recording career, all with the same gravitas he'd grown to project when he spoke of his father's meat hook.

After this, Wayne graduated to a full-blown outcast. The eye patch was one part of it—how it was always frayed and filthy around the edges—but the bigger part was how Wayne shoehorned Elvis into even the most casual conversations. He knew all of his songs and had seen all of his movies. He claimed that "E" enjoyed unlimited access to large-breasted women: models, actresses, and best of all, groupies. Once, while Wayne and I were waiting for our turn in kickball, he told me that he had it on good authority that once "E" had thrown himself a private party in the "jungle room" of his Graceland mansion and had invited *only* groupies. Dozens of them—every race, creed, and color—and as Wayne understood it, every one of the groupies had hips that swiveled as freely as a slaughterhouse meat hook.

As fate would have it, the Monday after I fell in love with Doris, Wayne and I were teamed together for an end-of-the-year science project—our small part in the group project was to chart how quickly water percolated into topsoil. After school, I pedaled my bike across town to the Clarks' house—ostensibly to get a jump on the project—and rang the doorbell. Wayne opened the front door and led me inside. As I stepped into his living room, I'll confess that I had a pang of self-doubt concerning our (and by extension, Doris') different stations in life. I lived in a house/bakery. It was utilitarian. We had three stoves, metro shelving, and empty bread flats stacked in the corner of our living room year-round. The Clarks' home looked as though it had been professionally decorated.

Their living room had olive-green shag carpeting, mustard-colored walls, a bay window, and a stone fireplace with an oil painting of the entire family propped on the mantel. (Whether consciously or unconsciously, the artist composed the family portrait with Wayne's eyepatch as the painting's focal point.)

Wayne motioned for me to sit on the sofa, then scampered from the room. When he returned a moment later, he had on a pair of too-large, navy-blue swimming trunks. His chest and feet were bare. "Elvis likes to lounge around the house in just swim trunks," Wayne said. He snapped his fingers and his younger sister, Brie, stepped into the room and presented me with a glass of iced sweet tea. Without further comment, Wayne moved to his parents' stereo cabinet and pulled an Elvis record from a pile of albums. He removed the vinyl disc from the paper liner with such grace that I couldn't help but be impressed. He studied the empty jacket for a second, then handed it to me. Big and small Elvises covered the front in a repeating pattern, like Elvis wallpaper. Along the top, the album read *50,000,000 Elvis Fans Can't Be Wrong.*

"You like Elvis?" I asked.

"Yes," Wayne said. "Elvis wore a lazy-eye patch when he was my exact age—twelve. And on the same eye. My parents have told me this repeatedly," he said. He hitched up his massive swimming trunks and lowered the stylus onto the record. The crackle of needle touching vinyl flowed through the speakers. He peeked at me from the corner of his uncovered eye. "Soon, my vision will be powerful. More powerful than anyone can imagine. I'll see tiny things—things that other people miss. Common house ants will appear as giants to me. The exact same way that they appear as giants to Elvis."

"Wouldn't that be scary?" I asked. "Ants the size of giants?"

Wayne closed his good eye and considered this for a moment.

"To me or Elvis?"

I'd witnessed enough to know that Wayne liked being lumped in with Elvis. "To both of you," I answered, managing a smile. "You *and* Elvis."

"Everything would appear as giants—so the effect would be neutralized."

I let it go at that. I shut my eyes for a second—not really shut them—more like I just blinked slowly, and in that time, an image of Doris bending over to tie her shoelaces flashed in my mind. I took a sip of my iced tea and glanced out the bay window. "Anybody new move into the neighborhood?"

Wayne shook his head. "Only the people next door."

I felt the same ping in my loins that I had felt at the farmers market. "Any kids?" I asked.

"A girl. She's a year ahead of us."

"What's her name?"

"I think I heard them call her Dolores. Or maybe just Doris."

From that moment on, I had a new best friend.

I biked to Wayne's house every day that summer. Regardless of when I arrived, Brie would meet me at the front door with a glass of iced sweet tea, stare directly into my eyes, then silently guide me into the living room. Fairly early on, Wayne sensed that I was visiting him because I was infatuated with Doris. At least once a day, he'd break off what he was doing and spout some absurdity clearly designed to test me. "Elvis likes capes," he said completely out of the blue one day in early June. "Elvis is cool. Therefore, capes are cool."

This was long before I knew what a logic syllogism was, so Wayne's reasoning seemed sound to me. "You'd have to be stupid to argue the other side," I said.

"But do you too like capes? Do you too think that capes are cool?"

"Yes," I said, nodding. "Yes. Capes are cool."

Apparently, through this exchange, I gave myself away. From that moment on, every single shared action became an elaborate negotiation. For example, I could stare out the bay window at Doris' house for a few minutes, but in exchange, I would have to listen to a new Elvis song Wayne had discovered—some barely tolerable deep cut off of some crappy soundtrack album. Or we could walk past Doris' front door, but then I'd have to help inflate Brie's wading pool. Somewhere along the line, Wayne began to spy on Doris and her family. As distasteful as this was to me, I hung on every word as he detailed each fresh discovery. Wayne told me that "Mr. Messinger" sold restaurant equipment and was on the road for days on end, and when he returned home, he and Mrs. Messinger fought with the same ferocity that the audience women fought with when "E" whipped one of his sweaty scarves into the crowd. Once, Wayne informed me that he was one-hundred percent sure that Doris—and he was positive now that her name was Doris and not Dolores—slept in the nude, or "in the raw like a groupie" as he phrased it. He had seen her slightly pudgy figure silhouetted against the curtain in her bedroom window at night and, as far as he could tell, she was both naked *and* getting ready for bed. For that nugget, I had to help Wayne change the strings of the acoustic guitar his parents bought him—a Martin D-28, which Wayne claimed was not only "absolute top of the line," but an exact replica of the guitar Elvis played on stage during his triumphant 1968 comeback tour.

One sweltering day in late June, Wayne answered the front door instead of Brie. For a tenth of a second, I didn't recognize him. He was wearing a white cape. Under the cape, he had on a white jumpsuit with an Aztec motif stitched across the chest. Around his waist, he had a black plastic belt with a rhinestone buckle the size of a deck of cards. His hair was still blond—he hadn't done anything crazy like blackening it with shoe polish—but it was styled like Elvis' hair circa 1958, parted neatly to the right and coiffed high in the front. He stared at me without emotion, his lips as straight as if he'd penciled them on with a ruler.

"I have important information about Doris, but it's going to cost you," he said.

I felt a jolt. It was the first naked acknowledgment that our friendship was based on multiple layers of deception on both of our parts. I needed proximity to Doris. Wayne needed a soft audience: someone to lend normalcy to his outlandish behavior. The irony was that over the past few weeks, I'd begun to think of Wayne as not only my friend but my best friend. Ever. "Is this how best friends treat each other?" I asked, fighting back a sob.

It must have been how my voice cracked when I said "best" because Wayne's features softened and he motioned me inside. He snapped his fingers and yelled, "Brie!" In a flash, Brie appeared from around the corner and handed me my ice-cold glass of iced tea.

"Is it cold enough for you?" Wayne asked, leading me by the shoulder across the olive-green rug to the sofa. "What about the sugar? Is the tea sweet enough for you?"

I took a sip and nodded.

Despite the pleasantries, Wayne had the leverage, and he knew it. He pulled his Martin D-28 from its case and lifted the strap over his neck. He put an Elvis album—*Live in Vegas*—on the turntable and lowered the stylus onto the spinning vinyl. The unbroken swell of a thousand bee-hived women screaming filled the room. Wayne let the din flow from the speakers for a few seconds. Then he lowered the volume to mimic the crowd falling quiet in anticipation of The King's entrance.

He moved to the center of the living room and flashed a boyish smile. "Thank you. Thank you very much," he said. He waved his hand in appreciation so convincingly that I looked over my shoulder, thinking that perhaps Brie was standing behind me with a second glass of iced tea. When I spun my head back, Wayne was holding a guitar pick above his head. He stood frozen for a beat, then slashed the pick across the guitar strings. He let the chord echo for an instant, then curled his lip and, with one quick gyration of his hips, launched into the first line of "Heartbreak Hotel." His guitar playing sounded rough—he sped up and slowed down, and once or twice he had to stop to re-position his fingers over the strings, but his vocals were solid. More than solid—they were good. If nothing else, the songs sounded how they were supposed to sound; he went up where the melody went up and he went down where the melody went down, and if that was what people meant by singing in tune, then Wayne was doing just that.

When Wayne finished, he dropped into a karate stance and threw a flurry of punches directly out from his diaphragm. He froze, crouched motionless, holding his fist straight out from his stomach in a completed karate punch. After a long beat, he motioned with his uncovered eye toward the stereo console and whispered, "Put the applause on again."

I jumped from the sofa and repositioned the stereo needle to the beginning. I turned the volume up and let the bee-hived women scream for a full five seconds, then hustled back to my seat in a crouched half-scamper. Wayne recoiled his fist in slow motion, then came out of his karate stance and flashed another Elvis smile. "Me and the boys from Memphis are going to slow it down now," he said, and without a hint of self-consciousness, he slipped into the first, tender notes of "Can't Help Falling in Love," singing the lyrics with all the emotional nuances of a man who'd been slapped silly by his unchecked propensity to fall in love. When he finished, he stood frozen with his head bowed as the last chord echoed into nothing. I couldn't help myself; I stood and clapped.

"Thank you. Thank you very much," Wayne said in a dead-on Elvis voice. He put his guitar in its case, removed his cape, and carefully folded it. Then he turned to me. "Doris is leaving. Her parents are sending her to fat camp."

"Fat camp?"

"She's fatter than they want her to be. There's a special fat camp near Harrisburg—across the river. For fat kids. They're sending her at the end of August and you're never going to see her again."

I slumped back into the chair and let out a truncated bleat. I felt defeated: outmaneuvered by a cosmic irony that, until that moment, I never knew existed. "It's over," I said. "Once she gets to junior high, some eighth-grader will snatch her up. I won't have a chance."

"I've been sitting here giving that some thought," Wayne said.

"And?" I asked, leaning forward.

"I think I have a plan."

The elementary school I attended in first grade was still under construction when the academic year began on September the 4th. I was six years old and discombobulated, but I distinctly remember that the auditorium was filled with scaffolding and dusty workmen. I also recall that the sheets of drywall stacked in the annex seemed to be a significant source of concern to the faculty, as was the dust that the workmen tracked from the auditorium to the drinking fountain between the boy's restroom and the girl's restroom. The cafeteria was finished, though, except for the dish-washing machine. It was sitting in a warehouse somewhere in Chicago. At least, that's the story Principal Burkholder fed us. As a result, we used disposable silverware and paper plates during the first few weeks of school. After we finished eating, we threw everything—food scraps and all—into a pair of fifty-gallon garbage cans.

I'd always been a persnickety eater, but I was content enough with the school lunches until the end of the first week when the cafeteria served us beef stew. After sitting with my tray, I discovered that the beef cubes were an unpalatable gray. What's more, the meat's natural fibers were constricted, as if the cubes had been brought to temperature in a pot of boiling water and then immediately rinsed off with cold tap water. I held a cube of meat up in my spoon and inspected it. I touched it with my finger. It felt rubbery. It wasn't the meat's fault. The fat marbling was decent. In fact, it was more than decent—it was exemplary. Beyond exemplary. Nearly perfect. By the time two more seconds passed, I had convinced myself that the marbling was perhaps the finest example of fat distribution in a cut of meat since the dawn of man.

I squeezed my hands into tiny fists and sat with a scowl on my face while my clueless classmates feverishly spooned up their crappy meal. When they put their spoons down, I put my spoon down. When they stood, I stood. My plan was to loiter by the garbage can with a solemn look on my face until my homeroom teacher, Ms. Fungi, spotted me and came to my aid. This would give me the opportunity to express my contempt for the cafeteria workers. All the cafeteria workers—not just the line servers, who clearly were just going through the motions, but also the chef, who, in my opinion, had failed his chosen vocation on a level previously unknown on Planet Earth.

The first step of my plan worked perfectly. Ms. Fungi, of whom I recall nothing except that she favored shapeless, solid-colored polyester dresses, placed her hand gently on my shoulder and asked, "Do you need help, Jim?"

I had my response formulated. I began to answer, but was quickly overcome with emotion. All I could get out were a few strangled bleats and a single word: marbling.

By the time she led me to the nurse's room, I was hysterical. By the time my father arrived at the school's office, I had collapsed. I came to on a folding cot in the nurse's station. My legs were covered with a thin, sky-blue blanket, and my sneakers were poking out from under the blanket. The room smelled of disinfectant. From the hallway, I heard Nurse Darcy and my father talking in hushed tones.

"Yes, yes. He gets plenty to eat at home," my father said.

"That's not what I'm concerned about."

"What then?" my father asked.

By the length of her pause, I could tell that the nurse was hesitant to answer my father. I heard her shoes titter on the linoleum. I lifted my head from the pillow. To put the moment in perspective, this was September of 1969. A few weeks earlier, American astronauts had landed on the moon. It was a new world. Bravery was in vogue. The girls received a pass, but suddenly the internal fortitude of every six-year-old boy was measured against the courage of grown men willing to be hurled into space in a tin can. Inevitably, we were found wanting. I was no exception—even before the trash can episode. Just that morning, I'd had difficulty grasping the concept of counting by fives. And earlier in the week, my inability to identify my own jacket had marked me as a slacker, a victim of mental sloth, and quite possibly in need of an eye exam. The nurse's feet quieted and she cleared her throat.

"Your son seems preoccupied with creature comforts, Mr. Dubbs. *Food.* Your son seems preoccupied with food."

"Who isn't?" my father shot back without missing a beat.

"Many people. Certainly, our brave Apollo astronauts," she said, and if the naked patriotism in her voice were any indication of her posture, her spine would have been as straight as the titanium flagpole that Neil Armstrong planted on the moon three weeks earlier.

A second passed. "Look," my father said in a thin voice, "I'm willing to concede that my son shouldn't have questioned the passion of the cafeteria ladies, but our family is in the food industry. We set up at the farmers market in town. And if Jim said the meat was ill-prepared, then I'm sure there's merit to that. And if he said the marbling was—"

"Mr. Dubbs, we're speaking of gluttony."

I heard another pause, long enough this time that I knew my father had given up arguing on my behalf. The next sound was Nurse Darcy pushing into the nurse's station. She handed me the lightweight jacket that now bore my initials on the inside tag.

My father and I walked past the drywall in the annex and out the door to our Econoline van. On the road, my father curled his lips as though he'd just tasted something bitter. He peered at me a few times from the corner of his eyes. My dad was twenty-six years old at the time, a few years older than I am now, and I'm sure he was contemplating how each step of his life had led him to this moment. I'd only been in school for four days. Ms. Fungi had already sent home one note concerning the jacket mix-up. Now this. He peered at me again and asked, "What was *that* all about?"

I'd never called him anything other than Dad, but at that moment, something told me to call him "Papa." I pressed my hands between my knees. "I don't know, Papa," I said.

This seemed to affect him. He looked as if the bitter taste had dissipated and left him with something else—something not altogether unpleasant. When we got home, my dad said, "Before we go in, put your jacket on."

My mother met us inside the door. "What is it?" she asked.

My father steered my shoulder toward the steps and gave me a gentle push toward my room. "He's got the chills," he answered.

All this to establish that not only were my parents accustomed to weird flights of indignation on my part, but also that I've held a lifelong affinity for food. So, when Wayne said, "I think I have a plan," I instantly grasped the entire thrust of his plan. "A reverse diet?" I asked.

Wayne nodded.

"How much weight do you think I'd have to gain to get into that fat camp?"

Wayne rubbed his exposed eye and pondered this for a moment. "At least thirty pounds," he said. "If you want to be safe, thirty and change."

"I have six weeks, but I'll need at least two of those to convince my parents to send me. So really, it's closer to four weeks."

"A pound a day—that doesn't sound outside the realm of possibility," Wayne said. Then, and I can't guess as to why, he dropped into his Elvis voice.

"No, it doesn't. No, sir, it most certainly doesn't."

That night I prayed for the first time.

I began my reverse diet from a position of strength. First, I was already a tad husky. And second, my dad had taken a part-time job at the Sigma Nu Fraternity house. He short-order cooked breakfast, then returned mid-afternoon and prepared a sit-down dinner. Barely a night went by that he didn't come home with a few pounds of roast beef wrapped in tin foil, a wheel of Longhorn cheese, or a lunch bag filled with frozen, individually wrapped Chicken Cordon Bleu. Whether this was an official part of my dad's compensation or whether he was pilfering foodstuffs to help make ends meet, I had no idea. I didn't care. The point is that between the frat food and Little Martha's unsold baked items, I had unlimited food. The moment I woke up, I'd gobble down an apple sweet roll. Then, while I sipped a tall glass of extra-thick chocolate milk, I'd prepare myself a lumberjack breakfast: buttermilk waffles, scrambled eggs, home fries, and either sausage or bacon. After that, I'd eat every ninety minutes until dusk, when I'd pop a gigantic batch of popcorn and drizzle an entire stick of melted butter over it.

By the middle of July, I realized that despite my best efforts, I wasn't packing on weight fast enough. A pound a day hadn't sounded like a lofty goal—I'd seen plenty of women's magazines advertise "lose a pound a day" diets, so the opposite had certainly seemed plausible. But I'd only gained eight pounds. True, I was burning a ton of calories biking back and forth to Wayne's house twice a day, but to my mind, the larger problem was the restrictions of the circadian cycle. A dieter could diet twenty-four hours a day; I, on the other hand, had to sleep. In effect, by rotating on its axis, the earth was stealing a full one-third of my reverse-diet opportunity each and every day.

That's when I invented "sleep-eating."

The concept was simple enough. I'd walked in my sleep when I was younger, and my family had always treated my nocturnal activities as an amusing event. I had no memory of the episodes, but apparently, I performed mundane tasks in my sleep. I swept the kitchen floor. I adjusted the TV rabbit ears. And once, I carried the ottoman out the front door and deposited it on the curb alongside the garbage cans. So, what, I reasoned, would stop a periodic sleepwalker such as myself from eating high-calorie food in his sleep?

My family caught me the first night. After everyone went to bed, I tip-toed down the steps to the kitchen to prepare myself a cheeseburger. I'd checked the refrigerator earlier in the day and knew that we had a package of ground beef in the meat drawer. It was 90/10—far too lean for a top-notch burger—but I had every confidence that I could work with it. I took a stick of butter from the freezer and used a serrated knife to saw off an inch-thick chunk. I pulled the beef from the refrigerator and fashioned a patty around the frozen butter chunk. Then I laid the patty on a piece of waxed paper and seasoned it with salt and pepper.

I was preheating the skillet when my mother stepped into the kitchen. She tightened the sash around her robe and crossed her arms. A few seconds later my father followed her into the room. Then Trez. I had anticipated this moment. I was naked except for my underpants and two black dress socks—both of which I had on my left foot. I counted the double socking of my non-dominant foot as a touch of genius: visual proof that I was functioning in the hazy nether land between sleep and consciousness. I dropped the patty into the frying pan. While my family watched, I cut a slice of beefsteak tomato and gently deposited it into a separate saucepan, the entire time keeping my eyes focused straight ahead as if I was under the influence of a hypnotist. When the tomato began to sizzle, I jiggled the saucepan to free the tomato slice. Then, with a flick of my wrist, I somersaulted it onto its unseared side.

Trez took a step toward me.

"No! Don't wake him," my father hissed, grasping Trez's shoulder, "It's not safe."

I placed a thick slab of pepper jack onto the patty and covered the pan. While the cheese melted, I applied a light toast to a Kaiser roll. I plated my creation (with a pickle spear and a few potato chips on the side) and walked droopy-eyed to my bedroom, all the while holding back a case of the giggles.

I held back giggles the next morning, too, when my mother asked me if I remembered anything about the previous night.

"Should I?" I asked.

Likewise, I kept a straight face the following morning when she held up the garlic press I'd dirtied just a few hours earlier while preparing a full spaghetti dinner. "Do you recall anything about last night, Jim? Anything about garlic bread? Or wearing your clip-on tie as a tail?"

"Should I?" I asked.

The sleep-eating worked. Whether it was simple math—calories consumed versus calories burned—or whether my metabolism simply waved the surrender flag, I had no idea. The third week of my reverse diet I gained nine pounds. The next week I gained twelve. My transformation was stunning. I looked like a fat kid who kind of resembled me. While I considered my weight gain a blessing, I confess, I did suffer a bevy of troubling side effects: my face was a tad ruddy; I woke up multiple times a night gasping for air; and my feet felt as if someone had driven a carpenter's nail deep into the highest, most sensitive part of each instep. More troubling, a glistening sweat that both smelled and tasted like hot dog water had begun to trickle down the back of my neck so relentlessly that I'd taken to draping a white bath towel across my shoulders.

Somewhere along the line, I'm guessing late July, my body—having exhausted every other available space—began storing fat on the back of my neck. Trez noticed it first. I was in the kitchen searching for something to tide me over until dinner. More accurately, I was standing splayfooted and motionless in front of the refrigerator with my towel draped over my shoulders, staring at a Saran-wrapped portion of leftover Chicken Cordon Bleu, wondering if my mother would miss it if I quickly scarfed it down. I must have dozed off standing up because suddenly Trez was beside me.

"Holy crap, even the back of your neck is fat," he said.

Trez reached for my neck towel. I pivoted to run, but my center of gravity had shifted so dramatically over the past fortnight that I pitched to one side. I righted myself, but it cost me a step. Trez was on me before I cleared the refrigerator. He yanked my neck towel so violently that it snapped my head back. At that moment, my parents entered the kitchen.

I tried to push past them to the hallway, but Trez blocked my path. "He's storing fat on the back of his neck, now," he said, pointing at me. "That's probably why he started wearing that towel."

My mother gasped. My father averted his eyes.

At that moment, it dawned on me that there'd been an entire ongoing family discussion concerning my weight gain. Call it pride, but I began to whimper.

Trez looked at my parents. "I saw him over in Twin Oaks at that kid's house again. They were standing in the wading pool eating hot dogs. And they were wearing capes."

"Wayne was wearing a cape—not me!" I blurted out.

Trez turned to my dad. "Don't let him lie to you. He was wearing a cape, too. I saw it."

My father looked at me the same way he looked at me after I'd passed out over the ill-prepared beef stew six years earlier. His lips curled into a grimace. "What's *that* all about?"

"Well it's not a character flaw," I said. And for some reason, I let out a series of truncated bleats.

"No one is saying it's poor character," my mother said.

I felt ashamed, embarrassed, humiliated. But I also recognized my chance. "Maybe you should enroll me in a fat camp?" I said, pitching my voice higher on the last syllable.

"There is no such thing," Trez said, pointing at me again.

"There's one in Harrisburg. I heard another kid talking about it in school. It's for fat kids. It's called Camp Eden—I think they named it after the Garden of Eden. Like in the Bible."

No one said a word.

So I added, "They put you on a scientific diet. It's foolproof."

My mother tilted her eyes toward my father. In the time it took her to fold her arms, something passed between them. My father ran his fingers along the back of his neck. "Money would be the thing," he said.

"Do they keep any loose cash at the Frat House?" Trez asked.

My father ignored him. Walking off with the occasional case of Chicken Cordon Bleu was one thing; rifling through the frat's petty cash drawer to send me to fat camp was something else entirely. He stroked his chin. As his eyes settled on my midriff, I could see him calculating the pros and cons. My stomach *did* resemble over-proofed dough—he had to admit that. On the other hand, I'd only been "fat" fat for a few weeks, which wasn't enough time to develop any serious obesity-related health issues. Still, he *had* noticed more and more customers eyeing me with disdain, and that reflected poorly on the product. And the last thing he wanted to do was instill trepidation in the customer base: it would squelch sales, thereby affecting Little Martha's ability to turn a profit. He took his hand off his chin. "We're not made of money," he said. "Maybe we can handle this in-house. Limit his access to food. Stay up overnight in shifts. That would put an end to the sleep-eating episodes."

I began to see it all slip away. I repositioned my neck towel. "I used to eat to celebrate," I said. "I'm not celebrating now. I need help."

And then I said the single word that sealed my trip to Camp Eden: "Please."

EPISODE TWO

Title: *This Humble Life*
Time: 42 *minutes*
Synopsis: *Jim makes a startling discovery at fat camp.*

Two Saturdays and $285.00 later, my dad, Trez, and I drove to fat camp.

I sat in the front of the van with my dad. Trez sat in the cargo area on top of his blue flannel sleeping bag, which I was borrowing because just before we left, I'd thrown a fit about packing a proper sheet set and blanket. (I thought the other boys would make fun of me). The trip to the far side of Harrisburg was reminiscent of the ride home after the beef stew incident. Every few miles, my father would peer at me. Then just when he looked poised to articulate a thought, he'd close his eyes and shake his head as if he were erasing an Etch A Sketch. It made for a long, tedious trip, and if someday I have reason to recount it to a psychiatrist, I'm sure that he will make a gigantic deal over how when we finally got to Camp Eden, my dad left the van's engine running.

In truth, I couldn't have cared less. If my fatness embarrassed my father to the point that he wanted to make a quick getaway, so be it. I'd already won. Doris' love was within my grasp—it felt predestined—and as I lugged my enormous suitcase along the camp's trampled dirt path to the last cabin at the end of cabin row, I had just one thought in mind: the impending use of the contraband I was smuggling into camp.

What contraband?

Two days earlier, I'd bicycled seven miles to the Distelfink Drive-in Restaurant. The drive-in was a 50s era burger joint with outside seating and a huge, neon Distelfink sign perched at the edge of the parking lot.

I coasted across the parking lot to the picnic table closest to the restroom door. According to Wayne, the men's room had a coin-operated "rubber" machine. (He'd seen it when his family stopped for ice cream one Sunday after church.) I leaned my bike against the table and pushed through the door. Just as Wayne had described, the shoebox-sized condom machine was bolted to the wall between the urinal and the sink. Above the machine's dented coin slot was a full-color decal of a man and a scantily clad woman. They were in a passionate embrace. Above the man's smiling face, the words: *When you're feeling tender, think about the hellbender* were written in purple script.

I had no idea what a hellbender was. An erection? A bratty child to be avoided with the help of a condom? Possibly some aspect of love-making which I had no knowledge of and would therefore be incapable of preparing for? This last thought troubled me so deeply that as I fed a quarter into the machine and twisted the knob, I panicked and paused mid-turn. The machine's release mechanism produced a halfhearted click. Then nothing. I rattled the knob. Still nothing. I let out a pleading, desperate bleat—loud enough to echo off the cinder block walls. As if reacting to my pleas, the machine slid a two-inch square cellophane package down the delivery chute. I snatched it up and turned it over in my hand. I had a cursory knowledge of the condom's function, but the actual nuts and bolts of putting it on were beyond me. Then I thought: I had an entire pocket full of quarters. What would prevent me from running through the whole process a few times on my own? A to Z. Just to be prepared. I slipped another coin into the slot and gave the knob a twist.

So now, on Saturday morning, August 17th, 1974, as I lugged my belongings toward my assigned cabin (#15) with my dad and Trez trailing three steps behind me, I had the last surviving condom wrapped in toilet paper and snugged in the battery well of my transistor radio, which in turn was wrapped in the folds of my freshly laundered neck towel, which in turn was buried in the deepest recesses of my comically oversized suitcase.

I mounted the cabin's steps and pulled open the screen door. The cabin was empty. The only sign of life was the counselor's bed, which was neatly covered with a fitted and flat sheet. To the left of the bed, on a shelf constructed from two wire milk crates and a slab of wood, sat a three-piece stereo system—receiver, tape deck, turntable. Two humongous speakers stood at either end of the makeshift shelf—each one big enough to bury an adult German Shepherd in.

"What a dump," Trez said, following me into the cabin. "It smells like mushrooms."

I dropped my suitcase at the foot of the bed closest to the door. The cabin was little more than a plywood shack, studded out with gnarled, mismatched 2x4s so randomly spaced that the overall impression evoked images of The Three Stooges in contractor overalls. Ancient, metal bunk beds lined the perimeter of the room. On each bed rested a dingy, cloth mattress that looked as if it had been purchased second-hand from an orphanage. At the far end of the room, a faded green curtain served as the bathroom door.

"Where's everyone else?" I asked my father.

As if in response to my question, the toilet flushed. An instant later, a twentyish man with shoulder-length blond hair rustled through the green curtain. When he saw us, he froze in place for a long beat, then pushed at his round, wire-rimmed glasses and made an unintelligible utterance.

If the man's appearance (his jeans were so filthy they could stand in the corner by themselves) or the lack of even a single cabin mate gave my father pause, he made no indication. "So, I guess watch after the boy," my dad said, reaching out to shake my counselor's hand. "I'd stay to get acquainted, but I've got to get back home. My wife is watching the stand and I don't trust her to push the garlic knots."

The blond-haired guy made a second utterance, which if I had to guess was, "I'll try."

With that, my father and Trez walked out the door. It had begun to drizzle—just enough to nudge the cabin's depressing mushroom smell to another level. I stood at the screen door and peered through the rain as two-thirds of my family hurried through the camp's infield to the unloading area where the Econoline van sat, coughing out spats of blue exhaust. My father climbed in the vehicle first, and then Trez. Before my brother could close the passenger side door, my father accelerated away from the check-in area as if the woods were on fire.

Someday, I'm sure the psychiatrist will make a big deal about that too.

By the time I turned back around, my counselor's face had morphed into a goofy smile. He was wearing a wrinkled, gray shirt with a Superman emblem silk-screened over the chest. He pulled his hand across the cracked red and yellow emblem and said, "Ask me my name."

"What's your name?"

"Viking. Now ask me why my parents named me Viking."

"Why did your parents name you Viking?"

"I have no idea." He jerked his shoulders and let out a stifled "*kee*," as though he'd just made the world's funniest joke and he was choking off a giant laugh—freezing in mid-yak as it were—to give me ample time to appreciate it as such.

"What's with the Superman T-shirt, Viking? What's *that* all about?"

"You mean, Supra Man." Then he made the *kee* sound again.

"I thought that the counselors were college students on summer break," I said. "Aren't you a little old for a college student?"

Viking stared at me as if he were weighing the merits of a half-dozen wildly varied responses. Finally, he said, "I'm twenty-four. I look older because of how I part my hair."

His long hair was parted down the middle. Whether it made him look older was debatable. It certainly didn't make him look healthier. He had broad shoulders—I'll give him that—but his physique was less than inspiring for a fat-camp counselor. He was pale and pudgy. And not a normal, benign pudgy either, where just his face and stomach were bloated. His pudginess was uniform, as if someone had over-inflated him with a bicycle pump.

"Where's the rest of the campers, Viking? The rest of my cabin mates?"

He paused again. "There were six boys last week."

"What about this week, Viking? How many this week?"

"You're it, amigo," he said. He smiled at me and then squatted on the floor between his giant speakers. My brother Trez had a small stack of records, but it was nothing compared to Viking's collection. Viking had probably seventy-five albums propped against the wall in three perfectly straight columns, as if he was recreating a record store display. He flipped through the stack closest to him and pulled out an album: "Are you into Clapton? Derek and the Dominoes?" he asked.

I was on the verge of saying that I liked rock music but couldn't match specific songs to specific bands when a bell rang out—five perfectly spaced tolls. I looked at Viking. He pushed his hair back behind his ears, seemingly oblivious to the ringing. Then he held up the album cover for me to see. "It's a double album. Side one is my favorite," he said. "Everyone's into 'Layla,' but side one has the two best songs: 'I Looked Away' and 'Bell Bottom Blues.'"

"What's that ringing, Viking?" I asked.

On cue, the bell rang again. Viking lifted his chin. His face froze in panic mode for a moment, as if the sound's meaning were buried deep in his mind, just out of reach. "It's the camp leadership," he said finally. "They're calling us to assemble in front of the assembly hall."

"Are you sure?"

"It's copacetic," he said, nodding.

"Are you sure that you're sure?"

"Of course I'm sure. I'm your counselor."

Viking and I took an indirect route to the assembly hall—past the shuffleboard court and around the showers before we ambled up a small hill to the foot of the assembly hall steps where the rest of the campers were already standing in groups of eight or ten. Sheila, the camp director I met at check-in, was standing on the porch, clutching a clipboard to her chest. She was a thin, high-cheeked woman, and even standing in place, she gave the impression of barely contained enthusiasm. "When the hand goes up, the mouth goes shut," she said, raising her right arm.

A slow roll of silence overtook the eighty or so campers. I didn't see Doris anywhere, which in itself didn't worry me. She was there. (Wayne had called me an hour before I left and told me that Doris' family had just pulled out of the driveway.) As Sheila droned on, what began to concern me was that, except for a few staff members, Viking and I were the only males. I confess, as uneasy as this made me feel—I could already sense eyes on me—I couldn't help but feel titillated. Six dozen girls surrounded me, most of them were in shorts, and all of them were roughly my age. Granted, to a one, they needed to lose weight. But who was I to talk?

When Sheila introduced her assistant, Morty, the change in voices brought me back to the moment.

Morty slid over and took Sheila's place. He was dressed in a white tennis outfit and had a thick, black mustache that resembled a child's Halloween costume accessory. "All of you have given in to your worst instincts and in the process, allowed yourselves to go to seed," he said in a measured cadence. He paused, presumably to allow us a few seconds of self-reflection, then repeated himself: "To reiterate, each and every one of you has gone to seed."

I'd seen enough cop dramas on TV to recognize the good cop/bad cop routine. Sheila was the good blue fairy—the tender heart to turn to for encouragement; Morty was the drill sergeant tasked with flogging us back into reality. "Gone to seed" seemed harsh but not wholly inaccurate. We *were* in fat camp. For my own part, I'd added the weight of a lawnmower to my already chubby frame in slightly more than one lunar cycle. I reached down and rubbed my stomach. One of the unintended consequences of my reverse diet was that I'd trained my body to demand an eight-hundred calorie meal every two hours. I hadn't eaten since breakfast. It had been a gluttonous meal: a six-egg Spanish omelet, home fries, biscuits with whipped butter and raw honey, and on a separate, oven-warmed hotel serving platter, the holy trinity of Adams County breakfast meats (hog scrapple, sausage, and bacon). It had served as the final meal of the condemned, and as sated as I felt at the time, my digestive system had already done whatever it did with whatever I shoveled down my gullet—excrete it or burn it or direct it to whichever part of my body still had room to store it.

I leaned closer to Viking. "When do we eat?" I whispered.

"Later."

I looked at Morty. He was pacing back and forth across the assembly hall porch, systematically ticking off a multitude of fat-related illnesses—diabetes, asthma, high blood pressure, high cholesterol, gallstones, orthopedic and joint damage—that we'd collectively opened ourselves up to because, and he was forced to reiterate this point once again, each and every one of us had willfully "*chosen*" to go to seed.

I tapped Viking on the arm. "Why's he keep saying we've gone to seed?"

"It's a metaphor."

"Why am I the only boy in the whole camp?"

For a split second, I anticipated Viking saying *That's a metaphor too*, but he didn't. Instead, he said, "The girl campers always outnumber the boys."

"But eighty to one?"

Viking lowered his head discreetly and whispered, "Ask me where I'm from."

"Where are you from, Viking?"

"Amorphica," he said. "Get it? America, but *Amorphica*."

"That makes no sense," I said.

He lifted his hand to his pudgy midriff. "When the hand goes up, the mouth goes shut."

To compare Camp Eden to a WWII POW camp would be hyperbole. True, it was lacking in nearly every area—even something as basic as topsoil. (According to the brochure, the camp was built on the remains of a Depression-era strip-mining site.) But in fairness, we weren't prisoners. I personally had gone to great lengths to finagle my way through the camp's ramshackle front gates. That's not to say I was happy. By the third day, I realized that I'd made a terrible mistake. I'd laid eyes on Doris only twice: both times in the mess hall and both times with a gaggle of other campers between us. That in itself would have been enough to dishearten me, but alongside that tragedy, my body was teetering dangerously close to its breaking point. Morty had warned us—gleefully, I would argue—to expect an onslaught of maladies as our "badly-seeded" bodies fought to reclaim their health: sluggishness, fatigue, confusion, punishing headaches, unexplained flights of panic, anxiety, feelings of hopelessness, dread, anger, and almost certainly, spontaneous bouts of incapacitating gastrointestinal pains.

I had every one.

In a way, the gastrointestinal issues were a blessing. By day four, every tasteless, ill-prepared morsel of dreck that the kitchen staff fed us passed through my digestive system in minutes, which was a higher level of dignity than it deserved. I'd grown accustomed to real food: sticky buns, cheesecake, tuna melts, slabs of longhorn cheese the size of a matchbox car, and the poor man's eggs Benedict that I'd invented one rainy morning three weeks into my reverse diet. (I'd used a toaster waffle instead of an English muffin and substituted melted butter for hollandaise sauce.) At Camp Eden, breakfast was a clump of overcooked white rice and a single slice of canned peach. Lunch was the same white rice and *two* slices of peaches. Dinner was a third helping of rice, a palm-sized slab of the day's protein—chicken or fish or ham—and a half-scoop of mushy broccoli, so over-cooked that its texture resembled regurgitated baby food.

While the food was merely a shiv in the heart of every culinary pioneer since the discovery of fire, the exercise program was nothing short of Draconian. Three times a day, Viking ushered me to the camp shuffleboard court for calisthenics, where he stood in front of me in his faded Superman T-shirt, clutching a piece of notebook paper with my exercise itinerary hand-printed on it in thick, block letters. "It says to do twenty jumping jacks," he would say. Then he'd stand with his hands clasped, listening to me count off each repetition as I struggled to complete twenty jumping jacks. When I finished, he'd lift the notebook paper just high enough to rest his hands on his pudgy stomach. Then, he'd study it again and say, "It says here to do twenty push-ups." And the whole process would begin again.

By lights-out of the fourth day, I still hadn't talked to Doris. I was lying on top of Trez's sleeping bag with my neck towel draped over my stomach, listening to the mice scurry from one corner of the cabin to another, when Viking pushed through the door. (He'd left twenty minutes earlier to "make a run to his car.") His backpack was slung over his shoulder, and he had a stack of record albums in his arms. I watched him lean the records against one speaker and then strip to his underwear. Just as he plopped into bed, something small and gray darted from behind the stereo and raced across the cabin floor toward the bathroom.

"Kangaroo mice," Viking said.

"What?"

"They're not regular mice; they're kangaroo mice," he said in a lifeless monotone. "I saw a dead one yesterday—you can tell by their back legs."

I was pretty sure that kangaroo mice didn't exist, but I didn't argue the point. From outside, I could hear the faint flutter of the camp flag and the randomly timed chings of its pulley system against the metal pole. I was starving. Dinner had been a joke: the standard-issue rice, two peach slices, and an unseasoned slab of chicken breast so over-baked that it could have passed for a square of tree bark. "I can't sleep, Viking," I said. "I'm miserable. My legs are weak and my stomach feels like someone inflated a balloon inside it."

Three seconds passed. Then Viking asked, "What's your favorite meal, Jim?"

I'd been in Viking's charge for eighty hours and it was the first time he'd called me by name. I hesitated, thinking that it was a test. "Are you sure it's a good idea to talk about food?"

"I am your counselor. I say it's copacetic."

I laid my hand across my stomach. "If you're asking, I guess my favorite meal is Chicken Cordon Bleu with a side of Broccoli Rabe. And good Broccoli Rabe too, prepared correctly, with just a light toast to the pine nuts. I believe in the elevation of food. But at the same time, just regular saltine crackers are good, too. To me, there's comfort in simplicity. At the same time, it's important to do things correctly. Once, in first grade, the school served beef stew for lunch. The meat was beautifully marbled—well, at least it started out beautifully marbled—but then the cafeteria ladies and the so-called chef boiled it in a pot of water. I can't prove it, but I think they used a cauldron. It was a sin against humanity."

Viking raised his head from his pillow and looked at me.

"It's true," I said. "The natural fibers constricted. I made a big stink about it. I told Ms. Fungi, but the chef was never held accountable. They called my dad and the school nurse compared me to Neil Armstrong."

"Well, at least she thought you were being heroic."

I shook my head. "No. She found me wanting. The nurse said—" and I stopped for a beat because my voice was in danger of cracking. "The nurse said I was gluttonous."

Viking laid his head back down. For a long moment, the only sound was the slow, steady chewing of the carpenter ants as they gradually reduced the cabin's rafters to sawdust. Then, Viking cleared his throat. "I think the pizza from Sal's in the mall food court is my favorite. I'd get two slices every day for lunch at work. One Hawaiian and one with bacon and fresh sliced tomato."

"Do they salt and pepper the tomato?"

"Sure."

"But do they grill the tomatoes?"

"Oh, yeah. If Sal didn't, I'd insist. Sal's a good guy. He knows me by name."

Now I lifted *my* head. The notion of someone as important as a pizzeria owner knowing Viking by name impressed me. In the thin light, I could just make out Viking's face. He was smiling, presumably at the thought of Sal's pizza. I closed my eyes and conjured up an image of Sal: early 50s, olive skin, white T-shirt, tossing a round of pizza dough into the air and catching it on the back of his lightly floured hands, stretching the gluten strands until they almost snapped, then ladling on his family's signature sauce—a recipe smuggled into America (under penalty of death) from the old country by his great-great-grandfather. Finally, I envisioned Sal spreading his thick, meaty hands wide and greeting Viking each day in an Italian accent so outrageous it would embarrass Chico Marx: "*Hey-a, how-sa my Viking today-a? You want I-a make-a you a special a-pie-a?*" Then, of course, a grinning Viking in his John Lennon glasses standing there taking three seconds too long to respond.

"Wait a minute," I asked. "What mall?"

"The mall in Philly. Where I work."

"I thought you worked here."

I laid my head on my pillow and waited for Viking to respond. I'd acclimated myself to his weird question-pause-answer rhythm. The first few days, I'd assumed that he was purposely slow to respond—that parsing his words was a vital function of his counseling responsibilities, the thought being that one reckless syllable on his part could short circuit my weight loss and send me home so fat that my parents would have no choice but to strip me naked, smear my sides with butter, and use a crowbar to wedge me back into the house. But since then, I'd concluded that the three-second pauses were part of Viking's natural speech pattern. Still, this particular pause dragged on so long that I assumed he'd fallen asleep until he said in a voice a full notch crisper than I'd ever heard him speak, "I took the summer off."

"Why?"

"It's stressful working in a mall."

"Were you one of those rent-a-cops?"

"No. I worked at Tower Records."

It fit. And, it would explain the ridiculous number of record albums. Suddenly, I had a thought: Viking was worthless as a fat-camp counselor, but maybe he could still be of help to me. I turned toward him and asked, "Would girls come into the store?"

"Oh, yeah. All the time. I'd sell them records."

"Did you ever use the store to ask a girl out on a date?"

"Yeah."

"Listen," I said, leaning on my elbow, "I have a confession. I'm not really fat."

Viking reached out with one hand and tilted the stereo speaker closest to him on its edge, then let it rock back. It thumped on the floor. He tilted it and let it thump again. Then, slowly—as if he was testing how lethargically he could run through each step of the task and still have it work—he thumped the speaker a third time. Finally, he said, "Do you even know what a confession is? It's when you admit to something that's not readily apparent. Something that casts you in a poor light. That's why confession is good for the soul. Saying that you're not fat isn't even true, much less a confession."

"Then I guess the confession part is that in real life, I gained all this weight to impress a girl that I met at the farmers market. She's here at camp. Her name is Doris."

"Bullshit!" Viking said. He sat up and pointed his index finger at me. "You can't bullshit a bullshitter, Jim."

"But—"

Viking raised his hand. "When the hand goes up, the mouth goes shut."

I couldn't fault him. I understood how far-fetched it must have sounded. I stretched out on my back. My stomach clenched, then emitted a long, rushing gurgle. In the dark, I couldn't help but think about Chicken Cordon Bleu and Broccoli Rabe with toasted pine nuts and how I forgot to tell Viking that the perfect cap to my favorite meal was a ginormous slice of Boston Creme Pie. And that made me think about Doris and how much I loved her and how amazing it would be to eat Boston Creme Pie with her. And as amazing as that would be, it would be even more amazing if she dropped her fork and had to bend over and pick it up. Maybe that's what a hellbender was: when a girl bent over and it put you through hell. I was just dozing off when I heard a rustle. Then, I heard crinkling and a second later, feverish crunching. I picked up my flashlight and cut a beam through the darkness. Viking was sitting up in his bed, clutching a king-sized bag of Utz potato chips. Our eyes met. He froze for an instant; a burglar caught with his greasy fingers in a jewelry box. Then he lifted a single chip in the air. For a split second, I thought he was offering me a taste. Then, he shoved the potato chip into his mouth and crunched down.

I woke up the next morning thinking about Doris. Viking was lying on his bed in his underwear. His sky-blue blanket was bunched at his feet and his midriff was slowly rising and falling. On cue, he touched his stomach and moaned. I pulled myself up onto my elbow. The empty, crumpled bag of potato chips was on the floor to the side of his bed. Farther away, as if he'd whipped it halfway across the room in a fit of self-loathing, lay his filthy Superman T-shirt. In the folds of the shirt sat a mouse.

"A huge kangaroo mouse is sitting on your Superman shirt," I said.

"You mean Supra Man," Viking said without a trace of *kee*. He reached back and hammered his fist into the wall so violently that something toppled off the bathroom shelf. Other than to lift its head, the mouse didn't move. I sat up and drove the side of my fist into the wall. This time, the mouse turned and shuffled toward the bathroom in such an indifferent totter that it read as if the creature had completely lost its natural fear of us.

"What the hell's wrong with that mouse?" I asked.

Viking sat up too slowly to even dislodge the potato chip crumbs from his chest hair. He let out a second groan that lasted a good twenty seconds and would have lasted even longer if not for the interruption of the assembly bell ringing. Viking twisted his head on the last ring and looked toward the sound.

I looked too. It had become a Pavlovian response—to loll our heads in the direction of the bell as though its tolling signaled the coming of some new, unimaginable suffering. "What would happen if we never went to anything? Would anyone even notice?" I asked. "Do you think that would be copacetic?"

"I can't allow that. I'm your counselor." He looked through his glasses from a distance before putting them on, then he said, "It's creek hike day. Wear your old sneakers."

"The entire camp is going? Together? Girls too? All of us side by side?"

"That's my understanding," Viking said, turning to me. His eyes were cheerless. He gathered his bottom lip under his teeth. For an instant, I thought he was going to apologize for eating the potato chips in front of me, but instead, he stood and scooped up his Superman T-shirt. He gave it a shake, presumably to dislodge any flecks of mouse dirt, before slipping it over his greasy blond hair.

"Come on, Jim," he said with a sigh. "Let's go."

Sheila stood on the top assembly hall step and peered through the female campers to where Viking and I were standing. "Perhaps our two gallant gentlemen will volunteer to lead the creek hike," she called out.

All eyes turned to us. It was the first warm day since we'd arrived. The sky was cloudless and the scent of hemlock trees was thick. The girls, to a one, were wearing shorts and tank tops, their arms and legs exposed to the sun. Viking and I were in the back, ten feet from the closest female. Viking was wearing his Supra Man shirt and baggy blue jeans. I was wearing a hooded sweatshirt. We both had on old sneakers. A couple of girls giggled. I instinctively shifted my eyes to the spot by the bell pole where Doris stood with her cabin mates each day. She looked down, seemingly in response to the giggles, and folded her arms. I turned back to Viking. His eyes were panic-stricken. He licked his trembling bottom lip and started to say something, but he stopped midway through the first syllable. In a different time and place, his reaction may have passed for comical, but this was fat camp. Viking was my counselor, and my fortunes were tied to him for good or bad.

"I don't want to get us lost," Viking finally stammered.

"If you get lost, just turn around and follow the stream back," Sheila said.

Another round of giggles.

Viking stood motionless for a good ten seconds. Then, as though his mental tumblers suddenly clicked into place, his expression became resolute. He pushed his John Lennon glasses up on his nose and made a windmilling "follow me" motion with his right arm. In the next instant, Viking was marching the entire population of Camp Eden away from the assembly hall and downhill past the counselor's lodge to the camp's lone stream. Without breaking stride, Viking hopped off the tiny bridge and landed flat-footed in the clearing by the stream's edge. One by one, the campers jumped off the bridge, landing as Viking had landed, flat-footed and arms spread, as though he'd been instructing them.

When all the campers were standing in the clearing, Viking lifted both hands over his head. "When the hands go up, the mouths go shut," he said.

To my astonishment, every camper fell silent—and not the slow-rolling, eventual silence that overtook the collective tomjammery when Morty or Sheila raised their idiotic good cop/bad cop hands in the air; this was an immediate, shut-up-or-else quiet.

"I *am* your leader," Viking said, tilting his chin up.

I'd lived Viking's pause-laden speech pattern for four days, so I knew that his proclamation wasn't a stand-alone sentence. Plus, I knew Viking was incapable of stringing together multiple sentences without using the word "copacetic" or making some esoteric reference to Supra Man, Derek and the Dominoes, kangaroo mice, or any of a few other, very limited number of topics. So, while the girl campers stood in the warm sunshine awaiting further instruction, I'd already narrowed Viking's next utterance to either: *"And this is Amorphica,"* or *"Ask me why I'm your leader."*

Instead, he surprised me. Viking gave his hands a victorious pump. "And as your leader, I say we rest for a few minutes and catch our breath."

"Afraid not, Leader," Sheila shouted from the back, "we're on a tight schedule. Get them in the water."

"Water then," Viking said, giving his hands another pump.

I had no idea if the other camper's existence had been as miserable as mine, but as the first cluster of girls stepped from the gravel bank into the rippling, sun-drenched creek, a palpable sense of joy filled the air, first as isolated whoops, then as a chorus of excited yelps. I stepped into the water. I can't swim—I'm a tad aquaphobic—but I felt a flit of excitement as the ice-cold water infiltrated my canvas sneakers and ran between my wiggling toes. At that instant, standing in the rushing water, the appeal of a creek hike was unmistakable. It was a rebirth. Not only was it physically stimulating, but it was mentally liberating. I was willfully breaking the rules. I was soaking my sneakers and socks, and it was okay. More than okay—it was copacetic. For the first time since I'd arrived at Camp Eden, I laughed.

When I looked up, Doris's nose was six inches from mine.

A second passed. In that time, the tiniest trace of breeze lifted a few of Doris' bangs and set them back down again. As much as my life had orbited Wayne's reverse-diet scheme for the past six weeks, I'd never given a thought as to what I'd say to Doris when we were finally face to face. I felt a surge of panic. Should I offer up something tied to the moment, something like *Cccooooold,* or *Is this your first creek hike?* Or, should I swing for the fences and try to establish a deeper bond with a line that touched on our shared fat-camp misery, something like *I see you're here to lose weight, too—bummer, huh?*

As it turned out, I didn't need to say a word. Just as I tried to buy myself some time by smiling, Doris stuck her finger in my face and simultaneously began and ended the conversation. "Tell your loser Elvis-friend to stop spying on my parents' house," she said.

I didn't cry as we hiked back—at least I sucked it up that much—but as soon as we cleared the lodge, I broke ranks. I lolloped through camp in my water-logged sneakers, clomping past the front of the dining hall and across the shuffleboard court and I didn't stop until I reached cabin row. I was crushed, but by the time I made it to my cabin and shut the door behind me, a strange calm had washed over me. I felt unshackled. The charade was over. I didn't have a chance in hell with Doris—not here at fat camp or back home in school or anywhere else on the face of the earth. Standing there with my back against the door, I felt my shoulders relax for the first time in weeks.

Ten minutes later, I was collapsed on my filthy mattress, fighting through an onslaught of hunger pangs when Viking slammed through the door. His cheeks were red. He threw himself onto his bed, landing with such a violent thump that it shook the cabin walls and sent whatever toiletries were left on the bathroom shelf tumbling to the floor.

"Seething and festering!" he sobbed into his pillow.

I peered out the window for some indication of what may have happened. Nothing appeared out of order. Morty was standing by the shuffleboard court with a clipboard in his hands, and a few girls were walking toward the pool with towels wrapped around their waists. I climbed off my bed and moved to Viking's side. "There, there," I said in as calming a voice as I could muster through my hunger.

Viking lifted his head. He sniffed hard and looked at me as if he had tuned into my suffering for the first time. "You're languid," he said, wiping a tear away.

"Maybe so," I responded, trying to appear thoughtful through my hunger. I had no idea what languid meant, but the "lang" part sounded like a blend of long and pain, which felt appropriate. "Maybe I am languid."

"Nobody gives a damn about us," Viking continued, "not one of the counselors. And that Sheila's even worse. How's it possible to smile and belittle someone at the same time?"

"There, there," I said. "Don't worry about them. You led the creek hike like you'd been doing it your entire life. The other counselors should be proud of you."

"That's where I just was."

"Where?"

"Trying to hang with the counselors at the lodge."

I didn't say anything. Apparently, the other counselors had ostracized Viking somewhere along the line. The possible reasons were endless. The Supra Man thing, for one. The Amorphica thing for another. And I'm sure his refusal to follow the staff dress code played into it. Judging by the rest of the staff's clean-cut appearance and pedantic attitudes, I'm sure they must have considered Viking a communist or a hippie or some nefarious combination thereof. I tapped his mattress. "If they want to act like that, it's their loss," I said. "I vote we skip the shuffleboard court today. It's not like anyone ever checks on us. Let's just stay in the cabin and seethe and fester together. We'll listen to records."

"I'd enjoy that," Viking said.

"What's your favorite record?"

He let out something between a sob and a laugh. "You know it's Derek and the Dominoes."

"Well, then we'll put on Derek and the Dominoes," I said. I slid the album from the sleeve without touching the grooves, just how Wayne had taught me, and placed it on the turntable. Then I lowered the needle onto the jet-black vinyl. The record hissed for a few seconds before the opening guitar riff of "I Looked Away" spit out of the speakers. Viking pressed his hands between his knees, and we sat on the floor with our backs against the plywood wall, our sneakers creating tiny puddles under our feet.

"We're dripping on the floor," I said after a moment.

"Couldn't care less," Viking answered. "Seething and festering—remember?"

Halfway through "Bell Bottom Blues," I noticed that we weren't hearing all the music. I was no rock and roll expert, but I'd heard this particular song on the radio ad nauseam, and I could tell that half of the guitar sound was missing. I turned to Viking. "Why are we missing some of the music?"

He stared at me—way longer than his pause-laden speech pattern would typically dictate. "I'm tired of all my records," he said finally. "Do you ever flip through your record collection and think, *I'm sick of all these—I want to hear something different?*"

"I don't have a record collection," I answered. "I can't imagine ever having one."

"But you have a transistor radio. We can listen to the radio."

"There are no batteries in it."

"They're dead?"

"No. There were never any batteries in it." I climbed to my feet and got my radio, then I sat down again and slid off the battery cover. I pulled out the condom I'd bought at the Distelfink and showed it to Viking. "Ask me what it is," I said.

"What is it, Jim?"

"It's a Distelfink condom," I said.

I handed him the condom. He turned it over in his hand, examined both sides, then handed it back to me. "What's a Distelfink condom doing in the back of your radio?" he asked.

Like the mice, I no longer felt the need to defer to Viking. We'd seen each other at our worst, and as a result, we were equals. So I told him the entire story about the farmers market and how I fell in love with Doris at first sight—how from that second on, I couldn't tell my brain and my heart apart anymore. Then, I told Viking about Wayne and how we'd cooked up the reverse-diet scheme and how he'd told me about the Distelfink's condom dispenser. I ended with, "And the worst part of this whole sappy movie is that after four miserable days, I finally get close enough to Doris to talk to her, and she rips into me for something I didn't even do. So, you can see why I'm seething and festering too."

Viking pulled his knees to his chest and stared at me. "This morning at breakfast, I saw that Doris girl watching the back of your head."

"That's because she hates me."

"I don't think so, Jim," Viking said, and he said it so convincingly that it made me scoot up. "Tell me again what she said on the creek hike."

"She said, 'Tell your idiot Elvis friend to stop spying on my parents' house.'"

"But nothing about you?"

"No. Not a word. She directed the warning towards Wayne."

"And all the spying happened when you weren't there—so, in her mind, you're not complicit."

"What are you thinking?"

"I'm thinking that maybe things are copacetic—that maybe you're in the clear."

"Really?"

"Trust me. I am your counselor."

When the bell sounded for the three o'clock exercise period, Viking gave me the notepaper with the list of exercises and told me to work through them myself. He had something important to do—counselor work. I didn't see him again until dinner. I was sitting at our table alone, forking a clump of dry, room-temperature rice into my mouth, when Viking pushed through the mess hall door and strode to my table. He shot a glance toward the serving counter, then leaned in. "Why are you eating this slop?"

"I need it to stay alive," I answered.

"It's slop. You understand that, right?" He straddled the bench and stared at me. Not his usual, hapless, fog-of-war stare but a probing stare. Like he was testing me.

"Yes," I answered. "Yes, it is slop. It's devoid of even the slightest hint of culinary nuance. And the presentation is an affront to humanity."

"Then I've got a secret to tell you," Viking said.

"Okay."

"It's a confession."

"Go ahead."

Viking took a deep breath. He tapped his fingertips on the dining hall table and then looked around the room again, stopping to study each staff member's face. "Not here," he said. "Back at the cabin where no one can hear."

In the cabin, Viking opened his mouth into a super-sized *kee*. "Ask me what my confession is."

"What's your confession, Viking?" I asked.

"I'm a camper. Just like you," he answered.

Viking *kee'd* again, then he turned and swan-dived onto his filthy mattress. Two mice darted from behind the stereo and raced each other to the bathroom. He rolled over and exhaled as if he'd been testing how long he could hold his breath. "Oh, my goodness. What a relief. You have no idea how good that felt—finally telling the truth."

"Bullcrap. There are no campers here your age," I said.

"That's the whacked-out part, Jim. That's what I've been trying to tell you all along. That this is Amorphica—a place where you can morph into anything you want."

I scowled and crossed my arms.

Once it was clear that I was going to wait him out, Viking sat up and swung his legs over the side of his bed. He touched his Superman emblem as if he were drawing strength from it; then, slowly, he began to tell his story. What he'd said the first day about the six boy campers was true. I was a late registration. So last second that the camp bent the rules to let me in. Apparently, I was supposed to have a doctor's note attesting to the fact that I was fat. (I can't even begin to imagine the humiliations that office visit would have offered. I envision my entire family huddled in the tiny, sun-drenched room as the doctor examined me: my mother holding my neck towel, my father checking his wallet, Trez stepping forward to ask the doctor, "What would cause an otherwise normal person to wear a cape? I mean even if he *wasn't* fat?") And because my parents registered me so late, it was impossible for the camp's only male counselor—Viking thought his name was John Something—to reschedule his vacation plans. As a result, the camp's administration was in a quandary. They didn't want to turn away a paying customer; at the same time, they didn't have male supervision. That's when Viking wandered into the story. He'd registered for the September adult fat camp, but he'd gotten the dates fouled-up and arrived at Camp Eden just a few hours before I arrived. Morty, who was prepared to step in as my counselor, saw the surprise arrival of Viking as his out. I would have an adult male as my cabin mate. The program pretty much ran itself. What could go wrong?

Viking took his hand off his chest. "So, when your father mistook me for an actual counselor, I played along," he said.

"So all this time you were supposed to be doing calisthenics with me? Not just standing there reading off the next exercise?"

Viking nodded. "I'm sorry, Jim. So now if you go ahead and forgive me, we can get to the next part. The important part," he said.

"The only way I'm forgiving you is if you give me the Superman shirt."

"You mean Supra man," Viking said, as though he was delivering the punchline to a joke.

I held my ground. "The shirt or no forgiveness."

Viking made a soft, whimpering sound, then pressed his open palm against the cracked, red and yellow emblem. "To be honest, I'm surprised you can't see there's no right or wrong here. No good or evil."

"Then why were you so happy when you told me the truth?"

Viking gathered his bottom lip under his teeth. He let out a pained sigh and pulled his shirt off, knocking his John Lennon glasses ajar in the process. He held the bunched shirt in his hands as if he was clutching some essential part of himself, then he sighed and tossed it into my arms. "The rest of *my* story is that I'm not taking a break from the mall. I quit my job. I needed a new start. My life is pathetic and I've gone to seed and I haven't lost a single pound since I've been here and it's my own lousy fault. So you can have my Supra Man T-shirt, Jim, but not because I wronged you. You can have it because you're my only friend and I want you to have it."

He sighed again, lifted his eyes, and a smile overtook his lips. "Hey, do you know why you never heard the second guitar on Derek and the Dominoes?"

I shook my head.

"For the same reason the mice are no longer afraid of us," Viking said. He spun the speaker closest to his bed around and pried off the back panel. An avalanche of food toppled onto the floor: Twinkies, Ring Dings, Big Wheels, cupcakes wrapped in thin foil, packaged pudding cups, individual-sized bags of chips and a few cookie-like things I'd never encountered before. "Ask me where all this came from," he said.

"Where did all this come from, Viking?"

"Morty doesn't lock the kitchen door after dark," he said.

My anger toward Viking dissipated by the third Twinkie. We were leaning against Viking's bed with an empty Frito bag and a scatter of Devil Dog wrappers strewn on the floor between us. The first side of The Allman Brothers *Live at the Fillmore East* had played through. Other than the crackling of the needle riding the record's play-out groove, the only sound was the distant overlap of voices from the pool and the occasional sonic splash of someone cannonballing off the diving board. "I've been thinking," Viking said. He stopped mid-thought to pull a Ding Dong from the speaker and unwrap it. He held it to his mouth and then lowered it without taking a bite. "I've lost everything. My job, my apartment, my chance at weight loss. I'll have to move back with my parents—at least temporarily. And they're Quakers."

"What's wrong with Quakers?" I asked.

Viking scrunched his face. "I never bought into the whole Society of Friends thing. When I was little, the Sunday school teachers would give us this whole big speech about how we were brothers and sisters, and then outside afterward the older boys would beat me up. That's why the whole Supra Man thing. And Amorphica."

I tore the wrapper off another Twinkie. It seemed to be idle talk—important on Viking's end, but of no real consequence to me—until Viking said, "So at the very least, I want to see how this whole sappy movie ends."

I adjusted my neck towel. "It ends with us going home fatter than when we came."

Three seconds passed. "I mean the sappy movie about you and the Doris girl."

Maybe it was the sugar revitalizing my synapses, but I was experiencing clarity of thought for the first time in days. I had no chance to win Doris' love. If my pursuit of her was a movie, then the plot wasn't only sappy, it was stillborn. Everything—the reverse diet, the spying, the Distelfink condom—were all for naught. And now, because my fake counselor had discovered the staff's hidden cache of Ring-Dings, I'd be lucky if I lost the fat stored above my eyebrows. "It ends in failure," I said.

But Viking just kept smiling at me.

"What?" I asked.

He made his laugh-stifling *kee* sound. "I spoke to the Doris girl on your behalf."

Viking convinced me—or "counseled" me as he insisted on saying—not to wear my neck towel on my date with Doris. This was probably wise for numerous reasons, not the least being that the white towel, as dingy as it was, most certainly would have caught someone's eye as I scurried behind cabin row and through a small sweep of hemlock trees to the unlocked door at the far end of the darkened mess hall. I was in deep—well past the point of bailing. When Viking spoke to "the Doris girl" on my behalf, he had slathered it on thick. He told her that Wayne had gone rogue and spied on her family without my knowledge, and that I was every bit as horrified as she was to find out about it. All I wanted was a chance to apologize and present a peace offering, namely food: protein, starches, sweets, and the cold beverage of her choice. Plus, and I confess that this part worried me, Viking told her that I had called her "cute."

I was in the kitchen, crouched behind the serving window contemplating how Doris could use our shared fat-camp experience against me at school if things turned sour, when the mess hall's side door squeaked open.

"Jim?"

I poked my head out of the serving window. "Doris?"

She pushed through the swinging door into the kitchen. I'd left the lights off—Viking had warned me about attracting attention—still, enough ambient light existed for me to make out Doris' face. It was a perfect oval, like the football plates the local diners serve breakfast on. Her bangs were combed to one side and held back with a pink, butterfly-shaped plastic barrette. She tip-toed toward me. "It's beautiful in here," she said.

"I know," I whispered. "It's the stainless steel. It shines even with the lights off."

She moved to the grill and ran her hand along the edge. "My father sells commercial restaurant equipment. I've grown up with the catalogs. I look at them all the time. Sometimes he takes me with him on sales calls and lets me write up the orders."

"Do you know my favorite part of a commercial kitchen?" I asked.

Doris shook her head.

"The smell of the walk-in refrigerator."

"I know!" she said, barely able to keep the hush in her voice. "Nothing else smells like it."

"Sometimes I smell it, then go outside and take a few quick breaths so I can come back in and smell it all over again," I said. "It's like . . ."

"Like how heaven smells?" Doris whispered.

"Yes," I whispered back.

We stood in the semi-darkness for a long moment, both periodically shifting our feet. Then, Doris looked down. "I apologize for the creek hike," she said. "It's just your Elvis-friend has our family creeped-out. We caught him spying on us a bunch of times."

"I had no idea about Wayne," I said. "I'll put a stop to it when I get home—I promise."

"That's a relief."

"I saw you at the farmers market," I said.

"I know. I saw you too."

Doris clasped her hands together. "So, your counselor—that Superman guy—said that he'd been deputized to speak to me on your behalf. He said they had real food in the kitchen."

"The staff has been *eating it*," I said as if I was filling her in on some nefarious plot that had been churning along unimpeded behind our backs. "There're leftovers from meals we've never had access to: eggs, lunch meat, pie, cake, snack foods. This is our chance to eat anything we want, but I've always found that nothing calms me more than properly prepared meat. Would you like me to make cheeseburgers?"

"What if someone walks in?"

"Easy—we pretend we're sleep-eating."

Doris didn't respond. Perhaps she was instantly on the same wavelength. Or, perhaps she was so transfixed by the anticipation of sinking her teeth into red meat that she logged my comment as curious but not worth clarifying. It didn't matter. I twisted the knob to light the griddle. "I love the smell of a well-seasoned flat top heating up," I said. "It evokes the memory of every single meal that's ever been grilled on it."

I reached for a spatula, then held my hand over the grill. It wasn't even warm. I touched it. It was stone cold. "It didn't light," I said.

Doris reached out and took my hand. "It's a Vulcan 960," she said. She put my index finger on the plunger and together we pushed. "You have to spark it."

I molded a handful of ground beef into a ball about the size of my fist. Then, I laid the meat on the hot grill and squashed it with the spatula until the air filled with the scent of caramelizing fat. While I busied myself forming a second ball, Doris moved close to my side. She brushed against my shoulder and smiled. Then she brushed against my shoulder again and this time, when she smiled, I smiled back.

I toasted two buns on the flat top in a puddle of hamburger grease. I would have preferred pepper jack or an extra sharp cheddar for cheese, but all the camp had on hand was American. I melted a double slice on each patty and plated the burgers.

Doris took a bite of her cheeseburger and chewed slowly. She started to take a second bite, then stopped. "You're not going to tell, are you?"

"Tell?"

"At school."

I had no idea what secret I was to keep. The hamburger? Our date? Camp Eden in general? "Who would I tell?" I asked.

"It's just I've never started a new school, and I'm nervous."

"Start by just blending in," I said. "No one will make fun of you if you don't stand out."

"It's not that easy," Doris said. She set the hamburger down and gathered her hands in front of her. "My mother is incredibly social. She didn't want to leave New Jersey. She cried when we drove past the cornfields outside of town. She kept asking my father why he was doing this to her. So just blending in isn't enough. I have to be part of the 'in-crowd.' That's why I'm here. I have to make a good first impression with the right girls."

Doris stopped talking for a moment. She shook her head. "When I was ten, my parents—my mom mostly—took me off whole milk. Do you know how horrible skim milk tastes?"

"That's because fat equals taste," I said.

"Do you know how it feels to think you can't do anything right?"

I instinctively understood that Doris had opened a door to a more private, vulnerable side of herself. I also knew that she was inviting me inside, but at a cost. She needed something in return—an offering of *my* pain. I also understood that my pain had to be a lesser pain than hers. I put my hamburger down. "I know what it's like to be unfairly compared to an astronaut," I said. "And to come up wanting in the comparison."

"I'm sure that wasn't pleasant."

"No. It certainly wasn't."

"Why can't people accept us the way we are, Jim?"

And this was the inception of my Art of Intuition. The entire concept took maybe a tenth of a second to construct in my mind. How should I respond to Doris? Don't think. Just abandon all intellectual thought. Let the conversation flow like water and the perfect line will spill out.

I touched her hand. "I think you're perfect the way you are," I said.

Doris didn't look flattered or embarrassed and she didn't smile; she just slowly tilted her head and stared at me, like she was staring into the deep end of a pool at a shiny penny.

"Are you still hungry?" I asked.

She nodded. "I've been hungry for days. The girls only get *one* peach slice at dinner."

"Then I have something I've always wanted to try—a food game. Do you want to try it?"

"If it involves food, yes."

If it was possible to look beautiful in a paper-towel blindfold, Doris looked beautiful. She sat cross-legged on the floor by the flat top while

I scurried around the dark kitchen filling a serving platter with food. "Jim?" she called out, twisting her head to listen for my footsteps. "It's kind of hot by the griddle. And I can't see. What are you doing now?"

"I'm back," I said, sitting down on the linoleum floor in front of her. "The point of the game is to have fun and to eat but also to fine-tune your palate. The person wearing the blindfold's part is to guess what the other person puts in their mouth."

I loaded a spoon with peanut butter and touched it to Doris' lips. She opened her mouth and closed it around the spoon. "It tastes like peanut butter."

"Correct."

Then:

"Chocolate Cake?"

Then:

"Hmm. This one is tough." She licked her lips and lifted her index finger to her chin. "It can't be—not here—but it tastes like cold shrimp."

It wasn't, but she was close, at least taste-wise. It was leftover scrambled eggs dipped in ketchup. She was so happy with her guess, though, that I played along. "I can't believe it. That's three out of three."

She smiled and clapped her hands. "Okay, Jim. I'm ready for another."

I didn't plan what happened next. It just happened in the flow of the moment. I was looking at Doris, thinking how beautiful she was with her paper blindfold on, when the thought struck me: my plan had actually worked. I chuckled. *Of course it had worked.* Every single scene—beginning with our chance encounter at the market to that morning's creek hike—had played out the only way it could play out. It was fate. The same cosmic irony that had crushed my hopes seven weeks ago was now smiling down on me. Before I could stop myself, I leaned in and pressed my lips against Doris' lips. I let them linger there, ever so lightly, for just a second before I pulled them away.

Doris tilted her head. "Is it tofu?"

"Try again," I said. And this time I gave her a movie kiss. And just like in the movies, Doris pulled back for one snippet of a second—just long enough to fool the audience into thinking she was protesting—and then she kissed me back.

Doris pulled her blindfold off. "Your turn," she said. She got on her knees and tied the paper-towel blindfold around my eyes. I'd barely had a chance to acclimate myself to the loss of one of my senses when Doris put her hands on my cheeks and kissed me.

To this day, I cringe at the next part of the story—and not a quick, fleeting cringe, but a sustained, semi-somatic cringe where I scream a tortured, unending bleat, cover my privates, and collapse onto the floor into the fetal position. When Doris pulled her lips from mine, I slid my hand into my front pocket and wrestled out the Distelfink condom. Still blindfolded, I held the condom out to Doris. Then I said, "When it's time to be tender, think about the hellbender."

Five seconds of silence ticked by—enough time for me to fantasize a half-dozen scenarios, all of which ended with me marrying Doris in my parents' back yard—before Doris made a wretched, choked-off sound that, while I can't begin to fully describe, has none-the-less never left my memory. I knew instantly that I'd overplayed my hand. The worst was yet to come, though. Apparently, Doris had taken karate lessons in New Jersey. She let out a sharp, piercing cry. The next instant her fist landed just above my right eyebrow. My balance tipped and I toppled backward. On the way down, my arms flailed, seemingly in slow motion, and the Distelfink condom left my hand.

At this point, any normal person would have pulled their blindfold off. I did the opposite. I reached up and secured it over my eyes. I rolled over onto my hands and began groping the floor for the condom. What was I thinking? Given my panic in the moment, it's impossible to reconstruct my exact thoughts. Maybe I was trying to recover the evidence. Maybe I was hoping that if I tucked the offending two-inch packet back into my pocket, Doris would forgive my temerity and we could continue our date, which until that point had been the best thirty minutes of my life. All I know for certain is this: from my position on the floor, I heard a familiar sound coming from the grill. A sound like a hamburger sizzling—only interspaced with the sound of bubbles popping. I sniffed the air and there it was—the smell of rubber burning.

At that moment, someone opened the kitchen's back door. I heard excited voices: Morty, Sheila, and three or four others that I couldn't identify. I heard the scuffing of shoes on linoleum close in on us, then stop. As frightening as those sounds were, the next few ticks of silence, with nothing to fill the air except for the seething of melted rubber on hot steel, truly terrified me.

What broke the silence was not the thundering voice of authority—Morty or Sheila or whomever else was present—screaming and admonishing us in a horrible clamor of threats and accusations. That would have been preferable, as would any one of a million other sounds I can imagine, up to and including Camp Eden's doomsday whistle, which Morty had told us on the first day would only sound in the event of a nuclear attack on the United States. No. What ended the silence was Doris' voice. And it wasn't the overwrought, pleading voice of a modern-day Juliet begging the powers that be to take pity on the plight of two famished, love-struck teenagers. No. It was a harsh and loud and declarative voice, and despite my being blindfolded, I knew that Doris was pointing at me.

"It wasn't me," she yelled. "It's him. He's a big fat jerk!"

EPISODE THREE

Title: *The Rebel Trez*
Time: *58 minutes*
Synopsis: *Jim, Trez and Mandy embark on a road trip to
  Graceland.*

Two days after Viking, Doris, and I were frog-marched out of Camp
Eden, I pedaled my bike to Wayne's house in Twin Oaks. I coasted
around the corner of Oak Lane just in time to see a tall, dour man with
white hair hammering a Century 21 Real Estate sign into the Messingers'
front yard. I watched from the end of the block, drawing my breaths
in short pants while he tied three helium balloons to the sign and then
drove away.

Wayne swung the front door open before I knocked. He waited for
Brie to hand me my iced sweet tea, then filled me in. When Doris returned from camp, there had been a ruckus, first inside the house and
then outside. Immediately after that, Mr. Messinger confronted Wayne's
parents about the spying. My name came up. First as an accomplice, then
as an overall nefarious influence—the seed of low-life farmers market
vendors who sold crappy, over-priced spinach garlic bread that wasn't
nearly as complementary to pasta as they led everyone to believe. For
his part, Wayne denied everything, and, so he claimed, offered a spirited
defense of my character. He was at a disadvantage, though. Something
had obviously gone horribly wrong at fat camp, but he had no inkling as
to what. And as he explained to me, he could only ad-lib so far without
fear of contradicting any subsequent lies we may be forced to tell to cover
our tracks.

Then I told Wayne about fat camp: the creek hike, Viking passing himself off as a counselor, the staff's secret food cache, my kissing Doris on the lips, and finally the tragic, ill-timed destruction of the Distelfink condom. I edited only Doris' last words—I left out the "he's a fat jerk" part.

Wayne leaned back and rubbed his uncovered eye. "Well, at least Viking sounds cool. The way he wore John Lennon glasses and tricked you into thinking he was someone else."

"I have a sneaky feeling I still have a chance with Doris," I said. "We connected. She kissed me. Twice. Everything else was just bad timing."

Wayne stared at me with genuine puzzlement. He shook his head, then picked up the telephone and walked to the bay window, trailing the long beige cord across the shag carpeting behind him. He pushed the drapes open and squinted at the Century 21 placard. "That's your problem," he said, dialing the telephone number, "you never know when to give up."

"Question about the Twin Oaks property," Wayne said into the phone. I sat on the sofa and listened while he let out a few "hmmms" and "sounds goods." He managed to look both bored and impish at the same time. He rubbed his eye patch and began to improvise, morphing from a generic grown-up voice into his young, aw-shucks, Elvis drawl. "That's a mighty fine house . . . Uh-huh . . . Uh-huh. Yes, sir, my mama surely would like that house." By the time Wayne finished, he was in a full-blown Elvis impersonation. "Thank you. Thank you very much," he said, then he slammed the receiver down as if he'd just asked the other end if they had Prince Albert in a can.

"What did they say?" I asked, pressing my knees together.

"Motivated sellers."

Extremely motivated, it turned out. The same dour-faced agent returned on Sunday to host an Open House. The next morning, he hammered a SOLD sign in the ground next to the FOR SALE sign. An hour later, Doris and her mother drove off. An hour after that, a trio of jumpsuit-clad men backed a box truck into the Messingers' driveway. Throughout the long afternoon, the men carted the family's furniture and appliances out through the front door and into the back of the truck. Then they drove off. The father remained in the empty house just long enough to close escrow.

The evening that Doris' father left their house for good, Wayne and I were in his front yard throwing the football. It was the tail-end of a perfect September day—the sky was clear, the air had a fall crispness to it, and the towering scarlet oaks that gave Twin Oaks its name had just a trace of autumn red to their leaves. We heard the grind of the Messingers' garage door opening. I stopped in mid-throw and watched as Mr. Messinger backed his car into the road. As the garage door closed, I felt something vital lift from my body—like a sparrow flying away. In that moment, part of me still believed that Doris and I were destined to be together. The "fat jerk" remark aside, she *had* kissed me. Twice. I turned the football over in my hands. Perhaps her father would jot down his family's new address for me. I wasn't much of a letter writer—the subtleties of a one-sided conversation escaped me—but if personal growth was required on my part, then so be it. I had just lifted my hand to flag Doris' father down, when he caught sight of Wayne and me. He stared at us for a moment, then rolled down his window and motioned for us to come closer. Wayne and I shared a glance, then walked to the car. Doris' father leaned out the window, and with as clear diction as he could possibly muster, he said, "Fuck both of you."

Three years later, by the start of the 1977 farmers market season, my brother Trez had undergone a transformation far more dramatic than my Summer of Doris-inspired weight gain. From one summer to the next, he'd morphed from a wiry, slightly buck-toothed all-American boy in baseball spikes and football pads into, in my father's words, "a stinking, low-life communist."

In truth, Trez was more of a 50s era bohemian with a scatter of Marxist-leaning platitudes tossed in for good measure. He grew his hair out. He wore a choker fashioned from handmade filo beads (a gift from his girlfriend, Mandy). And he walked in a slow, semi-slouched shuffle. Gone were his Converse sneakers and Baltimore Colt T-shirts. The new Trez refused to wear anything except sandals and solid, neutral-colored T-shirts. He'd grown tired, he said, of being used as a shill by huge, faceless corporations that would just as soon put a bullet in his head as pay him a fair day's wages for a fair day's work. And to my parents' chagrin, he was done with farmers markets. Not physically: he still had to help—but he'd distanced himself emotionally. He couldn't care less about the success of Little Martha's Bakery or the economic well-being of the markets in general. They were bourgeois, as were all consumables. Especially bread, which he considered a blatant manifestation of capitalism—empty calories produced for no reason other than to keep the poor, hapless proletarians on their poor, bedraggled feet just long enough to serve the interests of the oppressive landowners. The landowners in this case being our parents, Bill-n-Mattie Dubbs.

The apex of Trez's transformation came at the beginning of August. He quit the high school football team despite being the team's best player. He wasn't quarterback—again, that would be poor storytelling. My brother played wide receiver and he returned kicks. He touched the ball seven or eight times a game, but the team's fortunes soared each time the coaches put the ball into his hands. He was playing against stiffer competition, so this wasn't like middle school when he would seek out contact for no reason other than to punish his would-be tackler. Now, he used his speed and agility to outrace everyone to the end zone. So, when Trez asked to address the team in the locker room on the first morning of two-a-day practices, Coach Baylor likely assumed that my brother, as a senior, wanted to deliver a pep talk to the underclassmen. And when Trez began his speech by saying, "I like to drive fast with the windows down," I'm sure his coaches thought that my brother was gearing up to deliver some Knute Rockne tripe about playing the game with reckless abandon.

They were wrong. Trez paused to let his topic sentence resonate. Then he told the team he was quitting. The rest of them could still play if they wanted to, but he was done. It was time to put away childhood things. He was older now and it had been a slow awakening, but he had developed wanderlust of the soul. He'd heard stories about old hipster guys on the other side of town who didn't have jobs and stayed up until daybreak playing jazz. He didn't like jazz. He was still into Zeppelin—rest assured of that—but he felt intrigued by the concept of jazz because jazz musicians made it up as they went. They changed keys by a consensus of feel. And it was that consensus of feel that he now wanted to explore. Who knew? Maybe this moment was *his* key change. Maybe he would become a jazz musician himself and stay up to all hours of the night smoking tea. And by tea, he explained with a subtle smile, he meant marijuana, which he'd been dabbling with for the past few months, and now, over the past three weeks, had been *more* than dabbling with; he was smoking twice a day to build his stamina—the same way the rest of them were now practicing in pads twice a day to build *their* stamina.

At first, everyone thought that Trez was joking.

His teammates, most of whom were standing in front of their lockers in various stages of undress, exchanged grins. A few boys laughed out loud. Then, in the span of maybe two seconds, a consensus of feel similar to the one that moved jazz musicians to modulate keys prompted every single boy in the room to fall silent. Trez rocked back on his heels. He had intended the "tea" comments to be the crescendo of his speech. In his mind, he had foreseen himself pulling on his street clothes while his stricken teammates, and maybe even a few coaches, lined up to shake his hand and offer him well-wishes. But when Trez surveyed the gobsmacked faces staring at him, he concluded that he needed one final, grand gesture to mark the moment. That's when he lifted his football helmet as high as he could reach and let it drop onto the concrete floor.

And that's also when Coach Baylor walked over to Trez, laid his hand on my brother's shoulder, and said, "Son, get the hell out of my locker room."

After that, Trez was either a hero or a shithead, depending on whom you asked. The school's social outliers (druggies, misfits, artists), all of whom had long viewed my brother as a standard-issue, brain-dead jock strutting through the hallways like he owned them, now called out "*Hey, man*" and "*Right on*" to him between classes. The other, far more conventional herd of jocks, preppies, and social climbers treated him as though he'd deposited a giant bowel movement upstream of the town's lone water supply. All of this was the ideal outcome for my brother: he loved the dichotomy—that Gettysburgians from every level of the social strata were pissed off at him only confirmed in his mind that he was on the right path. "You can live your safe, bourgeois life as a hapless cog in the wheels of industry if you so desire," my brother said to multiple people every day, "but as for me, I wouldn't want to live a life without severe misgivings—like Stalin, I'd consider it a loss."

My parents were okay with Trez quitting football until that Saturday's farmers market. By the middle of the nine o'clock rush, a cloud of disgrace had settled over Little Martha's Bakery. The market was bustling, but our product wasn't moving. The sweet stuff—sticky buns in particular—languished on the table. The garlic knots and challah may as well have had a label that read "Includes Arsenic!" A few regulars passed by our stand without breaking stride. Then a few more passed. Around ten o'clock, some elderly, boot-faced woman whom none of us had ever seen before, shot Trez a dirty look, then proceeded to lecture my parents at great length about the societal benefits of corporal punishment as a means to control their wayward offspring. "A firm hand!" the woman spat out, pointing to the meaty, heel part of her palm to illustrate her point. "And a taste of the knuckle if it comes to that!"

After that, my parents told Trez to take a walk until it was time to break down the tent.

I went with him. We strolled down the sidewalk toward the 7-Eleven, then turned toward the college and cut across the railroad tracks to Carlisle Street. Trez wanted to stop at The Philosopher's Stone. The Stone was a one-room head shop on the ground floor of a tiny, two-story clapboard building. The shop sold a few record albums for appearance's sake but mainly trafficked in drug paraphernalia: bongs, hash pipes, rolling papers, Joss Sticks, et cetera. Local myth held that the owner—a bearded, middle-aged man who wore a fringed poncho and kept his dog (a sad-eyed bloodhound named Jimi) in the store with him for company—would hang a tie-dyed T-shirt in the store's picture window to alert the local pothead community that a fresh shipment of tea had arrived. And it was that T-shirt that Trez, winking at me, pointed to as we arrived at the store's facade.

I was nervous about entering the shop. It was more than the fear that a regular farmers market customer would see me and report it to my parents. I'd already been inside—three weeks ago with Wayne. We had heard from a guy at school that the shop had a full-sized poster of a naked woman tacked to the ceiling above the record display. Wayne's and my plan, hatched over a week's worth of study halls, was to casually enter the store and make our way to the records. While I flipped through the handful of albums, Wayne would nonchalantly gaze up at the naked woman. When he looked down, I was to wait five seconds, then take my turn.

So three weeks ago, in keeping with "the plan," we ventured into the shop and slid directly to the record display. Wayne covered his formerly eye-patch eye—ostensibly to give his uncovered eye increased focusing power—and tilted his head back. Immediately, he began to emit a weird sound. At first, the noise was innocuous enough; it sounded as though he was trying to clear phlegm from his vocal cords. When his throat clearing escalated into a raspy gargle, I couldn't restrain myself any longer. I looked up at the poster. My cheeks flushed instantly. Tacked to the ceiling was a full-sized poster of a naked woman. She was lying in a bed of white, undulating sheets, and she had one thin arm tucked under her flow of long red hair. My mouth gaped open. I sucked in three quick breaths, then launched into a long, piercing bleat that rose up and down the scale and built to such a high-pitched crescendo that it could have easily passed for the doomsday siren at Camp Eden.

This went on for a full ten seconds, which in itself would have been spectacle enough, but at the eleven-second mark, Jimi—the dog—padded to my side and began to howl along with us. That's when the owner strolled up behind Wayne and me, put a firm hand on each of our shoulders, and ushered us out the door.

So, when Trez pushed into the shop, I inched inside more or less in his shadow. If the owner recognized me, he didn't change his posture. He had a copy of National Lampoon open on the counter in front of him and he was leaning over it. Trez made a show of inspecting a ceramic Buddha incense holder, going so far as to tip it back to inspect the felt bottom. Then, still eyeing the incense holder, he said, "I see the tie-dyed T-shirt is hanging up."

It didn't take a genius to read the man's facial clues: the slow blink, the tongue pushing at his cheek, the way he lifted one corner of his mouth when he flipped the magazine to the next page. "No idea what you're talking about," the man said.

We scuffled back outside into the harsh sunshine. The owner's response was a slap in the face, and a quick one at that—the entire scene lasted less than thirty seconds. My brother never allowed humiliation to mar his self-confidence for long, though, so in a series of quick steps that could have served as poses for the ascent of man diagram, he abandoned his lethargic, stooped-over shuffle and puffed out his chest like the touchdown-producing Trez of old. We had an hour to kill, so we followed the railroad tracks to the indoor antique market a few blocks from the square. Trez thought that his girlfriend, Mandy, might be poking around the booths. She had the day off work, so it was more than plausible we might find her wandering the aisles of the dusty, sprawling antique market. (For weeks she'd been fixated on finding the perfect pair of battered old work gloves to sketch in charcoal.)

"Dad's mad about you squelching sales," I said as we walked.

"Couldn't care less and neither should you," Trez said. "Farmers markets are bourgeois. It's a great big, huge world out there and mom and dad have reduced it to the circumference of a sweet roll."

Trez's assessment seemed harsh to me. I loved sweet rolls—especially the raspberry—and I was hoping that there would be at least one left unsold so I could warm it on the skillet and top it off with a scoop of vanilla ice cream. I let it go, though. Inside the antique market, we split up. I went upstairs to scout around for a cheap typewriter—preferably an old Royal. I wanted one with heft to the keys, something that would make a thunderous clap when I typed my short stories. Trez stayed downstairs. He was on his own scavenger hunt. For most of the summer, he'd been babbling about finding an old, 50s era tweed suitcase: one that (in his mind) had belonged to some impoverished, lonesome traveler. He idolized the Beat writers, "idolized" being a charitable description. Every time he tried to read *Dharma Bums* or *Naked Lunch,* it ended the same way; he'd plop down on the sofa, barefoot, read two or three pages and then wander off, having already lost interest. It didn't diminish his vision, though. He had this whole elaborate fantasy about escaping Gettysburg the second graduation ended—he even told me he was going to walk across the stage to accept his diploma carrying his "beat" suitcase.

When I caught up with him ten minutes later, he was standing in front of a wooden table piled high with salvaged hardware. He was holding an oil-stained cigar box filled with a jumble of old, discarded keys. He stood there transfixed, examining the contents, and at one point, dug an ignition key from the box and stroked his chin with it. Suddenly, he jerked his head up to the old man sitting behind the table. "All these keys—how much for the entire box?" he asked the man.

"What do you want those for?" I broke in. "You're throwing your money away."

But it was too late; before the man even answered, Trez was digging into his pocket for his wad of crumpled bills. "These," he said, picking up one of the keys and dangling it in front of my face, "these are the weapons of a working-class hero."

I was raised on The Last Scone Story. As many times as I've heard it, though, my mental images aren't of the story itself; they're of my father telling the story. My mother's bowling pin story is different. I've only heard it once—when I was eight—but every time I replay it in my mind, I can picture every detail vividly, down to the thin, orangish-beige color of the mud caked in the bowling pins' glue-seam cracks. My details are details borne from a lack of repetition—I've expanded and filled in the empty spaces with my own imagination—and as a result, my mother's story has become far more real to me.

During the early 1950s, my mother and her mother lived in a rented house alongside Opossum Creek in the tiny village of Aspers. Their home sat next to a creaky, one-story wood-working plant that produced bowling pins. The sides of the building were clapboard with white, peeling paint, and the windows—which ran the entire length of the factory—were metal-framed six pane units. At both ends of the long, rectangular building were twin dock doors that swung open like the entrance to a barn.

Six or seven men worked at the plant. Every Monday, Tuesday, and Wednesday, my mother would wake to the sound of the factory's two-ton duplicating lathe chewing into the maple wood blanks. Listening to the machine over the years, my mother learned to tell how close the pins were to their final shape by the sound the lathe made as it carved the wood; a steady thumping sound meant that the workers had just loaded the blanks; a smoother, softer sound meant that the lathe had nearly finished shaping the blanks. On Thursdays, the men painted the pins, and on Fridays, they lacquered the pins. My mother loved Fridays. She sat on her mother's splintered back porch while the factory's colossal exhaust fan flushed the sticky over-spray into the neighborhood. To her, the lacquer smelled as sweet as honey.

One September day in 1955, the remnants of Hurricane Flossy stalled over Pennsylvania. After dark, the town flooded. Inside the factory, the week's production of bowling pins rose in the flood water and floated to the end of the building, where they bobbed in the dark. Just after midnight, the latch on the downstream doors gave way, and, in my mother's words, it sounded as if God had thrown a strike. A few seconds later, every downstream resident heard bowling pins battering the sides of their defenseless homes like torpedoes fired from a battleship.

Once the deluge receded, the villagers found water-swollen pins deposited throughout town: beached in their front yard, wedged into bushes, buried in the mud. Somehow—to everyone's puzzlement—a few pins even found their way into one family's basement. By mid-autumn, every Aspers resident had at least one bowling pin perched on their front porch. My mother wasn't content with just one pin. All fall she spent her after-school hours walking through town searching for lost pins. Before the weather turned cold, she found thirty-three of them. A few of the pins, by the time she rescued them, looked old and decrepit—maybe even the victims of some previous, long-forgotten flood. It made no difference to her. Mismatching or not, she lined them up on the front porch, where they sat throughout her teenage years.

Then one day in early June of 1958—it was the first Friday after school had let out for the summer—my mother was sitting on the back porch with a glass of ice water, fanning herself. The sun had just cleared the treetops, and tiny house-wrens were frittering in the undergrowth bordering the house-side of the creek bed. My mother heard the factory's exhaust fan kick on. A few seconds later, the smell of lacquer—so thick she could taste it—wafted across the yard.

"They're lacquering!" my mother called out to her mother.

My grandmother ambled out the screen door and stood on the back porch. She gave the air a sniff to determine its safety, the same way the astronauts in science fiction movies sniffed the air after crash-landing on an uncharted planet. She frowned. "Martha, what you see in this nasty smell, I'll never know," she said. "And it's not like—"

She stopped mid-sentence.

My grandmother stopped because she heard an odd sound. It wasn't coming from the factory—the hum of the lathe, the buzz of the bandsaw, the rattle of the exhaust fan's worn-out bearings. Those sounds were part of her daily existence, no more foreign than birds chirping. This was a tapping sound—steady but at the same time irregular. And it repeated itself—like a looping Morse Code distress call. "What is that, Mattie?" my grandmother asked. "That tapping sound?"

"I hear it too," my mother said.

My mother looked downstream. Just past where the ripples emptied into a deep section, the current was lapping against a tangle of storm-downed branches. Trapped in the debris was a single bowling pin, bobbing helplessly in the swirl of water.

My mother scurried down the back porch steps. She kicked off her shoes and waded into the stream. By the time she got to the branches, the water was past her waist, and she could feel the mud and silt suck at her toes. She wrestled the bowling pin free and pressed it to her chest. With her free hand, she broke off a branch and used it to steady herself as she made her way back to the creek's bank. My grandmother was standing at the edge of the creek by this time, with one hand shading her broad face as she watched my mother trudge up the mud embankment. "Mattie, why'd you wade all the way out there for that worthless thing?" she asked.

"It needed me," my mother replied.

My mom named the rescued pin "Daisy" and painted a face on it. By the time I started school, the bowling pins resided in the attic of our home. All except for Daisy, whom my mother kept on the mudroom floor beside the second refrigerator. One day—it was the first week of summer vacation—my mother was pulling boxes of butter from the second fridge and handing them to me one by one. She reached out to shut the refrigerator door, and when she did, she caught a glimpse of Daisy. "I don't feel any older," she said, "but looking at Daisy, I guess I am. Either that or somehow Daisy's growing old while I'm staying the same."

I can't remember my exact words. I was eight years old—plus I think that on some level I regretted what I said in response and pushed it to the back of my mind—but the gist of my words were along the lines of, "If Daisy makes you feel old, why not put her in the attic?"

"I like to rescue things," my mother said.

That's when she told me the story of the bowling pins, starting with the bowling pin factory and the flood and ending with her wading into

Opossum Creek and wrestling Daisy from the tangle of branches. She finished with, "And don't tell—this is our secret—but I rescued your father too."

"You rescued Dad?" I asked.

She nodded. "Only I could. I know it's hard to imagine, but your father didn't have even the tiniest bit of confidence when we first met. And from the moment he asked me on a date, I knew if I said yes, I'd have to say yes forever."

She squatted down and picked up the bowling pin doll. For a long moment, she studied the dried mud that still filled its cracks. Then she said, "I'd do it all again too. I used to think that it'd be wonderful if we all had two lives to live. One to practice with and then one to get perfect. Then I realized—the practice life would most certainly be the far more interesting of the two." She put Daisy back on the floor and looked at me. "So who in their right mind would ever choose the perfect one?"

I have no idea whether my mother ever told Trez the bowling pin story. My feeling is, probably not. I'm guessing that she understood Trez would never need encouragement to live the practiced life, the same way she realized early on—probably around the time I came home sick in first grade—that I would need to hear her bowling pin story. Just once.

On August 16th, 1977, two weeks after my brother bought the cigar box full of keys from the man at the antique market, Elvis died of a heart attack. It was a Tuesday—an off day for Little Martha's. Trez and I were standing in the front yard, barefoot on the jaggy, rain-starved grass, throwing the Frisbee. We had the stereo speakers propped in the open window and our beloved hard rock radio station, 98 ROCK, had interrupted its regular playlist for an Elvis song: "Burning Love."

"I'm almost eighteen years old," Trez said. "Jack Kerouac hitchhiked back and forth across America a dozen times before he was eighteen."

I glanced toward the house to ensure that neither of my parents were within earshot. "That junk you're smoking is destroying your brain," I said.

Trez turned on the balls of his feet and crouched down by the hedge to look for the Frisbee I'd just whizzed past his kneecap. Every thought he'd articulated over the past half-hour had been slow and circular, like water swirling down a half-clogged drain. Now, after telling me for the third time in five minutes that he was eighteen and still hadn't done anything Kerouac-like, he lifted his hands in frustration and yelled, "I can't find it!"

"It's right there!" I pointed.

Trez pulled the disc from the welter of branches and fired it back at me. "All morning, they've been talking about burying Elvis beside his mother," he said, motioning to the speakers. "Do you want to go?"

"Go where?"

"The funeral."

"Isn't Elvis bourgeois?"

I knew how Trez would answer. The Who, Led Zeppelin, Black Sabbath, Pink Floyd, The James Gang, Neil Young and Crazy Horse, Jimi Hendrix, Humble Pie, Traffic, Yes, The Rolling Stones: those were the bands Trez loved—not some phony, Vegas lounge-lizard like Elvis. But instead of responding, Trez just held his hands out for me to toss him the Frisbee. I could see by the tilt of his head that he'd already made up his mind. It would be perfect. Attending Elvis Presley's funeral could only enhance the Trez mythology. That, and serve as undeniable proof that he was operating on a level of satire well beyond the grasp of even the most enlightened members of the local tomjammery.

"We leave this morning," he said. "Around ten or so—before it gets hot."

I looked around as if I'd missed something. The hottest, most miserable part of the day had come and gone. What's more, it was time for me to start dinner. My mother let me prepare the evening meal every Tuesday and it had become one of my simple joys. "What do you mean *we*? I can't go. I'm making prison meatloaf and scalloped potatoes for dinner. Mom traded for extra onions so I can practice my knife skills."

Trez shook his head. "You're fifteen. The highlight of your Saturday night shouldn't be practicing your knife skills."

"It's Tuesday," I said, whipping the Frisbee back as hard as I could. "Thanks, but no thanks. I already have the breadcrumbs soaking in milk. That's the secret to prison meatloaf—to over-saturate the breadcrumbs."

For a moment, I anticipated Trez saying *the highlight of your Saturday night shouldn't be over-saturating breadcrumbs*, but instead he said, "I'm sure Mandy will come. You like Mandy. And she likes you. I've been thinking that you two should spend more time together."

Trez twisted his mouth into an innocuous smile. He knew that I had a crush on Mandy. She was the most beautiful girl in school, far and away. And to make her beauty even more Mandy-like, she was attractive in such an unconventional way that a cynic could make an equally compelling argument that she was homely. (She had a wide bump on the ridge of her nose that was chronically red—like the skin across it was in a constant state of irritation from being stretched too tight.) Mandy was also the most talented artist in school, and whenever I hung out with her and Trez, she lavished all her attention on me—explaining at great length the most minute nuances of her latest artistic epiphany. Trez had no problem with this. It was as if he'd pawned off the tedious, non-sexual part of their relationship on me. For my part, I never tired of her attention. Mandy showed me whichever new watercolor or charcoal she was working on, and since I recognized reciprocity as the foundation of any relationship, I showed her each new version of a story I was working on—a short piece about a man who wakes one morning and feels compelled to search an abandoned pearl-white building for a part of himself he perceives to be missing. Mandy had called my latest version of the story "Kafkaesque," which I took as a compliment even though I had no idea what "Kafkaesque" meant.

"Mom and Dad are never going to say yes," I said. "And even if they did, what are we going to use for money?"

"I've got twelve dollars."

"That's not enough. Where would we sleep?"

"We'll sleep by the river," Trez said.

"What river?"

"There's always a river."

"What about food? We can't go without eating."

Trez smiled. He pulled the keys to his 69' navy blue Super Nova out of his pocket and gave them a jingle in the sunlight. "It worked once," he said.

I considered "it" to be despicable. Trez was right, though. It *had* worked once. Flawlessly. Two days after Trez bought the ratty, oil-soaked box filled with keys, he drove to downtown Hanover, parked, then walked into some hole-in-the-wall diner. He sat at the counter and ordered the cheapest items on the menu—a grilled cheese sandwich and coffee. His bill came to $1.45. When he went to the register to pay, he tapped his pockets front and back and told the cashier that he had accidentally left his wallet in the car. "I'll tell you what," he said. For the woman's benefit, he stroked his chin as if he were double-checking this thought process. Then he handed her a cluster of three fake keys bound together with white string. "If it's okay, I'll leave my car keys here as collateral while I run outside and get my wallet, that way, you know I'll be right back."

Now, standing in our front yard, Trez dangled the keys to his Nova in the sunlight until I nodded. "Go to the attic and gather an armful of those bowling pins," he said.

"Why?"

Trez tossed the Frisbee toward the front porch steps. "Just don't let Mom or Dad see you."

"But why take bowling pins?"

"Because we might have to barter our way into the funeral."

Our dad, of course, considered a trip to Graceland to be a fool's errand. "Is that idiot, Elvis-freak friend of yours mixed up in any of this? That one-eyed kid who wears a cape and spies on people?"

"No. He hates Elvis," I said. "He's into The Allman Brothers now." Even as I was saying it, I knew that I'd made a mistake—the type of clumsy misstep that I'd trained myself to avoid. For as long as I could remember, I'd grasped that my father's mental faculties were at an odd angle to the general thought-line of normal society: in short, his every thought revolved around the farmers markets—specifically, our family's ability to turn a profit at them. So even as I was saying "The Allman Brothers," I knew that my father would hear it as the "Almond" Brothers, and in his mind, the "Almond" Brothers would morph into The Osmond Brothers. From there, The Osmond Brothers would evoke thoughts of the Mormons, and Mormons would conjure up disturbing images of squeaky-clean young men in white dress shirts and black ties handing out religious tracts at the farmers market—squelching deals and agitating the customer base by their very presence, thereby reducing the profitability of Little Martha's Bakery.

"I don't like what I'm hearing," my dad said.

"Straight to Graceland and back. Just to pay our respects," Trez said. When my father only furrowed his brow, Trez pulled out the big guns. "I'll be eighteen in two months—old enough to die for my country and I won't have to ask permission to do anything."

Our father looked across the kitchen to our mother. My mother was far more tuned into reality than my father. She understood that we weren't driving 900 miles to Memphis in a rusted-out Chevy Super Nova to pay our final respects to Elvis. We were using the King's death as a pretense for a road trip—an excuse for God knows what. Our mother was in a bind, though: from the time we were toddlers, our father had preached The Last Scone Story to us, and with it, the corresponding notion that letting the brass ring circle out of reach was life's only true tragedy. "What about Mandy?" my mother asked.

"I haven't seen her in weeks," Trez lied. "We're on the outs."

My mother crossed her arms.

That's when I stepped in. Literally. I took a single, full stride as though I was stepping forward to recite my line in a school play. "The practiced life," I said to my mom. Then I repeated it, this time with as much inflection as I could muster. "The *practiced life*, Mom."

I'm sure that my dad and Trez heard my words as a total non sequitur, but they both turned to my mother for her response.

"Straight there and back," she said. "And no Mandy."

We picked Mandy up in front of The Gettysburg Hotel. She was dressed in sandals, cut-off jean shorts, and the oversized, white dress shirt she wore as a smock when she painted. Otherwise, she had nothing—not even a purse. She leaned in through the driver's window and kissed Trez. "I'd almost given up on you," she said to him.

"No baggage?" he asked.

"I have everything I need, Lover," she said. Then Mandy did what she always did when I was along: she crawled into the back seat and slid so close to me that our thighs touched. "Do you see that, Jim?" she asked, pointing across the quadrant to Wolfe's Pub.

I leaned forward. The streetlights hadn't clicked on yet. The Pub's green and white striped awnings were mired in shade, muting their color.

The building's peak was silhouetted. Above the peak, in the twilight, the sky was a deep, pensive blue, and a few early stars were visible.

For weeks, Mandy had preached "the emotion of light" to me. I knew that she wanted me to mouth something like how the soft evening light evoked a completely different set of emotions than the harsh light of day. "Do you mean the light?" I asked. "How meditative it is?"

"It's poetry," Mandy said. "I love the first stars. It's like this whole secret world is poking through with all these hidden little wants and needs."

I let a moment pass to give the impression that I was reflecting on light and the first stars and their relationship to some latent truth concerning the human condition. In reality, I was allowing enough time to elapse so that my next line would sound unscripted. I'd written a joke about Mandy's favorite painter, Vincent Van Gogh—I just needed to maneuver her into mentioning him. "So, who would do a good job painting that light?"

"Monet. Rembrandt, maybe, but in a different way. He lit his paintings from within—that was his genius. I guess, first and foremost, my lovely Vincent."

"Do you know the best thing about Van Gogh's paintings?"

"What?"

"The paint is still wet."

Mandy angled her head back and studied my face. "How long have you been saving that one?"

"It's a joke," I said. "The absurd non sequitur."

"I know, and I get it. I love it to death. The paint can't possibly still be wet, but it *is* Van Gogh, so perhaps . . ."

Trez backed out of the Hotel's parking spot and steered the car onto York Street. At the first stoplight, he hit the brakes a tad hard and the bowling pins in the trunk shifted with a sustained, rolling clatter. Trez looked over his shoulder and said, "Attic bowling pins," to Mandy, as if that explained everything, then he pushed in an 8-Track tape—Deep Purple's *Machine Head*.

"So, what's this all about?" Mandy asked. "For real."

"Road trip," Trez answered. "You've got to take the train off the rails once in a while."

"Like it's Amorphica," I said.

Trez's eyes flashed in the rearview mirror. "What?"

"Amorphica—a new beginningness," I said. "It's America but an America where anyone can morph into anything they want. This Quaker guy, Viking, told me about it."

"Amorphica," Trez said. Then he repeated it, "*Amorphica*. I dig it. Just morph into whatever you want. That's what Kerouac did. And Trotsky and Engels and Marx too. Then they tested it against the status quo. Only then could they recommend it to the poor bedraggled masses whose hapless, life-giving blood greased the endlessly turning cogs of industry."

"Holy cow," Mandy said. "You better be careful you don't fall off that soapbox."

"Thank God I have it," Trez said.

Mandy looked at me and rolled her eyes. "What about you, Jim? Are you ready to take the train off the rails?"

"I'm hungry already. Plus, I'm a tad concerned about the sleeping arrangements—I'm against the whole idea of sleeping by the river. I wake up gasping for air sometimes and I don't know how the river will affect that," I said.

"See—that's what I love about you. You're without pretense. And you have an artist's heart. I can tell because your thought process isn't ABC. It's ADCBA, and then who *knows* what? Maybe a Q or Z thrown in. That's why I can talk to you about light. You get abstract concepts."

"I most certainly do," I said.

She touched my arm. "And I love that you're growing your hair out. The only thing is that the curls cover your ears and your ears are way too cute to cover."

I closed my eyes and let my Art of Intuition feed me a line. It took me a split second to get out of my own way because Mandy's fingertips were making tiny swirls on my thigh, but when I managed to clear my mind, it came to me—the perfect line for Mandy. "Such is life," I said.

We sped down Route 116 toward Memphis as though we'd hopped the fence. We had all four windows rolled down and the radio blasting so loud that Trez had to ease back the treble to keep the speakers from blowing out. The afternoon heat had dissipated, and the last rays of daylight were thin slivers of fuchsia clinging to the hills in front of us. Then, in the span of two songs, "Life in the Fast Lane" and "Ramblin Man," the sky gave way to stars, and in the thin twilight, it felt like we were gliding along the highway, an inch off the asphalt.

We were almost through Maryland when Trez lowered the radio and called out, "Check the map."

I spread the map across my legs—no easy feat given the wind ripping through the windows. "We stay on 116 all the way to 81," I said. Then I added, "We're getting close to West Virginia."

As if to underscore my point, our beloved 98 Rock radio station, which had been teetering in and out for the last twenty miles, faded into static. "It was only a matter of time," Trez said. "It's either Deep Purple again or a new station—and they'll be playing Elvis."

"I can do without Elvis," Mandy said.

"You mean 'E.' People called him 'E' after he got famous," I said.

"How do you know that?" Mandy asked.

"A friend of mine used to be infatuated with Elvis—he told me stories."

"Let's hear one."

I squinted out the window. "Well, it's not a full-blown story, but Elvis had a twin brother and he died in the womb. He got the umbilical cord wrapped around his neck and suffocated."

"Elvis had a twin brother?" Mandy asked.

"Yes."

"And he died?"

"Yes."

"What if the wrong Elvis died?"

"I'm not following you," I said.

"What if the wrong Elvis died? What if the Elvis that died could sing circles around the real Elvis? What if the Elvis that died was the better Elvis in every way?"

Trez used the rearview mirror to look at Mandy. "The problem with that is you're assuming there would be a good Elvis and a bad Elvis."

"Not at all," Mandy said. "It's the *what if* that interests me. You could just as easily ask what if both had lived? Would Elvis still have been Elvis but just Elvis with a brother? Or since he had a brother, would he have grown up to be someone totally different? Maybe he'd still be alive and working in a factory, living in a small house with the love of his life and every day would be a poem that only they could write."

"Or he could have killed someone just to watch them die," Trez said.

"That's my exact point—that we each have the capacity to live far more lives than we could ever possibly have the time to live."

Trez shook his head. "I believe in Amorphica—like the Quaker guy. We morph into what we want and create our destiny in the process. Take me: I quit the football team because I have wanderlust and I've never once looked back—even after that old lady told Mom and Dad to beat me because I had the audacity to point out the eternal class struggle inherent in a capitalist society. Now, I'm on a road trip just like Jack Kerouac because of it. I have my filo beads. I have my Zeppelin. I have my girlfriend. I'm driving fast with the windows down. And you know what? This feels exactly like who I'm supposed to be."

"That's because we live our lives forward and remember them backward," Mandy said. "That's why *now* feels exactly right—because it's *now*, so it can't help but feel right."

Trez shook his head. "All just more of your wine and cheese talk. I don't think anyone's life changes based on one event or one decision because it's just one of tens of thousands. There're a hundred possible ways to get to Graceland. In the end, each one takes you there and when you get there—by your own argument—now is now, so any *single* event or decision is irrelevant."

Mandy leaned forward. "But what if we take a wrong turn? I mean a *really* wrong turn? How far off the path can you wander and still find your way back? Or even *want* to find your way back? Is there a point when you've wandered too far—maybe you've drifted into some horrible, decadent period of your life where now is now but now doesn't feel right—and it's impossible to find your way back? Or maybe you do find your way back, but it turns out that you went off the path at the exact wrong instant and you missed the one singular moment that may have led you to be who you were supposed to be?"

I scooted up in my seat. "So maybe Elvis—at least the version of Elvis we're going to pay our respects to—was never even *supposed* to exist," I said. "Maybe he was the unintended consequence of an accidental turn by someone he didn't even know who got so lost they never found their way back to where they were supposed to be."

"Exactly," Mandy said.

"Or maybe Elvis himself took a wrong turn and, right now, we're unintended consequences of that wrong turn," I said.

"It boggles the mind," Mandy said. "It's like your short story about the man who wanders into the pearl-white building."

"What story?" Trez asked.

"The short story your brother wrote."

Trez didn't say a word.

"How in the world can you not know Jim wrote a story?" Mandy asked.

"I don't know every damn thing he does," Trez said.

"That's funny, since we're all expected to hang on every single syllable the rebel Trez utters."

"It's not an insult," he said, his voice clenched, "I simply don't know anything about it."

"Well, you should. I love his story to death. It's *really* good."

"Okay—so it's really good! I'm not saying it isn't. I hope it is! What's it about?"

Mandy turned to me. In the dark, a set of headlights emerged from behind a crest in the road and zipped past us. I cleared my throat. "Okay, the title is *Doors and Windows*. In the story, this guy wakes up one morning and feels compelled to go inside this pearl-white building because he feels a massive void in his life. Once he's inside, he discovers that the building is empty—no people or furniture or anything, just rooms, and every time he goes into a room, it's warmer than the rest of the building, but it's still empty. He wanders around for awhile, but he can't find his way out. Eventually, he finds a window and gets right to the edge and looks down at the door he entered, but when he thinks back over his steps, there's no possible way that the door could be located where it appeared to be. So, he wanders around some more and even calls out for help. In the end, he stumbles upon an interior door at the end of a long hall. He thinks, finally, this is the room he's destined to go into, but something is blocking the door from the other side. There's some give to the door, but he can only open it a tiny bit. When he finally pushes it open enough to squeeze through, he sees what's been blocking the door: it's a dead body."

"And tell him who's face it is," Mandy added.

"Nobody's. When he turns the body over, where the face should be, it's completely smooth. There's nothing on it that would even pass for nose holes."

"It's Kafkaesque," Mandy said.

A few seconds drifted by with nothing to fill the silence except for the hum of tires on the interstate. Then Trez asked, "Why is the building pearl-white?"

"You really *are* incapable of interpreting art," Mandy said. "It's symbolic!"

"Symbolic of what?"

Trez's face was in the rearview mirror again, waiting for my response. I could tell that Mandy had hurt his feelings. I felt a pang of guilt. The truth was that the building was pearl-white because I needed an adjective and pearl-white was the first adjective that leaped to mind. I plugged it in, and it worked rhythmically and tonally. Unfortunately, Mandy had assigned a deeper meaning to the color choice—as she had with the entire story—so I was screwed; I couldn't admit that the color choice had no meaning, nor could I ad-lib some brilliant, multi-layered explanation as to what it represented. So, I did what anyone would do. I let out a hurt "umph" and said, "You wouldn't understand even if I told you."

We hit a rough seam in the highway just as we passed the *Welcome to West Virginia* sign. Nothing horrible—not enough to snap any essential part of the car's suspension—but big enough to rattle the bowling pins in the trunk. A mile down the road, Trez took an off-ramp and a mile farther down the road, he guided the Nova through a small town and into the parking lot of a 7-Eleven. The streets were empty. Trez slid out of the front seat and squatted down to inspect the shocks. A second later he popped his head up. "It's okay," he said.

He looked at the 7-Eleven and then back at Mandy. "I'm going in for a soda," he said. Then he stood there, as if there had been an ellipsis at the end of his sentence.

Mandy wrapped her arms around her shoulders. After a second, when she realized that he was waiting for a reaction, she said, "So go in, then."

"Do I need to get anything? Protection?"

Mandy shot me a glance and then averted her eyes. "I have one in my pocket."

Trez walked into the store. Just as he cleared the door, Mandy reached down for one of Trez's shirts. She draped it over her bare legs and let out a sigh. "Did Trez ever tell you about my mother?" she asked.

He hadn't, but I knew the story. It was common knowledge in school. Mandy's father owned a funeral home. The day Mandy turned thirteen, her mother ran off with a coffin salesman—leaving all of her personal belongings, even her pocketbook, behind. Since then, her father had suffered from melancholia, so much so that by the time Mandy started ninth grade, the day-to-day running of the funeral home, including consoling grieving families, had fallen on her shoulders.

"You mean your mother's leaving?"

"Sometimes I daydream about finding her and bringing her home."

"Would that work?"

"I don't know. Probably not. What people want one day they might not want the next. There's fire then smoke and then no smoke. I think that's what happened to my parents—at least my mom."

A moment passed. Inside of the 7-Eleven, we could see Trez standing by the soda rack, talking to a scroungy-looking man in a khaki army jacket.

Mandy pulled the shirt up on her legs. "I just wish I had my sketching pad," she said.

"You're bored already?" I asked.

"No. The front of the convenience store," she said, pointing.

I lifted my head for a better view. "You want to sketch a common, everyday 7-Eleven?"

"There's nothing everyday about it. That 7-Eleven is a reflection of us. We see it right now through the prism of everything we're feeling at this exact moment. And this exact moment—with you and me right here right now—will never come again. So, the question is, if you were painting 'right now,' what emotion would you paint?"

I scrunched my lips and studied the 7-Eleven. Nine hours ago, I was tossing Frisbee in the front yard and thinking about scalloped potatoes. Now, I was two-hundred miles from home, sitting in an empty parking lot in the backseat of my brother's pox-marked '69 Chevy having a wine and cheese conversation with the coolest person I'd ever known—that I would probably *ever* know. A chill shook my shoulders. "Is feeling cool for the first time in my life an emotion?" I asked.

"It is."

"So how would a painter paint feeling cool for the first time?"

"It all depends. That's why art is art. A million artists can paint the same grain of sand in a million different ways. That's why the building in your story is pearl-white and not purple or gray or orange. We fill in the blanks with little bits of ourselves and if we're lucky, we learn something about ourselves."

"I'm not sure I want to know more about myself."

"Why?"

"What if I don't like what I find out?"

"Then change it. Or turn away from it. Or accept it and wallow in it for a season."

I looked at Trez inside the store again, then shifted my eyes to Mandy. "What emotion would you paint?"

The moonlight caught her face, and a slight smile touched her lips. She closed her eyes and kept them closed as she reached down and pushed Trez's shirt off her bare legs. "Are there really bowling pins in the trunk?"

I turned and looked at the upholstery as if I could see through it into the trunk. "Yes, a whole bunch. But they're no longer functional as bowling pins."

"Grab the keys," she said.

The trunk latch was tricky. For it to release, whoever was opening it had to place their hand directly above the lock, straighten their arm, lean into it with all their might, then slowly twist the key at the exact right speed. I was good at it—better than Trez—but I could feel Mandy's breath on my neck, so it took me three tries before the latch finally popped.

"No longer functional indeed," Mandy said. She pulled a pin from the trunk and handed it to me. I grasped it around the base while Mandy dug into her pocket for the condom. In one quick, deft move, she tore open the wrapper and rolled the condom over the head of the bowling pin. Then she wedged the pin, condom end up, between the rest of the pins so that when Trez popped the trunk, it would be the first thing he laid his eyes on. She took a step back and planted a hand on each hip as if she were admiring a piece of art. "There you go, Lover. Interpret the symbolism of that."

When Trez pushed out of the 7-Eleven door, he had company—the man in the army jacket. They climbed into the car. The man's head was bald and misshapen. (It swelled out and up at the top, like a flesh-colored balloon.) He wiggled in his seat, then reached down the neck of his T-shirt and pulled out a set of dog tags and let them bounce off his chest.

"What gives?" I asked Trez. "Who is this guy? Why's he in the car?"

"Kenneth here knows a man," Trez said, laughing.

"He knows a man for what?"

Apparently, my question wasn't worth answering. Trez cranked the ignition, and as he backed out of the parking space, he and Kenneth swapped a series of grunts and looks and muffled snickers. Mandy cleared her throat. "No, really, Trez? Who is this guy? He's like forty-five."

"Tell them what you told me, Kenneth."

"What?"

"That joke you told," Trez answered.

Kenneth angled his balloon head toward Trez. His thin lips were frozen in a smile, as though he couldn't quite remember what he'd said, but he was positive that once he did remember it, it would be funny as crap. A few seconds passed. Then in the darkness, Kenneth laughed. "Oh, yeah," he said. He turned and draped his forearm over the seat and stared at Mandy. "A hammer always finds a nail," he said.

Kenneth and Trez both laughed.

When Kenneth stopped laughing, he twisted his torso so he could see us better. He let out a second, more controlled laugh as if he was trying to convince us he harbored no ill-will. Then he turned back to Trez. "What's your name again?"

"Trez."

"My guy only fronts, Mr. Trez," Kenneth said. "But he might have some loose."

"That's cool. I trust you," Trez said.

Suddenly, I realized why Kenny was in the car. "I'm not smoking pot," I said. "It'll destroy my palette."

"Don't worry about him. My brother is part of the bourgeois class," Trez said.

Whatever Kenneth thought bourgeois meant, I couldn't guess, but he looked at me with a hint of respect. "What about the dark-haired girl back there?" Kenneth asked. "Is she bourgeois too?"

"She's just along for the ride," Trez said.

Kenneth nodded and pointed out the windshield. "Turn off onto this dirt road, then it's up here a little bit," he said.

Trez steered into the turn, and we drove through a wooded stretch until we crossed over a wooden bridge and the trees opened up into a clearing half the size of a softball field. A cinder block building was sitting in the clearing, and directly in front of the building, an American Legion flag was flying from an in-ground flagpole. We rolled to a stop. "The American Legion? Are you kidding me?" Trez said.

Kenneth slapped Trez on the back, "Don't worry, Mr. Trez, there's some grade 'A' bad-asses in this here building."

"Don't be long," Trez said. "We're on a schedule."

"Right," Kenneth said, trying to look solemn. "You're on your way to a funeral."

"So don't be long," Trez repeated, handing him the ten-dollar bill.

"Got it. Let the engine run. I won't dilly-dally." Kenneth looked back at Mandy. "What about the bourgeois girl? If she really *is* as bourgeois as you say, maybe I should take her along to help close the deal."

Trez turned around and looked at Mandy as though he was giving it serious thought. "I don't think she'd be much help. She's an artist."

As Kenneth trotted off toward the building, I could sense Mandy's shoulders tense. I'd witnessed her tear into Trez a few times over the past year—always when she thought that Trez was getting too cocky. I cringed in the darkness, waiting for her to erupt. Instead, her shoulders relaxed, and her anger seemed to drift away, like the thin smoke from a dwindling fire. We sat there in the dark for a long time. Then, just as Trez eased the radio volume up a tick, she leaned in close to me and whispered into my ear, "Your brother picks his nose after sex."

We sat in the gravel parking lot idling away our gas. After ten minutes, it was obvious that Kenneth wasn't coming back to the car. Whether he'd snuck out the backdoor into the woods, or whether he was sitting inside on a barstool drinking beer and waiting for us to drive away, I couldn't have cared less. He'd exited our lives and taken his freakish, flesh-colored balloon-head with him. It was a blessing, and if it cost us our last ten dollars, then it was the best ten dollars I'd ever had a hand in spending.

Trez wasn't as pleased. He puffed his chest like the Trez from The Philosopher's Stone—the one who acted like humiliation had no effect on him—and shifted the car into drive. A few miles down the road, the trees gave way to open fields and the highway widened into four lanes. It was well after midnight, but traffic was buzzing in both directions. A mile further, the fields gave way to parking lots and small, squatty storefronts with glowing neon signs. The scene felt like a mirage. Whatever we'd stumbled upon was zoned commercial—a mini bypass for a town somewhere on the periphery. To the left was a Turkey Hill and a mini strip mall. To the right was more or less the same thing, plus a gas station and a tiny diner with a few cars parked in front of it. We stopped at the first of a series of traffic lights. Trez drummed his thumbs on the steering wheel and let out an impatient blast of air through his lips. He looked into his side mirror, then pulled out of line and drove on the gravel shoulder for a few car lengths before pulling into the diner's parking lot.

"Why are we stopping?" Mandy asked.

"Yeah, Trez. Let's put some miles between us and that Kenneth jerk."

Trez killed the engine and pulled the cigar box of keys out from under the seat. He tossed a small clump of fake keys onto my lap. "I'm tired of doing all the heavy lifting. It's your turn." Then, he pulled the keys from the ignition and tossed those on my lap. "And if you two don't like the way I drive, then drive yourself."

It was an idle threat—I didn't even have my learner's permit—but if that was what it took to make him feel in control again, I let him have it. I stuffed both sets of keys into my front pocket and followed Trez and Mandy across the parking lot to the diner.

Inside, there was only a smattering of customers. Still, it took the waitress a few minutes to hobble out from behind the counter to our table. She appeared to be in her late forties. She had long, metallic-orange hair that framed her face like a pair of heavy drapes, and her hand—her writing hand—was shaped into a claw, like she was clenching it around an invisible tennis ball. In a progression of long, torturous movements, the woman pushed the top sheet of her pad forward with the pencil's eraser and slid her curled index finger underneath it. Then with the middle finger of her good hand, she flipped the paper over to the underside of the pad. Once she'd accomplished all of this, she looked at us and nodded.

"Grilled Cheese and coffee all the way around," Trez said.

The waitress lifted her crippled hand off the pad to jot down our order, and when she did, the page flipped back over to its original position. She began the whole process again.

Trez pushed his hair back from his forehead and raised his hand. "Excuse me. I'm a member of The People's Communist Party. I can't help but notice your hand. Does the owner of the diner take care of you? Are *his* hands deformed from working long, fruitless hours as a beleaguered pawn of industry?"

The waitress didn't lift her eyes from the pad. "My brother-in-law owns it here."

Trez took a deep breath. "Tell me—your brother-in-law—is he a landowner?"

"Leave her alone, Trez," Mandy broke in. "She's helping family. And her hands are perfect—they're a glimpse into the poetry of her soul." Mandy turned to the woman. "The painter Vincent Van Gogh would see your hands as the manifestation of your personal dignity. If he was here today, I'm sure he would ask for the honor of painting them."

This didn't affect the woman one way or the other. She wrote our order down, the only sound being the pencil lead scratching the order blank. I cleared my throat. "I had my heart set on prison meatloaf tonight, but from what I see, I'm not confident that your kitchen is capable of soaking the breadcrumbs thoroughly, so I guess a grilled cheese will have to do," I said. "Can you tell me what cheese the chef favors?"

"American."

"Swiss is a far more nuanced melting cheese. Not as good as either Manchego or Gouda, but certainly something the chef would have on the prep table. Also, if it's not too much to ask, can the chef sprinkle some capers across the cheese? Something on the order of one caper per square inch? I prefer my foodstuff enhanced, although once I ate an entire sleeve of saltines in the driveway."

"I don't know what a caper is," the waitress said.

"They put you in mind of a tiny, pimiento-less olive masquerading as a canned pea. They're a bit pungent, so as you can imagine, they'll play well off the Swiss cheese."

"I can have him brush some mustard on the cheese."

"What mustard does the chef favor?" I asked.

Trez dropped his fist on the table so hard his fork jumped. "Holy hell. Just bring him the capers on the side and use whatever mustard the guy uses."

The waitress stared at Trez as if she was memorizing every line of his face, then turned and disappeared into the kitchen.

"What the hell's the matter with you?" Trez asked in a harsh whisper. "Why can't you just shut up for once in your life? We're not paying. Remember? Trying to stay inconspicuous? Thirty years from now, she's going to be able to describe the freak who asked for capers."

"What about you?" Mandy broke in. "The People's Communist Party? Maybe it's time to give the whole 'Rebel Trez' act a break—it's getting a little old." She leaned forward and pointed at Trez. "And don't think I don't know what this is all about. That Kenneth weirdo played you and now you're taking it out on the waitress and her crippled hand and Jim and me and everyone else. And you know what? You told that weirdo I was just along for the ride—like I'm nothing. You called *me* up and asked *me* to come along. And I can guess why, too. Isn't that right, *Mr.* Trez?"

"If you're mad at me, just say."

"I'm mad at you."

After that, we sat in silence until the waitress limped over with our cheese sandwiches. Mine was intolerable. Apparently, the chef had tried to ad-lib with the cheese. I'd asked for Swiss and would have settled for Gouda or even a halfway decent slice of Havarti. Instead, I got Mozzarella. To add insult to injury, the sandwich was tragically under-cooked on one side. I forced down a tiny, rubbery bite, then let out a disheartened bleat and tossed it onto the plate in disgust. I picked up my coffee and downed the last two inches in one long, unbroken gulp. Then I raised my cup.

The waitress didn't move. She had already done the math: three snot-nosed kids ordering the cheapest item on the menu in the middle of the night equaled zero tip. I waved my cup in the air. Then I waved it again. Finally, the woman meandered across the linoleum tile with the coffee pot in her hand. She filled my mug—halfway to the brim—and asked, "Are you finished? We need these tables."

We looked around the half-empty restaurant.

"Did your brother-in-law tell you to say that?" Trez asked. "Is he trying to get rid of us because I'm a Trotskyite?"

Trez gave her a moment to consider his question. When she didn't reply, he said, "Listen to me, the unfortunate truth is that you're a member of the proletarian class and your brother-in-law is a member of the bourgeois class. Despite what you may think, the two of you are mired in constant conflict." Trez held his forearms parallel to the table and made two fists. Then he bumped them into each other to demonstrate the eternal class struggle that the woman was unknowingly ensnared in.

"The good news is that you can throw off your shackles—you have a choice. Just like I had a choice when I quit the football team. Wouldn't you much rather play free-form jazz with unemployed hipsters who modulate keys by a consensus of feel? I know I would. I haven't done it yet. I can't play an instrument and I'm too busy to learn one, but I plan to. Not just for myself but everyone. You and Jim and Mandy here and even that foul-mouthed old hag at the farmers market who tried to talk my parents into beating me."

The woman looked down at the coffee pot, its weight clearly wearing on her arm.

Trez leaned back and threw his hands up in frustration. "Do you like to drive fast with the windows down?"

Nothing.

"Have you ever wanted to sleep by the river?"

Silence.

"What about Elvis? I don't suppose you're an Elvis fan?"

The waitress let out a pained gasp. She reached out with her free hand to steady herself against our table. "Oh, that poor man," she whimpered. "That poor man and his poor, dear, dear bride." She blinked once, fighting back tears. Her bottom lip began to tremble. She blinked again, this time like she had something in her eye, and when she did, a lone tear broke free and ran down her cheek. She tipped forward another six inches, and for just a millisecond, I could picture the waitress as a much younger version of herself—a love-struck teenager draped over the edge of the stage, arms stretched out, screaming herself faint while Elvis reached his Elvis hand out to her and crooned, "Can't Help Falling in Love" as if she were the only girl on earth.

"Are you okay? Do you need to sit down?" Mandy asked.

The waitress turned her head toward Mandy in robotic, one-inch clicks. She made a loud utterance—a drawn-out *e* sound. For a long, torturous moment, she twisted her mouth as she struggled to articulate a thought. Just as she seemed on the verge of succeeding, her lips opened into a perfect circle and she let out a long, agonizing howl that over its ten-second duration both slowed and lowered in pitch, like a piece of machinery seizing up. Then, she just froze. Her hand was on our table and her mouth was still open, but aside from her chest slowly expanding and deflating, she was, in essence, a statue. I exchanged glances with Mandy and Trez, and then I turned my eyes to the coffee pot. Carved from stone or no, the waitress' arm was tiring and the coffee pot's spout was dipping toward the floor. A second later, steaming coffee began to trickle onto the woman's shoes.

That's when Trez reached up to take the carafe from the woman.

Unfortunately, when his hand touched the waitress's hand, it had the same effect as flipping a tripped breaker. The woman's mouth snapped shut and she jolted forward, shattering the coffee pot against the edge of our table. She blinked once; then, in a series of one-second pulses, her eyes returned to the moment. For a long beat, she studied the orange plastic handle in her hand and the broken shards of curved glass at her feet. Slowly, her eyes narrowed. "Now see what you made me do!" she yelled, glaring at Trez. "Damn you. Someone has to clean that up!"

She turned on her heel and disappeared through the kitchen door with a dexterity that I heretofore would have guessed impossible. From the other side of the door, we heard a commotion: a loud crash, the waitress's hysterical voice, a man's unintelligible voice punctuated by the sound of the "order's up" bell being slapped in anger over and over again. Then, most unsettling of all, there was a brief moment of respite from all noise. Three seconds later, the cook slammed through the swinging door.

The man walked directly to Trez. He was wearing a grease-stained apron and a white cook's beanie and he was holding a spatula. Beyond that, he was nondescript in every way except for his ears, which looked as though they'd been grafted on from a much larger individual. He pointed the spatula at Trez. "Are you the little shit communist who broke my coffee pot?"

"Yes, I am," my brother answered. His eyebrows dropped and he leaned forward. I took a deep breath. I knew Trez's next line. I knew it as well as I knew our shared line in The Last Scone Story. *Do you control the means of production?*

Trez hesitated, though. His eyes shifted to our waitress, who'd re-emerged from the kitchen and was clutching a mop handle in her deformed hand, and something—maybe it was his version of The Art of Intuition—told him that if he uttered those words he would forever feel like an ass. In the end, he just clasped his hand in front of him and said, "I'm sorry."

The man pointed the spatula toward the door. "Pay your bill and get the hell out."

He straightened his cook's beanie and followed us to the front of the restaurant. At the register, Trez and Mandy looked at me for a moment, then began inching toward the exit. It took me a few seconds to remember that we didn't have actual money—only three fake keys on a loop of white string. "Oh, my goodness," I said, pasting a shocked look on my face. I patted my pockets. "I left my wallet in the car. I'll leave my car keys here as collateral while I run out and get it. That way—if I leave the keys—you'll know I'll be right back."

Without breaking eye contact, I reached into my front pocket and set the keys down. The man, for his part, made no move to pick up the keys. I backed away from him until I felt the door's panic bar press into the small of my back. "Just one moment, sir," I said, holding up my index finger. "I'll grab my wallet and be right back."

When I got outside, Trez and Mandy were already beside the car. Trez snapped his fingers. "Give me the damn keys!"

I looked down at the keys in my hand. Then I turned and looked back to the diner.

"Come on," Trez said, snapping his fingers.

I turned back toward the car. "Trez . . ." I managed to stammer out. And that's all I could get out, so I said his name again—this time in a voice even more choked with emotion—and held out my hand to show him its contents. Three useless keys on a loop of white string.

The gravity of my mistake took less than a heartbeat to grasp. Both the cook and the waitress could describe us in detail. They knew our first names and probably had a rough idea of our relationships to each other. They knew Trez was a communist. They knew my cheese preferences. They knew Mandy's favorite painter was Van Gogh. They'd probably even put two and two together and figured out that we were heading to Graceland.

"I screwed up, Trez," I said, choking back a bleat.

We stood in the parking lot for a moment, our feet forming a perfect triangle. A cluster of cars eased to a stop at the traffic light. The traffic light buzzed for a second as if some internal mechanism was struggling to draw enough power to change the light from red to green. Then, with an audible click, the light changed. The cross-traffic pulled forward, and when it did, the motion spurred Trez into action. He clapped his hands the same way he clapped them on the football field when the offense broke the huddle. He took one quick lateral step—like he was trying to fake out a defender—and in the same amount of time it took him to run a pass pattern, he was inside the restaurant and out again with the keys to the Nova.

Before the traffic light changed again, Trez, Mandy, and I were back in the car and speeding down the highway towards Memphis.

We didn't notice the police car until the inside of the Nova lit up flashing red. To this day, I have no idea as to what was going through Trez's head when the police officer strode up to our car. All I know is that when Trez handed the officer his driver's license through the window, my brother said, "We didn't do anything wrong."

The cop rubbed the back of his neck and lowered his hands to his belt. "You were driving with your headlights off," the officer said.

I was sitting directly behind Trez. He shifted. Suddenly, the road in front of us brightened. The cop reached into the car and tapped his nightstick on the steering wheel. "Turn your lights off. Don't touch anything unless I tell you to," he said.

The cop studied Trez's license for a moment. "You kids are a long way from home."

"We're on our way to Graceland," Trez said. "To the funeral."

"Been drinking tonight?"

"Just soda," Trez answered.

The officer pointed to the soda can on the passenger's side floor. Kenneth's can—the one he'd had in his hand when he walked out of the 7-Eleven. Trez handed it out to the cop.

The cop held the can to his nose. "One more time. Have you been drinking tonight?"

"I gave a guy in an army jacket a ride—that's the soda he had with him."

"Get out of the car."

The police officer peered into the back and motioned for me to roll down my window. He pointed at Mandy and me. "Exit the vehicle on this side and sit on the curb with your hands on your lap."

Mandy and I moved to the curb under the streetlight. We watched while the police officer held his flashlight a foot from Trez's nose and moved it side to side.

"What if that cop arrests Trez?" I whispered to Mandy. "We'll be all alone."

"What? You don't want to be alone with me?" Mandy asked.

I've since learned what an intrusive thought is. It's an unwanted, shameful thought that comes out of nowhere—for me, in this case, a sudden, highly-detailed vision of my brother's girlfriend and myself entwined in a motel bed. I squeezed my eyes shut and pressed my hands between my knees. When I opened my eyes and turned to Mandy, some residue of the thought must have still been on my face because she stared into my eyes, and even after I looked away, she tilted her head forward and continued to study my face. Then she reached up and pushed my hair back from my ear. "You know," she whispered, "one of these days, I'm going to nibble on that cute little ear of yours."

A car passed us slowly, going in the opposite direction. We heard the cop rap his flashlight on the Nova's trunk. "Pop open the back, please."

Trez pushed down on the trunk just above the lock and twisted the key. The cop stood behind him with his flashlight pointed at the lock. On Trez's third try, the trunk popped open and their faces disappeared behind the blue metal. I followed the beam of the cop's flashlight as it bounced back and forth in the crack. Then, the light froze. At that instant, I remembered the condom that Mandy had stretched over the bowling pin and left propped upright in the trunk for Trez to discover. I heard the cop make a choked-off, disgusted grunt. The trunk slammed shut—violently—and in the harsh, unnatural glare of the streetlight, I saw Trez's face. What Mandy had preached to me about light was true; the light exposed the emotion, and the emotion told the story. Trez's face was soft and stricken: the face of a frightened boy. "I . . . I," Trez managed to get out.

The cop flicked his flashlight off and pointed it toward the road. "Get the hell out of my town."

EPISODE FOUR

Title: *I Never Knew How Much a Man Needed a Woman*
Time: *41 minutes*
Synopsis: *Jim falls in love with a religious girl.*

We never made it to Graceland and Mandy never nibbled on my ear.

Traffic ground to a stop four miles from the Memphis exit. As it turns out, 50,000,000 Elvis fans can't be wrong, but they can cause one hell of a traffic jam. We sat in what amounted to a twenty-acre parking lot until a police officer walked over and told us that we didn't have a prayer of making it to the cemetery. "The city's infrastructure is overwhelmed. The President called out the National Guard a few hours ago," he said.

"But we drove all night," Trez said to the policeman. "We've endured a lot."

"You and everyone else," he said, looking off into the snarl of traffic behind us. "My advice to you is to turn around and drive home."

"I think my car's overheating," Trez said, his voice cracking. "The needle is in the red and I don't know what to do."

"Turn the heater up full blast. That'll cool the engine," the officer said, and then he turned his eyes back to the stalled traffic to give Trez a second to compose himself. The officer tapped his knuckle on the car's side panel, just below the window. "You're going to be alright," he said. And then he walked off.

We sat for another hour on the hot asphalt with the car's heater blasting and the August sun baking us. Just when I felt like I was going to faint, a Pinto station wagon in front of us lurched forward enough for Trez to inch the Nova out of line. He didn't hesitate; he drove across the grass median to the empty northbound lane. Within seconds we were flying down the interstate at seventy miles per hour, and while Mandy and I didn't realize it in the moment, by the time we cleared the southbound traffic the Rebel Trez was every bit as dead as Elvis.

The next day I slept until noon. While I was eating breakfast in the kitchen, Trez walked in through the back door. I didn't recognize him at first. His hair was gone. He had a tight crew cut and he was clutching a stack of Air Force recruitment pamphlets to his chest. He went straight to his bedroom. I watched him pull out the half-baggie of pot he had stashed in his baseball glove and flush it down the toilet. Then Trez got our dad, and they went into our parents' bedroom together. When they came out, Trez and my father drove back to the Air Force recruitment office. That evening, Trez slipped on his old cleats, and he did what he did every summer to get ready for football. He jogged across town to the Lutheran Seminary, then sprinted the long, grassy slope to the top of the campus—up the hill for power and down the hill for speed—over and over until the sun disappeared below the horizon.

I have no idea if Trez and Mandy ever officially broke up. It didn't matter. There was never any animosity between them, nor was there any attempt to get back together. Trez just moved on. And as for Mandy, she was never the kind of girl who needed an emotional off-ramp to leave a relationship; she just went her own way too.

When school started, Trez and my relationship slipped back to what it had been. We were brothers, but we weren't friends. As for Mandy and I, we never interacted again in any meaningful way, not about art or the emotions of light or anything else. It sounds horrible, but it wasn't. We still passed each other in the hallways. For a week or two, we said hi. Then we just nodded. Then we just kept walking. That's where it stood until a few days before Trez graduated. I was cleaning a year's worth of forgotten papers out of the bottom of my locker when Mandy sidled up beside me. My heart skipped a beat as she pushed the hair back from my ear and leaned in so close I could feel her breath on my neck. "I liked your brother better when he was a communist," she whispered. And then she was gone.

My parents quit the Gettysburg Market at the end of the 1980 season. It had been a horrible year. The unemployment rate was 8%; the inflation rate was 13%; and something the evening news called "the misery rate" was a soul-crushing 21%.

From the opening weekend, the market's foot traffic was way down. To make matters worse, a trio of Amish vendors joined the market. It started slow. First, one family from Shippensburg joined for "just a few weeks" to sell their excess garden crops. By mid-July, the family was peddling—at dirt-cheap prices—everything and anything: baked goods, flowers, plants, meat, fresh-squeezed lemonade, popcorn, crocheted hot pads, and one day, inexplicably, a handmade loom. A second Amish family joined the market a few weeks later. By the time the third Amish family joined in early September, the long-honored vendor's code had deteriorated into everyone for themselves.

The last market day of October was beautiful. The morning sky was slate blue with just a scatter of clouds to give it depth; the dogwood trees were losing their leaves; and the air had a late autumn chill to it—just enough to awaken in the customer base the ancient call to store fat for the upcoming winter months. In short, it was a perfect day to sell baked goods. Despite this, my father was so dispirited that he made only a token effort to up-sell the scant number of customers who stopped at our tent. Halfway through, he turned his back to our table and gazed around the square. My mother moved to his side and wove her arm under his arm. I'm not sure what was going through their minds as they stood there, but I imagine it had something to do with the British man and the last scone and how that May morning in 1961 proved to them that they were young and strong and capable of earning a living without kowtowing to the man. And I'm sure that they were coming to terms with that season of their lives being over. They stood motionless for a long time, watching the cars circle the square. Finally, my father turned to my mother and said, "Mattie, I think we're at the end."

My mother tried to cheer him up. "Billy, wouldn't it be something if after all these years that British man showed up again and he wanted a scone?" She wrinkled her nose. "It'd be just like you and I were playing a hunch all over again."

My dad didn't even smile. He just let out a disgusted grunt. "He'd probably walk right by us and buy a whoopie pie from the Amish," he said. And his voice wasn't angry, nor was it sad. It was just thin and dispirited and played out, and for the first time in my life that I'm conscious of, my dad let out a sigh. Then he looked at me as if I'd let him down somehow and said, "And the next iteration of Jim would be born Amish."

So Little Martha's Bakery liquidated. Shutting down amounted to selling the twelve-quart mixer to the Aspers Fire Hall and unloading our sun-bleached, collapsible tent to Earl the Cheese Guy, who said that he'd take it because it wouldn't hurt to keep it stored on the garage rafters as an emergency tent. My dad wanted ten dollars for it, but Earl was a barterer by nature. In the end, the two men settled on a swap: the tent for the wheelchair that Earl never returned to the hospital after his wife toppled down the basement steps and broke her femur. The transaction crushed my father; the tent had set us apart from the other vendors in the early days—a visual testament to our commitment. Seeing it reduced to an emergency tent worth nothing more in trade than an ill-gotten wheelchair brought a mist to his eye. In the end, though, he just thanked Earl and had me load the wheelchair into the van. As soon as we got home—as if my dad couldn't bear to drag it out any longer—we packed the remainder of Little Martha's equipment (the rolling pins, the half sheet pans, the carbon-blackened muffin pans, the scone pans) into cardboard boxes and carried the boxes to the attic, where we stacked them in the corner beside my mother's rescued bowling pins.

My parents were devastated, but I took it in stride. I'd managed to graduate in the top ten percent of my class despite having no interest in attending college. I was tired of jumping through other people's hoops. I wanted to focus on what interested *me*. For example, my record collection. I started it the day after Trez left for the Air Force. In addition to buying two albums a week at either Ginny's Roundabout Records or the Hanover Mall, I enrolled in The Columbia Record Club under three different permutations of my name and address. I also joined the far-crappier (but easier to fool) Atlantic Record Club a staggering seven times. My motivation was uncomplicated: I wanted a crap-load of records and I wanted them fast and cheap and the introductory offer of twelve albums for one cent plus shipping was a bargain, especially if I had no intention of ever fulfilling the enrollment agreement that I signed.

Also of interest to me during my first months of post-school freedom: going to the movies (I shared none of my dad's stinginess—I paid to see

Apocalypse Now at The Majestic Theater four times), watching back-to-back episodes of The Galloping Gourmet PBS cooking show every Sunday morning, and hanging out with Wayne at the Gettysburg College's sandwich shop ("The Bullet Hole") while he fidgeted and twitched and waited for his turn to play his D-28 on Open Mic Wednesdays.

Of course, my paramount interest was girls. More accurately, "Girls! Girls! Girls!" which, in addition to being the title of a crappy Elvis movie that Wayne forced me to watch repeatedly during The Summer of Doris, was also the exact numerical representation (three) of the number of girls with whom I'd had sex: Beth, Melissa, and Lex.

None of those girls were ever officially my girlfriend. When a relationship hit the tipping point—the sixth or seventh date—I'd pull back. I didn't want to get bogged down. Since Mandy, I'd cobbled together a style all my own. I was no Cary Grant, but I had thick, curly hair that girls couldn't resist touching. And I had The Art of Intuition. Plus, I'd perfected a few tricks. I'd nod my head three times (no more, no less) when a girl talked about herself. And I'd do my right eye, left eye thing—that's where I would tilt my head and look at a girl with just my right eye and then tilt it again and look at her with just the left eye. That one was gold. The best one, though, was to call a girl by a shortened version of her first name. This worked exceptionally well with Alexis, who had no real interest in me until I called her Lex.

To these techniques, I added a few go-to lines. Nothing obvious—no coarse pickups or clumsy double entendres. My lines were as soft and innocuous as the soft, innocuous underbelly of romance itself. They carried with them the subtext of vulnerability and shared humanity. Recently, I'd enjoyed considerable luck with the word "handmade," especially when I juxtaposed it alongside an emotion. *"Love is handmade." "Tenderness is handmade."* And inevitably, *"Forgiveness is handmade."*

My only problem was I didn't have a job. Before Little Martha's fell victim to the economy, it had given me the pretense of employment and a little jingle in my pocket. Not much, of course, but enough to buy two albums a week and have a credible answer when someone asked where I worked. Each day I checked the paper's help-wanted ads. In the meantime, I applied at all the usual places: Dal-Tile, Fairfield Graphics, The Gettysburg Times, and all three of the dilapidated furniture plants in

Littlestown. I even drove to tiny Aspers to see if the bowling pin factory was still in business. It wasn't.

It took me a few months to realize that I was never even going to get an interview, much less a job. In desperation, I attended a recruitment event at ERA Real Estate. I figured why not? I had a decade of sales experience. Plus, unlike baked goods, I'd be selling something the consumer both wanted *and* needed. How hard could it be? I'd seen real estate agents in action. The Century 21 guy did next-to-nothing to sell Doris' house; he planted a FOR SALE sign in the front yard and hosted an open house. The sad truth was that by showing their daughter a condom at fat camp, I'd done more to sell the Messinger's house than anyone.

For my walk-in interview, my plan was to set myself apart from the local tomjammery by showing my true colors. I dressed in Viking's old Superman T-shirt. Over that, I wore the army jacket I'd bought at the Army Surplus Store in Hanover. As for pants, I opted for my denim overalls, which I thought evoked a certain everyman vibe. On my splayed feet, I wore what every boy my age in Adams County wore, ocher-colored work boots with leather laces.

As soon as I walked through the door, I realized I'd miscalculated. The office's decor was professional: framed landscape pictures, recessed lighting, and ten feet inside the front door, a built-in receptionist's desk with a clipboard for guests to sign in. Before I could pick up the pen to scribble my name, a middle-aged man in a dress shirt and tie stood and walked across the carpet to me as though he'd pulled the short straw. "So, you're thinking about the real estate game?" he asked.

"You bet," I answered.

"What's your handle?"

"Jim Dubbs."

He put his arm around my shoulders and smiled at me like I was his long-lost nephew. "Jim. Jimmy. Jimmy-James," he said. "Rubba-Dub-Dubbs."

I recognized the name-memorizing technique from the markets— ask a customer their name and repeat it back to them—in this case taken to its most absurd extreme, as if the man was reenacting a sketch from Monty Python's Flying Circus. "Well, Jim Jimmy-James, Rubba-Dub-Dubbs, do you have a girlfriend?"

"Not presently, sir," I answered. "I like to play the field. The whole footloose and fancy-free thing."

If my comment registered, he ignored it. "Then I want you to promise me one thing, Jimmy Dubbs," he said, touching my arm. "Promise me that when the day comes for you and your beautiful bride to buy your first home, you'll let your old buddy Neal Ruff take care of you."

"Who?"

He held out a business card. When I reached out to take it, he held his end of the card tight. A long, awkward second passed in which neither of us spoke. "I promise," I muttered.

Only then did he release his grip on the card. "You have one helluva future in front of you, young man," he said. "I accept your promise."

In June, I got a job with Seven Turns Orchards. The owner, Larry Anderson, called me just after supper one evening. He'd run into my dad at the grocery store and my dad had told him I needed a job. The work was spotty during the first part of the week—the occasional day picking string beans or berries when the field workers didn't show up, and I'd log a few hours every Wednesday hauling produce to the auction in Shippensburg. The weekend was different. I single-handedly ran Seven Turns' farmers market operation. This meant a seventy-two-hour stretch every weekend without sleep. Beginning at mid-day on Thursdays, I'd prep the vegetables and tree fruit for the next day's Open-Air Market in Harrisburg. It was a long, hot, grueling process, so I paced myself. I'd fill my Igloo cooler with iced "poor boy juice" (grape Kool-Aid with an extra cup of sugar) and blast Deep Purple or AC/DC from Trez's cassette player while I hauled lug after lug of produce out of the cooler and sorted through the containers, picking out all of the "rots" and "ugly sisters" (which I tossed into a galvanized tub to feed to the chickens). Then, after a sandwich and a Snickers bar, I'd pick bush fruit—raspberries, blackberries, blueberries—until it was too dark to see my hands in front of me. After that, I'd bundle shallots and garlic scapes under the dusk to dawn light. This lighter, more meditative work called for a change in music, so I'd play something mellow (Cat Stevens or The Grateful Dead). Finally, around 4 a.m. I'd load the truck, being careful to keep the brown eggs directly over the axle.

The Friday market was a marathon. It ran from nine in the morning until seven at night, so I'd leave the farm just after daybreak and not get back until dark. Then, I'd start the entire process over again for the Gettysburg Market on Saturday morning. After Gettysburg's final bell, I'd whip everything into the back of the truck and drive straight to the McDonald's on Steinwehr Avenue for three Big Macs and a large Coke. Then I'd push through the entire sleepless rig-a-ma-roll one last time for the West Frederick Market on Sunday morning.

For this, Larry paid me $200 a week in cash.

The last weekend of September, after I got home from the Fredrick market, Larry told me that I looked tired and that he'd unload the truck if I ran a quick errand for him. He wanted me to deliver ten bushels of yams to a church outside Gettysburg. The pastor's brother owned a restaurant in Maryland, and the brother sold sweet potato pies at the local Harvest Festival every fall. My job was to drop the potatoes off at the church and pick up the check.

I got there just after two o'clock. The church was a small, rancher-shaped building, bordered along the back by a vast cornfield. I'd assumed that the service would have long been over, but the parking lot was jammed. Beside the parking lot, a Winnebago was parked in the shade of a maple tree. The words THE COLE FAMILY were painted on the side of the vehicle. I eased Larry's truck along the road frontage and parked on the grass. Then, I flicked on the four-way blinkers and carried the crates to the church's front overhang and stacked them in the shade.

I heard music and clapping from inside the church. I tip-toed in and stood along the back wall while The Cole Family played. It wasn't my kind of music. There were six people on stage (parents, four teenage kids). They had the right instruments—guitar, bass, piano, drums—but their playing had a lilt to it that reminded me of AM radio, which is to say that it was the musical equivalent of wallpaper—in this case, religious wallpaper.

The pastor waved to me, then circled back along the church's outer wall and handed me an envelope.

"Larry threw in a couple of extra yams," I said.

The pastor nodded and said, "Why don't you hang around? We're having a potluck. You're welcome to get yourself something to eat."

I let out a slow ruffle of air and slumped my shoulders. "I'd love to, but I'm running on empty," I said.

"Are you sure?"

The family started another song. A blond-haired girl about my age was behind the piano, playing chords and singing. Her hair was long and perfectly straight, and when she lowered her head to glance at the piano keys, her hair caught the overhead lights. Suddenly, the band pulled back a little. The girl stopped singing, and instead she began to speak over the softer music—some hard-to-follow sales pitch about life being like a tapestry. When she got to the end of her "testimony," she looked across the room, and for just an instant—maybe half as long as it takes for a door to swing open—our eyes met.

I tilted my head toward the pastor and said, "Maybe I will stay. Just let me go out and turn off my four-ways."

I was pushing a slotted serving spoon into the three-bean salad, wondering if it would've killed whoever prepared it to sprinkle in a little finely chopped dill weed, when I heard a girl's voice behind me say, "I really like your church."

I knew who it was before I turned around. "Thank you," I said.

"Everyone's so welcoming," she said, holding out her hand. "I'm Angela."

I took her hand and gave it a gentle shake. Normally, my introductory repartee is spot on—especially if food is involved and I can work in the word "handmade" organically, but standing in the warm sun, I froze. Not just because she was beautiful—it was something more. A second passed before I was able to work my mouth into a smile. "Jim," I managed to get out.

"Are your parents here?"

"Parents?"

She nodded.

My stomach clenched. I had a sudden, horrifying image of introducing Angela to my father. I could picture him rocking back and forth on his heels, barely able to contain himself while I introduced her, then, the second the last syllable left my mouth, launching into some long, disjointed tirade about the Amish not following market bylaws. Or more terrifying, he'd go the other way. He'd try to connect with Angela by speaking to what interested her and blurt out some nonsense like *I guess*

God's okay, what with the divine intervention and all. And I suppose it's a good thing he sent his son to die for our sins, although I would have done it a bit differently.

"I'm an orphan," I said.

She lifted her eyebrows in empathy.

"I guess not technically an orphan since I've reached the age of legal consent—at least that's what the lawyers tell me," I said, breaking eye contact.

"It must be a struggle."

"I have people who care," I said, motioning to the congregation. I nodded. In the bright sunshine, wide-eyed children were scampering to and fro. The men were strong and tall, and the women, to a one, were demure and beautiful. The picnic tables were fully stocked with wholesome foodstuff: vegetables, fruits, grains. I felt myself drifting into one of my weird flights. Did these people do this every Sunday? Pool their resources and feed each other? My guess was yes; yes, they *did* do this every Sunday. They were the best of us—willing to embrace the most loathsome traveler and shower him with kindness and unconditional love. Feed him. Clothe him. Wash the disgusting farmers market dust from his scuffed, ocher-colored work boots. My throat tightened. "This is my real family," I managed to get out. "They took me in when no one else would." I wiped a tear away from my eye. Then I let out a handful of bleats, each weaker than the one proceeding it until they tapered off completely and I just stood there for a long moment feeling flushed and light-headed.

"That's a beautiful testimony," Angela said.

I sniffed hard. "Well, in my small world, I guess—not on a global scale."

"It's always on a global scale."

I had no idea what she meant, but I said, "Maybe so."

"I saw you walk into the back of the church when I was singing," she said.

"Your voice drew me in," I said. "It's new and old at the same time, like the handmade quilts the Amish women sell at the farmers market."

She tilted her head, trying to see me from a more telling angle. "There's something different about you, Jim." A smile spread across her lips and then—as if she was summoning a smidgen of bravery—she said, "Do you want to sit down together?"

We filled our plates and sat on the swings. Two boys, maybe four or five, sped by us on their way to the garbage can. We watched the boys toss their paper plates and plastic forks into the gray waste can and then tear off in the general direction of the cornfields. "That's what I love about little ones—they run everywhere they go," Angela said.

"It's how they're programmed," I said. Then I added, "By God."

Angela paused as though she was in deep thought. "Don't laugh at me," she said, "but whenever I picture Jesus, I picture him as a toddler."

I chuckled to give the impression that toddler Jesus was my favorite Jesus, too. "Oh, yeah. Don't you love the whole image? Pronouncing his r's as w's. Tooling around the house like a hellion—teasing the dog, busting stuff. The whole terrible twos and all."

Angela gave me an odd look.

I cleared my throat. "But a didactic version of the terrible twos. Where he would break his parents' fine china, but it was for their own good—to teach them that they could be happy with less. And once they'd heeded his word, he would miracle the plates back together as good as new. Like he was being didactic but at the same time having a laugh at their expense."

Angela smiled. "I think that you're having a laugh at *my* expense."

The same two boys sidled up and stared at us. They were close enough in appearance to be twins. They had the same bulbous nose, the same Mr. Spock haircut, the same short-sleeved, blue dress shirt. The only discernible difference between them was that the smaller of the two had a weird glint in his eyes, like he was destined to grow up deranged. I peeked at Angela, then furrowed my eyebrows at the boys and gave them a quick "beat it" scowl.

In unison, both boys took a step back.

"You know these little guys?" Angela asked.

"Oh, yeah," I said. "Sure. Everyone knows the twins."

"I think we're in their spot," she said, climbing off her seat.

The boys scampered onto our swing seats, and we gave them each a push. Angela was in a short-sleeved summer dress. Every time she braced to give her twin a giant push, she'd look at me and laugh.

"So, what's it like traveling?" I asked.

"It's the only life I've known. We live in the Winnebago."

"Like the Partridge Family," I said.

"They sang at your church?"

I gave my kid another push. "No. It's an old TV show. It's color—not black and white—so it doesn't have the timeless feel of *The Twilight Zone* or *The Honeymooners*, but for what it is, it's okay. It's about a family that drives around in an old school bus and they're a pop band and they play the oldest son's songs. It's a little far-fetched because the youngest boy, Chris, is about the same age as the twins here and he plays the drums professionally."

She gave the deranged kid one last, giant push and stepped back from the swings. "I guess I miss out on certain things like TV shows, but it's a small price to pay when I get to give my testimony to people."

"Your testimony was the best one," I said. "It was amazing how you built to a crescendo."

"Really?"

"I'd love to hear it again," I said.

I stepped aside as if we were in a movie and I was stepping out of frame. Then, and maybe it was the effects of seventy-two hours without sleep, I felt as though I was watching Angela through the lens of a movie camera.

She closed her eyes and held her hands out over an imaginary piano. She started to sway gently, moving to the rhythm in her head. Then she began to speak. "Sometimes, no matter how hard you try, you can't recognize your life for what it is. It's like you're looking at the back of a tapestry. It's like you see all the knotted-off ends of colored bits of material and they're just a jumble that makes no sense at all. But that's when you have to believe. You have to believe more than ever. You have to believe that each one of those knots has a purpose. And you have to believe in that jumble—even when none of it makes sense and everything is going wrong and your heart is desperate and broken and you don't know who you are and you feel like you can't take one more step. Even then, you have to have faith. More than ever. Because someday we'll all know in full what we only now know in part. And someday, God will spin the tapestry around and we'll see that beautiful picture and we'll see all those knotted off ends for what each and every one of them are—God's perfect plan for us!" Angela opened her eyes. For a split second, she looked unsure of herself, but then she raised her fisted hands over her head and yelled, "And that is that!"

"And that is that!" I cheered, standing on my tiptoes and raising my fists.

"Ow-ee," Angela cried. She let out a deep breath and folded her hands over her heart. "I've never said 'and that is that' before. It just came out. It was . . ."

"Extemporaneous?"

"Exactly! It was extemporaneous!"

"That was the best part," I said.

And just like we were in a movie, Angela looked at me as if she didn't know whether to smile or to avert her eyes. Finally, her smile won out, and she said, "You inspired me, Jim."

And even if I could have spoken, I wouldn't have said a word. I recognized The Art of Intuition when I heard it.

We walked the perimeter of the church grounds a dozen times. She told me about her life on the road with her family. I told her about farmers markets and working at Seven Turns and how Larry was a good boss because he trusted me enough to give me my own set of keys to his work pickup—a rusted-out '59 Ford with a hood as cratered as the surface of the moon. As we strolled along the edge of the cornfield for the last time, I finished with, "My favorite part of the market season is the last few weeks of October. The days are shorter and cooler and the leaves are changing and the hard work is mostly over. It's a time to finally just relax a little. I love it—it makes everything worthwhile."

"I never met anyone who knew so much about farmers markets," Angela said. "Especially how you can read the customers' 'tells.' It's amazing how you know what people are going to buy before they even pick it up."

"I have a talent for it," I said. "And I saved the best 'tell' for last. Whenever someone looks back at their car, it means that they are going to buy a watermelon."

"Why?"

"Because no one wants to walk around carrying a watermelon."

"But why do they look back? Presumably, they know where they parked."

I wanted to say because people are idiots, but I wasn't sure how it would play, so I just shrugged my shoulders and said, "Beats me."

Angela shook her head and said, "Just amazing."

I waited a long beat. "So, does your boyfriend worry about you? I mean being on the road all of the time?" I asked.

"Are you asking if I have a boyfriend?"

"I am."

She looked down at the space between her feet. "A few years ago, we were staying at a pastor's house. Outside, in the garden, they had a rose bush. The roses were the most beautiful red, and they smelled like perfume and the petals felt so delicate and cool when I touched them with my fingertips. I was standing in the sun admiring them when the pastor's wife came out and said I could pick one if I wanted. I stared at them until I found one that I thought was perfect. I cut it and took it inside, and I pressed it in the pages of my King James Bible. First Corinthians Chapter 13 of course—the love chapter," she said. "It's still there. I'm going to give it to the boy I love," she said, lifting her head and meeting my eyes. "Does that answer your question?"

"The '*going to*' part does."

"And?"

"Don't think I'm too forward, but my friend Wayne is performing at a restaurant tonight. Not really a restaurant, a pizzeria—Claudio's. Wayne and I eat there all the time. Sometimes his sister Brie tags along. I'm going because he needs me there for moral support. It's kind of my second, unofficial job—supporting Wayne and his music."

"Are you asking me for a date?"

"If that's copacetic," I said.

Angela didn't say a word; she just walked over to the Winnebago where her family was sitting in a circle on folding lawn chairs. In unison, they turned toward me. I shot them a wave. The father said something to her in a muffled voice. Then, the mother. A heartbeat later, Angela turned and hurried back across the parking lot to me. "What time?" she asked.

When I got to Wayne's house, he was sitting on the sofa in the living room polishing his Martin D-28 with a cloth diaper. "Tell me again," he said without looking up. "Why's this girl think you're a Christian?"

"Because I told her I was."

"So, you told her that *you too* were a Christian," he said as if he was internalizing my comment. He lifted his guitar to eye level, then angled it and peered into the soundhole. "What I don't understand is why? I don't get why you're on a church kick all of a sudden."

"I told you. I'm in love with a church girl."

"Why didn't you just tell her you don't know anything about God?"

"Because life is a tapestry and everything's got a knot in it," I said. "You and Brie go to church every Sunday. I need your help to win Angela over. Give me a few tidbits of scripture I can sprinkle into casual conversation."

"To what end? You said she's leaving tomorrow."

"I have a sneaky feeling that she's going to ask me to leave with her."

"And do what?"

"Join their band."

"You can't sing."

"I could play the tambourine. Like the little girl in The Partridge Family. You could teach me."

Wayne shook his head. "You have an artist's temperament in that you're all over the place emotionally and you need other people's approval to feel good about yourself, but trust me, you have no artistic talent— musical or otherwise."

Over the past seven years, I'd learned to accept Wayne's lack of tact. He wasn't being mean just to be mean. He knew about my weird flights, and as my best friend, he considered it *his* second, unofficial job to re-tether me to reality—or at least to his version of reality. I glanced out the bay window and pressed my hands between my knees. "I'll fake it. The same way I'm faking being a Christian."

"You can't fake being a Christian any more than you can fake tickle yourself. Not ultimately. What are you going to say if she asks you how you know God exists?"

"She already did."

"And what did you say?"

"I said God's one of those things that everyone knows exists but no one's ever actually seen—like a flying squirrel."

"And?"

"I got a big laugh."

Wayne looked up. "Have you gotten any sleep yet? Isn't this usually when you're deep into your post-market fifteen-hour coma?"

"She said that she has a perfect red rose pressed inside her King James Bible. She's saving it for her one true love. I've got to convince her to give me that rose."

Wayne flipped his guitar over and started the long process of restringing it. He unwound the thickest string, then grabbed his pliers off the green shag carpet. "What happened to playing the field? The whole footloose and fancy-free thing?"

"I don't want to be fancy-free anymore."

Wayne laughed. Not a spontaneous laugh—more like [Wayne laughs] was written in a script. "All of this reminds me of when you decided to gain all that weight on purpose. Remember that? Remember getting kicked out of that fat camp? The shame and humiliation you put everyone through?" He tightened the E string and clipped off the excess line. "Do you want my advice? Forget about her. It's the whole forbidden fruit thing. That's your problem—everything always has to be forbidden fruit to you. Now you're cooking up this whole elaborate scheme to trick some poor religious girl out of her pressed rose. And why? All to prove a point. Do you really want to live with that? Is that the kind of thing you—"

Wayne went on from there, but I wasn't listening. I was thinking of Angela and how her bare arms looked as she pushed the deranged kid on the swing. How the pushing motion had caused her sleeves to ride up her smooth, beautifully tanned arms and expose more skin than she'd planned. Or, maybe she did plan to show it. I shook my head to dislodge that notion from my brain. Angela was an angel—the future mother of my children—and I didn't want to think of her deliberately exposing heretofore concealed arm skin for less than puritan purposes. Suddenly, I realized that Wayne had stopped talking and was staring at me.

"I'm going to ask if I can call her Angie," I said.

The sun was setting when I pulled into the church. I was running behind. I had my regular date clothes, but none of them felt right. My first impulse was to stay in my work clothes—not risk changing anything. Then,

I'd toyed with the idea of wearing Trez's old suit. In the end, I settled on a pair of nicely faded-in jeans and Viking's old Superman T-shirt, which I still considered a good-luck charm despite my humiliating rebuff at the real estate interview.

Angela was standing by the picnic table when I pulled onto the parking lot. "My father said to ask how long you've been a member of the congregation," she said through the passenger-side window.

"This is the only church I've ever attended," I answered.

She ducked into the front seat beside me. "You know how fathers can be," she said. Then Angela gasped and lifted her hand to her mouth. "Oh, I'm sorry."

It took a second to remember that I'd told her I was an orphan. I felt a pang of guilt. "Totally fine," I said. I pushed Fleetwood Mac's *Rumors*—my go-to first-date tape—into the 8-Track. I glanced at Angela. Despite the night being a tad warm, she was wearing a beige button-up sweater. It looked a tad old, and the sleeves seemed too short—they didn't reach her wrists—but she looked pretty in it. "You look nice in your sweater," I said.

"It's my mother's. She said I could borrow it for my . . ."

"Your date?"

Angela nodded and gathered her hands across her lap. In her top hand, she had a wadded Kleenex tissue. I motioned toward it. "Are you feeling poorly?"

She looked at her lap. "No. It's just a silly thing. I always feel better if I have a tissue in my hand—just in case."

I looked out the windshield at the road. Then I looked back at the Kleenex in her hand. I could see our future a million miles off. It was inevitable. Once I married Angela, I'd carry a crumpled tissue in my hand because that's what couples do—they morph into each other. And if somewhere along the line Angela felt compelled to carry a crumpled tissue in each hand, I'd follow suit. And it went without saying that our children would carry tissues from a young age, as soon as they could be trusted not to put them in their mouths. I eased Fleetwood Mac down. "Maybe I should carry a Kleenex too," I said. "That way, nothing bad will ever happen to us."

"I think you're having fun at my expense again."

For a second, I was stumped for a response. I didn't want to contradict her. At the same time, I didn't want to ask her to marry me just yet. A split second before the silence drifted into awkwardness, I muttered, "Just thinking out loud," which seemed to tide us over until I pulled into Claudio's parking lot.

When we walked through the side door of the pizza shop, Wayne was already on stage, leaning into the microphone singing a shaky, nervous version of Neil Young's "Needle and the Damage Done." Every patron in the restaurant was laughing, which was out of character for Claudio's, and Claudio himself was striding across the seating area with a self-satisfied smile on his lips. This was without precedent. He rarely ventured out from behind the counter, and when he did, he never lifted his head—it was more along the lines of a squirrel breaking cover to retrieve a dropped acorn, or in Claudio's case, a dirty serving platter that a customer had left on the table rather than properly returning it to the pick-up end of the counter.

I led Angela to the counter. "They only have Pepsi products," I said to her. "Is that okay?"

She nodded, and I ordered my usual date order: a six-pack of Pepsi in cans and two glasses filled to the brim with ice. Then I ordered a large pizza. I looked at Angela. "What toppings would you prefer?"

"It's up to you," Angela said.

"I recommend tomatoes. They grill them on the flat top with a little salt and pepper—just a light sear. That's of the utmost importance because Claudio doesn't put them on until after he pulls the pizza from the oven."

"That sounds wonderful," Angela said.

I led Angela to my regular table—the second table from the door—which to my mind was the most desirable booth in the restaurant. Wayne and I and sometimes Brie always sat there. The left side had an unobstructed view of the ovens. Claudio had a vintage three-stack gas model with the company's name, Vulcan, spelled out in script on the oven's crown emblem. According to Claudio, the stack was a 1952, which put its manufacturing date smack-dab in the middle of the pizza oven industry's golden age, which (again, according to Claudio) spanned from 1947 until roughly the end of 1956. As much as I admired the oven, I was truly taken with the pizzeria's wooden paddle. To my mind, the lifter had long ago morphed into pizzeria art. Not only was its beveled edge worn as smooth as driftwood by the sliding in and lifting out of untold thousands of pizzas and grinders, but its four-foot handle was stained a walnut-color hue by the family's collective hand-oils: Claudio and Claudio's father before him and Claudio's father's father before *him*. I guided Angela to the left side so that she'd have the best view, then slid in across from her. "This is the premier table," I said. "Table two."

Angela smiled and nodded. "I can see."

"I talked them into it," I said, breaking into a big grin.

"Calling it table two?"

"No. Grilling the tomatoes." A weird laugh escaped my throat. "I used to do it when I was little. Other than me and this other guy—Sal in Philadelphia—no one else has ever grilled tomatoes in that context before. And from what I know of the timeline, I'm pretty sure I invented it first."

"That was very clever of you," Angela said.

I felt my face color. "Well, it's not like I invented penicillin. I'm sure someone would have thought to do it eventually."

"Maybe not. You never know." Angela smiled and looked around the room like a first grader on a field trip. She nodded toward the tiny stage. "That's Wayne?"

I lifted my head. Wayne was between songs. He was sitting perfectly still, and his eyes were narrow slits. I knew the look. He was either upset or angry. It suddenly occurred to me that Angela might judge me by Wayne's performance—that if he bombed or did something over-the-top strange, it could tip her affection one way or the other. I cleared my throat. "Yes, that's Wayne. He's good, but he plays a different type of music than you do—more singer-songwriter type stuff. And he has a nervous tick—he says, 'Check mic one,' before every song. It's kind of an affectation. I don't think he realizes he's doing it anymore."

"He's your best friend?"

"Ever since the sixth grade when we teamed up on a water project," I said.

I cracked open a Pepsi and filled each of our glasses. The fizz climbed to the top. "What time do your parents expect you in by when you go out on a date?"

"I don't know. I've never been on a date before," she said.

"Your parents don't let you?"

She shook her head.

"What then?"

"No boy has ever been interested in me."

My heart fluttered. "How is that possible? You could have your pick of any guy."

Angela's cheeks turned red right before my eyes. She reached over to the napkin dispenser and pulled three napkins from it, one right after another so quickly that the dispenser followed her hand to the center of the table. She crumpled the napkins in her hand, and then, as if it took every last bit of courage she possessed, she flashed me a quick, minuscule smile before looking away.

If there was a single molecule left in my body that wasn't already in love with Angela, it surrendered at that moment. I leaned in and slid my hand across the table to her. "I'm interested in you," I said.

"I know," she said back.

Love can take the world's strongest man and reduce him to a pat of melted butter. And I was far from the world's strongest man. I was a pudgy, chronically exhausted farmers market flunky with tight, curly hair, a full-fledged chafing problem, and a penchant for weird flights of indignation that were totally divorced from reality. Far worse, I was a liar, and I'd lied to Angela. And not one of my go-to, tiny white lies—like saying I threw shot put in high school and made it to States my junior year. My lies to Angela were huge lies that spoke to my lack of character. First, I pretended to be a Christian and then I pretended to be an emancipated orphan. All because, for a few fleeting seconds, I saw an advantage to it. Sitting there, with my hand on top of Angela's hand, I felt nauseous. I was just ready to confess everything to her—I even had the first line formulated in my head: *Angela, love can take the world's strongest man and reduce him to a pat of melted butter*—when Wayne bellowed, "Check mic one" into the microphone and launched into the opening chords of Dave Mason's "We Just Disagree."

At first, the anger in Wayne's voice may have escaped the ten or twelve people scattered around the restaurant, but by the end of the first verse, every face had lifted from their pizza and was fixed on him. By the time he got to the chorus—the line about the song's two characters disagreeing—the hostility in his voice was unmistakable. He leaned into the microphone and spit out the words with such venom that they represented nothing less than an overt challenge to everyone in the pizzeria to agree with him, Wayne Clark, or get the hell out.

At that moment, Claudio strode to the mini-stage and pulled the microphone away from Wayne's mouth mid-note. He turned to the seating area. Then, like a stand-up comic delivering the punchline to a joke, he said, "Jim, table two's pizza is ready."

With that, Wayne stopped playing mid-song. He stood and fit his Martin D-28 in its case, buckled the clasps, and walked directly to Angela and me. His face was expressionless. "Come on—we're out of here," he said.

"We're on a date, Wayne," I said.

"That's fine. It doesn't bother me."

I looked at the counter. "Our pizza's ready."

Wayne raised his hand and snapped his fingers. "Put Jim's pizza in a box!"

Once enough time had elapsed for Claudio to box my order, Wayne walked over to the counter. He took a long moment to stare at Claudio. Then he said, "Jim and I will still come here for pizza because Jim loves looking at your stack ovens and paddle, but I'm never going to sing here again and one day when I'm a huge star, you'll rue the day you screwed me over."

Claudio squinted and set his jaw tight (this was the first and only time Claudio actually looked Sicilian to me), but Wayne waved him off. After that, it would have been far too awkward to stay, so I grabbed our pizza from the counter, and Wayne, Angela, and I walked outside to the parking lot.

"It's not even dark yet," I said to Wayne. "And we're on our date. We're not going to your house or my house, and we're not going back to the Winnebago."

"So eat in the car."

"We don't want to sit in the parking lot and eat. What's the fun in that?"

"Then eat driving around."

"We're not doing that, either," I said.

"How about the Eisenhower Tower?" Wayne asked. "I'll drive. We can hang out there if no one's up on the landing. That'll be more like a date."

I rubbed my eyes with my thumb and forefinger. The tower was a fifty-foot high, square, metal structure that looked as if the prototype had been constructed using a child's erector set. It was less than a mile past the edge of town. The battlefield closed at dusk, so we would have to park at the bottom of the hill and sneak up to the clearing. I'd done it many times. Everyone had. It was a rite of passage for boys to climb the steps (usually drunkenly) at night and pee over the side. "It might be okay if no one is up there," I said. "Is that okay with you, Angela? If we go to an observation tower named after President Dwight D. Eisenhower?"

Angela blinked a few times, then she said, "I don't know enough to say yes or no."

"Are your parents Democrats or Republicans?" Wayne asked.

"Republicans."

"Good. Then you'll love it up there," he said.

I'd forgotten how peaceful the landing felt at night. We were only fifty feet high, but somehow the air smelled crisper and the stars seemed close enough to touch. We each grabbed a slice of pizza and stood with our elbows on the safety fence, gazing out over the Gettysburg skyline. To our right was town. To the left was the battlefield. Every few minutes, on the battlefield side, the darkness came alive with the headlights of an oncoming car, dim at first and then brighter and brighter until they crested the hill.

"Remember when we used to play the game where you have to guess when the headlights are going to appear?" Wayne said to me.

"Sure," I said. "It's tower tradition."

"Can we play it now?" Angela asked.

"Sure. You only win if you yell 'now!' *exactly* when the headlights break the horizon," I said.

For the next ten minutes, we ate pizza and drank Pepsi and played the headlights game. I won the first two, and then Wayne won. After that, we let Angela guess until she finally won.

"You should go down and get your guitar," I said to Wayne. "Angela only got to hear you sing two songs."

"I've got greasy fingers," Wayne said. "It's a Martin D-28. The soundboard is solid Sitka Spruce, and if I get pizza grease on the frets, I'll never get it off—it'd be a sin."

I looked at Angela. "Are greasy frets a sin?"

Angela shook her head.

"See?" I said to Wayne.

Angela and I watched over the edge while Wayne clomped down the metal staircase to his car and pulled his guitar out of the trunk. "I like your friend," Angela said.

"He has a way of growing on you," I said.

"Why does he cover one eye all the time?"

"He's done that ever since we were little. It helps him see things more clearly."

"Does it work?"

I thought for a moment. "Yes and no."

Angela covered one eye and looked down at Wayne.

"What's he doing?" I asked, playing along.

"He just wiped his hands on the grass. Now he lifted his guitar case out of the car and he's looking up at us with his hand covering one eye." She uncovered her eye and then covered it again. "You know, it does kind of work. I'm going to have to try this when we drive to the next town. One of my all-time favorite things is sitting in the front seat of my family's camper when we're driving after dark. I roll the window down a few inches so I can smell the night air. It always makes me feel like I'm on the verge of something brand new—something wonderful."

Angela looked at me like she'd known me her entire life.

"I don't get it," I said. "You're just who you are. No pretenses. How is that possible?"

"I know how it all ends." She reached out and tapped my hand. "You know too."

"Well, if I do, it doesn't transfer into no pretenses. I know I give the impression that I'm laid back, but most of that's just because I'm a tad portly and carry it well. It makes people think I'm innocuous. Usually, I'm okay with that—people thinking I'm whatever they happen to see in me."

She took a sip of her soda and nodded.

"I guess what I'm trying to say is that for all intents and purposes, I'm tofu."

A second passed.

"Do you know what tofu is?" I asked.

She shook her head.

"It's bean curd."

At that moment, Wayne stomped up the steps. He set his guitar case down on the landing and cleared his throat. "Okay, I'm ready to talk about how Claudio betrayed me." He looked away from us and rubbed his hands up and down his thighs a few times before he continued. "What he did with your pizza—it wasn't the first time. Right before you guys came in, he grabbed my mic off the stand and yelled for table seven to pick up their order—right in the middle of 'Needle and the Damage Done.' It was humiliating."

"I'm sorry," I said.

Wayne waved his hand as if he was trying to downplay it. "It's okay. The worst part is that I had my setlist down cold and I only got to play for five minutes."

"We'd love to hear you sing now," Angela said.

Wayne pulled his guitar out of its case and slipped the strap over his neck. "I'm working on a falsetto in case I ever cover 'Taxi,'" he said, sitting on the metal flooring. "But it's harder than you might think—after a few notes, I run out of air."

"Push out with your diaphragm," Angela said. "My mother taught me that."

"Your mother knows stuff like that?"

"She was a voice teacher before she married my father."

Wayne lowered his arms to his side. "What else did she teach you?"

"All kinds of tricks. Like to always shape your mouth into a circle when you sing a word with the O sound in it."

Wayne strummed a chord. He opened his mouth into a flattened slot and sang, "Oooh." Halfway through the note, he reshaped his lips into a circle. Instantly, his tone sounded a million times better.

"What else do you have?"

"Don't lean into the rhymes. You have to sing like the rhymes don't rhyme."

"Why don't you two sing something together," I suggested.

It took them a while to find a song they both knew. Angela didn't know any Bob Dylan or Stones or Neil Young. And she'd never even heard of Gram Parsons. (Wayne suggested "Return of the Grievous Angel" because it had nice harmonies.) For his part, Wayne wasn't familiar with any of Angela's Christian singers. They had a few hymns in common, but Wayne said it wasn't a good night for hymns, not after Claudio ran him off the stage at the pizzeria in such a disgraceful and short-sighted way that it would surely lead to his—Claudio's—personal and professional downfall. Finally, more as a lark than anything, they settled on "Raindrops Keep Falling on My Head."

Wayne started strumming and without a word of planning, they launched into the song, trading off lines as if they'd practiced it a hundred times. Wayne has always had a good rock and roll voice—it has a scratchiness that plays well with the right material. Angela's voice was on a completely different level, though. It stood apart. It sounded timeless, like water flowing downstream.

Wayne strummed the last chord, then said, "I did the circle thing for the O sound, and I tried not to lean into the rhymes, just like you said."

"I heard," Angela said.

Angela and I rested our backs against the safety fence and sipped soda while Wayne played his setlist. After he finished his songs, he played his "trilogy" of instrumentals: "Stephanie," "Denise at 16," and "Penny For Your Thoughts." Then he closed his formerly eye-patched eye and just strummed chords while the moon climbed the sky and the traffic below us dwindled to nothing.

"I hate to say it," Angela said, "But I really have to use a restroom. I'm not used to drinking soda."

"Nothing is open this late on a Sunday," I said. "Maybe a gas station somewhere. Or we can run you home."

Angela looked around. "I don't want to go home yet. This is too much fun."

Wayne looked at the rail and then back at me. "It *is* a rite of passage," he said. "We could close our eyes and steady her."

"Steady me?"

"Ignore him," I said, shaking my head. "We'll find someplace open."

Finding someplace open for Angela to pee proved harder than I'd anticipated. We drove to the square, but the streets were empty, and the shops were dark. The Pub was still open, but it was a bar—there was no way they would let us in, even just to use the restroom. McDonald's was on the far end of town, but it was past eleven, and I was pretty sure they closed at ten.

"Keep going towards McDonald's," I said to Wayne. "Maybe they're still open."

"Guys, I really need to go," Angela said.

"She's really got to go," I said. "I think the Lincoln Diner stays open all night for the drunks. In fact, I know they do. I was there one time real late—the owner showed me the menu he puts on the tables after midnight. He jacks the prices way up since the customers are too intoxicated to notice."

"How far is it?" Angela asked.

"We'd have to turn around. Then three or four minutes. The bathroom is down a flight of stairs in a catacomb-type setting."

"I'll never make it."

"I'll run the lights," Wayne said.

"I'm not going to make it," Angela whimpered. She leaned forward and knotted her hands over her abdomen. "Pull over. Now!"

We were driving through Colt Park at the time. Before Twin Oaks broke ground, Colt Park was the most desirable subdivision in Gettysburg. Wayne pulled over in front of a small rancher. We sat in the car, horrified, as Angela disappeared into the darkness of the owner's backyard.

Almost immediately, a dog began to bark. A few seconds later, the porch light clicked on. I heard a gate slam, then I saw a flash of movement and Angela bolting through the front yard.

"Go, Go, Go!" Angela yelled, diving into the back seat. Wayne floored it and turned sharp at the same time. The back tires spun and the car fishtailed for a long second before straightening out.

"What happened?" Wayne yelled from the front seat.

"An elderly gentleman saw me."

"Peeing?"

"No. I'd just finished when the lights came on and there he was, standing in the doorway in boxer shorts and a white undershirt."

"Did he say anything?" I asked.

Angela nodded, but she was already laughing.

"What did he say?" I asked again.

"He said, 'Hey, that's not a bathroom!'"

Claudio's was closed by the time we got back to my Pinto. We climbed out of Wayne's car and stood in the tiny, empty parking lot beside the restaurant's dumpster. The street was quiet. A single moth was circling the yellow light bulb above the back door. Wayne pulled his guitar from the trunk and slid the case into the backseat. Then he stood motionless, staring at the darkened building as if he just remembered leaving something important inside. "Well, I guess I'll head home," he said, sighing. He turned to us. "Are you guys alright?"

"We're good," I said.

"Thank you for sharing your talent," Angela said to Wayne. She reached out to shake his hand and said, "Be of good cheer, Wayne Clark."

And that was the first time I'd ever seen Wayne speechless.

I drove Angela back to the church parking lot. It was late—well past midnight. I turned off the engine and rolled down my window. I put my hands on the top of the steering wheel, then slid them down to the driving position. I hadn't slept in seventy-two hours, but I felt wide awake. I looked at Angela. "Well, I'm sorry. Our date was kind of a disaster," I said.

"Are you kidding? This is the most fun I've had . . . ever."

"Angela?"

"Yes?"

"When is your family leaving?"

She leaned forward. "As soon as we wake up. Why?"

I didn't know what to say. And I knew my voice would crack if I did say anything, so I just smiled and shrugged.

She smiled back and then gave my hand a tap. "Don't leave yet, Jim. I have something for you."

My heart jumped. In a flash, Angela was across the parking lot and through the door of her parents' Winnebago. Inside, a flashlight clicked on. The light bounced around for a moment, then settled on one spot. I could picture Angela flipping through her King James Bible as quietly as possible, then letting out a muffled, almost silent squeal as she carefully pulled the pressed rose from between the pages of the "love chapter." I took a deep breath and looked up at the moon. It looked different—bigger and softer than on all those long nights spent sorting blueberries alone. I felt something tingle in my stomach. I had no idea what would happen—if I would go with Angela or if she would stay with me—but the result would be the same; everything would be different. From this moment on I'd find a new me. A better me. No more living a life of self-absorption. No more scarfing down multiple Big Macs. No more defrauding record clubs. And most of all, no more footloose and fancy-free garbage. I'd project exemplary character. I wasn't quite sure what the "best" me looked like, but with Angela by my side, I'd figure it out.

The Winnebago door opened. Like in a dream, Angela was gliding across the parking lot. She'd taken her mother's sweater off. She was wearing a flannel nightshirt now, and the moonlight lit her long blond hair from behind as she hurried toward me. She had a white envelope in her hand and she leaned in through the window and held it out to me.

"Thanks for a wonderful evening," she said, kissing me on the cheek. She kissed me again, this time closer to my lips, then darted back to the Winnebago as if we were playing hide-and-seek and it was my turn to count backward from ten. I turned the envelope over in my hand. I traced my fingertips around the thin lump in the center, then carefully tore the envelope open. Inside were five crumpled-up dollar bills and a torn-off scrap of notebook paper. I unfolded the paper. The note read, *For my half of the pizza.*

EPISODE FIVE

Title: *Decadent Times Part 1*
Time: *43 minutes*
Synopsis: *Jim surrenders to his worst instincts.*

When I get to Heaven, I'm going to have some specific questions for God: *What's the most disgusting thing that I ate by accident without knowing? Would it be possible for him, God, to invent a record album that wasn't one long, continuous groove?* And *were there any hot girls who wanted to have sex with me that I had no idea about?* Of course, those questions will be mere icebreakers, my boyish attempt to evoke a smile from The Creator of All before I sheepishly dig my big toe into the dirt and ask the only question that I've ever really cared about: *Where does love go when it's gone?*

How will God answer? Maybe that love is like sunlight and that even in the depths of the darkest, loneliest night, the sun is still reflected by the moon. Or maybe he'd launch into some lengthy explanation about love being like water: that in his wisdom, he created a finite amount of love—ostensibly to elevate its value—and it's endlessly cycled through different states. That when love goes, it evaporates and floats into the sky where it collects with a multitude of other poor bastards' vaporized love until it rains down again on two new, momentarily elated saps, thus beginning the whole cycle anew.

The only thing I knew for sure was that I had loved Angela and now I hated her. I spent the rest of 1981 and all of 1982 cultivating my hatred toward her. I'd let my guard down. In a moment of weakness, I'd strayed from my footloose and fancy-free policy and offered my heart to a she-wolf in sheep's clothing. One who—with malice of forethought, I would argue—scarfed my love up only to spit it back out. No matter how many times I turned it over in my mind, I could see only one option: to punish Angela, I'd allow myself to go even further to seed. It would be a steep price to pay, but my physical, moral, and spiritual tailspin would serve as a cautionary tale to her and the rest of her treacherous ilk not to fuck with honest people's affections.

Thus began my season of decadence.

By the time the 1982 market season started, I was tired of Seven Turns—tired of hauling produce, tired of waiting in line for hours at the auction every Wednesday, tired of pushing mushy berries that were past their prime. More than anything, I was tired of farmers markets and tired of working seventy-two straight hours without sleep for a measly $210 a week. In early May, I convinced Larry to hire Brie to help me on Fridays and Saturdays. Then, I guilted him into allowing me to sell a few baked goods at the Gettysburg Market "to help me make ends meet." I rescued Little Martha's scone pans from the attic and dug out my parents' old recipe cards, and beginning the third week of the season, I offered three different muffins as well as my parents' signature product, the sour crème and chive scone that had ensnared the British man in the pith helmet all those years ago (thereby paving the way to my existence).

I needed money. Not only had I bought a 1978 Ford Bronco on payments, but I'd also ratcheted up my taste in food to a level that now qualified as "high-brow." As evidence, I'd taken a liking to duck eggs—Welsh Harlequin being my duck egg of choice. As for mushrooms, I insisted on Shitake. When it came to cheese, I'd consume Tillamook or nothing. I saved my highest level of discernment for meat. I'd taken to wearing Trez's old suit to the grocery store. On each trip, I'd saunter to the cold case, slide on my over-the-counter 10X reading glasses and study each cut of meat's fat marbling before I committed to a purchase. And if Nurse Darcy had a problem with it, she could go straight to hell. I had the craps of pandering. As a result, I'd packed on an additional layer of dense, seal-like fat. The added weight deadened the spring in my step, but that was the point—to wallow in my own crapulence. My goal was to grow so fat that if Angela ever came back to me, she'd be forced to pull my corpulent body from room to room on a wooden dolly. It would serve as her penance.

All of that aside, I was content. The only real strife in my day-to-day life was foisted upon me by the Clark siblings, Brie and Wayne.

Working with Brie at the markets was like trying to put on wet socks. She seemed to be harboring some deep-seated anger toward me. I was her boss, but because she'd taken FFA (Future Farmers of America), she felt no need to defer to me or even to acknowledge that I was her superior. Every single task—from sorting out the "ugly sisters" to setting up the display—played out as a battle of wills. Worse, in just a few weeks she'd become far more proficient at our job than me. She worked harder than me, knew more than me, and cared more than me. More galling, though, Seven Turns' customer base—customers I'd painstakingly cultivated—preferred Brie to me. Especially the little old ladies, who waited patiently in line for Brie to help them while I stood there twiddling my pudgy thumbs.

Unlike his sister, Wayne's master plan was to never work a day in his life—at least not in the conventional sense. He'd started a rock band. His singer-songwriter days were over, he said. In addition to the genre being an artistic dead-end, it had become unmanly. Effeminate singers such as Dan Fogelberg and Dan Hill had ruined it with their insipid, self-pitying lyrics that only pale-lipped college girls with a Sylvia Plath mentality could stomach for more than five consecutive seconds. As for his band—and Wayne would never dream of demeaning himself or his bandmates, Bryon "Sky-Rat" Hartline and Jon Kilgore, by calling it a "group"—it had changed names six times since Wayne founded it ten months ago. When the band consisted of just Wayne, its working name was The Wayne Clark Project. Then when Jon joined, it became Kilgore, and then a week later, The Wayne Kilgore Project. When Sky-Rat joined in mid-October, Wayne rechristened the band Sky-Rat, which quickly morphed into Clark, Kilgore, and Sky-Rat, then The Sky-Rat Project, and then finally Three Guys Named Sky-Rat.

Three Guys Named Sky-Rat had played out twice. Both times were frat parties. Once, they played for free, and once, they played for a case of Rolling Rock. The first gig, their nerves got the best of them. The second, they hit their stride twenty seconds into the first song—CCR's "Sweet

Hitch-Hiker"—and never looked back. After their set, while they were packing up their amps, a guy from the lacrosse team invited Three Guys to play a third party for actual money: $25.00.

Wayne turned him down flat.

"Screw covering other people's songs," Wayne said at an emergency band meeting two minutes later. "It's fool's gold. Even if we were the world's greatest cover band, that's all we'd ever be—a cover band." They decided then and there that they would hole up and write their own songs. What's more—and they decided this point by unanimous vote—they would not play in public again until they had an entire set of original songs.

That's where Three Guys stood now, on hiatus until they had twelve original songs.

That's also where I came into the picture. As Wayne told me repeatedly, I was an integral part of his master plan. Terry Cool, the owner of the dilapidated Gettysburg Sulfur Springs Resort, had offered Wayne a sweetheart deal. In exchange for some light maintenance work, Wayne and I could live in two of the Resort's abandoned bungalows for $50 a month. According to Wayne, it was a Carpe Diem-type thing: we had to snatch the offer up fast or the opportunity would escape through our collective hands "like a half-captured lizard."

So that's where things stood on the first Saturday morning of June. It was damp and chilly, and Brie and I had pulled into the market a few minutes later than normal. I was dressed poorly for the cold: cargo shorts and a T-shirt. Brie was wearing the same outfit she wore for the first hour of every market: jeans, a T-shirt, a flannel shirt, a lightweight zippered sweatshirt, and her blue, corduroy FFA jacket. While she finished pinting the last of the root vegetables, I put my basket of baked goods on the table by the point of sale. I stood there for a moment, adjusting the price sign until I was satisfied that the angle would catch the eye of the most possible customers. Then, I stepped back and blew into my hands. "It's freezing," I said.

"You need to dress in easily removable layers," Brie said.

I blew in my hands again. "I'm walking down to 7-Eleven for two coffees. In the meantime, if some guy either wearing or not wearing a pith helmet walks up and asks for a scone and I'm not back yet, ask him to wait—I need to talk to him," I said.

"So, if *any* man walks up for a scone, ask him to wait?"

"He would be British—at least ostensibly—and he'll probably ask for a sour creme and chives. And he might appear out of thin air. Just make sure you ask him to wait."

"You're ridiculous," she said to me.

I bit my lip. For the past two weeks, that was Brie's go-to phrase whenever I tried to exercise authority over her. I was fed up with it. It wasn't even the "ridiculous" part. If she merely accused me of *being* ridiculous, I'd simply ignore it. But instead, she purposely presented it as my permanent and unalterable state of being. I crossed my arms and tried to look mad.

"No, I'm serious," Brie said. "You're ridiculous."

"Listen to me," I said. "I don't care if you took Future Farmers of America, and I don't care if you *were* the first girl to earn an American FFA pin. I got you this job and I'm in charge. Just make sure you greet the customers. And don't give away any vegetables to any of those college guys who hang out around here trying to talk to you. Especially the fingerling potatoes—people have been asking for weeks when they're coming in."

"When have you ever seen me give anything away?"

"Just don't lose any sales," I said, trying to drop my voice into a lower, more authoritative register. "If three or four customers come up at the same time, don't waste time on lookers. Focus on the buyers. Do you need me to go over the 'tells' again?"

"I know them," she said.

"Oh yeah? Customers other than regulars?"

"If they walk down the table naming off all the vegetables, they're never going to buy."

"If they ask you what time the market closes?"

"They're never going to buy."

"What if they say that everything looks wonderful?"

"They're never going to buy."

"And my muffins and scones?"

"All of the above, plus, if they touch their stomach, they're never going to buy."

"Because?"

"Because hands always go to pain, and your muffins and scones inflict the local 'tomjammery'—which isn't even a word—with such a painful internal conflict that they have no option but to touch their stomach and then scurry away as fast as their conflicted feet can carry them."

"I don't get it. You're so nice to everyone else. Why are you so disrespectful to me?" I asked.

"Because you're ridiculous."

I'll admit, calling me ridiculous a third time in thirty seconds ticked me off. I turned and started toward the 7-Eleven. I'd only taken a half-dozen steps when I heard, "Jim!"

I stopped and turned halfway back.

Brie was standing in front of the stand. Her face had changed from the obstinate, semi-adult Brie to the shy ten-year-old Brie who brought me iced tea at her parents' house. She took a step toward me. "Listen," she said. "Don't ever eat a banana in the orchards when Larry has the bees out pollinating. The banana-peel smell mimics the bee's natural attack pheromones. You'll get swarmed and might not be able to get away."

"I don't eat bananas."

"Well, even so, don't all of a sudden decide to try one."

It was classic Brie. Pick a fight and then babble on about some perceived safety concern—like the time she made a big stink about the fumes from rotting potatoes being toxic and my potentially dying from them. I made an "OK" sign with my fingers and kept moving. I took my time. When I got to the 7-Eleven, I pulled the new copy of Rolling Stone off the newsstand and scanned the record reviews, then I poked around the snack aisle for a few minutes before I poured two large coffees. When I got back to the market stand, Wayne was standing under the tent.

I was barely within earshot when he called out, "Cool wants an answer."

I handed Brie her coffee and took a sip of mine. "Tell me the deal again—what exactly is it?" I asked.

"$50 a month plus we have to fix the place up. Painting, a little groundskeeping, stuff like that—around our schedule. No big deal."

"That's what I'm worried about—the caretaker part," I said. "I drove out there yesterday. It's completely overgrown. I couldn't even see the bungalows from the road. Plus, there's a bunk of old aluminum siding back there just sitting on sawhorses. What's *that* all about?"

"That's why we're only paying $50 a month—plus the security deposit."

"Which is?"

"I told you, $200."

I raised my eyebrows, but it was just for effect. I'd decided days ago to move in. I'd already borrowed a slew of apple crates from Seven Turns to pack all my stuff in.

Wayne moved out from under the tent. "Back in the woods there's the burned-out ruins of a carriage house—just the stone foundation. Kilgore and I dug out a fire pit. Everybody's coming over tomorrow for a housewarming party. If you move in right away, you won't have to drive home. Just walk a hundred yards to your brand-new bungalow."

"Who's coming?" I asked.

"You, me, Brie, and Sky-Rat and maybe Kilgore and a few others."

"What others? That's everybody we know."

"Good others."

"What good others?"

He looked at Brie, then motioned for me to lean in so he could whisper. "Groupies," he said. And then, as if he needed to clarify further, he mouthed, "*Band* groupies."

The next afternoon, I loaded all my belongings into the back of my Bronco and moved to The Gettysburg Sulfur Springs Resort. The Resort was a scatter of dilapidated bungalows that sat off the highway three miles south of town. Legend held that both Nathaniel Hawthorne and Ulysses S. Grant had visited the sulfur springs for their medical benefits: a sickly Hawthorne to seek relief from "bad humours" and Grant to treat his swollen liver. In the late 1800s, the springs became the site of an up-scale resort with a tennis court, a restaurant, and a formal ballroom. The original buildings burned down in 1912 after being struck by lightning. A decade later, the owners built a cluster of tiny summer bungalows to take advantage of the uptick in battlefield tourism to Gettysburg. From there, it was a slow, steady downhill slide. By the late 50s, the property had fallen into its current state of disrepair. Seven of the nine bungalows needed to be razed; two bungalows—the two Wayne and I were to occupy—were habitable. A third building, an office-sized brick structure with a sun-faded CHECK-IN sign still fixed to the door, was in decent shape. That was the building Wayne planned to use as Three Guys Named Sky-Rat's rehearsal hall.

I'd only unloaded half of my stuff when I decided that moving in with Wayne was the coolest thing I'd ever done. My bungalow was one big, rectangular room divided into a kitchen side and a living room side. Back a three-step hallway was the bathroom and, across from it, a tiny bedroom with a bunk bed in it. After I carried my belongings inside, I set up my stereo. As a rule, I never stack albums on the spindle (when they drop, the records tend to hydroplane—as a result, the needle doesn't know what to do and you get that infuriating "wah-wah" effect), but I was so excited about my new pad that I made an exception. I put on *Dark Side of the Moon*, then Humble Pie's untitled third album, then the first Boston album. While Floyd played, I dragged the two filthy, half-rotted, twin-sized mattresses from the back bedroom into the living room. Then, I tore apart the bunk bed and stacked the pieces outside, behind what looked to be a maintenance shed. After that, I positioned one mattress against the wall as a sofa of sorts and dragged the second one back into the bedroom, where I unzipped Trez's old sleeping bag and spread it out as a comforter.

The kitchen was more of a challenge. The sink was ancient—the porcelain was worn so thin that rust spread out from the drain like a Rorschach test. The stove was decent enough, though, and the refrigerator kicked on without a struggle when I plugged it in. The cupboards were gone, pried off the wall and carted away by who knows whom, so in their place, I stacked Larry's apple crates against the empty wall. I made three stacks, five high, butted tight against each other. Not only did they cover the unpainted swath of wall where the cupboards once stood, but they also looked stylish and functional.

I placed all of my pots and pans on top of the apple crates. Inside of the top layer of crates, I arranged my dishes and utensils, my box grater, garlic press, ladles, et cetera. In the bottom two layers, I fit all of my dry goods and canned goods. On a whim, I flipped the highest middle crate around so that the back faced me. I tapped a nail into the wood two inches from the top and hung my beloved 12" Griswold cast iron skillet from the nail. The effect was stunning. It tied everything together—so much so that every few minutes, I paused my work just to admire the manly beauty of it.

Brie pulled up while I was still unpacking my clothes. Right after that, Sky-Rat and Kilgore barreled down the long, dirt driveway in Sky-Rat's Firebird, raising a humongous dust cloud that took ten minutes to dissipate (which set Wayne off—apparently, we were ordered to keep a "low-profile" at all times). An hour later, just before sunset, two girls showed up. And by "showed up," I mean that they suddenly were just standing by one of the dilapidated bungalows, as if they'd sneaked out of the woods while our backs were turned. Wayne was beside them in a heartbeat, accepting a bag of chips that they seemed to be in joint possession of. He directed their attention to me. "Jim, these are my special friends, Chloe and Tina," he said, winking.

Then Wayne introduced the girls to Jon and Sky-Rat.

"Sky-Rat?" Tina asked.

We turned to Sky-Rat. From the uninitiated visitor's perspective, I'm sure his appearance was a tad frightening. (His head looked flat and solid enough to use as an anvil, and his teeth—to put it kindly—were in dire need of professional attention.) "It's based on Duane Allman's nickname—Skydog," he said. "I just did a twist to it."

When Tina acted as if she couldn't fill in the blanks, Kilgore stepped in with, "He just replaced dog with rat and added a hyphen."

"And Kill-Gore is a nickname too?" Chloe asked.

"No, it's my surname," Kilgore said. Jon was small and pale. Since third grade, there had been a general understanding in school that his blood was abnormal. It didn't produce enough iron. Or, it produced too much and was slowly poisoning him—the doctors were never quite able to pin it down. "Kilgore is German," he explained. "You know—German—like the Nazis in *Raiders of the Lost Ark*."

"Okay, Jon. Thanks," Wayne said, stepping in. He clapped his hands together, effectively bringing the introductions to a close.

Together we walked back along the narrow footpath in the woods to the carriage house ruins. Burned-out was too lavish of a description. The site was a small clearing in the woods. The only remaining evidence of the original stall structure was the blackened, three-sided stone foundation, and even that was close to being swallowed by nature. It didn't matter, though. While Wayne and everyone else spread out the food and beer on the blankets that Jon had brought along, I leaned over the fire pit and held a match to the kindling.

"Before we start, I have an announcement," Wayne said. "I have a better name for the band. Don't say anything—just try to picture the name on an album cover." Wayne held his hands apart the width of an album jacket and gazed into the space between them. Then just above a whisper, he said, "Bum's Rush."

Wayne had told me the name a week earlier. I'd had time to consider it and my thoughts hadn't changed. It was the best, unused band name ever. So, I had the opportunity to watch Kilgore and Sky-Rat's face when Wayne unveiled it. Kilgore smiled. Sky-Rat's reaction showed a brain in conflict. He pushed his long hair back and focused on the fire. Bum's Rush was the far superior name—he couldn't argue with that. But right now, currently, the band bore his official name—or at least his official derivative of Duane Allman's official nickname.

"It's the perfect name," Kilgore said. "The problem with Sky-Rat has always been the hyphen. If you say it out loud, it sounds okay, but in print it looks like our name is the quote 'Three Guys Named Sky' and we're attributing it to some guy named Rat. Bum's Rush is perfect. 'Bum' because we're a working-class band and 'Rush' for a head rush, either from pot or our music. It works both ways."

"Exactly," Wayne said.

"It's such a cool name it seems someone else would have scarfed it up already," Sky-Rat said. "Maybe we should stick with Three Guys Named Sky-Rat just to be safe. I don't want to dick around and get my ass sued off."

"What's everyone else think?" Wayne asked.

No one said anything.

"It's what's best for the band—otherwise, I wouldn't dream of changing names again."

"Oh, I'm not saying it isn't better," Sky-Rat said. "It's just . . ."

Wayne waited a few seconds to give the impression he was allowing Sky-Rat the opportunity to make his case. "It's out there for the taking," Wayne said. "We just need to vote."

It was never really up for a vote, of course. It was Wayne's band. He was the engine that drove the dream forward, and on some level, both Kilgore and Sky-Rat understood that their names had only appeared in the band's name long enough to convince them to join. So, when Wayne called for a vote, it was such an obvious *fait accompli* that even Chloe and Tina raised their hands.

"This is a turning point," Wayne said, "I can feel it."

To celebrate, Wayne not only passed everyone—including Brie— a Heineken, he twisted the cap off each bottle before he handed it to us. One by one, we leaned against the stone foundation and raised the bottles to our lips. The night felt perfect. The beer was cold. The meat was hissing on the fire. And the evening sky held just enough light to silhouette the pine trees on the town side of the ruins. It was one of those rare, organic moments when the heavens permit a small gathering of friends to sit together as equals—no one better than the other—and feel totally free to voice any thought, no matter how unscripted, without fear of embarrassment.

So when Kilgore said that The Kinks made him want to be a better person, no one laughed at him.

And when Sky-Rat said, "You know, I don't agree with some of the artistic choices Led Zeppelin has made," we all hushed up and gave him our rapt attention, as if he'd just uttered the single most well-reasoned comment given voice since the dawn of time. "*Physical Graffiti* should have never been a double album."

"What songs are you thinking of leaving out?" I asked.

"All of side four. And probably 'In My Time of Dying' if they still needed to cut."

We kicked that around for a few minutes until Wayne leaned forward and raised his hand. When we all turned to him, he said, "You know— and I've been sitting here thinking this—Joe Walsh didn't join the Eagles, the Eagles joined Joe Walsh."

"I heard that!" Sky-Rat said, lifting his beer bottle.

And it went on from there, the sun dipping below the treetops, everyone sitting on the moss-covered foundation with a bottle of beer in their hands or at their feet. After a time, I knelt beside the fire pit. The coals were perfect. I rotated the kielbasa and nursed them along while Wayne pulled his guitar out of its case to play us the new song he'd been working on. "It's called 'My Way of Thinking,' and it has a minor chord progression," he said, strumming the chord pattern.

"I love it," Chloe said. "It's transcendental."

"I love it too!" Tina said, scooting forward with a tad too much urgency.

"I'll tell you this. When we hit it big, no way am I moving to California," Kilgore said.

"We're a Pennsylvania band," Sky-Rat said. "Nothing's going to change that."

"Don't worry, Jim," Wayne said to me. "We won't leave you in Gettysburg to rot—you're going to be the band's road manager."

"You'll regret it," I said. "That's the mistake bands always make. They hire their friends, and by the time they're done, they're not friends anymore."

"That'll never happen. You're part of this. You've been a part of this since the beginning," Wayne said.

I knew that he wasn't just talking about his Elvis concert or in high school when we'd listen to records for hours trying to find songs that would fit his voice; he was talking about after graduation when I sat with him at the sandwich shop while he nervously waited his turn to play. The truth is, I never really considered it a chore to sit with him. Why would I? It was my job: to be there when he messed up the rhythm or words and give him the single, reassuring nod he needed to nudge him back on track. I took a sip of beer. "How about if I'm the band's pastry chef?" I asked.

Sky-Rat let out his goofy laugh and held up his beer bottle. "I heard that! Jim can be the band's personal pastry chef."

"It's settled then," I said, moving the kielbasa to the edge of the fire.

I glanced at Wayne. He had one hand pressed over one eye, and he was alternating his gaze back and forth between Tina and Chloe. They were groupies. Or at least, in Wayne's mind they were groupies. I knew he was trying to make a decision. Tina was the more attractive of the two. She had blond hair and bangs that just covered her eyebrows. At the same time, Chloe had natural beauty. She looked athletic and she had a deep, outdoorsy tan. The big difference between the two was that Tina was far and away the more talkative—in truth, she talked non-stop. I knew that Wayne would consider that a deal-breaker, so I wasn't surprised when Chloe got up and moved to Wayne's side as if he'd summoned her.

An awkward moment ticked by with nothing to fill the silence except the crackle of the fire.

"Who are you?" Tina said, turning to me. "I mean, besides the band's pastry chef?"

"I work at farmers markets," I said. I looked across the fire at Brie. She was snuggled in her FFA jacket, poking the fire with a stick. The same beer that Wayne had handed her after the vote was sitting on the ground between her feet. She'd taken maybe two sips. Just two hours earlier, Brie had been beside herself with excitement. She had a full day and a half to herself, and she was going to do what *she* wanted to do, she said. She'd brought two dozen ears of bi-color sweet corn and was planning to roast them on the coals in a wet burlap sack. She showed me the sack Larry gave her ("I tried to pay him, but he wouldn't take it."), and she explained near breathlessly how she planned to prepare the corn. She was going to husk it, salt it, then arrange it in the wet sack with an entire stick of butter smack dab in the middle. In theory, the butter would combine with the wet burlap to "butter-steam" the corn. She said that part was her idea, and she had a sneaky feeling that I'd be impressed by it—maybe even wish that I'd invented it first. Then, she laughed for no reason. It was a side of Brie that I'd never seen. She was giddy. She even looked inside my bungalow without asking permission and then wanted me to put The Grateful Dead's *American Beauty* album on the stereo. She said we could dance to "Box of Rain" in our bare feet on my tiny porch.

Then Chloe and Tina showed up and Brie hadn't said a word since. It was at that moment—when I looked across the fire and saw Brie poking the fire with the stick—that I realized she'd never even taken the sweet corn out of her car.

"Have you met Brie yet?" I said to Tina, motioning across the fire. "She works at the markets with me. She knows everything there is to know about ambient temperature and sunlight and how it affects the sugar content in produce. She earned an American FFA pin. It's a big deal just earning the pin. She earned it as a junior and she's never even lived on a farm. Her dad's an inventor."

Tina glanced at Brie and then turned back to me. "So, you sell fruits and vegetables."

"Yes, and my baked goods too."

"What about meat?"

"I think Larry's looking into it," I answered. "Maybe down the road as some sort of co-op thing."

"You'd sell another animal's flesh?" Tina asked.

I began to sense the conversation going sideways. "Possibly," I said. "I don't know—it would depend on the market's interpretation of a co-op. My big thing is food preparation." I leaned forward with my beer. "It's about the integrity of it, and by that, I mean doing things correctly. One of my earliest memories is being sent home from first grade for complaining about the culinary staff's shoddy preparation of the beef in the beef stew. It was a sin. The meat had amazing marbling—maybe the finest I've ever seen—but by the time the so-called chef brought it to temperature, it was gray. I can't prove it, but I think he cut it into cubes and boiled it in a cauldron of water. They had to call my dad."

"Why'd they call your old man?" Tina asked.

"They overreacted when I complained," I said, attempting to shrug. "It was 1969 and a lot of things were in play. Neil Armstrong just walked on the moon. I was a little behind in math—they acted like I should be able to just walk in the door cold and be able to count to one hundred by fives," I said. My throat pinched tight. "The important part is that my father agreed with me about the beef marbling. It was a travesty to boil away that marbling. Fat equals taste."

"I hate fat," Tina said.

"All fat or just sub-par marbling?"

"I hate the harvesting of fat."

"But you don't have a problem with rendering fat, right? Rendering the fat off of bacon, for instance. You have to. No one can eat raw bacon," I said.

"Harvesting, rendering, it's all the same. Fat belongs to the fat bearer. Who am I to demand other lives be sacrificed to sustain mine? And who am I to arbitrarily render fat off of bacon like I'm some fat-rendering God? Do you think that's in keeping with Earth Mother's wishes?"

I looked around the ruins. Even Sky-Rat looked uncomfortable. I turned back to Tina and worked my lips into a smile. "Earth Mother?" I asked, sipping my beer.

It was a mistake. Tina talked without pause for the next ten minutes. She was a vegetarian, and she hadn't eaten meat since the seventh grade when she hit a piece of gristle in her mother's Salisbury Steak. In that moment, as she spit the gristle out, she experienced an epiphany: she was eating an animal—the offspring of whom she'd later come to know as Earth Mother. And since that day, she'd refused to eat anything with a face. Eggs were okay, as were milk and cheese because none of those things had a face. Mostly, she ate vegetables. But even then, she suffered moments of intense guilt. She'd seen a film strip in elementary school— the one where a scientist hooks a carrot up to a gizmo that prints out the carrot's brainwave activity. The printout showed the carrot screaming as it's pulled from the soil and then fainting when the scientist's lab assistant takes a bite of it. The barbarism horrified her. But what option did she have? She had to eat something.

But by the grace of Earth Mother, Tina met a kindred spirit. She met her Sister with a capital S: her pen-pal Matías from Guatemala. Their coupling had been fate—the result of a fourth grade Cultural Arts project where each student in Tina's class was assigned a pen-pal from a poverty-stricken country. The assignment was to exchange a single letter, but Tina and Matías hit it off and they'd been corresponding ever since. When Tina became a vegetarian, her Sister with a capital S followed suit. Only Matías took it one step further; she actively fought against the consumption of animal flesh in her small hillside community. Most recently, she had freed a flock of chickens from a farmer's chicken coop. And these weren't ordinary, run-of-the-mill chickens. These were adult chickens that the village priest had already blessed.

When she stopped talking, no one said a word. I looked across the campfire smoke to Wayne. "Wayne, thoughts on Earth Mother?"

Wayne didn't even look up from his Heineken. "It's the whole, *do dolphins swim around all day thinking about triangles?* thing," he said. We waited for him to elaborate, but instead, he held the bottle up and peered at the bottom of it. "Damn it to hell," he said.

It was a brilliant move. I'd seen Wayne execute it many times. It was his version of an octopus releasing black ink into the water. He would toss out a non sequitur, one esoteric enough to pass for brilliant insight. Then while everyone was mentally discombobulated, he'd quickly change the subject in such a dramatic way that the thrust of the original conversation was rendered inert.

"What happened?" I asked, playing along.

"You don't want to know."

I took it as my opportunity to escape. I tilted back the last of my beer and stood. "I'll be back in a minute," I said. I walked back along the path to the bungalows. I had five beers. Usually, I'm a cheap drunk—two or three bottles and I'm walking sideways—but I didn't have the slightest buzz. Inside my bungalow, I fixed myself a cup of jasmine tea with a splash of orange juice and a double teaspoon of Pete the Honey Vendor's raw buckwheat honey. (I'd grown fond of the honey's malty tone.) The cabin still had the lingering earthy smell of a groundhog's winter den. It'd only been half a day, but I already took comfort in the musky scent. It spoke "uncomplicated" to me—a life stripped of everything but the basics: food, shelter, friendship, farmers markets, my Hi-Fi and record collection, beer, and at this moment, a cup of honey-sweetened herbal tea.

The first side of Boston's debut album was still on the turntable. I lowered the needle onto the vinyl and unlaced my scuffed work boots. The opening chord progression of "More Than a Feeling" flowed from the speakers. My new home's acoustics weren't the best. The drop ceiling completely deadened the treble—but for the time being I could live with it. I took a sip of the jasmine tea and began pulling my records from the cardboard boxes and separating them into two stacks: bands and solo artists. From there, I divided the stacks into sub-stacks: rock, hard rock, southern rock, solo artists who had always been solo artists, solo artists who were still part of a band but had released a side solo project, and solo artists who had permanently left their original band. I'd just begun alphabetizing the sub-stacks when someone rapped on the front screen door.

Before I could respond, Tina pushed her way inside and leaned against the closed door. She folded her arms under her breasts and took a slow, deep breath. I hadn't fully appreciated it earlier—probably because I was distracted by all the "Earth Mother" yammering—but Tina was amazingly shapely. Her breasts touched each other, creating a natural cleavage that even the most voluptuous Hollywood actress would kill for. Her hips were in proportion to her breasts, and her legs were tanned and perfectly tapered, right down to her toenails, which were painted deep lavender. "Chloe's with Wayne," she said, rolling her eyes.

"That's Wayne," I said, trying to smile the appropriate amount.

"What are we listening to?"

"Boston."

"They're good," she said.

"Who do you listen to?"

"I like the way Etta James sings," she said.

I had never heard of Etta James. "Isn't she amazing?" I said. "Her voice has a handmade quality to it."

Tina maneuvered around my record stacks and sat down six inches from my side. She rubbed her fingers on the dank mattress. I'd covered it with a blanket, but even so, the mousy, mildew smell hung in the air between us. Tina puckered her lips as though she was in deep thought, then rotated her head to take in the room in a slow, ten-second pulse. When she finished, she leaned into me and sniffed my shirt above the shoulder seam. "You smell like campfire smoke," she said.

She held her arm up for me to smell. I lowered my nose to her wrist. "So do you," I said.

"Tell me something unbelievably personal about yourself," she said. "Some deep, dark secret that you've never told anyone."

I wasn't naïve or stupid. I knew that I was Tina's second choice, but this was the first time a girl had ever hit on me. And this was well beyond flirting—this was closer to the opening scene of a porn film. I recognized it as a trade-off moment. Of course, she hadn't offered her part of the trade, nor had she even made a token attempt to ease into it unless you counted her campfire-smoke line. Normally my Art of Intuition would have kicked in, but in the headiness of the moment, the only thought that came to mind was *fat equals taste.* Then it hit me. I took Tina's hand

and looked directly into her eyes. "I was conceived in public. At the farmers market right on the square in Gettysburg. My parents had sex in the back of an Econoline van while dozens of pedestrians walked past."

This seemed to please her. "Your parents were hippies?"

"More pseudo beatniks. It was '62. My dad always said that '57 was the best time to be counter-culture, but he'd missed it by a few years. Plus, there weren't any beatniks in Gettysburg back then—only Eisenhowers."

"You're funny," she said. Then, like an afterthought, she added, "Personality is important."

I understood the subtext: I was fat.

Again, not morbidly fat, but overweight. Something on the order of thirty-five pounds. I didn't give a crap, though. I was finished living my life to please other people. I had my own pad and a possible pastry chef position with a kick-ass rock and roll band that had the best unused band name anyone had ever heard. Wasn't this the entire reason I'd moved in with Wayne? So I could have sex with random groupies? Free of any gigantic, soul-devouring rig-a-ma-roll at the hands of a she-wolf? I looked into Tina's eyes. "I think it's cool that you're a vegetarian."

She didn't say anything. A long moment passed.

"And I think it's really cool that you have a Guatemalan pen-pal. And even cooler that someday you're going to follow her lead and take a political stance against animal suffering."

That seemed to do it. Tina pointed to the three-step hallway and asked. "What's back there?"

"The bathroom and the bedroom," I said.

Tina stood and disappeared back into the hallway. From my vantage point, I couldn't tell if she turned into the bedroom or the bathroom. The Boston album was still playing. I lifted the overarm so it would replay, then turned the volume up, thinking that if she were using the facilities, I'd save her the embarrassment of her knowing I could hear her pee. A second later, Tina yelled, "Jim!"

I eased the music down. "What?"

"Come here."

In the bedroom, Tina was lying on my bed, fully dressed except for her sandals. She reached up for my hand and, in one deft move, pulled me on top of her and wrapped her legs around my waist so tightly that

I felt my bottom two vertebrae realign. We rocked a few times until we were more or less balanced on the arc of her buttock. Within seconds, Tina was asleep. And within a few seconds more, she was snoring. And that was it. I laid there unable to free my arms, gently rocking, listening to side one of Boston play over and over again until I lost count of how many times I'd heard "More Than a Feeling" before I finally dozed off.

This went on for two weeks. Each night, fully dressed, Tina pulled me on top of her and wrapped her limbs around my midriff, pinning my hapless arms to my rib cage. We rocked gently. She fell asleep. I fell asleep. Eight hours later, I woke up beside her, thrown clear somehow during the night. If it was a porn film, it was the worst porn film in the history of the world.

I didn't consider what Tina and I were doing sex. Who would? It was more like we were mired in the early, awkward stages of some bizarre mating ritual, one known only to a handful of primitives residing in the deepest, most remote reaches of the rainforest. I'll confess, though, it wasn't the worst thing I'd ever partaken in. Which isn't to say I was proud of it—or even okay with it—because each night as we rocked lightly on the fulcrum of Tina's amazing, perfectly arced buttock, in the back of my mind I could hear Brie's voice saying, *You're ridiculous.*

Meanwhile, Tina moved her meager belongings into my bungalow. It started with just a handful of small, innocuous items: a macrame wall hanging of an owl, a candle, an ancient, plug-in hair dryer that looked as if it predated the Korean War. From there, she carted in a single cardboard box of clothes and a ratty, neon-pink bean-bag chair that smelled like mushrooms. Where her stuff had previously been, I had no idea. If we decided somewhere along the line that she was moving in, I'd missed it. All I knew was that she borrowed my vehicle to haul her stuff to the bungalow (except for the bean bag, which just mysteriously appeared one day while I was at work) and that each time she finished, I found a wad of crumpled Big Mac wrappers shoved under the driver's seat.

At the two-week mark, she walked through the door clutching a shoebox. She let out a lungful of air as if she'd just finished a Herculean task. "That's finally the last of it. What a relief to have everything moved in."

I looked around. The sum of her belongings, including the chair, could have easily fit into the back of my Bronco. Now Tina was standing in front of me, holding a battered shoe box. She lifted it for me to see. "These are my treasures. Every letter Matías has ever sent me."

"Who?" I asked.

Tina gave me a half smile, half frown and handed me the box. "They're all in here chronologically. All I ask is that you keep them in order," she said. Then she pointed to the ratty bean bag and disappeared back the hallway.

The message was clear.

I hadn't sat in the chair yet—it looked sticky—and when I did sit down, I was right: it *was* sticky. Worse, it smelled like a feral cat had marked it. I took a breath through my mouth, then opened the box. The letter in front was yellowed and torn at the folds. I unfolded it and read the letter from beginning to end, every single, misspelled word. Then I skimmed the next dozen or so letters. Almost immediately, two things became clear. First, Matías wasn't a sister with a capital S. He was a boy with a capital B. How Tina had initially missed this was easy to see: the only photograph he'd ever sent of himself was a long-ago group shot with one of the smaller, more androgynous-looking children—Matías presumably—circled in blue crayon. The second thing that became immediately apparent was that around the time Matías reached puberty, he began to consider Tina his fiancé. Since I only had half of the correspondence, I can only guess that somewhere along the line, Tina had inadvertently entered into a prearranged marriage agreement of some sort. From there, it worsened. The closer the letters got to the present time, the more apparent it became that grown-up Matías was a full-blown, enviro-terrorist. Beyond releasing the chickens, he wrote of one day master-minding a grand animal-rights gesture designed to cement his bond with Tina. ("Wrote" being a charitable description—Matías' language skills leveled off fairly early, leaving the second clump of letters to read as if they'd been penned by an incredibly cynical nine-year-old.)

I'd just folded the last letter and slipped it back into its envelope when Tina stepped from the shadows of the hallway. She was naked. She touched her hair, then rested one hand on her hip and slid her other hand as high up on the doorway arch as possible. She angled her head so only one eye was visible to me and asked, "Do I look like the girls in those magazines?"

My first thought was to stifle my natural impulse to bleat. My second thought: *Don't say anything stupid.* Mercifully, my Art of Intuition kicked in. "Yes," I said.

"Then what are you waiting for?" she asked.

In his 1941 film, *Citizen Kane*, Orson Welles depicted the souring of Charles Foster Kane's marriage by cutting together a series of increasingly loveless breakfast scenes. The only characters in the scenes are Kane and his wife, Susan. I can do the same thing with myself and Tina. The scenes have more settings and characters and play out over a shorter time— months rather than years—but other than that, the only significant difference is that instead of revolving around the breakfast table, each scene revolves around my perfectly seasoned, twenty-year-old 12-inch Griswold cast iron frying pan. The frying pan that Tina—my girlfriend, roommate, and constant companion—ruined beyond repair, all because she was too busy yammering about Earth Mother to listen to a single word I said.

● SCENE ONE ●

The morning after Tina and I first made love, I prepared a special breakfast for us. We'd passed into a new phase in our relationship. We were lovers. I'd seen her naked and she'd seen me naked and neither one of us had passed out or giggled. Therefore, a celebration seemed in order. I had four nicely aged, room-temperature Welsh Harlequin duck eggs sitting on top of the apple-crate shelving. I also had two medium-sized Yukon Gold potatoes that Bitner's Organic had gifted me for helping them break down their tent. Plus, I had some fresh scallions and a shriveled red bell pepper that still had some life left in it. While Tina showered, I heated three heaping tablespoons of bacon grease over a medium flame in my Griswold skillet. I sliced the potatoes and spread them out evenly across the bottom of the skillet. Over the potatoes, I spread chopped bell pepper and scallions. When the potatoes had a nice, golden-brown crust, I flipped them over and added salt and pepper. Over this, I poured the four lightly beaten duck eggs. Then, I killed the heat. To my mind, that was the beauty of cooking with a skillet as perfectly seasoned as my beloved Griswold—it held the heat, allowing me (in this case) to achieve a perfectly ephemeral set to the duck eggs.

I grated the last of my Tillamook Cheddar over my creation just as Tina strolled out from the bedroom. She had on my Superman T-shirt. I was taken aback for a second—the T-shirt had been precious to me ever since I'd demanded it from Viking as reparations for tricking me into believing that he was someone else—until I realized that Tina had nothing on underneath. She sidled up beside me and slid her arm around my waist. "Superman?" she said, pulling the shirt away from her body with her free hand.

"You mean Supra Man."

"You're funny," she said, and she kissed me on the cheek.

I knew she didn't get the Nietzsche reference. I didn't care. It felt good to have someone appreciate my sense of humor—even if I wasn't trying to be funny at that particular moment. A spark of electricity rippled through my veins. For the first time in my life, I felt like a grown-up. I laughed for no particular reason. Then I dragged my plastic spatula along the side of the pan to loosen the eggs. "Don't worry about a thing," I said. I let a boyish smile spread across my lips, "The integrity of your vegetarian diet is intact."

"What is it?" Tina asked.

"A vegetable frittata. The secret is the cast iron frying pan. It's never been washed. Ever. The history of every meal that's ever been prepared in it is all right here in the seasoning. My parents even warmed up my baby bottle in it," I said. I felt myself drifting into one of my weird flights. I bit my bottom lip to suppress a bleat. "The cooking surface is sacred—like the place where a hero fell," I said, my voice cracking with emotion.

"Oh, sweetie," Tina said.

She tried to weave her arm around my waist again to comfort me, but I waved her off. "I'll get you a fork," I said.

"Forks are for tearing. Like fangs. I only use a spoon," she said.

I pulled a spoon from the apple crate shelf. "A spoon for . . ." My mind rushed, sifting through the possibilities of how to finish the sentence. For a split second, I panicked. Our relationship had changed.

What were we now? Sex partners for sure—last night had proved that. Three and a half times. But what else? An instant before the pause bled over to embarrassment, I saved it. "A spoon for my Mademoiselle," I said, and then I handed her the spoon over my forearm, like a chubby waiter.

"You're funny," Tina said.

She dug her spoon into the frittata and lifted a bite to her mouth. Her eyes pulsed with culinary bliss. She licked her lips and actually said, "Mmm." I knew that it wasn't just the Griswold. It was the bacon grease. Bacon grease wasn't part of a vegetarian diet, but who was Tina kidding? Those McDonald's wrappers hadn't crawled under my car seat by themselves. I put my fork down and watched her eat. I have to admit, I was so enthralled with watching her devour our special break-fast that I almost didn't notice how she scraped the sides of the bowl long after the last morsel of food was gone and long, long after any normal, sentient human being on Planet Earth would scrape the side of an empty cereal bowl.

Tina and I spent the day hand in hand. I took her to the spot in front of Wolfe's Pub where my parents set up for the farmers market and showed her the exact parking space where I was conceived. We ate an early dinner at the Lincoln Diner (I got a gyro, Tina got a salad), then we drove to the Hanover Mall so I could purchase Tina an album. The only Etta James record the store had in stock was a tacky-looking greatest hits compila-tion, which set me off, but Tina studied the back and pronounced it worth the seven dollars because the song list included her two favorite songs, "At Last" and "Wallflower."

By the time we got back to the bungalows, the sun was behind the trees. Sky-Rat's Firebird was parked in front of the rehearsal hall and the lights inside were turned on. "I think they have all the cardboard egg trays tacked up on the walls—the acoustics should be pretty good now. Do you want to go in?" I asked Tina.

"It'd be the perfect end to the day," she answered.

We walked into the rehearsal hall and sat on the bare floor. True to Wayne's vision, Bum's Rush had been working exclusively on original ma-terial. Wayne had written six songs. They ranged from decent ("Whiskey Veins," "My Way of Thinking") to pretty good ("Sleeping Dogs Sleep,"

"Working Overtime," and "The Railroad Song"). Wayne's newest tune, "The Ballad of Bum's Rush," was his most ambitious. It clocked in at a massive twenty-six minutes and, according to Wayne, told the "true story" of Bum's Rush. The song worked in band introductions, a frenzied five-minute salute to the first British Invasion, a ten-minute guitar solo that Wayne claimed was based tonally on Bach's "Sleepers Awake," and not one, but two false endings. All before climaxing in a minute-long blitzkrieg of Sky-Rat's near incendiary cymbal bashing.

Tina and I listened to the band work through their set. When Wayne finished "The Railroad Song" with a guitar riff that imitated a train grinding to a halt, the only original they had left to play was "The Ballad of Bum's Rush." All twenty-six minutes of it. I looked at Tina. The vision of her standing naked in the doorway replayed in my frontal lobe for the seven-hundredth time since I'd opened my eyelids that morning. Waiting half an hour before I could have sex with her seemed intolerable. I stood up and let out an exaggerated yawn. For some reason—maybe it was an extension of the feeling I had at breakfast, that I was doing grown-up things for the first time in my life—I walked over to Wayne and shook his hand. "We're heading out, guys," I said. Then I shook Kilgore's hand and Sky-Rat's hand. And I guess that they were feeling a little grown-up too because they each returned my handshake without the slightest hint of self-parody and responded with a montage of, "Thanks for coming," "Get some rest, man," and "We'll talk in the morning."

I put my arm around Tina's shoulders and we walked along the footpath to my bungalow. The moon was low in the sky and our long, blended shadows raced out in front of us to the door. The night air smelled of pine trees. To make the moment even more perfect, just as I fit the key into the lock, somewhere up high in the darkness two barn owls hooted to each other. I didn't bother to flick on the lights. Two steps inside, Tina slipped her shirt over her head and walked straight to the bedroom. Just as I shut the front door, the opening riff of "The Ballad of Bum's Rush" echoed across the compound. Twenty-six minutes later, by the time Sky-Rat climaxed the band's opus with a cacophony of cymbal crashing that would have read as overkill to Keith Moon, Tina and I were finished.

• SCENE TWO •

On the third Monday in October, I discovered that the bungalow had no heat source. Bleary-eyed and more exhausted than when I went to bed, I ambled into the kitchen with my Carhartt sweatshirt draped over my shoulders. I put on a pot of coffee—a Kenyan dark roast that I'd recently taken favor to—and stood motionless while the water heated to a perk. I must have dozed off on my feet because the next thing I knew, the earthy aroma of the coffee was thick in my nostrils and I was salivating. I poured a cup and took a sip as I wrestled the kitchen drapes open. The morning sky was the color of granite. The branches of the oak trees along the driveway were bare. On the inside of the window, a thin layer of silver-white frost spread out from the bottom sash like lichen growing on a rock. I pressed my fingertips against the pane. It was ice cold.

I scanned the living-room walls for the thermostat. Nothing. I slogged into the living room and crouched down to look behind the television set. Still nothing. No electric baseboard. No heating vents. No radiators. I let out a "humph." Until that instant, I'd never given it a thought, but it made sense. The Sulfur Springs Resort was a summertime destination. Why invest in a furnace or baseboard heat or whatever the hell they had back then? Just winterize the plumbing before the first frost and be done with it. I filled my coffee cup, walked across the compound to Wayne's bungalow, and rapped on the window.

"Heat?" I asked when he opened the door.

He was wearing a jacket and his knit hat. "We'll have to make do," he said.

The first remedy was more blankets. I drove to my parents' house and borrowed two musty-smelling army blankets that I found buried in the bottom of the hall closet. When I got back, Tina and I drove to the Rescue Mission, and for five dollars we bought the thrift shop's only space heater—a prehistoric thing with the word "works" scrawled across the top in black Magic Marker. On full blast, the heater took the chill off the air, but we had to unplug it at night (only a lunatic with a death wish would leave it running unattended for more than thirty seconds). And since the bungalows weren't insulated, our breath became visible again within minutes of pulling the plug.

The worst was yet to come. Just after Halloween, the temperature dipped below freezing for three straight days, setting the ground as hard as concrete and touching off a mass migration of mice from the surrounding woodlands to our semi-warm home. The invasion began one afternoon as a single, fleeting glimpse of something dark and tiny and villainous darting along the baseboard behind the mattress-sofa. By evening, scores of rodents had overrun the bungalow. The idea of falling asleep that first night was a bad joke. Tina and I endured seven torturous, fully dressed hours stretched flat on our backs while dozens of tiny, hairless feet raced back and forth in the bedroom's drop ceiling. As unnerving as that sound was, what followed at daybreak was truly horrifying: an ominous silence—as though the mice had collectively exhausted themselves and fallen asleep.

Predictably, Tina and I differed over how to deal with the mice.

At first, Tina made a show of taking it in stride. "I'm perturbed at Earth Mother for sending these tiny souls to live with us, but who are we to hoard heat like some over-privileged heat God?" she said multiple times an hour. Then she'd point at the space heater and stare directly at me, waiting for me to expand upon her theme of collective survival.

I had my own thoughts. I took the mice as a symbol, and unlike the pearl-white building in my short story, I could explain the symbolism perfectly. The disgusting rodents represented all of the unwelcome things that had infiltrated my home: tension, freeloading, and the pretend hatred of meat, just to name a few. The novelty of living with a girl—even one with perfectly symmetrical breasts—had worn off. I didn't love Tina. For long periods, I didn't even like her. She snored. She was forever cold. She never offered to pay for food or gas or to help keep our living space clean. She broke things. She cleared her throat continuously. And in what had become her most exasperating trait, whenever I asked her a question, she would stare at me without the slightest hint of comprehension, then repeat what I'd just said back to me in the form of a question.

For example:

Me: "Can you give me a hand cleaning up?"
Tina: [A three-second, uncomprehending stare] "Can I give you a hand cleaning up?"

Me: "Yes. It'd be nice if you helped."

Tina: [A blank, even longer uncomprehending stare] "Are you saying it'd be nice if I helped?"

So, while Tina fretted about the tiny souls, I gleefully split their skulls open. I bought five dozen mouse traps at the grocery store and modified them into the most lethal mousetrap known to man. First, I flattened out the trip catch with a pair of needle-nosed pliers, effectively creating a hairpin trigger. Next, I WD40'd the hinges and the arm clasp. Then, I swirled a pinch of cotton into the bait (peanut butter) to make the mice more inclined to yank with their filthy, miserable little heads and trigger the spring trap. As the *piece de resistance*, I placed a tiny crumb of Earl the Cheese Vendor's extra sharp cheddar on top of the peanut butter. Every night, the traps worked their magic. So much so that after the third night—to protect the "mood"—I left the stereo playing to drown out the relentless din of traps springing and the occasional, partially-trapped-but-not-quite-dead mouse flopping around on the hardwood floor. And each morning, no matter how poorly I'd slept, I crawled out of bed first and gathered up all the dead mice and deposited them a few feet off the front porch, where they'd serve as a cautionary tale to any vermin contemplating a move into my domicile.

Tina's charity toward the invading force ended the second week of November, when a mouse the size of a hamster darted across our bed while we were having relations.

"Wouldn't we be safer with the mattress elevated?" Tina asked the next morning.

"Safe from what?"

"The visitor mice."

"You mean the brave little souls? Yesterday you claimed they were economic refugees."

"Where's the bed frame, anyway?"

"How am I supposed to know?" I snapped.

I pulled on my work boots and sat on the mattress-sofa, tying and re-tying my laces, giving Tina the chance to snipe back at me. I'll confess, the bickering worked to my advantage. Not only was it cathartic, but I'd discovered early on the joys of make-up sex—that Tina was open to a wide variety of new "levels of intimacy" after an argument. By the time I tied my laces a third time, though, she hadn't said a word. Then, I saw a single tear slide down her cheek.

That got me. "Look," I said, "I know I'm no bargain." I paused to show my sincerity.

"With guys, looks aren't as important," Tina said.

That's not what I was going to say, I thought.

I walked outside and across the compound to Wayne's bungalow. I pushed inside without knocking. He was on all fours with his head stuffed into the opening beneath the sink. "I think the mice are getting in around the plumbing," he said.

Wayne's bungalow looked as though burglars had ransacked it. Clothes were strewn everywhere, the cushions to his small sofa were on the floor, and in the corner, his bookshelf was tipped over. "You have to keep it cleaner in here," I said. "There're too many places for the mice to hide."

Wayne pulled his head out from under the sink and stood up. "The problem is that we can't kill them quick enough with traps. We need flour and concrete. Feed them and the first time they drink, the concrete will set up and they'll bleed out."

"I agree," I said. I tapped my foot on the floor. "Did I ever tell you that when Tina talks about someone dying, she says they 'moved on from the used-to-be' instead of just saying they died?"

"No, but it doesn't surprise me."

"What's that mean?"

"The 'used-to-be' is now if you've moved on from it. She's employing circular language because she can't cope with the idea of death. It's probably an extension of all that Earth Mother crap."

"Before she split, did Chloe ever talk about Tina?"

"Only that she's been around. All over the state and up north too."

"I'm thinking of kicking her out."

"Why?"

"She's a buzz-kill."

"What's the sex like?"

"I can't complain—everything's on the table. But then, sometimes if she has bad news, she breaks it to me during relations. Once, she told me she invited her mother to visit us for the weekend."

"In the middle of sex?"

"Yeah. And get this—she claims to be this devout, holier-than-thou vegetarian, but every time she borrows my Bronco, I find McDonald's wrappers under the seat."

Wayne put his hand over his formally eye-patched eye. He stared at the floor, deep in thought. "What you have on your hands is a self-loathing vegetarian," he said, pulling his palm away. "She's punishing herself for sneaking McDonald's. She wants to get caught. That's why she claims her mother is on the way every time you have sex—her old lady's not really on the way, but it gives her the sensation of punishment for betraying her belief system. It's about as Freudian as it gets."

"She doesn't say she's on the way. She says she wants to come for a visit."

"It's still Freudian."

"This was supposed to be easy. Instead, it's drudgery."

"That's because you forgot my steadfast rule. That's the whole problem with you—you always forget my steadfast rule."

He was right. I couldn't remember it. "Tell me again what it is?"

"Girls date me; I don't date them."

Tina was still in the kitchen when I walked back to my bungalow. "Did you get them?" she asked.

"Who?"

"The visitor mice."

"First of all, they're not visitor mice; they're kangaroo mice," I said. I waited a second so she couldn't help but catch the disdain in my voice. "But I wouldn't expect you to know that since you never roll out of bed until the middle of the afternoon."

Tina turned back to the sink and dipped her hands into the soapy water. She fished a steel sponge from the suds, shook it once, and dunked it back into the water. At first, I thought it was a bad joke (*she was doing dishes?*), so when a black object surfaced from the water like a baby humpback, it took me a second to process what I was seeing. "Are you scrubbing my Griswold with a steel sponge?"

Tina looked down at my skillet as if she was noticing it for the first time. "I tasted Salisbury Steak," she said. "You know—meat."

My eye twitched. "No crap you tasted meat. It's never been washed! Not even when my parents heated my baby bottle. The surface is sacred—like the place where a hero fell!" I shouted.

Tina stared at me. "Are you saying it's like the place where a hero fell?"

Since this is a confessional, I confess this: I bleated. A long, tortured bleat that carried with it the cumulative weight of every atrocity that had befallen humankind since God kicked Adam and Eve out of the Garden. And when I finished bleating, I turned and ran—yes, ran—down the hallway to Tina's and my bedroom where I dove onto our filthy, odious mattress and laid for the next hour, curled in the fetal position, sobbing.

I kicked Tina out of my bungalow the next morning. I told her that I was driving to my parents' house to visit and I wanted her and all of her crap out by the time I got back. When I returned home just after dark, Tina's ratty bean-bag chair was still in the living room, pulled next to the stereo. The Etta James record I'd bought her the day after we'd first made love was leaning against one of the speakers. The chair she might abandon—a mouse had chewed a quarter-size hole in it, and every time we moved it a few of the beans spilled out—but I knew she'd never leave Etta behind. I walked back the three-step hallway to the bedroom. Tina rolled over in bed. In the dark, I touched her shoulder. Her skin was soft and smooth, and I could tell that even in the freezing room, she was naked underneath the covers. I stripped down to my underwear and crawled in beside her. Her breaths slowly became audible in the quiet, then faster and louder as she turned onto her side and reached out for me.

That's when I discovered make-up sex taken to almost comical extremes.

⦿ SCENE THREE ⦿

After New Year's—January and February—everything went to crap. I had no work and no money; the TV reception was spotty; I was tired of all my albums; and I got sick twice. Once I got a sinus infection and had to borrow money from my parents for antibiotics, and the second time I picked up a stomach virus that left me bed-ridden for three days. It was no wonder I kept getting sick; the bungalow was forever damp, and some slimy, indestructible black mold had taken root in one corner of the bathroom. Plus, it was freezing. We'd found another space heater at the Rescue Mission. This one a 50s era relic that read as even less trustworthy than the first one and conjured up horrific visions of the entire Sulfur Springs compound engulfed in a wall of flames. And even though I spent my last four dollars on it, once we carted the heater home, I forbade Tina from ever plugging it in (which, of course, set off a big fight). In the end, the lone positive outcome of the punishing cold was that the mice were gone, having presumably frozen to death.

With Tina—my lover and girlfriend and twenty-four hour a day companion—the same grievances were still in play. She scratched my Allman Brothers *Eat a Peach* album; she used my neck towel without permission; and as I discovered one Saturday when I hauled our laundry out to my parents' house to get a break from her, she'd stretched out the neck-hole of Viking's old Superman T-shirt. For what nefarious purpose, I had no idea. All I knew was that it looked as if she'd repeatedly forced a basketball through the head opening.

So, the third scene in the *Citizen Kane* model is the shortest.

One February morning, I climbed out of bed to discover that it had snowed overnight. I peered out the window. A thick blanket of white covered the ground. I pulled a package of bacon from the fridge, peeled off a thick wad of meat, and laid it in the Griswold. I'd long since given up any pretense of accommodating Tina's vegetarian lifestyle. If sustaining my life meant sacrificing millions of smaller lives, then so be it. I didn't invent the food chain. I was merely abiding by an age-old system that had worked pretty damn well up to now. For that, I made no apologies—not to Tina or Nurse Darcy or that dickhead Morty or anyone the hell else. I stood for a moment listening to the meat sizzle. The sizzling sounded like rain pelting the tent canopy at the farmers market, and that made me think about Brie and how my favorite Saturday markets were the slow, rainy ones when it was just her and me for long stretches and we had plenty of time to play the misheard lyrics game she invented. That, and continue our unending debate over the proper way to dress for the market—she favored easily removable layers while I argued for the importance of comfort. Thinking about Brie, I felt something ominous lift from my shoulders—like a buzzard flying away.

Over the course of a few heartbeats, I smiled. Then, I let out a gleeful laugh. I eased the flame down under the Griswold while I did the math in my head. It would be four, maybe five weeks until Larry called me back to work. First, we'd busy ourselves with general spring clean-up and equipment maintenance. Then, we'd break the soil for the first plantings: onions, turnips, and potatoes. Then in the last week of April, the first farmers market would open for the season. Suddenly, in the time it took the bacon to crisp, I had hope—a light at the end of the long, desolate winter's tunnel. I plated the bacon strips, drizzled maple syrup over them, and, plate in hand, walked out across the frozen tundra and back down the footpath to the burned-out carriage house. The ruins were covered in snow. I stood by the fire pit, shivering while I ate my breakfast. When I finished, I walked back to the bungalow. Just outside the front door, I saw my frying pan sitting in the snow beside the pile of spent mouse traps. The snow around it was melted. I picked it up and turned it over in my hands. It was as curved as a shovel blade. I let out a horrified bleat. Then in slow motion, right before my eyes, the surface of my beloved, perfectly seasoned 12-inch Griswold split into two.

I blasted through the door. Tina was standing by the oven. "Get the hell out," I shouted. "And I mean it this time."

Tina stared at me for five seconds. "You mean it this time?"

"Leave and never come back."

Another pause, then, "You're saying to leave and never come back?"

That night we had the best sex in the history of the world.

EPISODE SIX

Title: *Decadent Times Part 2*
Time: *43 minutes*
Synopsis: *Jim takes desperate actions to rid himself of Tina.*

I've been in love three times. Each time felt different. To extend the earlier water metaphor, falling in love with Doris was a maelstrom powerful enough to wash away my existing topsoil. Mandy was an afternoon cloud burst that left my shirt drenched and matted to my body in a less than flattering way. And Angie was a gentle farmer's rain that coaxed the promise of growth from me, at least until she crushed my heart like a grape.

Tina was none of these things. I can't even conceive of a water metaphor for her. Ice, maybe. And that's only because by late February, it felt as though the longest, most frigid winter of my life was in danger of dragging on forever, and that I was one tiny misstep away from ending up encased in a block of ice for all eternity—like some slope-headed neanderthal who underestimated the treacherous gravel at the edge of a frozen pond.

I finally got rid of Tina, not because I summoned the carnal will-power to kick her out for good and make it stick, and not because I recognized the inherent dangers of meandering along the slippery edge of an ice-covered pond. I got rid of Tina because Wayne nearly killed Kilgore.

Let me start at the beginning.

Wayne had complained about Kilgore's bass playing since the band's earliest days. The exact nature of his objections escaped me—something to do with Jon only playing the root note on the one and three beats. That, and his unwavering refusal to play on the upper frets. As Wayne explained to me and everyone else at great length, Jon's "safe" approach might work for a band like the Eagles, who have three guitarists, but not a power trio like Bum's Rush.

"There's a ton of air to fill," Wayne would lecture Kilgore ten minutes into each practice, "I don't give a shit if there *is* something wrong with your blood. I need you all over that goddamn bass neck. And play with a little more energy, if you can stand it."

Each time Wayne berated him, Kilgore would nod, as if at long last he finally understood; then he'd say something along the lines of, "Okay. More notes higher up on the neck. And dance, too."

"No, I don't want you to dance," Wayne would say.

"So just kinda be-bop a little, then."

"Just try to look like you're not stapled to the floor," Wayne would say. Then he'd strike up the band and Jon would play his bass lines the exact same way.

Around the time Tina split my skillet in two, Wayne decided that if he couldn't extract any more animation from Jon, he'd rewire Jon's amplifier to give his bass playing more vim. The fact that Wayne had never rewired an amp before didn't faze him in the least; he viewed it as just one more skill set he needed to master in order to push the band forward. He set up a table in the rehearsal hall and spread out the amp's innards like a jigsaw puzzle. After studying the parts for two days, he bought all new vacuum tubes from an electronics store in York. Then he decided that switching out the tubes wouldn't be enough, so he drove back to York for a box of capacitors and a refurbished 12-volt output transformer that he had a hunch he might need. Still, he wasn't finished. On the drive home, Wayne stopped at the hardware store in New Oxford and picked up a small hand brush to whisk away the mouse dirt that accumulated on the table each night.

So, on a bitter cold Saturday night in late February, this was the state of our little universe: Tina and I were in a sexually-fueled mini-detente, Kilgore had his bass plugged into his reassembled bass amp, Sky-Rat was sitting behind his drum kit shirtless despite the rehearsal hall's sub-Arctic temperature, and Wayne had just finished a new song. "It's called '(Ain't Gonna) Phone it in Like Dylan,'" he said, slipping his guitar strap over his neck. "And the 'Ain't Gonna' is parenthetical."

He played the main riff at half-tempo. It was a bouncy eight-note blues riff—something that would slot in nicely with Dylan's post-Newport Folk Festival output. He played it a second time, slowly, so Jon and Sky-Rat could internalize it.

"It's that all the way—so just follow along," he said.

He flicked on his amp, and just as the first pellets of sleet struck the hall's windowpane, Wayne called out "Check mic one" and launched into the riff at tempo. Sky-Rat blasted in at the end of the second measure, setting down a 4/4 beat so solid it bordered on parody. Four beats later, Kilgore waded in with the root note on the one beat.

Ten seconds into the first verse, Kilgore's eyes came alive—it was as if the dozens of vitamin B12 shots he'd taken since first grade all kicked in at once. He jerked his head back and nodded a few times. Then, he stuck his tongue out and began to be-bop across the hardwood floor in a sideways, crab-like shuffle.

I put my mouth to Tina's ear. "Kilgore's coming out party?" I asked.

Tina stared at me as if she hadn't quite heard what I said, then a glimmer of comprehension sparked her eyes. "Yes. Yes! Kilgore's coming out party." Then she said something that I didn't catch.

"What?" I yelled.

"I said this is to Earth Mother's glory—like freeing captive chickens."

"Yes," I nodded. "It's tantamount to freeing chickens."

The next moments were a pleasure to behold. Kilgore slapped the bass strings so violently that his amp spit out a mini sonic boom. He grabbed the bottom of his bass and, in slow motions, as if it took every last ounce of his strength, he pushed it away from his chest. When he had his bass as far away from his chest as the strap would allow, he arched his back and posed like this—a newly-minted God of Rock and Roll—while Wayne launched into a twelve-bar guitar solo and Sky-Rat thrashed the cymbals as if he was fending off a shark attack.

From there, it only ratcheted up. After his solo, Wayne moved to Kilgore's side and mimicked Jon's pose. Then he lowered his pelvis into the same karate stance he'd used all those years ago for his Elvis living room concert and began to saw his strings against Kilgore's strings. The ensuing noise wasn't music. Not for an instant. But, that wasn't the point. The point was to push hard rock to the outermost edge of sanity—the last frayed second before the audience's brains melted into a puddle of liquid madness. It was a transcendental moment—the birth of Bum's Rush as a musical force to be reckoned with—and I was there to see it. Tina too. I reached out and took her hand. She smiled at me, and I gently lifted her hand to my lips and kissed her ring finger just below the first knuckle.

At that moment, an odd smell began to fill the room: like a hairdryer overheating. My first thought was that a mouse had chewed through some essential house wire and fried itself. I looked up at the drop ceiling. The lights pulsed—so imperceptibly that I wasn't sure that what I'd seen was real.

When I lowered my eyes, white froth was foaming from Kilgore's mouth. The lights pulsed again—this time a slow, undulating off and on. Wayne's guitar strings were still touching Jon's bass strings—they seemed welded together somehow—but Wayne's head was turned to me and his lips were twisting in slow motion, repeating the same pattern over and over again, like a goldfish struggling for air. Just as I raised my hands to cover my ears, Wayne choked out the words: *Switch. Off. Switch. Off.* At that instant, Sky-Rat slid across the wooden floor toward Jon's equipment, his face frozen in a mask of horror, his outstretched index finger on a collision course with the amp's power switch.

That was my last clear image before the flash and pop.

When I opened my eyes, I was still sitting on my folding chair but I was flat on my back, staring at the drop ceiling. My ears were ringing, and I had the sensation that minutes had passed. I looked to my left side for Tina. She was gone.

I pulled myself up just as Sky-Rat and Wayne were propping Kilgore up on a chair. His head was lolled to one side. He was breathing, but other than to twitch his arm when Tina draped a blanket over his shoulders, he was motionless. I looked at Wayne. I'd been in the rehearsal hall the past few days, watching him as he tore Kilgore's amp apart and reassembled it unendingly, and it was obvious that he had no idea what he was doing.

"What the hell happened?" I asked.

"We must have overloaded the 40-amp service," Wayne said.

"Is he okay?" I asked.

"I'd feel better if he opened his eyes," he said.

Without warning, Sky-Rat reared back and slapped Kilgore's face. Hard. It did the trick. Kilgore opened his eyes. He looked at each of us as if he was trying to place our faces, then he turned and looked at his bass amp and the blackened V on the drywall above the smoldering outlet. Slowly, while he was still turned to the outlet, a red handprint began to take shape on Kilgore's face. He rubbed his cheek. He began to cry, softly at first—just barely audible sniffling and a few random tears. Then his shoulders began to spasm, and he let out a long, slow wail that morphed into a single, unintelligible word.

"You shouldn't have slapped him that hard," I whispered to Sky-Rat.

"I didn't," he whispered back.

Kilgore took a deep, whimpering breath and motioned for Tina. She leaned over him and he whispered in her ear.

Tina looked up. "He's asking for soup."

Wayne snapped his fingers. "Jim. Quick. Soup."

Sky-Rat and Tina looked at me. The smell of burned wires was thick in the air. Sleet was pounding the building's roof and windows. I had my jacket with me, but it was across the room and I had the sense that seconds counted. I raced out the door to my bungalow and took a hurried inventory of my foodstuff. In the bottom apple crate, I found the can of chicken broth that I'd sent Tina to the store for when I had my stomach flu. I filled my saucepan with the broth and lit the flame. Working at top speed, I whisked an egg in a bowl. Then I chopped my last three scallions into quarter-inch lengths. I unscrewed the lid to the jelly jar I kept my ginger roots in and frantically grated a half-teaspoon of ginger into the simmering broth. Then, hands shaking, I drizzled the egg into the broth. To finish, I tossed in the scallions.

I rushed back across the treacherous, icy compound to the rehearsal hall and pushed open the door. Kilgore was still huddled under the blanket, slumped forward as if he'd been born without collarbones. "I whipped up some egg-drop soup," I said.

"There now," Wayne said, turning to Kilgore, "Jim heated some egg-drop soup."

Tina took the soup from my hands and knelt beside Kilgore. She dipped the spoon into the pan and held it up to Jon's lips. I turned to Wayne and gave him a dirty look.

"I didn't heat it up. I made it from scratch, except I didn't have time to strengthen the chicken broth because—"

He held up his hand to cut me off.

We all watched as Kilgore sipped from the spoon.

When Jon took a second sip, Wayne's lips spread into a tentative smile. "Well, I think it's best we knock off for the night and pick it up again tomorrow. Start where we left off. I have a second song I've been working on. I haven't finished it yet, but I'd appreciate some feedback."

On the word "feedback," Kilgore began to cry again.

Tina folded her arms across her chest. "Are you sure he's alright?"

"Oh yeah, he's fine," Wayne answered.

Tina looked into Kilgore's eyes. "Jon, honey, are you okay?"

"Oh yeah, he's fine," Wayne said again. "It's probably just his blood at this point. There's something chronically wrong with it—it makes too much iron. Or not enough. The doctors have never been able to pin it down."

Kilgore wiped his eyes. Fear and confusion had given way to anger. He was pissed, and not just at nearly being electrocuted. He was pissed at everything: Wayne's constant, unending criticism, the tongue-lashings, the cracks about his blood. He looked at his shoulders as if he were aware of the blanket for the first time. He furrowed his eyebrows and shook his torso until the blanket slid down his back and onto the hardwood floor. It was only then that we saw Kilgore had peed his pants.

"I quit," he said.

The image of Kilgore sitting in a puddle of his urine telling us to go to hell took a few days to push to the back of my mind. I couldn't escape the feeling that at that moment, Kilgore was the best of us. Naturally, Wayne didn't see it that way. Kilgore had blown a tremendous opportunity, he said. The band was ready to take off. They had nine original songs, five of which had "top-ten" written all over them. Especially "Up n' Coming," which he'd just finished and was a classic double-entendre rocker in the Aerosmith mold. And that Kilgore had gotten his nose out of joint and quit the band over a simple, common-placed wiring mishap was a life-altering mistake he'd damn well better be prepared to live with.

Still, Bum's Rush needed a bass player. We were sitting in Wayne's bungalow watching a rerun of *Get Smart* when he turned to me. "I've been sitting here giving it some thought. Why not go in-house for a bassist? You know the music. Maybe not the actual notes, but you know the emotional landscape of each song."

"I can't play bass. Art escapes me. You tell me that all the time."

"Just stick to the low frets and play the root note on the one beat."

"You tried to kill Jon for doing just that."

"I've already got it figured out," he said, ignoring me. "Your band nickname is going to be 'Trucks,' as in the vehicle."

"Plural? Like I'm more than one truck?"

"No. Plural as in a term of familiarity. Like your last name was Truck and for a while, we called you Trucksy, but then we shortened it to just Trucks."

"Why 'Trucks' at all, though?"

"Because your real name is phonetically uninteresting."

"I disagree."

"Of course you do. You're obstinate by nature."

"Why do I have to have a nickname at all?"

"Because it enhances the band's mythology."

"If I have to be Trucks, can we rename the band 'Three Guys Named Truck'?"

"No."

"Why not? Everyone else already had a chance to have the band named after them."

"Because."

I felt myself spiraling into one of my weird flights. It wasn't fair. Not by a long shot. I'd be damned if I'd be spoken down to by someone too incompetent to rewire a lousy bass amp. I'd quit the band first—the same way Kilgore did.

Wayne leaned forward and looked into my eyes. "You're having one of your weird flights right now, aren't you? That's another one of your problems—you go from being uninterested in something to being overwrought in a heartbeat."

"I just don't understand why we can't be called Three Guys Named Truck."

"Because we already have the best name in the world—Bum's Rush."

I couldn't argue with that one. Still, I didn't want to be in a band. It seemed like the kind of thing you had to be all-in on. At the same time, I saw an opportunity: Wayne needed a bass player; I needed to rid myself of Tina. I was at my wit's end. I'd kicked Tina out of the bungalow four separate times, and yet there she still was, scratching my records and using all the hot water and saying that the kangaroo mice "moved on from the used-to-be" instead of just saying in plain English that they'd died of exposure. I cleared my throat. "If I help you with your band problem, then you have to help me with my Tina problem."

"Just kick her the hell out."

"I've tried," I said.

"How?"

"Last trip to the supermarket, I bought nothing but salami."

Wayne looked at me with disdain. "That's your problem. You're too wishy-washy. That's been your problem since day one."

"And?"

"If you join the band, I'll get rid of Tina for you."

When I made the deal, I envisioned Wayne talking to Tina on my behalf: calmly explaining to my girlfriend of five months that the preponderance of evidence clearly showed that she and I were at an impasse and that it would be best if we parted ways. But of course, since Wayne was a modern-day Huck Finn, persuasion never even entered his mind. It would require an elaborate scheme. Otherwise, it wasn't worth his effort.

Fate provided an opportunity almost immediately. On March the 6th, two days after I rehearsed with Bum's Rush for the first time, John Belushi died.

Wayne and I were in his bungalow watching TV when the first reports broke that Belushi had been found—first unresponsive and then officially dead—inside of a rented Hollywood bungalow. I leaned closer to the television just as the screen flashed a black and white publicity photo of Belushi. He was wearing a toga and had one eyebrow arched. "He must have had a heart attack," I said.

Wayne sat up and tilted his head. "Just now I've been sitting here thinking. You went to Elvis' funeral, right?"

He knew the story. He even knew the epiphany of the story—that I'd had an intrusive thought, and for a tenth of a second, I'd pictured myself entwined with my brother's girlfriend. "We never made it there," I said. "The cops turned us around outside of Memphis."

"But you tried."

I nodded.

"That's my point. Unexpected things happen. Accidents. Given a certain set of circumstances, Trez may have been left behind."

"But he wasn't," I answered.

"But what if he had?"

The moment was eerily similar to the inception of the reverse-diet scheme. I instantly grasped the gist of Wayne's plan—drive Tina to John Belushi's funeral under the guise of paying our final respects and then abandon her somewhere along the way. The difference was that I was no longer the same naive thirteen-year-old that I was nine years ago. I'd lived a decade's worth of Wayne's schemes and I knew that every single one of them ended in disaster.

The television screen switched to a live shot of a coroner's ambulance parked in front of Belushi's rented bungalow. I switched it off. "I don't know . . ."

"I didn't want to tell you, but I think she's accustomed to it."

"Accustomed to what?"

"Getting dumped."

"What are you talking about?"

"Chloe said that Tina's mom kicked her out and that Tina bounces around a lot."

"I thought they were friends?"

"Chloe only met her a couple of days before we did. Tina latched onto her. That's what she does. She latches onto people and sucks the life out of them. Didn't you ever wonder about the guy who dropped off her bean bag chair?"

"What guy? The bean bag was just there one day, like it sprouted out of the floorboards."

"I saw him."

"Who?"

"The previous iteration of Jim."

"What did he look like?"

"Exactly like you, only not quite as gobsmacked."

I sat up. "I mean, was he better or worse looking than me?"

"Exactly the same. He was your doppelganger. Or you're his."

I gathered my lower lip under my teeth. "What did he do after he dropped off the chair? Did he come inside the bungalow?"

"He never got out of the car. He just sat there while Tina wrestled the chair out through the window. Then he peeled out and raised one hell of a dust cloud all the way out to the road, which kind of pissed me off. Cool says we're supposed to keep a low profile back here."

"Uh-huh," I mumbled.

I began to feel sorry for Tina. She wasn't all bad—at least not to the point that she deserved to be reduced to the role of permanent transient. True, she had zero qualms about freeloading off of me. And she did blather on about things no normal person would have the slightest interest in. And she *did* have a weird attachment to her idiotic macrame owl wall-hanging. But she was awfully cute. And her body. . .

Wayne must have read my face. "How long has it been since she told you that you were funny?" he asked.

"Just the other week."

"How long since she's meant it?"

I thought for a moment. "I'm not sure she ever did."

"Listen, John Belushi has moved on from the used-to-be," I said to Tina. We were standing next to my apple crate shelving and Wayne was standing a few feet away with his hands stuffed in his front pockets. "I loved the old *Saturday Night Live* cast and *Animal House* too, so I thought we'd zip up to Martha's Vineyard to pay our respects and then zip right back—the same way my brother and I zipped down to Graceland to pay our final respects when Elvis moved on from the used-to-be."

Tina looked at me. I could read her face—the slight pucker of her lips and the minuscule squint of her eyes. Why was this the first she heard of my attending Elvis' funeral? Did I have anything from the funeral? Anything she could appropriate? Or complain about? Or ruin by accident?

"What Jim learned from Elvis, though, was that when you go to a famous person's funeral, you have to pack for a long trip," Wayne said.

"So take all your clothes and personals," I added.

"What about Matías?"

"Who?" I asked.

"Yes, definitely bring your Matías," Wayne said, stepping in. "As many as you've got."

For the first seventy-five miles, I actually forgot about the plan and enjoyed the ride. It was nice to get away from the Sulfur Springs. Wayne was driving the first leg, so I had the luxury of watching the trees and hills roll past my window. Even if the trees were bare and the hills forlorn, they were a nice distraction. And the midday sunlight on my face felt rejuvenating. "It feels good to be out and about in fresh air," I said. "The sun is good for me. I think I might be suffering from vitamin D deficiency."

"It's called SAD," Tina said. "Seasonal affective disorder."

"That's a real thing?" I asked.

"The farther you live from the equator, the more likely you are to get it. I saw it every winter when I lived up north," Tina said. "Don't worry, Sweetheart. It's nothing that Earth Mother, in her infinite grace, can't cure. You just have to trust her."

"You lived up north?" Wayne broke in.

I knew what he was doing. He was trying to coax Tina into outlining everywhere she'd ever lived to remind me that abandoning her like an unwanted cat on moving day was not only in my best interest, but the humane thing to do. I cut him off. "I like the southern states better. I loved driving to Graceland. We had this whole big conversation about Elvis' twin brother dying in the womb and that maybe the wrong Elvis died."

"What do you mean?" Tina asked.

"We all assume the good Elvis survived, but maybe we're wrong. Maybe the good Elvis died in the womb and the world—in a cruel twist—got saddled with the sub-par Elvis."

"What did you decide?"

"That Elvis was never supposed to exist. Or if he was, then we weren't."

"What about John Belushi? Was he supposed to exist?" Tina asked.

"There's no way of knowing. That's kind of the point—no matter what, the evidence always points both ways."

Wayne let out an irritated sniff. "So, for famous people, life is like a dream," he said, giving the steering wheel a quick shimmy to take his octopus-ink distraction to another level.

"I have a dream," Tina said.

"You do?" he asked.

"Yes, I do," she said. "My dream is to make a grand gesture for animal rights that will live long after I've gone on from the used-to-be. It all started when—"

I knew it by heart: it all started when Tina hit gristle in her mother's Salisbury steak. She started out miffed at beef producers but ended up incensed at poultry farms. The farms—with their rows and rows of cages—were an affront to Earth Mother. Who would disagree with that? No one. At least no one who could still embrace the childhood joy of capturing fireflies in a mason jar. Therefore, Tina reasoned, it wasn't outside the pale to conclude that every chicken house in America should be burned to the ground.

"It's morally justified," Tina said as we zipped down the road. "Free the enslaved chickens so they can kiss the face of Earth Mother. Then burn their chicken prisons to the ground. And not for my glory—but the chicken's glory. The chickens would be the *real* heroes."

I'd long ago learned to resist the impulse to even blink while Tina blathered on about burning chicken coops to the ground, so I was sitting motionless, my face as inert as a slab of concrete, when she asked, "What's your dream, Jim?"

At first, I was unaffected. But by the time we traveled a hundred feet, I'd segued into indignation. For five months I'd listened to Tina's dream ad nauseam, and now, after spending nearly every moment of the past half year sequestered together in our tiny, mold-infested hovel, she'd finally mustered enough interest in me to ask about my dreams. My jaw tightened. "I have no aspirations of any kind," I answered.

"Don't lie," Wayne said. "That's one of your problems—you lie even when you don't have anything to gain by lying. Tell her about your movie script. The one where you think 'reclusion' is a real word."

I met Wayne's eyes in the rearview mirror. "I've told you a bunch of times, 'reclusion' is a real word."

"It's easy enough to fix, so just fix it. Instead of 'reclusion is expensive,' just have your character say, 'The life of a recluse is expensive' or something like that," Wayne said. "Why insist on shoehorning a word that doesn't exist just to save face? It's distracting to the audience."

"You don't understand brevity," I said.

"It's not brevity if it confuses people. It's hurting your script. That's another one of the problems with you—you'll never write a movie that anyone would pay money to watch."

"You could say that about nearly everyone on the face of the earth, so you're not going to harangue me into admitting it's a character flaw," I said. "Besides, there are tons of movies out there that people refuse to pay to see—a little flick called *Star Wars* for one."

"Name one person who refused to pay to see *Star Wars*."

"They're out there," I said.

That shut him up. I should have left it at that, but instead I said, "I guess that shut you up."

"Not really," Wayne shot back.

"I'd love to hear about your movie, Jim," Tina said, breaking in.

"Forget it."

"No, really. I want to hear it."

So, I told Tina about my movie idea.

First of all, I said, if I did have a problem, it was that I had great ideas—stories *and* movies—but I could never come up with a satisfying ending. My first brilliant idea, *A Fistful of Hamburger*, was about two rival lunch wagons competing for the business of a small woodworking factory. It stalled out halfway through. My next idea, *The Clone and the 110 Year Old Man*, was set fifty years in the future against a backdrop of planet-wide overpopulation. I shelved that one early on because it turns out science fiction is a lot harder to write than people think.

The movie idea that Wayne was referring to was my current idea. In it, author J.D. Salinger, knowing that his heirs will sell the movie rights to *Catcher in the Rye* the second he dies, secretly hires Woody Allen to film his novel. Salinger has two conditions: first, that the movie's existence remain a secret until after his death, and second, that he, Salinger, be paid in advance. As he says in the story, "reclusion is expensive." Woody, long known for a tightly controlled set, films the movie. The actors and crew sign contracts with a bevy of draconian clauses, chief among them a confidentiality clause stating that if word of the film leaks, the negatives will be destroyed, and the guilty party will be liable for the cost of the entire production. The twist is that Woody needs an unknown actor to play Holden Caulfield. The actor, let's call him Jim, now has the best role in the history of movies, but he's screwed: he can't work again until Salinger dies. Five years? Ten years? Twenty years? Who the hell knows? So, Jim does what anyone in that situation would do. He decides to kill Salinger. My main problem with the story was that I couldn't think of a third act. All I had was the notion of a pivotal scene where the actor bursts into Woody's apartment, dumps Salinger's head out of a pillowcase onto the carpet and says, "Now release the damn film!"

Of course, that would kill the comedy and wipe out any goodwill the audience had for Jim. Plus, it all but guaranteed that Salinger's real-life lawyers would slap the project with an injunction post-haste.

"Anyway, that's my movie idea," I said. "I'm not saying it doesn't need work. What I really need is a Hollywood ending."

Tina averted her eyes as though she was embarrassed for me. Then, she folded her hands over her lap, and inch by inch—as if she were hoping I wouldn't notice—she rotated her face away from mine and set her gaze out the window.

"Wayne? How far to the funeral?" I asked.

Wayne and I took turns driving for the next three hours. Just across the New York border, Tina said she had to pee. Wayne shot me a look, then took the next off-ramp and pulled into a McDonald's. "Take your box of belongings with you, Tina," he said.

"Why? I only have to use the restroom."

Wayne looked at me.

I leaned over to Tina and whispered, "Maybe you should change clothes. You smell a little . . . stale."

The radio was playing "Soul Man." Wayne eased the volume down because that's what you do when you're just going to sit in a parking spot for a minute while you wait for someone to pee and change their shirt.

Tina grabbed her box of belongings and slid out the door. She took a couple of steps and turned back to us. "I'll be right back."

"Take your time," Wayne said, lighting a cigarette. "We're not going anywhere."

As soon as Tina disappeared into the McDonalds, Wayne idled away from the curb and inched to the stop sign at the edge of the parking lot. He sat there motionless, staring at the traffic while two gaps big enough to pull a school bus into came and went.

"Left," I said. "Why the hell are you waiting? Turn left."

Wayne looked up at the rearview mirror as if noticing its existence for the first time. He reached up and gave it a slight tilt upward. Finally, when both directions were completely clear, he said, "And that is that," and stomped on the gas.

I rolled my window down and tilted my nose to the stream of air. "Do you feel good about what we just did?" I asked.

"It's the whole, *do dolphins swim around all day thinking about triangles* thing," he said.

"For real, though?"

"What do you mean?"

"I mean, how'd we turn into this?"

"Just a minute ago I was sitting at that stop sign giving that some thought," he said. "And what I've concluded is that we were closer to who we were supposed to be back when we were little. Before society got a hold on us."

"We were never little," I said.

Wayne chewed on his lip for a second. "So, you're saying we've always been like this? When we were little, we were larvae destined to grow into what we are right now—and the same way no one could blame a fly larva for becoming a fly, no one can blame us for anything we do. Is that what you're saying?"

"No, not at all. I meant that we were never little *together*. We didn't hang out until sixth grade."

"Oh yeah. The whole Summer of Doris thing." He stared at me, keeping his eyes off the road a good two seconds longer than was safe. "That seems like forever ago."

"That's my point—our emotional growth is almost nonexistent."

Wayne let out a disgusted grunt and squished out his cigarette in the ashtray. "I don't think that we're that bad off. We have food. I have plenty of time to play music and write songs. You have plenty of time to walk around all day mumbling about what you're going to eat next and whatever the hell else it is you do. What more do you want?"

"It's like the race started and we're still trying to figure out which lane to get into. What's it going to be like at our five-year reunion? We won't be able to show our faces."

He shook his head. "See? Right there. That's the problem with you— you're always trying to win other people's approval. You should be more like me. All I need is my own approval."

"You can't give yourself approval—it's impossible—just like you can't tickle yourself," I said.

"You do it all the time. You try to do it by winning other people's approval, and I can prove it. Name one person—one girl—who you don't care about impressing."

"Brie," I said without hesitation.

"Brie doesn't count. Name someone else."

I had the perfect answer: Tina. I'd just proven it beyond all doubt. My arms felt leaden, like my blood wasn't circulating. My mouth began to water. I put my hands between my knees and closed my eyes. Without any conscious thought, a vision flooded my mind. I saw myself as a bloated, white larva, blindly devouring the leaves of whichever plant I'd been deposited on, then, mindlessly contracting my abdomen to push myself to the next helpless plant. I felt sick to my stomach. Tina was somewhere behind us. How long would it take her to realize that we'd ditched her? I could picture her searching the booths for us, ready to pounce on me for eating something with a face, then, when she couldn't find us, scouring the parking lot. Then, finally, wiping a tear from her eye as she walked out to the highway with her tattered box of belongings and poked her beautifully tapered thumb out at the passing cars.

"Pull over," I said. "I think I'm going to vomit."

Wayne steered onto the shoulder. I flung open the door and fell to one knee. I dropped to all fours and crawled across cinders and broken glass to the edge of the guardrails. The bank fell off sharply at the edge of the shoulder. Below, in the dried, dormant weeds, was a scatter of trash—paper, bottles, and a single, mangled hubcap. And there was something else: something dark and wet and matted down, and it had pinkish matter crusted to what remained of its flattened head. My stomach clenched. I arched my back and let out a series of retching heaves. On the fifth heave—just as a semi passed so tight to the shoulder that the draft lifted a cloud of dirt into my face—I puked up a tablespoon of bile.

I spit and turned toward Wayne. "You got me into this," I said. "You're no longer my best friend."

Wayne squatted down beside me. He lit another cigarette and stared straight ahead. "I know you can't see it right now, but it's for the good of the band." He took a puff of his cigarette and let the smoke escape his nose. "Think about it this way. If everything were good, then good would be nothing more than the ordinary state of things. Without the bad, there's no opportunity to rise above it."

"But we're the bad," I coughed out.

"Then there's no place to go but up," Wayne said.

I took a wrong exit somewhere near Scranton and we drove north for an hour before Wayne noticed that the town names were different. Then, once we turned around, I took a second wrong turn and we ended up on the outskirts of Allentown. It was as if the whole process was an exercise in determining how far we could wander off the path and still find our way home. The moon was descending by the time we got back to The Sulfur Springs. I took my foot off the gas and coasted down the dirt driveway. Just past the cattails, we saw a bloom of light emanating from the bungalows.

"Was Brie supposed to be coming over?" I asked.

"Not as far as I know," Wayne answered.

We parked in front of my porch. Every light in my bungalow was turned on. When I unlocked the door, The Moody Blues' "Tuesday Afternoon" was just fading out. For a moment, I thought that I'd accidentally left the stereo playing and the arm on repeat. Then I noticed the tea kettle. The burner was lit, and steam was blowing out of the spout. On the counter beside my favorite coffee mug rested a tea bag: my last bag of Shelly the Tea Vendor's special High Mountain Blend. It was like the old ghost story—the one where a missing freighter floats into dock twenty years later with a hot dinner on the table and not a soul on board.

Wayne looked at me. "Sky-Dog?"

"He hates The Moody Blues," I answered.

I walked to the tea kettle and killed the flame. When I turned around, Tina was standing in the hallway opening. Every synapse in my brain fired at once. Fight, flight, or freeze, and I froze. Tina had Trez's old sleeping bag draped over her shoulders. She was shivering. Her hair was a flat, lifeless mess, and her eyes had the same shallow, downcast, friend-or-foe? set of a lost dog.

"I can't get warm," Tina sputtered out. She rubbed her hands together, and then she lifted her eyes to mine. "You abandoned me."

After the shock of seeing Tina passed, my first thought was *how in the world did she beat us home with no car?* My next, more human thought was that even after what I'd done to her, Tina had returned to me. The bungalow was her home. *Our* home. We were boyfriend and girlfriend and we belonged together, for better or worse. My throat tightened. I slumped forward, and a few actual tears ran down my cheek. What would become of me without her? My life was pathetic. I was living in a plywood shack with no heat source and sleeping at floor level on a half-rotted, secondhand mattress. I was a loser and a dimwit and a fat-body. I was lucky to have Tina. She was hot. Plus, in bed, she was innately giving. Once she put something on the table, it stayed on the table, like a high-end buffet. I choked out a weak series of bleats. "I thought I'd lost you," I said.

Tina opened her arms and rushed toward me. "Oh, Jim."

I met her embrace. Out of the corner of my eye, I saw Wayne's face. Two polar opposite emotions were competing for the set of his lips: disgust and—let's call it professional—appreciation.

Tina kissed me and put her hands on my shoulders. She pulled her head back so she could study my face. "Will you give me all your tomorrows?" she asked.

And I'm not sure, either my Art of Intuition kicked in or failed me miserably because I heard myself say, "You make forever bearable."

I put my arm around Tina and guided her back to our bedroom. She didn't lay down so much as she collapsed onto the mattress. I kissed her cheek and pulled Trez's sleeping bag up close under her chin.

I walked back into the living room. "The poor thing's exhausted," I said to Wayne.

Wayne's hands were on his hips and his eyes were narrow slits. "That's your problem—you're too easily turned. She's not how she is because she doesn't have any friends. She doesn't have any friends because she's how she is. And that's not circular logic, my friend, that is that. My advice is to forget her. She'll only bring you sorrow—just like Angela. Remember Angela? She's that girl that you knew for a whole ten hours and have been moping around about for three years now."

"I haven't been moping."

"Wait!" Wayne said. "Shut up for a second!" He covered his formerly eye-patched eye with his hand and stood perfectly still, his face a weird mixture of concentration and enthusiasm. "I just got an idea for a new song," he said to me, uncovering his eye. "No chords or anything. It will be a cappella. I'll list off a bunch of ironic things and then after each one, we'll all chant, 'and that is that.' We'll use it for an encore and get the audience to chant along with us. We'll call it the 'And That is That' song."

I clenched my fists. "Listen to me, you son of a bitch," I said in a half-growl, half-whisper. "You're not writing a song called 'And That is That.' I forbid it. So you can just get that whole stinking idea out of your goddamn head right now!"

I walked back into the bedroom. In the dark, Tina lowered her head. I knew from experience that anything spoken in the main room was easily heard in the bedroom. How much had she heard? I tossed off my shoes and climbed under the covers.

I was almost asleep when Tina said, "If you love me—if it's not just a bunch of lies to sleep with me—then you'll help me burn down the chicken houses."

I pulled my parents' gas can from the back of my Bronco and Tina and I covered the distance from the top of the ridge to the chicken houses in a crouched, semi-run. In the moonlight, I could see the poultry coops were far older and far more decrepit than they'd appeared to be from the road. They were tacked together from reclaimed barn wood: gray, splintered planks that were no doubt as dry as tree bark. The air smelled rank. My encounters with chicken farms were limited to a few errands I'd run for Larry, but I recognized the odor—a thick, gaseous stew of bird droppings and airborne feather dander and wet, decomposing feed grain.

"Can they see us from the farmhouse?" Tina whispered.

"I don't think so," I said so softly that I could barely hear my voice.

The farmhouse sat a hundred yards away. The porch light was on, but the windows were dark. From somewhere in the shadows, a dog's chain rattled across the ground. I looked back at the outline of my vehicle and tried to estimate how many seconds it would take to cover the distance from here to there in my fat-hindered version of a full sprint. Twenty seconds? Maybe more? Then five more ticks to jump in and turn the engine over. "Let's do this and get the hell out of here," I whispered.

"Roger that," Tina said.

She'd been using faux military terms all day—we both had—ever since early that morning when we drove to The Army Surplus Store and Tina bought a pair of khaki pants and a black military beret. That's what she was wearing now: the pants, the cap, and my all-time favorite hooded Carhartt jacket (that she'd cut the sleeves off of without asking permission.) She'd even put a match to a wine cork and blackened her cheeks and forehead. Standing in the thin light, as terrified as I was, I couldn't help but think that Tina—who'd just two hours before had held the same 100% wool, French military beret tight to her head while we engaged in a multitude of carnal delights that could only be described as morally bankrupt—looked cute as hell.

"Roger that," I said.

I doused the side of the first coop with gasoline and moved to the second one, trailing a thin line of gas to act as a fuse. I splashed the can's remaining contents over the moonlit side of the second coop until the liquid formed a deep, glistening puddle in the dirt. Then I stepped back and held the box of matches out to Tina.

Of course, Tina being Tina, she couldn't pass up the opportunity to deliver a speech. "For Matías!" she shouted. Then presumably addressing the chickens, she raised her fist into the air and yelled, "Say goodbye to your servitude, my sweet sisters. Climb mountains and make a joyous noise unto Earth Mother. Her peace will bathe you like warm sunshine, and her love will ease your cares."

Then, Tina struck the match and flung it toward the coops.

I've since learned exactly why it's dangerous to start a fire with gasoline: it rolls. By that, I mean that lit gasoline can create an utterly unpredictable fireball which travels faster than the eye can follow. I've also since learned the concept of combustion as it pertains to enclosed spaces with highly flammable airborne particles, such as grain dust or sawdust or, in this case, feather dander. The particles burn instantly, and when they do, they light the surrounding particles. This causes a chain reaction that flashes through the dust cloud with explosive force. This phenomenon has a name. It's called deflagration.

But standing in the moonlight, I wasn't thinking about gasoline fire-balls or chicken dander or massive explosions. I had just one thought: expunging my shame for abandoning my girlfriend in the parking lot of a fast-food restaurant. So, when she flung the match—seemingly in slow motion—my eyes followed her bare, luscious arm as it extended toward the coops and then recoiled back through the ambient light to her per-fectly symmetrical breasts, and for maybe one-tenth of one second, I felt the soft, sweet kiss of redemption.

Then I heard the boom.

If the farmer had a hundred sticks of dynamite stored inside the chicken house, the effect wouldn't have been any different. The coop literally exploded. The blast knocked us off our feet. I landed flat on my back with Tina beside me. For a second, I lay crumpled in the dirt, staring straight up at the night sky, dazed and confused as to why I was laying in the dark in the middle of a field. The stars were close—so close that I could have reached out and flicked them away one by one—and the moon was pulsating with an amber glow. Slowly, I became conscious of a crackling, like a bulldozer crushing brush under its treads. I lifted my head off the ground just as a second boom filled the air. In the next heartbeat, a slab of metal roofing the size of a car door dropped from the blackness and crashed into the dirt beside me.

I staggered to my feet just as the second coop went up in flames. I grabbed Tina's hand and pulled her toward the Bronco. At the crest of the hill, we stopped and looked back. Half of the farm appeared to be ablaze. That would have been horror enough, but a second, more pro-found level of terror awaited us. We'd barely taken a breath when the first chicken house collapsed. An instant later, a globe-sized fireball shot from the flames as if someone had launched it from a catapult. Then two more. Then, in the time it took to raise my hand to my mouth, hundreds of flaming comets began to shoot from the ruins. At first, I didn't grasp the level of calamity I was witnessing. Then one of the comets shot directly toward us. Halfway up the grass bank, the fireball slowed and veered off in a semi-circle for its last few, staggering steps and fell over. For a second, it lay on the ground, smoldering. Then it jerked once and let out a single, pained death squawk. It was only then that I realized the full scope of what Tina and I had wrought: we'd forgotten the most important part of our plan—indeed the whole point of our grand gesture—we'd forgotten to free the chickens.

Tina and I didn't sleep that night, much less have the best sex of our lives. Nor did we revert to our early, primitive mating ritual, the one from the rainforest where we rocked on the fulcrum of her rock-hard buttock. Instead, we writhed under the covers with as much space between us as the putrid mattress would allow. At one point, Tina lifted her head and broke out sobbing, sputtering some unintelligible lament about missing Matías. For my part, I tossed and turned. I wasn't worried about the police—the farm was in the middle of nowhere and not a single car had passed down the road while we were on our ill-fated mission. I was worried about my health—I'd inhaled quite a bit of smoke. Not only were my sinuses burning, but every time I closed my eyes, my mind would default to an image of billions of tiny ash particles floating through my lungs and plugging my bronchial tubes like dead leaves choking off a downspout. Plus, a second thought gnawed at my being: who the hell knew what godforsaken chemicals the farmer had stored in those coops? Farmers were notorious for storing all kinds of long-ago outlawed shit on their property, and lying beside Tina, replaying the previous hours' horrific events frame by painful frame, I couldn't help but fixate on the thought that the jet-black smoke billowing from the second coop smelled unnaturally pungent.

So, it was a blessing when morning came. At least it was, until we turned on the television set. The Channel 8 morning news devoted the first eleven minutes to the story. If it bleeds, it leads, and this story had it all: blood, fire, loss, and a profound senselessness guaranteed to outrage even the most casual viewer. As an added bonus, the very real possibility existed that hundreds of chickens—and they were a breed called Aspas, so they were capable of a limited version of flight—were roaming the countryside, most likely cold and dehydrated and panic-stricken.

By the farmer's estimate, 1,200 chickens perished. Charred corpses were scattered across his farm, smoking like smoldering piles of leaves. The poor man's voice was quivering as he spoke, first in a voice-over as the camera zoomed in on what appeared to be a volleyball-sized clump of blackened rags, and then directly into the camera. He'd been in the Second War, and to his eyes, the carnage was comparable to what he'd witnessed in Dresden after the Allies bombed the German city into rubble. This weighed on him more, though, because the Nazis had it coming. To him, the most agonizing part was imagining the horror his birds must have felt as the fire closed in around them. He took solace, though, in the thought that most of the flock probably died of smoke inhalation before the flames reached them. "But maybe," he said, and here his stoicism failed him. He paused for a long, tortured second before he took a deep breath, "Maybe that's just wishful thinking."

By the noon news, sightings of the surviving Aspas had begun to filter in. One man claimed that a ratty-looking chicken fell from the sky and struck his windshield with the force of an airborne pumpkin. Two separate people—a college student and a middle-aged woman—reported seeing a fox trot across Route 30 with a chicken in its jaws. The woman, who declined to be identified, reported that the chicken in the fox's mouth appeared to be struggling.

Of course, all of this was somehow my fault.

I walked across the gravel to Wayne's bungalow. He was standing on the front stoop, wearing his knit hat and smoking a cigarette. He tapped the ashes off his cigarette and smiled. A huge smile. Ear to ear. "I'm eating this up with a spoon," he said.

"What?"

He pointed over my shoulder. By the edge of the driveway were two white clumps, about eighteen inches apart, so inert they may as well have been landscaping stones. While Wayne and I watched, a third chicken—this one very much alive—bobbed its head out from the thick brush. "If I believed in Karma, I'd say this was Karma," Wayne said, "but it's far more probable that the terrain is funneling the chickens in our direction somehow."

I shifted my weight.

"What are you doing now?" Wayne asked.

I shrugged.

"This is the perfect time to be practicing your scales," he said. "We're a power trio. I need you all over that goddamn neck."

I walked back to my bungalow. Tina was sitting in her bean bag chair. A few Styrofoam beans were on the floor at her feet, and she was staring at one of Matías' letters. "Don't freak out, but one of those Aspas is pecking in the dirt outside," I said.

Tina didn't say a word. She didn't even repeat what I said back to me as a question. She just folded her pen-pal's letter and carefully slid it back into its dingy, yellowed envelope. I waited for her to say something, or maybe even break down sobbing again, but she didn't make a sound. She just unfolded the next letter and held it up to read.

Wayne and I were outside by the rehearsal hall, trying to chase the Aspa out of a welter of scrub pines when Tina emerged from the bungalow. She zipped up my Carhartt jacket and walked out the long, dirt driveway towards the road—no doubt off to McDonald's to mitigate her sorrows with a Big Mac and fries. No sooner had Tina cleared our view when a police car inched past the cattails and came to a stop twenty feet from us. We watched as two police officers climbed out of the car more or less in unison and walked toward us.

"Don't worry. We're renters. We have a right to be here," Wayne said to me.

I didn't recognize the tall officer, but I recognized the short, thick one. His face had an incongruity about it that was indelible. His eyelashes were ridiculously thick, like he used lash thickener; at the same time, his massive chin was nothing short of a squared-off slab of concrete. He straightened his utility belt and looked past us, focusing for a long moment on the bungalows. "How you boys doing today?" he said in a thick New York accent.

The instant I heard his voice, I placed him. He'd bought one of my muffins at the market a few months earlier. He was dressed in regular street clothes, and he walked up to the table with a pained expression, as if the idea of walking through a farmers market was an affront to his masculinity. He had a boy at his side who looked to be about eight.

"You want a cupcake?" he had asked the boy.

"Actually, they're muffins," I said. "Bran muffins with pineapple chunks and a smidgen of lemon zest to wake them up."

Other than giving me a contemptuous look when I said "smidgen," the cop ignored me. He bent at the waist to speak to the boy. "It's either the cupcake or the popcorn from before," he said.

"You mean muffin," I corrected.

The boy opened his mouth into a wet circle and pointed to the bran muffin. The cop pushed the boy's hand down. "No pointing," he said. "You gotta speak if you want it. I know the crud my sister lets you get away with. If you want a cupcake, you say the word."

The boy hesitated, then said, "Cupcake."

The cop reached into his wallet for a dollar and smiled at me. Not a real smile, but a smile that said *I'm going to call your goddamn muffin a cupcake and you're going to goddamn stand there and take it.* He held a dollar out to me. "We'll take the cupcake, Chief."

Now, five months later, the cop was standing in front of me. "How are *you* doing?" I said, holding my hand out. "Remember me?"

The cop studied my face for a moment. "Hey," he said, "I *do* know you." He let out a staccato laugh and snapped his fingers as though he was trying to remember. "Aren't you that guy who sells cupcakes on the square?" He turned to the taller cop. "Hey, this guy here sells cupcakes."

"Muffins," I said. "You knew goddamn well they were muffins."

He held the laugh posture, but slowly, over the span of a few seconds, he twisted his mouth into a look of disdain. "They're both round, Chief," he said.

Wayne stepped up beside me. "What's the charge, officer?" he asked.

The cop had the upper hand, and he knew it. He put his hands on his hips and looked across the remnants of The Sulfur Springs Resort. The cluster of buildings didn't just look decrepit—they'd looked that way all along—now, after six months under Wayne's and my care, the entire compound looked to be the victim of willful neglect. Not only had Wayne and I never lifted a finger to uphold our end of the repairs bargain, but we'd ignored even the most routine grounds-keeping duties. Windblown trash—newspapers, soda cup lids, empty plastic bags—was snagged in the overgrown brush. Dozens of spent mouse traps were piled just off my bungalow's front porch. And the bundle of aluminum siding that was sitting on the sawhorses the day we moved in was sitting in the same spot, untouched. Only now, rain-soaked cardboard hung from its sides like tattered drapes, and at the center point, where the bundle sagged, a small maple tree had taken root in the debris. To add a final, farcical touch to the scene, a single dead leaf was clinging to one of the sapling's tiny branches.

The cop took his hands off his hips. I knew enough not to say anything—either he had legitimate police business, or he didn't. Unfortunately, the silence proved too much for Wayne. He coughed into his hand and then said, "I front Bum's Rush."

It was a mistake. It gave the cop an opportunity to extend the moment without stating his purpose. He repeated Wayne's words in his heavy New York accent, "I. Front. Bum's. Rush." He angled his massive chin toward the taller cop. "For the life of me, I can't put any meaning to that sentence," he said. "Hell, I'm not even sure it *is* a sentence. I mean, where's the verb?"

He turned his head back to Wayne and bared his teeth. "Where's the verb, Chief? No verb, no sentence. Didn't they teach you that in kindergarten?"

At this point, the taller cop stepped in. "Do you gentlemen have a copy of the occupancy permit for these dwellings?"

"No, sir. Our landlord, Mr. Cool, would have the paperwork. He's letting me and my friend live here because he believes in my band—it's his way of helping to keep rock and roll alive." Then he pointed to me. "This is Jim. He's my bass player."

The taller cop rubbed the back of his neck. "Well, the truth is Mr. Cool enjoys playing a little trick on the township every couple of years. He loans these shacks out for free labor. I'll give you boys credit, though. You hid back here pretty good. If we hadn't stopped to scrape those dead chickens off the road, we'd never have spotted you."

"Free labor?" Wayne asked.

"You work on these buildings in exchange for rent. He buys the supplies and you live here for free and do the work. That's the story every time."

"Oh, I see the confusion now, Officer," Wayne said. He let out a single, truncated laugh, as if he'd just figured out the tiny but crucial bit of information required to clear up the entire misunderstanding. "This is different. We have a legitimate rental agreement. We pay $50 a month plus electric, and *we* purchase the materials to improve the dwellings. He's giving us a cherry deal because he believes in my band and he—"

Wayne stopped mid-sentence. He made a weird noise and then another barely audible noise. I watched his face lose all elasticity as the truth sank in. Cool didn't give a crap about rock and roll. Or Bum's Rush. Or Wayne. It was all a ruse, and we'd fallen for it.

And since this is a confessional, I confess this: even as I watched Wayne's heart split into two, my heart filled with joy—my Tina problem was over.

EPISODE SEVEN

Title: *Walden or In Which I Reset My Beingness*
Reading time: *39 minutes*
Synopsis: *Reeling from recent events, Jim seeks to reset his life by moving into the woods.*

The cop with the thick eyelashes and square chin gave us twenty-four hours to vacate the property. I didn't need it. I scurried around the bungalow, whipping my belongings into Larry's apple crates as if a monsoon were closing in on The Sulfur Springs Resort. I loaded my stereo equipment into the front seat of my Bronco and padded it on all four sides with blankets. Everything else—Trez's sleeping bag, my clothes, records, pots and pans, all my remaining foodstuff, including my jar of ginger roots and the last of the maple syrup—I jammed into the back. As for the decrepit space heaters, I left one in the bungalow and one on the front porch. I figured that Wayne could use it if he decided to stay one last night. The mattress that Tina and I had slept on for the last six months, I abandoned.

I found Wayne in the rehearsal hall. He was pulling the cardboard egg trays off of the back wall and stacking them inside each other. "When are you getting our security deposit back from Cool?" I asked.

"I already got it."

"Let's divvy it up, then."

"I got it a long time ago."

"What are you talking about?"

"I borrowed against the security deposit to finance the demo tape," he said.

"What demo tape?"

Wayne reached for another egg carton. I took a deep breath and let it ripple out between my lips. I was flat broke—literally down to a mason jar full of change. Half of $200 would have kept me in gas and pizza until I cashed my first Seven Turns paycheck. I didn't have it in me to be mad at him, though. Whatever had happened with the demo tape, the anguish he was experiencing in the here and now was far more life-altering than my temporary poverty. Twenty minutes ago, he was on the upward trajectory of a dream—the lead singer, lead guitarist, and undisputed creative mastermind behind a kick-ass band with nine original tunes and the best unused name in the history of rock and roll. Now, in less time than it took to perform "The Ballad of Bum's Rush," he'd lost everything.

"Just leave the egg cartons," I said. "Screw Cool—he can pull them off the walls himself."

Wayne met my gaze for the first time since I walked in. His nose was running and his eyes were puffy. "These egg trays are mine, and I'm taking every single goddamn one of them."

I drove my Bronco out the long driveway. Fast. At the cattails, I stomped on the gas until my back wheels dug into the loose dirt and raised a thick, billowing dust cloud dense enough to obscure the Sulfur Springs compound in my rearview mirror. When I got to my parents' house, no one was home. I couldn't bear the thought of moving back into my old childhood room, so I carted my belongings up the stairs to Trez's old room. Then I made up his bed and collapsed onto it.

This was seven days before my father watched *Star Wars* on television, seven days before I heard The Last Scone Story for the final time, and seven days before I walked out the front door to the mailbox where I found a postcard. The postcard was a colorized black and white photo of Rehoboth Beach. At first glance, it seemed odd—who visits the beach this time of year? I flipped the card over. It was addressed to me. The message wasn't signed, but I recognized Tina's handwriting. It read: *I used to love you but now I hate you.*

When I think about my time at the bungalows, I think about dirt. Not just the ordinary, everyday household dirt that accumulated on the walls and floors and in the crevasses of my home of nine months. I think about personal dirt—dirt on my hands and feet, dirt in my armpits, dirt behind my ears, and even the thin, almost imperceivable layers of dirt dirtying my fat, dirt-encrusted eyelids. On my first day home, I showered three times, running away all of the hot water each time. The second day I showered four times and I brushed my teeth compulsively, something on the order of once every forty-five minutes. I felt sullied by my season of decadence. I knew what I needed. It wasn't as if the answer was hiding from me. I needed to cleanse my soiled beingness, and not just with a quick wipe down, like I was sponging spilled milk off the countertop. What I needed was a grand gesture.

The answer came to me fully formed one morning as I was digging out the can opener to take the lid off a can of sliced peaches. AMORPHICA. *Duh,* I thought. What better way to cleanse myself than to bathe in Viking's Amorphica? And what better way to bathe myself than to ride a motorcycle to every last, hidden corner of this vast and bountiful country?

Local precedent existed, albeit on a much smaller scale. The spring before graduation, my friend Joey Stemper bought a motorcycle. As he told the story to us one day in study hall, he walked into the Honda dealership along Route 30 on the second Saturday of May at 8:01. The salesman was standing behind the counter, half-asleep, sucking from a foam 7-Eleven coffee cup. Without a word of niceties, Joey slapped twelve crisp, uncirculated $100 bills on the counter and told the salesman, "I'll take the 750 in the corner with the sunburst tank, and you're going to throw in *that* helmet for free." The salesman didn't say squat. He just set his coffee down, walked over to the helmet rack, and asked, "This one?" An hour later, Joey was speeding through Westminster on his way to Rehoboth Beach to purchase a new hermit crab. Except for the hermit crab part, it was the most bad-ass story any of us had ever heard, and the last few weeks of school, we begged him to tell it over and over again.

Joey was AWOL now—even his parents were clueless as to his whereabouts—but I was determined to one-up his hermit crab story, and if none of my old high school friends were still left in town to beg me to tell the story over and over again, so be it. I'd tell every last, stinking detail to Wayne or Brie or Trez or my own children someday. Ad nauseam. It'd be *my* Last Scone Story.

My plan was to buy a used motorcycle and ride it to all four corners of the lower forty-eight. I had an entire, elaborate fantasy worked out. On the first leg of the journey, I'd neither bathe nor shave. I'd sleep on the ground and survive on the goodwill of strangers. Somewhere in there, I'd develop a heavy limp. In each town, I'd seek out a farmers market. Out of spite, I'd say nasty things to the market vendors as I staggered by, dragging my bad leg behind me as though it were a splintered-off tree limb. Slowly, as my ravaged psyche healed, the impulse to insult random strangers would pass, and I'd feel hope begin to bud in my heart. I'd purchase a razor and shave my beard off over the sink of some filthy gas station restroom. I even pictured a cathartic moment when I'd coast to a stop at a crossroad in the desert. I'd peer out across the sand as the last rays of sunlight painted the barren landscape a burnt orange so beautiful that I'd have to close my eyes and open them again to convince myself that it was real. I'd cut the motorcycle's engine, pull my helmet off, and give my long, curly hair a quick shake. I could turn east or I could turn west. East, I would ride into the morning light. West, I would continue to outrun the darkness. In the distance, above a cluster of scrub cactuses, a lone eagle would soar across the blue sky, its wings lifting it higher and higher into the horizon. I'd remember how I told Angela that the wind would stop to listen to her sing. I'd ponder this, thinking of my life and of everything that I'd found and everything that I'd lost. Slowly, a flicker of understanding would color my eyes as I came to terms with the cosmic irony of life. I'd slip my helmet back over my noodle and kick-start my bike's engine. Which direction would I travel? East? West? It didn't matter; either way would work as a metaphor.

So on March 26th, after the final credits of *Star Wars* scrolled across the television set and my dad finished The Last Scone Story with the amazed smile he reserved for his epiphany about life being like a tapestry, I announced my plan to cleanse myself.

"What the hell's Amorphica?" my father asked.

"It's America, but an America where you can morph into anything you want. Viking told me about it."

"What Viking?"

I let that one go. "Haven't you ever wanted to feel unfettered, Dad? To enjoy a modicum of freedom?"

"I *had* a modicum of freedom. Your mom and I both did—when we sold that last scone. Then you kids ruined it by doing crap like getting kicked out of fat camp and turning into communists."

I began to sense the conversation going sideways. "Look, I need to borrow $500 to buy the motorcycle," I said. "And another $25 for a helmet because I probably can't leverage the guy into giving me a free one when I'm only buying a used bike."

"Do you even know how to ride a motorcycle? Motorcycles have a clutch. Remember when I tried to teach you to drive stick?"

I remembered. I kept stalling out. And every time I ground the gears, I let out a tortured, gut-curdling bleat. Then, when after an hour I finally managed to circumnavigate the block, I drifted back at a stop sign and banged into some guy's fender.

"I'll get Joe Stemper's brother to show me," I said.

"We don't know any Joe Stemper," my father said. He leaned forward in his chair and pointed at me. "It's time you straighten the hell out. If I had to grow up, then so do you."

I turned to my mother. Her hands were folded over her lap. She had an exasperated look etched into her eyes. I asked anyway. "What do you think, Mom?"

"Starting out $500 in debt doesn't sound like freedom to me," she said.

That ended my motorcycle fantasy. For the lack of a better idea, I toyed with the notion of visiting Trez in Fairbanks. The problem with Alaska was that winter lasted seven months, and recent history had taught me that cold temperature negatively affected my ability to function as a normal member of society. Plus, Trez and I had nothing in common anymore. Since he had joined the military, it was as if the memory of his high school persona was so unpalatable that he overcompensated in an attempt to obscure it, shunning every last ounce of the duality that had made him not only the "The Rebel Trez" but also my brother Trez. It was sad. So much so that I now considered him "The Ghost of Trez."

Whether it was a psychosomatic reaction or merely a coincidence, the instant I dismissed the idea of visiting Trez, my mouth began to water. I didn't even make it to the commode. I puked in the mudroom, right beside Daisy. For two days I couldn't keep anything down, not even liquids. On the third day, I made myself a cup of weak tea—an herbal mint blend that was easy on the digestive tract—and I ate a cracker. On the fourth day, I made myself a piece of dry toast. The day after that, I made myself two slices of toast and spread orange marmalade on them.

At the one-week mark, I was balancing a cup of tea on a saucer and pushing open the door to Trez's room when my eyes settled on his fishing rod—an open-faced model that he'd used to float worms down Marsh Creek during his all-American boy phase. I set the saucer down and walked across the room to the wooden bookcase where the rod was leaning. The top shelf was lined with books that "The Rebel Trez" had stolen from the school library: Kerouac, Burroughs, Salinger, and at the bottom, a worn paperback version of Thoreau's *Walden*. I knew the story—or at least I knew the gist of it. Thoreau had withdrawn from society to build a cabin on Walden's Pond and revel in nature's good tidings. Once there, he lived the simple life for—and to me this was the intriguing part—two years, two months, two weeks, and two days. Why that duration? Not having read the book, I could only guess that it had something to do with his heart being trod upon by a woman.

I picked the book up and fanned through the pages. Just like the motorcycle trip, the solution to each and every one of my problems came to me fully formed: I would reset my beingness by living in the woods like Henry David Thoreau.

Instantly, I felt better. I hurried back down the steps to the kitchen and swung open the refrigerator door. In the meat drawer, I found a small helping of 80/20 ground beef. I checked the cupboard. We were out of rolls, but we had a single hot dog bun. I got the skillet going, then dumped the hamburger into a mixing bowl. I spooned a glob of mayonnaise on top of the meat and added chopped onion and salt and pepper. I found some cilantro in the fridge, so on a whim, I chopped it ultra-fine and threw it on top of the mixture. I molded the concoction into the shape of a bratwurst and deposited it into the scalding hot pan. Once it had a nice sear all the way around, I lowered the heat and melted pepper jack cheese over the top. I slipped it into the hot dog bun and—working solely on instinct—topped it with a double spoonful of raspberry jelly and a sprinkle of finely chopped jalapeno.

I took a giant bite of my creation; instantly, the chills went away.

The next day I sold two boxes of used records to Ginny at Roundabout Records for one-hundred and ten dollars. It was all stuff I could live without: The Marshall Tucker Band album that Columbia House sent me by mistake, the first two Elvis Costello albums, and all of my David Bowie (including a rare Japanese pressing of Ziggy Stardust). Plus, I sold her a few dozen records that Trez had left behind. I figured they were fair game—that no one who enlists in the Air Force and moves to Anchorage to fly fighter planes ever returns home to reclaim their old Mott the Hoople albums.

From Ginny's, I drove to the Army Surplus Store in Hanover where Tina and I had bought her beret. The only person in the store was a guy about my dad's age standing behind the sales counter. I picked a hatchet off one of the metal shelves—I'd need it to build my cabin—and walked over to the cash register. Up close, the salesman looked odd. It took me a moment to put my finger on it, but then it hit me: the cornea of his left eye was the color of skim milk. Not only that, but a glob of yellowish puss was balanced on his bottom eyelid, right by his tear duct. I set the hatchet on the counter and reached into my pocket for my money.

"Figuring on camping?" the man asked me.

I saw no reason to conceal my plans from him. "I'm going to live in the woods. Like Henry David Thoreau in *Walden*."

"Why?"

"I'm going to cleanse myself so I can reset my beingness."

"Is that so?"

I nodded. "Plus, I'm going to gawk at the hand of God. I've already decided."

The man stared at me for a beat, then wiped his infected eye with his thumb. He reached under the counter and pulled out a hand-crank radio. "Well, you're going to need this, then. It pulls in AM, FM, and all your lower band television stations—2 through 13. Hell, I even picked up a ham signal from the Philippines the other day. Some guy speaking Mandarin."

"Can I try it?" I asked.

He jumped a cigarette out of its package with a flick of his wrist. "You're not going to pick up any signals in the store, not with that warehouse across the street."

I rotated the crank a few times, then twisted the tuner knob. He was right. Nothing but static.

"Told you," he said.

"But it works?"

"If I'm lying, I'm dying."

I flicked the radio off. "I don't know. I'm on a tight budget."

He wiped his eye again. "So, you're going to gawk at God, huh? What are you going to do if God gawks back?"

"He'd gawk back?" I asked, my voice tapering into a weak bleat.

"It's a distinct possibility," he said. "One could even make the case that you're inviting it."

A truck rumbled past the store, shaking the front window. I shifted my weight and focused beyond the man's shoulder to the street traffic outside. An unbroken stream of cars and trucks were passing by the store on their way downtown. As they slowed to a stop for the traffic light, each individual face behind each individual steering wheel came into focus. It was a weighty thought: God gawking back. I hadn't considered this—that alone in the woods with nothing to distract God's attention away from me, I would be inviting scrutiny. I'd spent my life *avoiding* scrutiny. That's why I never complained to Columbia House when they shipped me the Marshall Tucker Band album by mistake: I didn't want customer service to check my address and stumble onto the collection of shell accounts I'd opened under every conceivable permutation of my name and Tina's name (seven in all—including three with the middle name Matías). And even if God was willing to overlook my desire to expand my record collection by any means necessary, he still had a multitude of other reasons to be ticked off at me—everything from gluttony to mental sloth to the gleeful killing of kangaroo mice. In my defense, though, I was disgusted with myself to the extent that I was moving into the woods to begin a life of self-imposed exile. Outside the store window, the street traffic lurched forward. I shifted my eyes back to the man behind the counter, settling first on his hand, which was collapsing the radio's antenna, and then his face and then his infected eye.

"I just need to get away for a while without dying," I said.

"In that case, let me show you what *I'd* take into the woods."

I left the store with the hatchet, the hand-cranked radio, a folding shovel, a lantern, a case of water-proof matches, chlorine tablets to purify my drinking water, a first-aid kit, three muskrat traps, 100 feet of twine, a 20-pound bag of white rice, a 3 ply, 22 mil thick plastic tarp guaranteed not to crack, fray, or rip, and a pair of cowhide shoelaces that looked so bad-ass against my scuffed work boots that I bought a second pair to give to Brie as a present. Finally, without any input from the man behind the counter, I purchased a new cast iron frying pan: a nine-inch, double-spouted Lodge, which was by no means comparable to my old Griswold, but needed only to be seasoned at low heat on the bottom rack of my parents' oven to be serviceable enough for my purposes. The total came to $109.35.

On April 23rd, Brie borrowed Larry's ancient Ford pickup and helped me move to the Michaux State Forest. We loaded my army surplus survival gear, my stereo system, records, a used 12-volt car battery (to power the stereo), Trez's sleeping bag and cassette player, my neck towel, and a few food staples (shortening, tea bags, salt, pepper, a half-dozen chocolate bars) into the truck bed. Then, since we still had room, we loaded my twin-sized mattress into the back.

I was in high spirits as Brie drove us into the mountains. To my mind, I'd deduced the answer to all of life's problems by using stone-cold logic. And, it wasn't like Wayne's erroneous syllogism about Elvis liking capes. My syllogism was unassailable: nature was clean; I would live in nature; therefore, I would become clean. I hung my elbow out the window and took a long, deep breath of the piney air. I turned to Brie. "It smells like a Christmas tree up here."

"Are you okay?"

"To be honest, I've never felt more clarity of purpose. My days of willful decadence are behind me. Win, lose, or draw, I'm a frontier man now—no different than Davy Crockett."

Brie eased off the gas and steered around a branch on the road. "These woods are dense. Aren't you scared of snakes? Or falling and breaking your leg and dying before you can crawl to help?"

"Not at all," I answered. "There's an ancient pull to these hills. I'll be safe here, just like my ancestors before me and their ancestors before them. I'll harvest the earth to my advantage. It's all about Manifest Destiny—nature exists to conquer. Thoreau said so."

"Really?"

"It's in the book."

"What are you going to eat?"

"Wild carrots are everywhere out here. And berries."

"What about protein?"

"I'll fish and hunt," I said. "I have Trez's fishing pole, and the guy at the Army Surplus Store showed me how to set the muskrat traps. Muskrats are abundant up here. Just slow-roast them and the meat falls right off the bone. The bigger ones compare favorably to brisket."

"Who told you that?"

"The Army Surplus guy."

"It might not be as easy as you think."

"You're kind of ruining this for me. I know you like to think everything through ten million different ways, but haven't you ever wanted to live life a tad more dangerously? Besides, the last thing you have to worry about is me starving. I'm famine resistant," I said. I grabbed my stomach with both hands and gave it a shake to prove my point. "See? Famine resistant."

Brie was wearing her FFA jacket with her cherished American FFA badge pinned to the front, directly over her heart. Under her jacket, she had on her brother's old Grateful Dead T-shirt—the beige one with the cover of *American Beauty* on the front and a group picture of the band's extended family on the back. Wayne loved the shirt. He'd worn it long after it was too small for him. I'd assumed that he threw it out, but apparently Brie had rescued it from the rag bag. To complement her shirt, she had on her white granny skirt (pulled up over her knees so she could drive) and her steel-toed work boots, which she'd laced with the leather shoestrings I'd given her as a gift. On any other girl, the attire would have presented as a failed attempt at satire, but this was Brie, so it more or less qualified as her uniform.

"I'm not worried about you starving to death," she said.

"What then?"

She waited a moment. "I think you know."

"What?"

"You're not the most focused person I've ever met," she said. "You kind of just meander along and drift into what everyone else is doing."

"Like tofu?" I asked, my voice cracking.

Brie was well aware of my weird flights—she'd witnessed more than a few at the markets—so she knew enough not to feed me any line. She let a moment pass, then asked, "Is the stereo going to run off a car battery?"

"Why wouldn't it?"

"Why do you need a stereo at all?"

"To drown out the sound of nature."

"Like Thoreau?"

"Yes. He found the ambient chirps and leaf rustling tedious—again, in the book."

It suddenly dawned on me that Brie had probably read *Walden*. English was her favorite non-FFA class, and Mrs. Colestock was her favorite non-FFA teacher. "It doesn't matter," I said. "The important thing is that I'm going to write. I have two yellow legal pads and a dozen pens. I'm going to keep meticulous notes. What I eat. How I obtain it. How I build my log cabin. And most importantly, what I learn about myself. Nature is the best therapist's couch—the Army Surplus guy told me that. The trick is to document everything. Plus, I'm going to write supplemental treatises. I've got a sneaky feeling there's a book in all of this."

"You mean like *Walden*?"

"I know you think I'm a big fat tofu joke, but I'm dead serious about this. I've already written my first treatise." I reached into my backpack and pulled out a legal pad. I flipped it open, and as we drove along the shaded mountain road, I began to read aloud.

Ten Albums Essential to a New Beingness
by
Jim Dubbs

In the spring of 1984, I entered the untouched, sapling-laden woods of the Michaux State Forest in the Commonwealth of Pennsylvania to live a simpler life—to, like Henry David Thoreau, experience a new beingness unfettered by the influence of a coddled and materialistic society. But what then, you may ask, of the better, more noble parts of the society I was leaving behind? Generosity of mind and spirit? Innate gallantry? Altruism? And what of the humanities? Art is and always will be the fruit of the human soul. It seems to me, to cut myself off from said fruit would ultimately prove counterproductive if I wanted to cleanse my soul of a certain "tofu-ness."

For this reason, O' Gentle Reader, I decided to take my Hi-Fi equipment into the forest with me. Of course, with regards to chattel, the inherent frugality of timberland dwelling requires a bevy of tough decisions—the first being how many albums to allow myself. In the end, I decided that ten was the perfect number. This, however, created a new set of problems, not least of which, what albums made the cut. Greatest Hits compilations, with a few glaring exceptions, such as Jethro Tull's M.U. The Best of Jethro Tull . . . *do not withstand repeated, engaged listening. First, there is no continuity of sound; listeners can experience virtually any song in a better context on its original record. I submit as the perfect example: David Bowie's greatest hits package. Are you really prepared to sit there, O' Gentle Reader, earphones slid tightly over each ear, listening to* ChangesOneBowie, *and tell me that "Space Oddity" and "Rebel, Rebel" belong on the same album?*

The question of how to treat double albums also presents itself. Since I'm the one choosing and have two double albums on the list, I've decided to allow double albums to count as one selection. Without further ado and in no particular order, here is my list of the ten albums essential to a new beginningness:

1. Neil Young. Live Rust. *Always the album I'm going to put on the turntable when I want to hear Neil rock out.*

2. Graham Parker and the Rumors. Squeezing out Sparks. *"Local Girls" and "Waiting for the UFOs" would be enough, but "You Can't Be Too Strong" clinches the argument.*

3. Led Zeppelin. House of the Holy. *Hard to limit myself to one Zeppelin offering, but this album, especially "Over the Hills and Far Away," is the realization of Jimmy Page's vision of Led Zeppelin as "an army of guitars."*

4. The Allman Brothers. At Fillmore East. *With twin juggernauts "Whipping Post" and "Statesboro Blues," it's impossible to imagine—*

Brie stopped me there.

I was ridiculous, she said. Plus, I'd lost narrative tone halfway through and the overall language was pretentious. And "beingness" wasn't a word.

Nor was "tofu-ness." I couldn't just add "ness" to any word and make a new word. She'd heard me make up words at the farmers market and was tired of just letting it slide. "Wayne said that's what's wrong with you—you're always trying to save face when you misuse a word," she said, steering the truck around a tight corner.

I let out a derisive utterance. "Your brother knows what's wrong with everyone but himself. And 'beingness' is most certainly a word because I've used it before on tests and in book reports, and Mrs. Colestock never marked it wrong."

That shut her up. We drove in silence through the forest until we passed a tiny general store. I pointed to a gravel pull-off at the base of the mountain. "This is it," I said, "Pull off here."

Brie pulled onto the gravel and killed the engine. She peered out the windshield at the side of the mountain. "How far is your campsite?"

"Two miles straight up through the woods."

"Well, let's get a move on, then," she said, opening her door. "You're going to need one heck of a head-start if you plan to outrun yourself."

Brie believed in starting any job with the hardest task, so we began by carrying my mattress straight up the side of South Mountain. This proved much harder than I'd imagined. By the time we wrestled the mattress through a two-mile expanse of brush to the clearing that would serve as my personal Walden, my quads were burning and I was out of breath. Brie and I pushed the mattress over on the ground and flopped onto it. We laid there on the soiled cotton, staring up through the tree canopy until Brie said, "Those bell-shaped mushrooms growing everywhere— they're Death Caps. Don't eat them."

"Why not?"

"You really can't figure it out? *Death* caps? If you eat one, you'll die. Your tongue will start to itch, and then you won't be able to move your legs and your brain will melt like candle wax."

"Got it," I said, fanning a mosquito away from my face. "Don't eat the Death Caps."

"And these mosquitoes—they mean there's standing water nearby," she said. "You know enough not to drink standing water, right?"

"Of course," I said, fanning another insect away. "You need to trust me, Brie. This is my home now—standing water and all. It may sound odd, but I welcome the insects. It's all copacetic. The more bugs there are, the more things that eat the bugs. And the more things that eat the things that eat the bugs. It's the food chain and I'm at the top of it. You could make the argument that these insects are here to sustain me and me alone. That the Michaux State Forest is God's finest four-star restaurant, and I've reserved the best table—no different than table two at Claudio's."

Brie twisted her head toward me. "So what's this all about? Really?"

The trees' highest leaves fluttered in the breeze for a few seconds. "I need to lay fallow for a while," I said. "I need to build myself back up and hopefully start over at the beginning. Let's face it; I'm no bargain. I *am* like tofu. I have zero personality and I overcompensate because of it. Your brother is right. I try to shoe-horn things that don't belong. I'm fat. I'm scruffy. I'm persnickety. At times I'm willfully insolent. I'm dimwitted to the point that when I see two similar jackets, I have no clue which one is mine. I pass out over fat marbling, and after all this time, I still break into a blind panic when I have to count by fives. Nurse Darcy had me pegged. I'm overly concerned with creature comforts—so much so that I've stunted my emotional growth."

"I think you're being way too hard on yourself."

"It's all true."

"So what if it's true? What if those things are what make you unique?"

"Then I'm pathetic."

"What if someone said they like you the way you are?"

I forced a mocking laugh. "Then I'd say they're *way* too innocent for their own good."

Brie didn't say anything. After a second, I twisted my head to look at her. The instant I did, she turned her back to me. "See! Right there! That!" she said over her shoulder. "That's your real problem—you can't see that innocence has value."

I looked at Brie. I wanted to reach out and touch her and tell her that she was wrong. That I did value innocence—her innocence—and I didn't want to damage it. But I didn't reach out. Instead, I wrapped my arms across my chest and gazed up past the leaf canopy into the pale blue, and just as I did, a lone bird flew across the sky, no doubt on its way to someplace far better.

It took three trips to trudge the rest of my belongings up the hill. The stereo equipment and records were one trip. The survival gear and food were another. The last trip—just odds and ends—was the lightest but far and away the most tiring. We dropped everything on the ground and I handed my canteen to Brie. "You know what?" I said, "It occurs to me now that we should have brought Earl the Cheese Guy's wheelchair along. We could have used it to push everything up the hill."

Brie handed me back the canteen. "I've got something to give you," she said. She opened her backpack and pulled a folded hand towel from it. "It's a flare gun," she said, unfolding the towel for me to see. "And four flares."

I took it from her and turned it over in my hands.

"You need to get to a wide-open space. Like the stream—the widest spot. You don't want to set the woods on fire. You might get turned around in the flames and not be able to escape," Brie said.

I nodded. "This must have been expensive—you shouldn't have spent money on me."

"You were nice enough to buy me those leather shoelaces."

"The second I saw them, I knew they'd be perfect," I said. "They had Brie written all over them."

"You know enough to point the flare away from your face, right?"

I gathered my bottom lip under my teeth. It was so Brie—buy me a thoughtful gift and then accuse me of being too stupid to use it without blowing my eyebrows off. I could have feigned offense, but I knew that Brie couldn't help herself. "Point it away from my face—got it," I said.

Brie gathered her hands in front of her. "So, how long is it going to take to purify your soul? I mean, if you had to put a timeframe on it?"

"It took Thoreau two years, two months, two weeks, and two days, so I'm guessing at least that long and maybe a good bit longer. I don't want to belabor it, but I'm pretty messed up in the head."

"Do you want me to spend the first night with you? We can build a fire and play the misheard lyrics game—the new version I thought up. We can take turns standing watch."

"No one stood watch for Thoreau."

"Aren't you a little scared?"

"No."

"Do you want me to come back tomorrow to check on you?"

I put a hand on Brie's shoulder. "I know you have to get back," I said.

"Aren't you at least going to say goodbye to me?"

I slid my hand off her shoulder and tried to paste a melancholy smile on my lips. "Thanks for helping me, Brie," I said.

The afternoon sun caught her chestnut-brown hair as she turned around. I watched her navigate the first dozen steps down the hill and I was surprised at how quickly she disappeared into the thick welter of rhododendron bushes. And, I was surprised how quickly the rustling of dead leaves quieted. Most of all, I was surprised at just how quickly I felt totally alone.

I can recall my first day and my last day in the woods in vivid detail. Other than that, there are entire swaths of time, and at one point, a string of at least four days of which I have no memory. What stands out most is just how quickly—virtually from the moment Brie disappeared—I abandoned any pretense of self- discovery.

Luckily, I have my journal to help cobble together the series of events that led to my disastrous encounter with the shopkeeper in the trading post. As a whole, my journal entries are unsettling to read, not only because the coherence of my note-taking falls off sharply after the third day (as dehydration set in), but also because by the seventh day, my handwriting had grown to resemble the frantic, panic-stricken scrawl of the last survivor of a doomed Arctic exploration team.

What follows is an abridged version of my diary. I've edited it for repetitiveness, non sequiturs, and entries that are, from beginning to end, incomprehensible. I've also tamped down the profanity and the many, many references to a "toad-like stare" (whether I was fixated on the idea of a toad-like stare, or whether I was attempting to document occurrences of said stare, I have no recollection). Finally, to preserve the record, I've left my last entry unedited. It appears in these pages exactly as it appears in my journal and serves (sadly) as a clear reflection of my frayed mental faculties in that moment.

DAY 1.

Greetings and salutations from my own private Walden. I can only describe my first day in the Michaux State Forest as ethereal. Second growth evergreens and towering oaks co-mingle with saplings of indeterminate species, forming a moat of solitude around me that can only aid my return to beingness. The air is fresh, O' Gentle Reader, just as God intended it to be. Both the temperature and dew point are the exact equal of my unfettered skin, producing a sensation of non-existence that I can also, in a very real sense, only describe as ethereal. The woods themselves are accepting. A bevy of woodland creatures (chipmunks, birds, a scary, three-legged thing that may have been a deformed marten) have shown the good grace to welcome me to their home. Meanwhile, the quadra-phonic sounds I encountered as I transported my scant belongings to my campsite—rustles, chirps, a weird, untraceable tapping sound—have quickly become the soundtrack of my healing, as essential to life as my own heartbeat.

A few minor setbacks to report, O' Most Kind Reader. The car battery is dead. In hindsight, I should have tested it before I lugged it two miles up the side of a mountain. Consequently, my stereo and the ten albums that I painstakingly selected are now nothing more than clutter—worse, they're clutter I must keep dry. While a lesser man may have suffered the momentary sting of self-doubt, my enthusiasm remains uncurbed. I have the cassette player I took from Trez's room as well as a handful of tapes from his mellow period: Cat Stevens, James Taylor, and The Grateful Dead. Not Led Zeppelin or the Allman Brothers or AC/DC, to be sure, but the fruit of humankind's shared humanity nonetheless.

Also, I can't help but feel that if I'd read Thoreau's book, I'd have some inkling as to his work process as he built his cabin dwelling. After my faithful she-servant, Brie, disappeared down the long and winding mountainside to return to the safety of a rabid and underachieving society, I began the task of constructing my log cabin. Unfortunately, felling and de-limbing even a dwarfish tree proved far more difficult than I'd anticipated—it took the entire afternoon—leaving me famished and in dire need of a Snickers bar.

In its place, O' Trusted Reader, I've constructed a lean-to. I used twine to fasten the felled dwarf tree across two larger trees about ten feet apart; then, I stretched the nylon canvas across the suspended tree and pinned the tarp's corners down with a small cairn of rocks. With luck, it will see me through my first night. Good night and God bless.

DAY 2.

Greetings and salutations. I captured a fish today. I say "captured" rather than "caught" because I didn't catch the fish in the sense the word is used in the fishing vernacular. I was completing my mid-day security sweep when I stumbled across a fish that had somehow trapped itself in a shallow offshoot of the stream at the foot of the mountain. It was a trout, perhaps nine inches long, and it exhibited no natural fear of me. (Was I the first human being that its non-binocular eyes had ever encountered?) After two dozen or so attempts, I managed to fling the fish onto the bank with a trident-shaped stick. Not wanting to see the poor creature suffer, I attempted to end its life quickly by bringing my ocher-colored work boot down on its head. Unfortunately, this proved more difficult than capturing the fish in the first place. It wasn't until a frenzy of glancing blows left me on the brink of exhaustion that I was able to finally, mercifully, square the poor thing's noggin up with the heel of my boot.

As with life in general, O' Most Trusted Reader, the good news is often tempered by bad news. I've come to the sad conclusion that the Army Surplus guy is/was a charlatan. The hand-cranked radio that he sold me is a piece of [expletive]. Actually, it *was* a piece of [expletive]. For two days, no matter how Herculean my effort, the only station I was able to pull in was an AM station out of Allentown, and even then, the station was only audible if I cranked the handle as fast as I could without pause. Then, this afternoon as I was cranking the handle furiously to try to catch a weather report (rain is coming), the [expletive] handle snapped off in my [expletive] hand.

DAY 3.

Greetings, Dear Reader. I've decided to hold off on building a cabin. Foraging for food has proven to be far more difficult and time-consuming than I anticipated. The muskrat traps are useless—more proof that the Army Surplus guy was a crook. Plus, the wild carrots that appeared so abundant when I scouted the location a few days ago have turned woody. For now, I can survive on rice.

I'm finding sleep difficult. The tapping sound is unnerving. It seems to come from both everywhere and nowhere at the same time. I understand now why Thoreau hated the forest. Also, a few quick comments regarding my water situation. I was pretty sure that running water was okay to drink, but Brie had me so paranoid that I'd been boiling all of my drinking water. As it turns out, it takes a hell of a long time and a whole lot of wood to boil even small amounts of water. And after my experience with the piece of crap wind-up radio the infected-eye guy unloaded on me, I didn't trust the chlorine tablets that I'd purchased from him (at what now seems like a suspiciously low price). So this morning, when I was unable to light a fire and had no choice but to drink stream water, I used twice the amount of recommended tablets in half the water, creating what might have been a lethal dose of chlorine if I hadn't puked it up within seconds. More proof the infected-eye guy sucks.

DAY 4.
(Entry rendered unreadable by water damage)

DAY 5.
Woke up this morning clutching the flare gun to my chest and sobbing . . . The weird tapping sound has continued unabated . . . It rained all night . . . My bungalow mattress has turned sodden and the deluge has coaxed a nauseating petroleum smell from the tarp . . . More proof the infected-eye guy blows . . . On the plus side, I've decided to call my settlement "Woody Creek" as a homage to Hunter S. Thompson . . . I've also decided to write in more fragmented language and jam ellipses between each sentence in my journal entries, again as an homage to HST . . . I am, after all, a professional.

DAY 6.
More rain today . . . I think I may have fallen asleep standing up again . . . I rationed out my rice on a large, flat piece of bark that I pulled from a dead tree . . . One fistful of rice per day . . . I have enough to last out the month . . . Maybe . . . Beginning to wish that I'd read Thoreau's book . . . That would have been the thing to do . . . That would save me . . . To read it one day at a time so that my experiences ran concurrent to his . . .

It would answer my nagging question . . . How did he deal with the tapping sounds . . . How did he find food . . . And did he encounter some sort of mentor in the woods? . . . A spirit teacher, perhaps.

DAY 7.

More rain again today . . . Three straight days now . . . Harsh and unforgiving . . . Hellish rain pelting my bedraggled tarp . . . To my chagrin, I've developed a toad-like stare . . . Small Fries are everywhere, having invaded Woody Creek . . . Every minute I spend in the lean-to I get weaker . . . Every minute the Small Fries crouch in the bush they get stronger . . . Even my piece of tree bark appears water-logged, which to me is [illegible] . . . The canvas is holding—despite the smell—but my mattress has sponged up so much water from the ground that I have been forced to [illegible] against a tree . . . More bad news . . . Small Fries have decimated the Earl Grey loose leaf tea and the Singell Darjeeling . . . Only the Russian Caravan has survived unscathed.

DAY 7. (SECOND ENTRY)

Disaster has struck . . . While I was performing my security walk an animal got into the rice . . . I'd taken to suspending the bag from the lean-to crossbeam with a piece of twine . . . When I got back, the twine was ripped in two and the rice and the slab of bark I sort it on had been dragged outside the lean-to . . . The bag was ripped open . . . Most of the rice spilled onto the wet ground and is ruined . . . Have been forced to suspend the remaining rice from the lean-to crossbeam by using my belt.

DAY 7. (THIRD ENTRY)

More disturbing news . . . I've discovered that the shortening has turned rancid . . . Sleeping is a chore in futility . . . I fear that [illegible] before help arrives . . . More tapping sounds . . . Unabated . . . [illegible] and the bacteria that most assuredly would be harbored in it . . . Hard to pin down as they seem to emanate from everywhere and nowhere . . . I've taken to scanning the horizon, waiting for my spirit teacher . . . One hand over my eye, watching for him or her . . . For now I wait . . . In the meantime, I've fashioned a Robinson Caruso belt from the last of the twine . . . [illegible] likely leaving the trading post at the bottom of the hill as the only option if I'm to survive.

DAY 8. (NO ENTRY)

DAY 9. (UNEDITED)

Greetings an salutations . . . toad-like stairs from the grate unwashed! . . . I drug my mattress back to the lean to. I fear that it is a silent killer waiting to infect my lung-scarring bacteria . . . still no signs ov my spriit teacher . . . t a foot from the north wall On par with rotting potatoes . . . the toad-like stair again . . . I had no choice because they said there pox was before that time . . . Small Frys have raided my tea once more . . . their boxes as pristine as the day I'd drug it down into a small clearing and propped up up in the sun so that I could air could get to both sides, but It had never completely dried out . . . Atfer that I bartered for them from Shelly, the tea and vendor v nd herbs the first night had moved into the stuffing

My journal entries abruptly end there.

My last day at Woody Creek is vivid in my memory. I'm guessing that my body, sensing the end was near, tapped into some deep fat-store to restore a measure of lucidity to my brain. I was lying on my back on the damp ground. I had a hand over one eye, and I was staring up through the same hole in the leaf canopy that Brie and I had stared through when we were lying on the mattress. The air was still, but the tops of the trees were fluttering. The leaves and the sky beyond them had a weird, weak green and blue hue—like the fading colors of an old Polaroid. I began to think about how Brie had pointed out a couple of mushrooms and warned me not to eat them because eating them would cause my brain to melt like candle wax. I began to feel like my brain *was* melting, even though I knew for sure I hadn't eaten any mushrooms. Then, I realized that the source of the sensation was emanating from outside of my body. To my left. At ground level. I lifted my head and looked at the cassette player. Cat Stevens was singing "Peace Train," but his voice was garbled and the music was slow. On cue, like a dying man, Cat held onto one last undulating note for a few tortured seconds before the tape dragged to a stop.

I pried off the cassette player's back cover and turned the batteries over in my hand. The weight seemed roughly the same as when I bought them. Did batteries lose weight as they ran down? The whole entropy thing? It seemed logical. On a hunch, I dug up the two dead D batteries that I'd buried behind my lean-to and held them in my other hand. Then I extended my arms—in essence forming a scale. As close as I could determine, the batteries' weight was identical.

My legs began to tremble. I could live without food, but music was different. It was the spring well of my soul. Then, I remembered the trading post at the gravel turn-off. Surely it would have size D batteries. I stood and cinched my rope belt tight. A second later, I was lolloping down the mountainside.

I stood splayfooted in the trading post's empty parking lot, panting through my mouth. The tiny store was the main feature of the weed-infested lot. To the right was a three-sided shed with a small forklift parked inside. To the left, beside what appeared to be an outhouse, sat a decrepit swing set, so rusted and gnarled that it would evoke fear in even the most lackadaisical parent. I unscrewed the top of my canteen and took a sip. The water tasted metallic. I pulled my neck towel tight around my shoulders and stepped onto the front porch and through the post's wooden screen door.

The shopkeeper—a slab-faced man of indeterminate age—was standing behind a wooden counter. His shoulders were round, and a foam-gray ruff of chest hair poked out from the neck of his undershirt. He looked at once both bored and irritated. He squinted at me. "Do I know you?" he asked.

I smiled at the man. "I've been camping," I said. When he didn't respond with anything more than a slight backward tilt of his head, I added, "Up on the ridge," as if alluding to what I guessed was a common landmark would lend me credibility and mark me as an experienced woodsman on par with Lewis and Clark or John Muir.

"You living up there?"

"Oh yeah."

"On federal land?"

"Not technically living—not in the conventional sense. More doing research. I've written a of couple treatises: *Squirrels In, Squirrels Out* is probably the best, but *Ten Albums Essential to a New Beingness* is pretty darn good, too, if you're not going to quibble about whether or not 'beingness' is an actual word."

I sensed the man focusing on my twine belt. I'd added to it just that morning. One end of the belt now extended to my knees. The other end, the one closest to my waist, was knotted off in a lumpy, tangerine-sized ball—the result of a sudden, ill-advised burst of inspiration concerning a hoop and ball system that I thought would simulate a buckle. I cleared my throat so he would refocus on my face. "I know. Woods. Record albums. I rationalized bringing music because art is the spirit cry of the human soul, and to cut myself off from said spirit cry would be counter-productive if my ultimate goal is to be less tofu-like."

At that point, I think I may have drifted into my toad-like stare. Either that or I dozed off on my feet again because when I refocused on the man, I had the sensation that a few minutes had passed. He was standing farther back than I last remembered him and his pupils were dilated, as though he was mired in some sort of fight or flight response.

I panicked and repeated the last thing I remembered saying: tofu-like. When this didn't seem to mitigate the panic in his eyes, I asked as slowly as I could, "Do. You. Carry. Size. D. Batteries?"

A few seconds of silence followed, about the length of the gap between two songs on a record. Then the man pointed to a shelf along the back of the store.

Unbeknownst to me, shortly after I scurried splayfooted and cackling from the store with a paper sack full of D batteries pinned to my chest, Brie's telephone in the wooded section of Twin Oaks rang. It was the shopkeeper. As Brie later told me, after she'd hiked back to Larry's pickup, she'd talked to the man and paid him $20 to watch for me. A retainer, she called it. She figured that I'd snap, so it was no surprise when her telephone rang and the voice on the other end said, "I think I just saw that fella you told me about."

Back at my lean-to, I was playing side one of The Grateful Dead's *Workingman's Dead* on the cassette player and measuring fistfuls of rice onto a better and, in my mind, more trustworthy slab of tree bark that I'd found propped against a rock just that morning, when I heard my name. I froze. A slight rustle filled the air. I covered one eye and scanned the undergrowth for movement. Nothing. Then I heard it again—unmistakable this time—a female voice calling my name. "Jim?" I heard something big kicking through the leaves, and suddenly a young woman was standing in the opening. She was wearing an FFA jacket and a white granny dress. The sun filtering through the treetops gathered behind her and illuminated every strand of chestnut-colored hair that had escaped her pigtail. She was beautiful. More than beautiful. She was stunning—the kind of pristine, spiritual apparition about whom Thoreau had surely written. I instinctively scrunched down. "Are you my spirit teacher?" I asked.

"You're ridiculous," she said.

EPISODE EIGHT

Title: *Finale—The Last Farmers Market*
Time: *64 minutes*
Synopsis: *Jim and Brie search for Angela.*

I've since learned the physical and mental effects of severe dehydration. Physically, it causes a build-up of acids in the body that clog the kidneys with the protein myoglobin. When someone dies of thirst, this is what kills them. On the mental side, prolonged dehydration impacts the sufferer's mood and ability to concentrate. Memory is affected (which is why I can't recall giant chunks of time), as is the ability to communicate coherently (my encounter with the owner of the Trading Post). Acute dehydration also produces an altered level of consciousness resulting in everything from abrupt, trance-like drowsiness (toad-like stares) to full-fledged hallucinations (the Trading Post's gnarled swing set, which in reality was an abandoned hand pump). The condition's very worst effects—fear, anger, anxiety, depression, and paranoia—I was spared. To this, I attribute the very real possibility that God was, in fact, gawking at me and, no doubt sadly shaking his head.

Of course, at the time, I didn't possess the wherewithal to realize that I was dehydrated. I felt fine—or thought I felt fine—until I recognized my spirit teacher as Brie. Something inside of me clicked. It was as if I were laying eyes on my campsite unhindered by familiarity—an anthropologist parting the thickets and taking his first, clear-eyed view of a tiny, unexplored village. My mattress was on end, wedged tightly between two trees; my lean-to was sagging heavy at one end; and the car battery that I'd lugged up the hill was tipped upside down in the middle of the clearing, encircled like a shrine by randomly sized chunks of bark. I let out a weak, flailing bleat and toppled onto the forest floor in a flaccid heap. My face hit the dirt, bounced once, and came to a rest beside the empty paper sack that just an hour ago had held sixteen brand-new D batteries.

Brie helped me to my feet. She draped my army blanket over my shoulders and led me downhill along the stream pass and across the ridge to the foot of the mountain. At the bottom, I turned and looked back into the thickets. "My neck towel is still up there. And the bark I sort my rice on." I took a staggering step back toward my campsite, but Brie caught me by the arm and guided me toward the gravel turn-off.

She sat me down inside Larry's pickup and held a water bottle out to me. "Don't gulp it. Take a sip and then count to ten before you take another."

I took a sip and silently counted to ten, then I took another sip and wiped my mouth with the back of my hand. "How long have I been missing?" I asked.

"You were never missing."

"Then how long have I been gone?"

"We drove up here April twenty-third. Today's May the eighth."

It took a moment, but I did the math in my head. "I made it," I said. "Two weeks, two days, and judging by the sun, two hours. I survived hardship—like an Apollo astronaut."

"You need to keep drinking, Jim. Your eyes are sunken in."

"I'm not thirsty."

"That's what's scaring me. Do you remember the last time you peed?"

"I don't know. Maybe this morning."

"Was it dark?"

"I just told you it was morning. The sun was up, but it wasn't directly overhead yet."

"I'm asking if your urine was dark?"

It suddenly dawned on me that Brie was talking to me the same way she spoke to the woman we thought was having a stroke at the farmers market—the older woman who fell over in the middle of buying a zucchini. "I don't know—I think it came out brownish," I said.

I could tell by Brie's face that it was the wrong answer. She placed her hand on the bottom of the water jug and eased it up to my mouth.

"I'd much rather have iced tea. Remember? My reverse diet? How every day you'd hand me a glass of ice-cold sweet tea at the front door? Although it seems to me now that the fatter I got, the less sugar you stirred in. Is that true? Did you cut my sugar?"

Brie shook her head. "I don't have any iced tea, Jim. And if I did, I wouldn't give it to you. Caffeine is only going to dehydrate you more."

"You gave it to me back then," I sputtered, suddenly mad.

Brie eased the jug back up to my mouth. "Don't talk," she said, letting out a sigh. "And for just once in your ridiculous life, do what I say."

I sat in Larry's pickup truck, sipping water and picking burrs off my mud-caked pants while Brie hiked to my camp and hauled back anything of value: Trez's cassette player, his tapes, a few clothes, my shovel, and the flare gun and flares. The records were ruined, and my stereo was nowhere to be found—apparently, I'd carted it deep into the woods at some point.

"I left the car battery and the mattress," she said. "It just looks like an abandoned hobo camp now."

"Did you get my neck towel?"

"You have it. It's around your neck."

"What about my special bark—the curved one by the stream for handfuls of rice? I need that."

Apparently, this didn't warrant a response.

She backed out onto the road, and we drove downhill past the small outpost store. The shopkeeper was standing by the open screen door, and he turned his head to follow us as we drove by. I craned my neck and looked back at the store, trying to catch a second glimpse of the man. "I knew I should never have trusted that bastard," I said.

"He saved your life."

"I was perfectly alright."

"I know."

"I could have done that indefinitely."

"I know you could have."

"I didn't need help."

"I know you didn't."

I took a sip of water. "How come Wayne didn't come along to help get me?"

Brie let out a truncated gasp and wiped the back of her hand across her eyes. I lowered the water bottle into my lap. "How come Wayne didn't come along to get me?" I repeated.

"He's gone."

"What do you mean, gone? Where did he go?"

Brie kept her eyes fixed on the road. I leaned forward. "Brie, where is Wayne?"

"No one knows," she sputtered. "He disappeared."

Gone, disappeared, vanished. All of Brie's words and none of them described Wayne's status. He'd taken his guitar and driven away in his car—they'd pieced that much together—but his motivations for leaving, as well as his whereabouts, were a complete mystery. As bad as my kidneys hurt, I insisted that Brie show me Wayne's bedroom before she drove me home to my parents' house.

Wayne room looked as if a bomb had gone off. His poster of Humble Pie was ripped and dangling from one thumbtack. Records were out of their sleeves. And in the far corner—just like in his bungalow—he'd dumped the contents of a shelf onto the floor and then flipped the empty shelf back upright. The only sign of order in the chaos was the cardboard egg trays, which Wayne had stacked neatly by the closet door.

In the living room, Wayne's father asked me, "Did he say anything? What was his frame of mind?"

Over the years, I'd only ever exchanged a few hundred words with Mr. Clark, and almost all of them concerned his meat hook contraption. I gathered my bottom lip under my teeth. I hadn't noticed it until that moment, but the living room looked exactly as it had in 1973. There was the same olive-green carpeting, the same beige drapes, the same faux-walnut stereo console parked in the same spot against the same mustard-yellow wall. The room felt sad and faded and lost in time, and while I was formulating my response, my attention drifted to the Clark family's portrait above the fireplace mantel—the one that featured Wayne's frayed eye patch as the painting's focal point. I shifted my focus back to Mr. Clark. "He seemed fine to me," I said.

"How did he feel about losing his condo?" Wayne's mother asked.

I looked at Brie.

"The condos at The Sulfur Springs Resort," Brie said. Then she nodded a few times.

I forced my lips into a reassuring smile. "You know your son," I said. "I think he saw it as an opportunity."

My near death from dehydration wasn't without its perks. The first day I was home, my dad treated me with his kindest hand—going so far as to make my bed while my mother dug out the sick bell for me to ring if I needed anything. I spent two days in my sweatpants, drinking water and eating tiny amounts of protein every two hours: a spoonful of peanut butter, half a hard-boiled egg, et cetera. The third day, I dragged Earl the Cheese Guy's wheelchair out of the attic and sat in it on the front porch. I set one of Seven Turn's apple crates beside it—a convalescence table of sorts—and on the crate I set the sick bell and my drink. I spent the rest of the week sitting quietly in the wheelchair with my neck towel draped over my legs to ward off the chill, waiting for Brie to check in on me on her way home from work and offer the latest news—or lack thereof—concerning Wayne's disappearance. In the evening, I'd brew a pitcher of iced coffee in preparation for the next day's sitting. I couldn't afford a high-end coffee bean, but instinct told me that an off-the-shelf Peruvian bean would serve just as well. Of course, I needed a sweetener. Simple syrup was the obvious choice, but again, I was counting pennies, so I opted for a more cost-efficient substitute—a splash of flat Pepsi.

Around mid-afternoon of the seventh day, I was on the porch sitting in Earl's old wheelchair, thinking about my record collection (specifically, how much would it cost to buy every record Jeff Beck ever played on?) when I realized my iced coffee needed sweetened. I gave the sick bell a jingle.

"I think my iced coffee needs another splash of Pepsi," I said to my mother, holding my tumbler out to her. When my mother didn't move, I gave the tumbler a wiggle to prompt her into action. "Just a little more," I said. "Just a smidgen."

My mom took the glass inside, and a few seconds later, she reappeared with it. I took a tiny sip just as she disappeared back into the house. It still needed the least little bit more Pepsi—maybe just half as much as would fill an upturned bottle cap. I gave the bell another ring.

From inside, I heard a heated exchange. I'd heard my parents argue before—many times—but this had a completely different tone. It seemed to be missing at least two ingredients of a squabble. First, it was missing coherent words. They were communicating in choked-off grunts. And second, there was a lack of conflict. Their verbal contortions rose and fell in perfect harmony, as if they were commiserating in song. The screen door slammed open, seemingly by itself, and in the next heartbeat my father was towering over me. "Get the hell out of that wheelchair," he yelled.

In my defense, to face my father, I had to twist toward the sun, and the sudden, unanticipated change in his demeanor coupled with the punishing sunlight combined to discombobulate me. For one long moment, I fumbled with his words. *Get. The. Hell. Out. Of. That. Wheelchair.* The sentence itself made perfect sense, but its deeper meaning escaped me. *Why* did he want me to get out of the chair? I had to sit *somewhere.* Perhaps he was still concerned about my health: that I would develop deep vein thrombosis from sitting in one spot too long. Or maybe, unbeknownst to me, he'd bartered for a better wheelchair. Maybe Earl's wife had fallen down the basement steps again and Earl had failed to return a newer, more ergonomic wheelchair—one with a cup holder.

"What wheelchair?" I asked.

The effect of my question was similar to when Tina flung the lit match at the gasoline-soaked chicken coops. Only it wasn't the chicken coops that exploded; it was my dad's head. He let out a string of garbled curse words, including the F-word, which he began and choked off three separate times. Then, he lifted the wheelchair by the handles and dumped me face-first onto the wooden porch slats. I laid there for a second, stunned, until my dad flipped the wheelchair upside down and shook it over me as if to dislodge any flecks of Jim debris that may have embedded in the seat fibers.

I rolled over and let out a weak bleat. "But . . . I needed that," I said.

"You sure as hell did," my father answered.

That afternoon, I drove to Seven Turns and discovered that Larry had given away my job. Actually, "discovered" doesn't quite capture the scene's tone. Larry was pissed. So pissed, that he whipped the shovel he was holding across the gravel before I could even shift the Bronco into park. Without so much as a syllable of preamble, he told me that he couldn't have some [expletive] dimwit employee just not show up without any [expletive] explanation. And that I could [expletive] keep the [expletive] apple crates that I [expletive] stole from him. Then, he fired me. More accurately, he told me to "get the [expletive] off his [expletive] property and never come the [expletive] back."

As humiliating as it was, Larry's tongue-lashing was a blessing of sorts. I wasn't tempted to backslide into my old ways and squander the one thing of value I'd returned home from Woody Creek with: a trimmer body. I'd lost twenty-six pounds in my two weeks, two days, and two hours of Walden-inspired hell. When I added in the nine pounds that I'd lost from the stomach flu before I moved into the woods, I'd shed thirty-five pounds—the exact reverse of my Summer of Doris reverse diet.

So while I was without a job, I felt primed for life in a way I hadn't in years. Not only had my center of gravity shifted north about eight inches, but the dehydration reset my system. I got restful sleep, my chafing problem receded into a bad memory, and for the first time in years, I could see my ankles without pushing my stomach in with both hands and pitching my head forward. Two days after Larry fired me, I rooted through Trez's dresser and found a ton of clothing that fit me, including a tank top and a pair of running shorts. That evening, I jogged to the Lutheran Seminary and ran the long grass slope to the top of the campus—up for strength and down for speed—over and over until the sun disappeared behind the hills. The next day, I ran the slope again. The day after that, I put together a weight program using just my body weight: push-ups, chin-ups, deep knee bends, et cetera. It may not have counted as the new beginningness I'd climbed the mountain in search of, but for the first time since I was seven years old and leaped to my tiny feet to scream my shared "Limey" line in the The Last Scone Story, I felt spry.

Then on the third Saturday of May, my dad died.

He was fixing himself a tuna fish sandwich for lunch and a second later, he was crumpled on the floor with the lid to the mayonnaise jar still in his left hand.

My memories of the next few days are scattered. I had a sense of time passing, but it was as though I was in a vast, empty room filled with fog and I was floating in the fog and every now and then I'd touch the floor and my feet were moving ridiculously fast—as if the whole time I been pedaling my feet faster and faster to try and find the floor.

And when I did find the floor, the fog would thin for a few seconds, and a jumble of short scenes would come into focus.

I remember running to get my mom.

I remember a delay in the funeral home picking up my dad's body. And when the funeral director finally came, I knew him even though I'd never seen him before; I knew him because he was large and he was melancholy and he was Mandy's father.

Then I floated for a long time until the fog thinned out and Trez was in our living room. He was wearing his Air Force dress uniform. My mother was sitting in her chair, and Trez was bent down on one knee in front of her, holding her hand.

On the third day, the fog thinned out except for a few wisps, and the background filled in with walls and windows and trees, but the colors weren't right. Especially outside. They were the supersaturated reds and yellows and blues of a child's plastic beach ball. I remember thinking I had to drink water like when Brie rescued me. And when I went to the kitchen for a glass of water, I noticed that the can opener that my dad had used to open the tuna fish was still sitting on the counter exactly where he set it down. It was the last thing he did on this earth. It seemed impossible. Every single thing my dad ever said or did or thought or felt since the instant he was conceived all progressed in one long unbroken moment and culminated in his putting the can opener down on the counter. And the opener was a small thing that meant nothing, but it was still there. I'd have to put it away. Or my mother would. Or Trez. And then the chain would be broken forever, and I remember thinking that if Trez put it away, then maybe he wouldn't realize that it was the last thing Dad ever touched and he wouldn't have to think about it for the rest of his life.

Then, the afternoon of the fourth day, the fog cleared completely. My mother, Trez, and I were sitting in the funeral home's tiny office when Mandy walked into the room. She was wearing a plain pantsuit, and her dark hair was combed straight back and gathered behind her head in a plain, everyday barrette. She was only a year older than me, but she could have passed for thirty-five.

"I guess we can skip the getting to know each other part," she said, moving behind the desk.

We all talked and then we all stood up together. Mandy's father led our mother to another room to sign some papers. After he closed the door, Mandy, Trez, and I stood in the middle of the office with our hands stuffed in our pockets.

Mandy cleared her throat. "So, how have you been, Jim?"

"Okay—writing some," I said.

"That's right," Mandy said. "I remember you wrote a poem I thought was really good."

A long, awkward moment passed. Trez and Mandy shared a glance, then looked down at their feet for a moment before returning their gaze to me. Trez's eyebrow was arched. "Oh," I said. "I'm sorry. Let me get out of your guy's way and let you catch up." I pulled my hands out of my pockets and turned to leave the room. Just as I twisted the doorknob, I couldn't stop myself. "You mean a short story. You said that it was amazing," I said without looking back, then I walked out the door.

On the day of the funeral, the fog came back so thick and impenetrable that I didn't have any sensation of my feet moving. Instead, they were leaden, and when I did land on the floor, it was with a thud. I only have one memory of the service, and it's this: Brie standing by my side, looking as if she hadn't slept for days, and the entire time she stood beside me, she never said a word until we turned to leave the graveside and make our way back to our cars. She said, "So okay then, Jim." And I said, "Okay then, Brie."

The house was quiet after Trez flew back to Alaska. My mother and I spent countless hours "going through boxes" and walking from one room to another for no real reason. And answering the phone. For a few days at least. That's one thing I learned: the phone rings off the hook the day after a funeral. Then the phone calls are cut in half each day until four or five days in when the telephone goes completely quiet and you keep catching yourself looking at it, praying that it will ring because now it's over and everyone else has moved on and you're totally alone.

The first Saturday after the funeral, I woke up just after six o'clock. I walked downstairs to the kitchen. My mother was sitting at the table stirring a cup of tea. The back door was open, and the morning sun was shining through the screen door. "It kind of makes a giant hole in everything," I said.

"We'll be okay," she said.

"Are you sure?"

My mother looked past me for a moment, then she said, "I asked your father that once. Just after you started school. You got off to a rough start. The first day, you came home wearing another boy's jacket. Then a few days later, you got sick and your father had to pick you up. He brought you home, and after you went to your room, I looked at him and said, 'Billy, are you sure we're going to be alright?' He didn't say anything. He just stood there looking back the hallway toward your room. Then he said, 'I guess we have to. The boy just called me "Papa."'"

I watched her stir her tea. "Mom?"

"Yes?"

"Was dad proud of me?"

"Very much so."

"Why?"

"Because you're exactly like him."

* * *

By the fall of 1984, I'd quietly surrendered any notion of a new beginningness.

I was working at Dal-Tile in the kiln room. Dal-Tile was a workplace version of the Eagle's "Hotel California"—you could check in, but you could never check out. Not that I or any of the score of lifers who worked there would ever hear an Eagles song at work; radios were prohibited, as was anything that could conceivably bring an ounce of joy to the workday. For forty hours each week, I loaded unfired ceramic tile onto carts that traveled along a circular track and disappeared into the mouth of a giant, glowing tunnel. During July and into August, the kiln room touched 110 degrees. I cut off my curls—it was either that or suffer a heat stroke. And I shed the last, stubborn traces of the blubber I'd packed on during the Summer of Doris—the kiln room's heat rendering it off my body like bacon fat, which would have either pleased or disgusted Tina.

I rented a one-room efficiency on Chambersburg Street for $175 a month plus electric. When I moved in, it smelled weird—and not the weird but comforting groundhog smell of my old bungalow. This was a pungent, old lady smell that attacked my upper nasal passages and reeked of slow death. (Two days after I moved in, the downstairs tenant confirmed to me that my unit's former occupant was, in fact, a little old lady who had, in fact, died in my apartment a month earlier.)

I bought a CD player at Sears, and since I had a new address and nothing better to do, I joined the Columbia Compact Disc Club four times and the far-crappier BMG Compact Disc Club three times. The discs played clean, but—like when Viking played "Bell Bottom Blues" after the creek hike back at Camp Eden—I couldn't shake the feeling that the music flowing through my speakers was missing some essential element. It took me a few weeks to figure it out; when I finally did, I couldn't un-ring the bell. The missing element was the comfort derived from time spent together. All of the skips and scratches and dust pops that had been birthed from our shared listening experience had been replaced by a digital perfection that made me long for the imperfections of my old vinyl collection.

As for my love life, by early September I'd dated four girls: Lisa, Georgia, Tina 2, and Kimberly. I had no problem getting the first date— I used all my tried-and-true Romeo techniques—but an hour or so into the evening, when the "even trade" moment presented itself, I bailed. I had my own heartache to offer, but it felt way too personal to serve up willy-nilly just to advance some random first date to the next level. I had to say something, though, so it usually played out something like this:

TINA 2: "My best friend ditched me in 12th grade. It was beyond traumatic. My parents had to put me in therapy."
ME: "I invented the idea of salt and peppering tomatoes."

Or.

KIMBERLY: "I'm scared to love—I've been hurt too many times."
ME: "God's like a flying squirrel—no one's ever seen either."

It was pathetic.

And since this is a confessional, I'll confess this: after each of those four miserable dates, I drove slowly past the church for a one-second, moonlit glimpse of the picnic table where I first met Angela.

The last Friday of October, I woke up dreaming about the snagged bowling pin from my mother's flood story. I laid in the dark for a long time, fully awake. When my alarm clock sounded, I hit snooze. When it sounded a second time, I turned it off. Forty minutes later—ten minutes before I had to start loading tile at Dal-Tile—I pulled myself out of bed and called the shift supervisor at Dal-Tile and told him there was no way I could make it in to work: I'd been up the whole night puking and it took me every last ounce of strength to crawl to the phone and dial the number.

I didn't bother getting dressed, and for the first time in my life, I ate over the sink. When night fell, I left my sofa bed folded up. I made a double box of macaroni and cheese and sat up watching fuzzy, black and white reruns of *The Twilight Zone* and *The Honeymooners* on the only station I could pull in with my rabbit ears, channel 54. When channel 54 signed off the airwaves at 2 a.m., I put on Pink Floyd's *The Wall.* I had the compact disk—it was the first CD I'd ever bought—but I dug out the pockmarked vinyl instead and listened to all four sides, beginning to end, three times in a row.

When the sun came up, I pulled my last supermarket egg from the fridge and scrambled it in the Teflon skillet I found in the clearance aisle at the discount store. I was methodically pushing it onto a paper plate when I stopped mid-push. The egg looked pathetic by itself. What it needed was a slice of toast. Preferably sourdough. One with a nice chew to it. I felt something stir inside of me. What the dish *really* needed was home fries. Yukon Golds—sliced to a uniform thickness, seasoned with salt and pepper, and fried in re-claimed bacon grease until they had a golden-brown crust that could only be described, even by the most discerning culinarian, as toothsome. I didn't have any potatoes. I knew where there *were* potatoes, though. A copious amount of them. And I knew who was selling them.

I could see that Brie was dressed in easily removable layers from half a block away. She had on her FFA jacket, a hooded sweatshirt, multiple flannel shirts, and gloves with the fingers cut off. "You shouldn't display the potatoes next to the onions," I said as I walked up to the tent. "Onions cause potatoes to rot—remember?"

Brie looked up but didn't respond.

"It's been a while," I said. "How've you been?"

"Fine."

I reached up and ran my fingers through my hair. "I know I probably look a little rough. Last night I decided to stay up for seventy-two straight hours—like I used to."

"Why are you here?"

"What, I can't visit the market?"

"Suit yourself," Brie said.

I fixed my mouth into a smile. "I don't know if you know, but I've got an apartment. It's not as cool as the bungalows because I can't fix it up how I want to, and besides that, an old lady died in there and it still smells funky."

"Uh-huh."

"I bought a CD player. It's okay, but at the same time, I don't know . . ."

Nothing.

I tapped my fingers on the table. "So, I was thinking about driving out to visit the bungalows. Would you want to come along?"

"I don't think that would do either of us any good."

She had three rows of red onions on the table, but she turned away from me and began boxing more. It wasn't the reception I expected. I waited for her to finish, thinking that maybe then we'd slip into our old farmers market banter—maybe even play the misheard lyrics game like we used to on rainy days—but when she filled the last container, she kept her eyes down and reached for an all-but-empty lug of Brussels sprouts.

I cleared my throat. "Do you know what I've been thinking?" I asked.

"Yes," Brie said.

I thought she'd misheard me. "No, I said, do you know what I've been *thinking*?"

She lifted her head. "Yes. How could I not? I've stood under this tent for two years listening to it, and it's always the same old garbage. You're going to say that you can't help but think about Angela. Then you're going to ask if you ever told me the story about meeting her at the church picnic and how she had a special rose. And how you thought she was giving it to you and just like that your whole life was going to change. Then you're going to make that weird bleat sound you make and stand there like you've never thought of it before and say, 'A-duh, you know what I wish more than anything? I wish I hadn't squandered my big chance with Angela. A-duh.'"

"Go ahead," I said. "This is where you call me ridiculous."

I waited for her to fire something back, but instead she just picked up the lug and shook the last few Brussel sprouts onto the street.

I put my hands on my hips. "There's nothing wrong with pointing out that my life's been episodic—and as proof, I could mention a few things, but I won't because I don't think it behooves me. And what's more, if I want to daydream a little about how things could have been, then I think I've earned the right."

"You're going to miss what's right in front of you," Brie said.

"I can live with that," I shot back.

Brie turned to the truck. Her shoulders stiffened and she slid one foot forward, like she was centering her weight. She jerked the lug over her head and brought it down across the fender so hard that the crack turned heads all around the square. "Hey!" Brie yelled, pivoting back to me. "You know what *I* wish more than anything?"

I shook my head.

"That you were sitting in a wheelchair right now so I could dump you out of it."

I was ten strides away when I heard, "Jim!"

When I turned around, Brie was standing at the edge of the table. She took half a step toward me, then she stopped and lowered her eyes to the sidewalk. "Listen," she said, folding her arms, "good luck staying up like you used to, but I've got my life to live."

I made it out of Brie's line of vision and across the street to my parents' old quadrant before my legs lost all strength. I slumped against the corner lamp post, slid down a few inches, then clung with both hands to the ridged cast iron as if it were a lifeline. A truck rumbled past, vibrating the lamp post under my palms and blocking the sun for a beat. Brie was done with me; she'd made that much clear. I couldn't walk past her again—I'd rather take a bullet in the head—and I couldn't circle the opposite direction and just meander back to my apartment. What would be the point? There was nothing for me there: just a cold scrambled egg on a paper plate and a pile of unlistenable CDs and an old lady smell that was never going to dissipate no matter how many days I left both windows propped open while I was away at my crappy job. I turned toward the Pub. A couple was standing under the dogwood tree. The tree's foliage was reddish-brown—just like the end of every farmers market season since before I was born. The man was standing on the fallen leaves, sipping from a Styrofoam coffee cup. The woman beside him was cradling a long neck pumpkin in her arms. Just down from them, beside my parents' old spot, Jessica the Flower Vendor was sitting on a lawn chair beside her chrysanthemums.

I walked over to her. "Hey, Jessica," I said, holding my hand over my chest. "Selling anything?"

She raised her hand to form a visor over her eyes. "Is that Jimmy?"

"It's me," I said.

"My goodness. It's been how many years?"

"I was just here last year—selling for Seven Turns," I said, pointing toward Brie's quadrant. "You probably just didn't notice."

"You look so different. Your hair. And you're . . . thin."

"Where's Shelly with her tea? And Earl the Cheese Guy?"

"Neither came back this year," she said, lowering her hand to her cheek.

"But you're here," I said. "You'll *always* be here. That'll never change."

"As long as these bones can stand it," she said.

I looked over my shoulder. "My parents' old space is empty. Did anyone set up there this year?"

"I don't believe so."

"So, it's just abandoned?"

Jessica looked to the far end of the quadrant as if she may have missed something. "I believe." She looked me over again. "Tell me, how are your parents? You know I love your father's sticky buns."

"Mom's doing okay," I said. "Hanging in there."

Jessica nodded. For a second, I thought that she'd caught her mistake. Then she said, "And your daddy?"

I looked at the empty spot again. "He's fine," I said.

I walked by The Hotel Gettysburg and down past the tiny building that used to be The Philosopher's Stone and across the college campus until I got to Claudio's. It was barely 9:00 a.m. When I peeked in through the door, Claudio was behind the counter, methodically slicing pepperoni on the meat slicer. I rapped on the glass and mouthed, "Pizza?"

He wiped his hands on his apron and unlocked the door.

"I'm not open, Jim."

"I know, but I could use one of my old pizzas, Claudio. One like you used to make me—with grilled tomatoes on top. Salt and peppered."

I sat at the counter while Claudio stretched the pizza dough. He'd changed his technique—no more tossing the pie into the air and catching it on the back of his lightly-floured fingers. Instead, he centered it on the pan and used the heel of his free hand to work the dough to the edge. When he'd stretched my order to size, he ladled on the sauce and covered the pie with cheese.

"Where's your paddle?" I asked.

Claudio looked down at the paddle in his hand. "Right here."

"I mean the good one—the one with the worn beveled edge and stained handle. You know. The cool one that your grandparents smuggled in from the old country?"

Claudio looked befuddled. "What old country?"

"Italy."

"I buy my paddles from the Restaurant Depot."

I let it go at that. I clasped my hands in front of me while Claudio slid my pizza into the bottom oven of his Vulcan three-stack. He cast me a sideways glance, then moved back behind the slicer. I watched him fill a hotel pan with pepperoni and then start to fill a second one. "Hey," I said, "I came in here on a date with a pretty, blond-haired girl four years ago. It was the night Wayne sang. Do you remember her?"

He looked at me. "Are you okay?"

"Why do you ask?"

"Because you're twiddling your thumbs and you keep making weird sounds."

I looked down. My thumbs were moving in little, interlocking spirals. I squeezed my hands together to stop them. "You know, I just remembered—someone's waiting for me," I said. "Can you box my pizza to go?"

No one was waiting for me. No one anywhere. I had a pizza, though. And a six-pack of cold Pepsi. And if Brie didn't want to visit the Sulfur Springs with me, there was no law saying I couldn't drive out there by myself.

I parked in front of my bungalow. The door was locked, but that didn't stop me. I slammed my shoulder into it and it popped open with the sound of splintering wood. The musty, groundhog den smell hit me like a punch in the face. I took a breath, pulling the stale air into my lungs until my ribs ached, then I flicked on the overhead light. The living room was empty, all except for a trail of white polystyrene pellets on the floor. The trail led from the far corner—where Tina always sat in her bean bag chair when she listened to the Etta James album I bought her the day after we first made love—to the front door. I stared at the beans. The chair was worthless, even before the mouse chewed a hole in it, but Tina had apparently dragged it with her to wherever she ended up—probably at great effort.

I was retracing the pellet's path when the refrigerator's compressor kicked on. I was positive that I'd pulled the plug before I left. I walked to the refrigerator and opened the door. A Big Mac box was sitting on the top shelf. I picked the box up and opened it. Inside, next to a smear of dried sauce and two confetti-sized pieces of lettuce was a half-eaten hamburger. My guts twisted. There was no way that Tina would have walked back to the compound carrying a McDonald's bag the day I left—she still thought that I thought she was a vegetarian. She must have stayed in the bungalow for a day or two after I left. I let my mind expand on this notion for a millisecond, which was a millisecond too long; in that micro-flash, I pictured Tina, her face puffy from crying, sitting on the bare wooden floor, waiting for her boyfriend to return home and tell her that all was forgiven. I set the box back on the shelf, then I reached behind the refrigerator and gave the plug a quick jerk.

There was no place to go except for the church. When I got there, a rusted Volkswagen Beetle was parked in the gravel. I walked to the swing set and sat down. I didn't push off with my feet—that would have felt too pathetic. Instead, I sat quietly on the white plastic slat and stared out over the withered field corn while I chewed on a slice of pizza. I was sipping from my soda when I heard, "You have my brother's yams?"

It was the pastor. "I'm surprised you remember me," I said. "I needed someplace to sit and eat and think. I hope I'm not trespassing," I said.

"You're fine," he said. "What are you thinking about?"

"Life. Farmers markets. Elvis. Mostly that. And the practiced life."

"I don't know what the "practiced life" is."

"My mother told me once that when she was a teenager, she wished she had two lives. One to practice with and then one to get perfect. She said she finally figured out that of the two, she'd much rather have the practiced life. But I don't know. What do you think?"

"Well, I'm a pastor, so I'm always going to say you can't have one without the other. That's pretty much how it's set up."

I gave my swing a tiny push. "Would you like a slice?" I asked.

He didn't even hesitate. "Definitely."

I pulled off a slice and handed it to him. "Hey," I said. "When I was here before, you had a traveling family of singers at the church."

"The Cole Family."

"They had a daughter my age."

"I remember."

My pulse quickened for the first time in months. "Are they ever coming back?"

He shook his head. "That was serendipitous. They called us out of the blue and asked if they could perform. I'm not sure, but I think I still have the thank you letter they sent us—I can look for it if you need me to."

We walked inside to his office. It took a while—he'd look, take a bite of pizza, look again, take another bite—but eventually, he found the letter buried deep in the recesses of his desk. He handed it to me. It was short and to the point—thank you and perhaps we can do it again in the future. But then, and I had to shut my eyes and open them to make sure I wasn't hallucinating, the last sentence read, *Thank you again—our family had a wonderful time, especially our daughter Angela.*

"Can I write down this phone number?" I asked.

"I'll tell you what," the pastor said, "I'll trade you the letter for another slice."

I called the telephone number from my apartment. I suppose I could have explained everything to the elderly woman on the other end of the phone, but I thought it'd be easier just to pretend that I wanted to book the family to perform. "Are they singing in Pennsylvania or anywhere close any time soon?" I asked. "It's probably better if I talked to them in person—it feels predestined to me."

"I don't believe in predestination," the elderly woman said. I heard her open a drawer and then shuffle some papers. "They're singing at— hold on. Yes, here it is. They're singing in Harrisonburg. That's in Virginia. Tonight."

"What venue?"

She shuffled the papers again, then she said, "A farmers market."

My plan was to beg Brie to help me find Angela. When she opened the door, I had both hands in front of my chest in a "don't yell at me" posture. "I know it's your post-market nap time, and I know that you're done with me, but just hear me out," I said. In a flurry, I told her that I had a deal for her: next week, I'd help her set up at the Gettysburg market and then tear down at the end. Plus, if Larry weren't around, I'd unload the truck at Seven Turns. I'd do it myself. She could just stand there and watch and even laugh at me and call me "ridiculous" as many times as she wanted to. In exchange, she'd help me find Angela. It'd be a road trip. She could listen to the Grateful Dead the entire way there and back—I promised. I ended with, "I know this sounds ridiculous, but I've always believed I was destined to find my perfect love at the farmers market, and I think this is my last chance."

The entire time I spoke, Brie stood in her parents' doorway with her arms crossed. When I finished, she said, "I think you're exactly right. This *is* your last chance."

"And?"

"Wait in the driveway," she said.

I sat in the Clarks' driveway, tapping my thumbs on the steering wheel. After ten minutes, I did a K-turn in the driveway so I could pull straight out without wasting time. After ten more minutes, my jaw began to ache from clenching it. How the hell long did it take her to change into a Grateful Dead T-shirt? It had Brie written all over it—screw around and purposely hold me up when she knew I was on a tight schedule. I'd just raised my hand over the horn when she stepped out through the front door. She was wearing a three-quarter length granny skirt and she had her FFA jacket folded under her arm; no surprise there, but she had on a top I'd never seen her wear before: a sleeveless, white lace blouse with purple needlework down the front. And her hair was fixed in a loose braid and draped over her shoulder.

I couldn't help but stare at her as she climbed into the vehicle. Brie sat for a moment, peering at me out of the corner of her eye. "It's the end of October," I said to her. "Your arms are going to get cold."

"I guess I'll just have to live dangerously."

"I'm not sure I want you living dangerously," I said.

"Let's go," she said, snapping her fingers and pointing toward the road. "You better step on it if you're going to run down your past."

We sped southbound down Route 116 just as Trez, Mandy, and I had seven years ago. I flipped my visor up and accelerated into the fast lane. "So, on these trips, we ponder life. Usually, we let a subject float to the top naturally, but this is a short drive so we'll have to force it a tad." I stroked my chin. "Gee, I don't know," I said, "I can't help but wonder if everything is all attached somehow. Do we have free will, or are there forces we can't comprehend leading us around by the nose? And what about predestination? What's *that* all about?"

Brie just looked at me.

"Your turn," I said. "This is where you piggyback off what I said."

"Okay. If all of this is predestined, why is it so much work?"

"You're not playing right. You're supposed to ponder the great cosmic giggle and then act like it's mind-boggling. And you have to ask questions that lead the conversation into vast empty spaces so we can bloviate. It should feel like we're wandering through a labyrinth with wine and cheese in our hands."

Brie looked out the windshield. "What *kind* of cheese, Jim?"

I didn't fall for it. I knew that she was trying to trick me into digressing into some long, food-related tangent and then feed me more and more line until I eventually started to complain about the shoddy work ethics of the first-grade cafeteria ladies. "Why can't you just play along for once in your life?" I asked.

"You have to give me a prompt—like Mrs. Colestock used to."

"I just did. I gave you four rock-solid prompts."

"Give me a new one."

"Okay, was Elvis supposed to live or not live?"

"Live."

"Wrong," I said. "He was never supposed to live in the first place, much less at all. We figured that out on the first road trip to Graceland and then all over again on the Belushi trip."

Brie nodded and said, "That makes perfect sense," in a mocking tone. I accelerated past a slow-moving pickup truck. As I eased us back into the slow lane, a few miniature raindrops—the kind that fall from a clear blue afternoon sky—speckled the windshield. I pulled the wiper switch to make a single swipe just as Brie pushed her tape into the cassette player. I peeked at her from the corner of my eye. Other than her totally predictable refusal to play the game right, it felt good to have Brie beside me. It reminded me of driving to the market on Saturday mornings and how, maybe once every three or four weeks, we'd be the first vendors to show up and the square would be quiet and the sun would just be peeking out over the buildings and we'd seemingly have the entire town to ourselves for a few magical minutes—no other vendors, no pedestrians, no street traffic. It always made us giddy and joyous beyond all reason and we'd inevitably end up laughing and smart-alecking our way through some goofy conversation that bounced all over the place but flowed like water nonetheless. I loved it, and even though Brie never said it out loud, I knew she loved it too.

"Hey, Brie," I said, turning to her. "Remember that whole thing I said a minute ago about the labyrinth? I think I know why it'd be counterproductive to sell wine and cheese at a market to walk around with. Once the customers are sipping wine without a care, they're way too content—it deadens their buying impulse. Plus, it'd tie up both of their hands, so they wouldn't be able to reach into their pockets for more money even if you did manage to upsell them."

"Isn't that why we always left room on the table for a purse? So the customer can set down what they're holding and buy more?"

"No. That was so the Roy Orbison woman wouldn't plop her ginormous pocketbook down right on my baked goods and crush the living snot out of them like she did that one time. Remember? She just chucked it down and destroyed two cranberry-orange muffins. She didn't even offer to pay for them. It boggles the mind."

"Are we bloviating now?"

"No.

"Can we?"

"Are you going to play the game right?"

"Yes."

"Life is like a tapestry—true or false?"

"I think it's obvious. We belong to the tapestry and the tapestry belongs to us."

"So, you're saying that everything—life and who we are and everyone around us—is mired together in a symbiotic relationship. Like potatoes and potato bugs."

"I've changed my mind. This game is ridiculous and I don't want to play anymore," Brie said.

I fixed my sights on the road. "Fair enough. What do you want to do?"

"The misheard lyrics game."

"The new one or the old?"

"The new one—where we fill in what the other person was thinking," Brie said.

"Okay. I'll go first. The first time I heard Simon and Garfunkel's 'The Sounds of Silence,' I thought that he was singing *the songs of Simon.* And I thought . . ."

"You thought, how egotistical because this guy is like five foot two."

"Close," I said. "I thought that he was ripping on his own songs in a self-pitying way—the whole tortured artist claptrap. Go ahead. Your turn."

"The first time I heard Neil Young's 'Needle and the Damage Done,' I thought he was singing *meat on a damaged onion.*" And I thought . . ."

"I know exactly," I said. "You thought, if someone did, in fact, have a damaged onion, that it should be immediately sequestered from all undamaged onions."

"Pretty much."

I tapped my thumbs on the steering wheel. "So, for that 'meat on a damaged onion' thing you just said. I'm picturing a red onion. What kind of onion are you picturing?"

"One of those big Vidalia onions. The ones we recommend to people when they say they're going to try to make French Onion Soup."

"I love French Onion Soup. Except I hate when there's a big glob of Gruyere that hasn't melted and you almost choke on it. Don't tell anyone, but I'm pretty sure that when I wake up gasping for air, it's because I'm dreaming about eating French Onion Soup and in the dream, I hit a half-melted blob of Gruyere with the rind still on."

"Who would I tell that to?" Brie asked.

"No one, I guess," I said.

"Jim?"

"What?"

"Why do you think we don't have any friends?"

"It's the farmers markets—the markets are a demanding mistress. Or in your case, they're a demanding whatever the male equivalent of a mistress is."

"Do you really think that's why?" Brie asked.

"Sure. Who wouldn't like us? It's just no one ever gets the chance."

"Will they ever get a chance?"

I shook my head. "I'd like to say yes, but no. It's similar to the whole 'Elvis was never supposed to live' thing."

Brie put her finger to her chin, pondering this, then she said, "I don't think there is a male equivalent to mistress. It's a man's world."

I shook my head. "Women have all the power."

"As a woman, I can say that's one-hundred percent false."

I pointed to the map. "Then why am I driving two hundred miles to Harrisonburg?"

While the Dead's *American Beauty* played on the tape player, we drove up an unending mountain. My side of the highway was solid rock; Brie's side was a sea of red and orange autumn leaves. The road was long and winding, so we had to slow down on a few of the sharper turns. But every once in a while, we'd hit a long, straight, downhill stretch and we'd coast, picking up speed until our ears popped. At the foot of the mountain, I turned to Brie. "So still no idea about your brother's whereabouts?"

"None."

I tapped my thumbs on the steering wheel and let out a sigh. "It occurs to me that after all these years, I've never heard the whole story about when Doris got home after getting kicked out of Camp Eden—about her father accusing Wayne of spying," I said.

"You've heard it. Mr. Messinger came over and screamed at us."

"I never heard what he actually said."

"He said he knew your family was sub-par when he saw you sold bread in a parking lot for a living. Then he made a disparaging remark about the quality of your parents' baked goods."

"I figured as much. You should have seen him bang his stupid ring on our table at the market. I'm still amazed that my dad didn't clobber him," I said. "Wayne always told me he defended my character—did he?"

"Yes and no."

"What'd he say?"

"He said that you were a pathetic slave to your desires and he befriended you out of the goodness of his heart—the same way Elvis befriended a stray dog he found wandering loose outside of the Sun Recording Studio."

"What else?"

Brie hesitated. "I don't know that I remember."

"I promise I won't get mad."

Brie looked at me and put on a half-cringe face. "He said you were kinda . . . sorta . . . like tofu."

"Dammit!" I furrowed my brow for effect, but I wasn't really mad. Wayne was gone—what would have been the point?

"Well, I guess I can't blame him. That's always been the rap on me—that I'm tofu-like. And your brother *did* befriend me," I said. "And he did have you serve me iced tea every day."

"The first day. After that, I did it on my own."

"Why?"

"You looked thirsty."

"So how come the more successful my reverse diet was, the more you cut the sugar?"

Brie let out a snort. "I try to give you the benefit of the doubt—I do—but you really are an out-and-out idiot, aren't you?"

That ticked me off, so I hit eject on the cassette player and ejected Brie's tape mid-song. Then I turned the radio off. "I'm not an idiot," I said, staring straight ahead. "If anything, I'm a reverse idiot. And since we're on the subject of people saying stupid stuff, you're all the time rambling on about me not eating bananas. You know I'm not allergic to bee stings—I tell you every time we see a bee buzzing around and you bring it up. And you're always forbidding me from eating mushrooms and going on and on like a mental patient about me dying from breathing rotted potatoes—like that's even possible."

Brie didn't say a word. She just flicked the stereo back on and pushed her cassette back into the tape player. The second Jerry Garcia's voice was flowing through the speakers again, she folded her FFA jacket into a pillow and placed it between her head and the door; then she spent the next five minutes thrashing around and shooting me dirty looks, like it was all my fault that she couldn't get comfortable. Just when we merged onto 81 South and I thought she was finally asleep, she snapped her head up. "Oh, and don't think that I'm going to just let that go. Yes! You *are* an idiot. A big, fat, tofu idiot."

I was glad when Brie fell asleep for real, and not just because I was tired of her insulting me. It gave me a chance to think. Until now, reconnecting with Angela had been a fantasy. I'd never given any real thought to what I'd say to her if I ever saw her again. It had been four years. What Wayne had said in the bungalow was right; Angela and I had only spent a few hours together. I didn't even have a photograph of her. All I had was a mental picture that—even in my most delusional moments—I had to admit was growing more and more out of focus.

I could picture where we were going, though. Harrisonburg was a small, Civil War town. According to the woman who answered the Cole's telephone, the farmers market was set up on the town square, right in the heart of the historic district. So, in my imagination, I just plugged-in downtown Gettysburg. Visualizing the market was easy enough: tents, vendors, customers, etc.. As for Angela and her family, they'd be set up on a temporary stage and it would be located on the outer rim of the activity so as not to bottleneck the market's foot traffic. That was Farmers Market 101.

I let that image marinate for a few miles, then I injected Brie and myself into the scene. I placed us behind a hedge, crouched down, peering at Angela on stage as her family worked through a hymn.

"Is that her?" Brie would ask me.

I'd push the hedge apart and squint through the gap in the branches. "I'm not sure. It seems like she was taller."

"I thought you could never get her out of your mind?"

"Well, I guess not the height part. She was sitting down most of our date."

"You're ridiculous," Brie would say.

I'd give her a dirty look and say something like, "Just shut up for once in your life and hold my car keys while I go up there."

A semi-trailer passed me in the fast lane, breaking my concentration. It was just as well. I didn't like where my imagination was taking me with the scene. I cracked the window to draw a few breaths of fresh air into my lungs, then I tried again.

I'd push the hedges apart and squint at Angela on stage. "This is it—I'm going up there," I'd say to Brie. "Wish me luck."

Brie would cross her fingers and hold them up. "Luck," she'd say.

I'd step to the front of the stage as though I were walking on ice. Angela would look exactly as I kind of remembered her. She'd even have a pile of crumpled Kleenex on the piano lid. Her mouth would form a perfect circle as she sang an "O" sound, and I'd think again about how the wind would stop to listen to her sing. Then, just as her family collectively sang the song's last note, Angela would spot me. I'd be posed in anticipation of the moment: head tilted, hands stuffed in my front pockets, bodyweight on my non-dominant foot. I'd let a smile just touch my lips, and then I'd do the right eye, left eye thing. Angela would clap her hands in glee and blurt into the microphone, "Sorry folks—we're going to take a small break now."

I'd climb the stage steps and strike the same pose; except I'd leave out the eye thing. "Hello, Angela," I'd say.

"I always knew I'd see you again," she'd respond.

Just then, a little girl would toddle out from behind the piano. She'd have Angela's eyes and blond hair. Angela would put her hand on her daughter's little shoulder and say, "Lily, this is a dear, dear friend of Mommy's."

I'd stifle a bleat and squat down to the child's level. "That's a beautiful dress, Lily," I'd say. Then I'd go through the charade of looking left and then right before asking, "So, where's her daddy?"

At that moment, a man would walk across the stage. He'd be handsome, the same way a guy wearing wire-rimmed glasses and studying at the library would be handsome. I'd fight back the urge to kick him in the balls. Angela and her husband would exchange a knowing look; then he'd scoop Lily up and walk off stage with her, leaving us alone.

I'd say something like, "Is he a good man?"

Angela would dip her eyes and say, "Yes. The very best," and it would be impossible to miss the sadness in her voice. Then she'd ask, "What about you? Is there someone special?"

I'd shake my head and say, "No, but Brie and I have it figured out. It's not our fault. The farmers markets are a cruel mistress—people never get a chance to know us."

I didn't like the direction that scenario was taking either, so I cranked the window down another inch and tilted my face into the stream of chilly air. Then I tried again.

All the aforementioned would happen, but after her husband wandered off, Angela would say, "I wanted to give you the rose—the one I had pressed in the love chapter of my King James Bible. But, but . . ."

"I was ready to leave everything and come with you," I'd say.

"And I was ready to stay."

A long moment that carried the weight of our shared regret would pass, then Angela would say, "It's funny to think how our lives would be different if we'd both just said what we were thinking."

I looked at Brie. Her head was against her FFA jacket. I pushed rewind and found "Box of Rain" so it would be playing when she opened her eyes. I reached over and touched her shoulder. "Wake up, Brianna."

She lifted her head a few inches off the door and squinted at me.

"Brie, I'm sorry. When I saw how miserable you were at the housewarming party, I should have got up and sat beside you. I don't know what's wrong with me."

She closed her eyes and laid her head back against her jacket. "Oh, that's okay," she murmured.

"Are you awake?"

"Yeah. I'm getting up in a few minutes."

"Brie, why do you always say all that stuff about bananas and me getting stung?"

"Because I can't bear the thought of anything happening to you," she said. Then she was fast asleep again.

I had the wiper blades on medium when we rolled into Harrisonburg. The town was hopping, but we got lucky—a block off the square, an El Camino pulled out from a spot in front of the movie theater and I was able to pull right into it. Brie got out of her side without her jacket. I grabbed it, then climbed out my side and fed a handful of dimes into the parking meter. The town was exactly how I envisioned it—a smaller, less touristy version of Gettysburg. From the far side of the square, I could see pit beet smoke floating over the vendor tents, and, just faintly, I could detect the slightest whiff of animal fat caramelizing. From the same direction, I could hear someone tuning an electric guitar.

"This place is nuts. It's like a festival crowd or something," I said, scanning the throes of people around us. I held Brie's FFA jacket to her. "It's going to get cold once the sun dips down—especially in this drizzle."

She twisted her head away from me.

"What's the matter?" I asked.

"I can't believe you still want to look for her."

"That's the whole point. I thought you understood."

"So go, then. What do you need me for?"

I looked in the direction of the market, then turned back. "Brie, I can't stand the thought of you being disappointed in me."

"Too late. I've been disappointed in you and your fat, stupid face every time I've ever seen it."

"Why'd you come with me, then?"

"Because I felt sorry for you."

A second ticked by with neither of us reacting.

Suddenly, Brie's face darkened. "So go, then!" she yelled. A few heads turned toward us. Brie lifted her foot off the ground and stomped it at me, like she was shooing a dog. She stomped her foot again, this time so hard that her entire body reverberated. Then, just like that, she was racing down the sidewalk away from the market. I took a step to follow her, but she must have sensed it because she spun around and lifted her foot again. She held it in the air for a second, mid-stomp, as if she was daring me to take another step. Then, in less time than it took for me to reach my hand out toward her, Brie was gone.

Hands go to pain, and my hands were clasped over my heart. I stood on the wet sidewalk squinting through the drizzle until long after the strength drained out of my legs. People were still walking toward the market. Standing there, clutching my chest, I felt a tinge of panic. I had no idea what to do. I couldn't search the streets for Brie. If she came back and I wasn't where we'd parked, she'd assume I was with Angela. Or worse, she'd think I'd abandoned her. Then what would she do? Call her parents to come get her? Try to walk home? All two-hundred miles?

I took a few steps and ducked under the theater marquee. Every few minutes, I'd press Brie's FFA jacket against my chest and hustle up through the rain to the edge of the market, thinking that maybe she would double-back along a side street. I'd twist my head in both directions, frantically searching the crowd for a glimpse of her face. Then, just as quickly, a surge of anxiety would overtake me and I'd run back to the theater to wait for her under the marquee again.

An hour in, I began to ask passing strangers if they'd seen Brie. I stopped one woman who vaguely reminded me of the Roy Orbison lady. "She's barely five feet tall," I said, holding my hand chin-high, "and she dresses like a cross between a hippie and someone's grandmother. Her favorite song is 'Box of Rain' by the Grateful Dead because she loves the way the different instruments rattle in and out at the beginning."

"Can't help you," the woman said, hustling away.

I talked faster to the next group of people, so I was able to add, "She's completely oblivious to broad social trends, and once, she made me go back to the 7-Eleven and pay for a cup of coffee the lady forgot to charge me for. It ticked me off at the time but now I'm glad I did it."

After twenty minutes of nothing but contemptuous looks, my legs began to wobble. I was leaning on the empty ticket booth when a disheveled-looking woman wearing a ratty overcoat wandered past me. "I'm looking for my friend," I said weakly. I bleated once, then slumped against the booth as if every muscle in my body had turned to liquid.

The woman continued past me. Then she stopped and looked back. "What?"

I pulled myself up. "Maybe you've seen her. She's short and she spends a lot of time by herself, which I count as a good thing. And she loves the Grateful Dead. She saved her brother's old Dead T-shirt from either the trash or the rag pile. I never asked but I'm almost sure it was the rag pile because once she told me she felt sorry for rags. And I should have sat beside her at the house-warming party when I saw how miserable she was and told her I wanted to live the practiced life with her, but I didn't because I'm selfish and a pathetic slave to my worst instincts. I'm horribly flawed. The same way the whole idea of Amorphica is horribly flawed. And one day, I'm going to track Viking down and tell him just that. But right now, I'm worried about Brie. She stormed off and it's raining and she doesn't have her FFA jacket. She's wearing a thin blouse and her bare arms are bound to be freezing by now and I can't bear the thought of her shivering in the cold."

The woman looked behind her. Then she looked back at me. "Are you talking to me?" she asked.

After that, I gave up talking to strangers.

I was huddled against the building with my head down and my arms wrapped around Brie's jacket when I heard her voice. "Well? What did she say?"

"I didn't talk to her," I said.

"Why?"

"Because I've been trying to describe you to people and all I could come up with was that you're short."

"Gee, thanks."

"I mean, every time I tried to describe you, I couldn't. I'd go straight to the things that make you Brie and I couldn't say them fast enough. How you're innocent and smart and funny and far and away the most self-actualized person I've ever known." I stopped for a second because I started to tear up. "Do you know why I wouldn't say goodbye to you in the woods?"

"You wanted to hurt me?"

"No. Well, yes—that was part of it," I said, and then I bit my lip. "But the real reason was because I didn't want you to think about me anymore."

"Why?"

"Because I've never given the best of myself to anyone. What if there *is* no best of me?"

"Isn't that for me to decide?" Brie said.

I took a deep breath. "Would you be willing to give me a chance?"

She looked into my eyes for a long moment. Then, she reached with both hands for her American FFA pin. Slowly, she unpinned it from her jacket. "I may not have a rose to give you, but I have something."

"Brie, I can't take your American FFA pin."

"You're not taking it—I'm giving it to you." She gathered a handful of my T-shirt and fastened the pin through it. Then, she pulled her head back to inspect her work. "So, okay then," she said.

Her blouse was soaking wet and her arms were covered with goosebumps. "Look at you," I said. "You're chilled to the bone. All those mornings at market when you scolded me for not dressing warm, and now here you are shivering." I draped her FFA jacket around her and helped her slide her arms into the sleeves, one at a time. Then I snuggled the collar around her neck.

"What about you? You're cold too," Brie said.

"I'm fine," I answered.

"I'd give you my jacket but it's too small."

"I know you would."

"You could wear it over your shoulders."

"I know," I said.

Brie put her hands on my arms, just below the shoulders, and rubbed up and down real fast to warm me up. "It's this darn drizzle," she said. "It makes everyone chilly."

I took Brie's hand and gave the back of it a tiny kiss.

Standing there in the fading autumn light with Brie's hand in mine, that tiny kiss could have passed for a Hollywood ending, but our tapestry still had one last knot. When I pulled my lips from her hand, I asked, "Are you ready to head home?"

"It seems a waste," Brie said, looking toward the square. "We've come all this way and the market is still open."

I gave her hand another kiss. She slid her arm under my arm, and we walked to the market and made our way along the row of tents. We were standing at a pasta vendor's table when we heard the miniature sonic boom of someone tapping a microphone. Then an amplified voice called out, "Check. Mic number one. Here's an original tune I wrote. It's called, 'And That is That.'"

I looked at Brie.

"No—it can't be," she said.

A second later, we were running hand in hand through the street toward the voice. We pushed through the crowd to the front row. On stage, Wayne was be-bopping across the plywood in a restrained version of Chuck Berry's duck walk. Angela and the rest of the Cole family were accompanying him, laying down an equally restrained shuffle beat. The Winnebago was parked behind them. On its side, painted in three-feet high block-letters slanted forward to give the allusion of speed, was the band's new name: *The Cole Clark Project*. When Wayne spun to duck-walk back across the stage, he spotted us and broke into a wide grin. The second later, while the band was still playing behind him, he unfastened his guitar strap and leaned into the microphone. "We're going to take a little break, friends. God bless."

He was still five strides away when he called out, "I know you said I could never write a song called 'And That is That,' but I wrote it anyway."

"It's got 'top ten' written all over it," I said. I held my hand out, but Wayne surprised me. Instead of taking my hand, he hugged me—so long and hard that I had to pry him off.

"Holy crap," I said. "You've got to give me a chance to breathe."

"Where have you been?" Brie broke in. "Why'd you leave without telling anyone?"

Wayne turned and looked at the stage, then turned back to us. For a split-second, I anticipated him saying *It's the whole do dolphins swim around all day thinking about triangles thing*. But he didn't utter a peep. He just stood in front of us with a silly grin on his lips.

"Speak!" Brie shouted.

"Yeah," I said. "The whole disappearing without a trace thing? What was *that* all about?"

That's when Wayne told us his story.

After the short police officer chased us from the bungalows, he had a crisis of confidence. For the first time since he'd botched his show-and-tell presentation in kindergarten, he had self-doubts. He questioned not only his guitar playing but his vocal abilities. Every note he sang sounded flat—or sharp. He couldn't tell anymore. Plus, in a particularly lucid moment of self-examination, it dawned on him that he had no money and no marketable skills and no immediate prospects of obtaining either. Then, I abandoned him by moving into the woods.

So, one day when no one else was home, he grabbed his Martin D-28 and drove to the bungalows. He found the Sulfur Springs Resort in the same condition that I would find it a few months later: barren and decrepit and devoid of hope. The smell of the pines took him back to the house-warming party and how he had unveiled the name "Bum's Rush" to the band, and how he and everyone else thought that it was a turning point. He walked the path to the carriage house ruins and leaned his guitar case against the stone foundation. He didn't feel like playing, but he took his guitar out and strummed the chords of the first song he ever learned: "Heartbreak Hotel." Then he played it again, this time singing the words. From there, he sang all his old singer-songwriter covers—all except for "We Just Disagree," which he'd long ago vowed to never again sing. After that, he sang his rock and roll covers—the ones that Three Guys Named Sky-Rat played at the frat parties. Finally, he played all of his Bum's Rush originals. In the end, he felt a little better, but at the same time, he felt like shit, and by the time he drove his Nova out the dirt driveway to the main road, to his surprise, he felt even more like shit.

On a whim, instead of turning right, he turned left and drove through the evening into the night. He drove for days, untethered from everything he'd ever drawn comfort from: Twin Oaks, his dad's slaughterhouse contraption, Bum's Rush, the bungalows, and most of all, the dream that he'd cultivated since the sixth grade, to be a rock and roll god. The further he drove, the more the small details of his life began to elude him: the name of our elementary school art teacher, the title of the Elvis movie where Elvis lived in Hawaii, and as hard as he tried, he couldn't recall the exact date his dad's meat hook had received its utility patent.

Five days into his odyssey, he was sitting in his car at a crossroads in rural Ohio. His pants were filthy; his hair was matted to his head; and he had a lingering metallic taste in his mouth which evoked thoughts of the unused aluminum siding pile at the bungalows. There wasn't a house in sight—just roads and trees and uncultivated scrub fields. Wayne got out of his car and leaned against the front end. He didn't move for hours, even when a carload of college-aged guys pulled up and pelted him with insults. It started to rain. Then the rain turned into a steady downpour. Still, something told him to stay put. "It was weird. It was like I was awaiting further instructions," Wayne said. "I stood at the crossroads all night in the pouring rain, and just as the sun came up, a Winnebago pulled up to the four-way stop."

A family's name was painted on the side of the vehicle. Wayne didn't know Angela's last name—I'd never told him—but he took it as a sign. He followed the Winnebago to a tiny rec park on the outskirts of a small, flat town with a giant water tower smack in the middle of it. As the family unloaded their equipment, Wayne recognized Angela. Still, he hung back while a small crowd filled the grass seating area and the Cole Family began to sing. He was filthy and disheveled and sopping wet. People were staring at him, but he didn't care. He put his hand over his old eye-patched eye and slowly panned the stage; when his uncovered eye settled on Angela, he saw that she too had one hand covering one eye. Three days later, they were married.

Wayne turned toward the stage. "I spent all that time being myopic about Bum's Rush—trying to control every last aspect of it—and what I found out was that sometimes a dream doesn't end up looking like how you first pictured it."

"You need to call Mom and Dad," Brie said.

"I will," he said. "And I'll visit. We'll be within an hour of Gettysburg in a couple of weeks." Wayne tucked his hands into pockets. "But all of this gets better." He broke into a giant grin and turned his head toward the stage. "Ang!"

Angela stood up from behind the piano and walked gingerly to the edge of the stage with her hand resting on her enormous stomach. She inched down the steps onto the grass.

I put my hand on Wayne's shoulder and leaned in. "A little hellbender?"

"They're thinking twins," he whispered back.

"Are you sure you're ready for this?" I asked.

"Definitely," he said. He looked at Brie and me holding hands. "I could ask you two the same question. How long has this been going on?"

I hesitated, and when I did, Brie picked up on it. She lifted one eyebrow. What was the right answer? Five minutes? Eleven years? I was screwed. Whichever way I went, she would bust me on it. Just as I felt as though my only option was to let out a sharp, piercing bleat and double over in pretend pain, my Art of Intuition kicked in one last time. I pointed to the sky. "How long have the stars been part of the sky?" I asked.

"Wow. You got *sooo* lucky with that one," Brie said.

Wayne shook his head. "Well, I could say that it's about time, but I know how obstinate both of you are—that's the problem. With both of you. You're both too obstinate for your own good," he said, and as he said it, his eyes left us and he took a step forward to meet Angela. "Angie, I think you know this guy," he said.

"Congratulations, Angela," I said.

"Thank you," she answered, rubbing her stomach.

Wayne turned to Brie. "And this is my sister, Brianna."

Angela reached for her hand. "It's funny how life works. If Jim hadn't asked me on a date, I'd have never met your brother."

"The market is closing in a few minutes," Wayne said. "But we're supposed to play until the crowd is gone. If you want to stick around, we can go out and get some pizza."

I looked back in the direction of the Bronco. I hadn't slept since Thursday night, but I felt a surge of energy—call it forward momentum. "I'd love to, but we have a long drive. Why don't we hook up when you get back to town?" I said. I shook Angela's hand, and when I reached out to shake Wayne's hand, I said, "When you get home, just so you know, I thought you were dead, so I joined Columbia House and BMG two times each under different permutations of your name."

"I wouldn't expect any less," Wayne said.

Brie and I watched Wayne help Angela up the steps of the stage. She slid behind her piano and Wayne lifted his guitar strap over his head. After a second, the rest of The Cole Clark Project joined them on stage, and together they began to play. It was an upbeat song I'd never heard, and by the way Wayne opened it with one of his signature five-note guitar riffs, it was a good bet that it was an original.

A handful of customers were still shopping the tents. Far more were just meandering around with food and drinks in their hands, listening to the music. "Are you noticing this?" I asked Brie.

"What?"

"The market. Not just this one. *All* the markets. This is how they are now."

"I know," Brie said. "People want a whole experience provided for them."

"That's my point. To me, that means opportunity."

"And?"

"I've been standing here thinking. What would stop us from starting a food truck? Not one like that crappy Smiling Pete's Lunch Wagon that parks on Baltimore Street. Pete's food is crap—it's tantamount to a slap in the face of everyone who's ever taken a mouthful of properly seasoned food since the beginning of time. I'm thinking of something refined—I'm thinking farmers market high-end casual. I already have our signature product—the cheeseburger dog. I invented it right before I left for Walden. Plus, I invented a raspberry jalapeno relish to put on it. And we can upsell side dishes—like that butter-steamed corn on the cob you invented. We'd grow everything ourselves. We'll even get Earl the Cheese Guy to teach us how to make cheese. That'll be our shtick. We'll paint it on the side of the truck. *Fresh and local and straight from our farm to your stinking face.* Except we'll leave the 'stinking' part out."

"I thought farmers markets were a demanding mistress?"

"We'll be together, so the effect would be neutralized. Like Elvis looking at house ants."

Brie shifted her weight. "We could sell at events and festivals, too. We could pull in the night before and sleep behind the truck—on the grass under the stars."

"It would give us a modicum of freedom," I said.

We both stopped talking for a moment. A middle-aged man and woman brushed past us. Directly above our heads, the streetlight flickered on.

"So, what do you say?" I asked. "What would stop us from starting a business together—like when my parents started Little Martha's Bakery?"

"I guess just the not being married part," Brie said.

Something inside of me lurched to one side. I instinctively reached out to steady myself, and when I did, I let out a long, panic-stricken bleat that climbed the scale up into a falsetto and then cascaded back down into a lower pitch and ended abruptly—like someone lifted the needle off a record mid-song. I slumped over and stayed that way for a long moment, gasping for air. When I straightened my legs, Brie was laughing at me.

"What's so funny?"

"You're being ridiculous."

"*Being*? So, there's hope for me?"

Brie took my hand. "Come on. Let's walk through the market and watch the vendors tear down. That's always my favorite part."

"Really?"

"Absolutely. There's a whole story hidden in things people just walk by. You of all people should know that—you were conceived at a farmers market."

Brie and I walked side by side through the market. The rain had stopped, and the last traces of October sky were almost gone. Along the sidewalks, vendors were packing their goods and breaking down their tents. Whether they had a good day or not, I couldn't tell for sure, but I could guess. To a person, they looked content. And it was a contentment that couldn't be swayed by a few dollars more or less. I knew the feeling. Brie was right. It was written into my DNA. I had left the markets and thought I was done with them, but I was back. And at the best time of the year too—the end of the season. I squeezed Brie's hand. "So, okay then," I said to her. She squeezed my hand back, and we kept walking down the street into the fading autumn light. Next spring would come soon enough, and after that summer and then fall. And some seasons would be good and some would be bad and they would cycle through without end. And some years would be good and some would be bad, and they too would cycle through without end. But that was okay. Better than okay—it was copacetic.

THE END

Acknowledgments

I'd like to thank my wife, Johanna, and my children, Hunter, and Abby, for their patience while I worked on this story. I'd like to thank my first readers, Marianne Drummond, Janet Vogel, Elena Bittinger, Bob Dubbs, and Virginia Grandorff for being so generous with their time. I'd like to thank Rachel Watson and Victoria Mitchell for lending their talents to the cover art. I'd also like to thank my editor, Taylor Berger-Knorr.

About the Author

Before finding success as a novelist, James R. Dubbs, earned his living in a myriad of jobs, including factory worker, newspaper writer, realtor, liquor store clerk, groundskeeper, customer service representative, and self-employed baker. In the 1990s, he left his Gettysburg home to study creative writing at The University of Alaska Southeast in Juneau. His first novel, "Life in the Lion's Mouth," was published in 2016. His short fiction has appeared in periodicals such as *Explorations, Wrinkle, and The Quiet Time Report*. When not writing, you'll find him listening to Led Zeppelin, practicing Tae Kwon Do, or strumming his beloved Taylor six-string.

Also by James R. Dubbs
Life in the Lion's Mouth
(available on Amazon.com)

Made in the USA
Middletown, DE
21 August 2022

71669504R00142